# BEST FRIENDS

# BEST FRIENDS

## John Fraser

AESOP Modern Fiction
Oxford

AESOP Modern Fiction
An imprint of AESOP Publications
Martin Noble Editorial / AESOP
28 Abberbury Road, Oxford OX4 4ES, UK
www.aesopbooks.com

First paperback edition published by AESOP Publications
Copyright (c) 2021 John Fraser

www.johnfraserfiction.com

The right of John Fraser to be identified as the author of this work
has been asserted in accordance with sections 77 and 78
of the copyright designs and Patents Act 1988.

A catalogue record of this book is
available from the British Library.

First paperback edition 2021

ISBN: 978-1-910301-75-3

# CONTENTS

# CITIES ON THE PLAIN, ON A HILL

'Asking questions no one else asks isn't genius. It's insane. If you're not unhappy ... let it go....'

'Not more unhappy than if.... And uncertainty – it's good for you.'

A really bad start.

Two males, no sex, live together – a decision to share everything.

Nothing is ever shared – not equally: one has the fresh, the other what's left. One the top, the other.... One what he can afford, the other.... They say 'shared', they must mean 'divide'.

\*

*Neighbours*: When the old man died, his wife let his bird starve to death in the cage – 'he would have wanted it,' she tells the daughter.

'No I wouldn't,' the old man shouts from the rackety cemetery, but he's crying – if he'd not cried, maybe he'd have been heard. But dying, and death – they're almost never described as being good experiences... You must expect some tears. Not being heard – that's common enough.

You can turn up to pray, no one ever asks about the bird, not so many about the old man.

\*

*Salvation?* The Americans had it easy – a big country conquered, against a handful of poorly armed people protecting their livelihoods, ignorant of the depth of those attacking armies. That's

7

how now they impress – some of them, a handful – with their slick use of language, their ingenuity. No one can rival them, and they still have motorcars, they drive all over meeting people with turns of phrase, and publish the quips and trouvailles, like smart alecs and party-heroes, the 'life and arse-souls' they are called.

*

'I'm not riding that bus,' the woman says.

'They've paid the bandits,' says the daughter, pushing her aboard, 'And there's the statue too.'

The bandits don't get them – it's the curve: – always been there, always take it slow and circumspect.

This kind of talk – it's everywhere

*

'There's bandits everywhere, nearly,' says Ahmed. 'Guerrillas gone bad. Or living on rich guys' vices – smokes and pills.'

'I could talk to guerrillas,' Nico says. 'They're used to talk. I know the texts. It's hard not to sympathise – they've not forgotten evil, if we have.'

'If they cut off your nose….' says Ahmed, laughing.

'Oh, then it's easy not to sympathise,' Nico says. He holds his long nose, spoofs with a twang, '"The bourgeoisie has stripped of its halo every occupation...." even clandestinity!'

'It's cheap living here,' says Ahmed. 'So you always feel you're nearly rich.'

*

'There's lots here who's come back from the war,' says Ahmed.

'Usually people wish you hadn't,' Nico says. 'That's maybe why they have these wars – send the horrible ones far off and hope they don't come back. I was in one....'

'One in Chechnya?' Ahmed asks. 'That was hard. Hard on everyone.'

'Sleep and a crap,' says Nico. 'Those are hard to get in war. Everything else – it's encouraged. Do it casual, it doesn't register.'

'Oh, I take sides,' says Ahmed. 'If you avoid the lines, you must know sides – it's geometry. If you don't have aeroplanes – for sure you are a terrorist.'

'I don't remember the humans,' says Nico. 'I remember the cats. There were thousands, scurrying, looking for the perfect hiding-place....'

'Are you sure you were there?' asks Ahmed. 'People write about where they weren't, and the language is wonderful. So maybe you weren't there, but have a tale.... Hunters must finish when it gets dark – then, narrative is what they do. Soldiers – think they have a home. It's all a fantasy. A silent cry. "Retreat!"'

'A hunter knows there's no return, no "back". They cover up their dirty deeds with lyrical embroidery.'

'If you come back, it makes no difference,' says Nico. 'And if you don't come back, it makes no difference. Reason has no opinion – I could have been where I say. Opinion – has no reason to suspect.'

So it rests, and Ahmed thinks Nico was in some combat, somewhere. He hopes it wasn't Chechnya – those pictures, that everybody shared. Divided. A horror, even if they were touched up.

*

'We must take the bus and see the forts. There's a desert carved all over – runes and animals, probably a calendar, or else astronomy. We must be stupid not to know which one it is....' And Ahmed chooses his clothing with some care – desert temperatures; and Nico laughs with some affection.

'Those lines,' says Nico. 'It is clear they were for irrigation.'

'There isn't water here,' says Ahmed. 'But of course, we're only now.'

'This is where the battle was,' the guide says. 'Men and dinosaurs....'

'That made it hard to change your side,' says Ahmed. 'One was what one was born.'

'They were all tiny then,' their guide goes on. 'The men – they rode alpacas. This surface – it's obsidian. They cut those tracks – a strategy, flank and outflank. The lizards – they just charge head on, maybe they don't see so well....'

'I see it all,' says Nico. 'War is terrible....'

'It's worse if you win,' the guide says: 'Look at us, stuck here, no money and no clothes. If you lose,you get to run away and find a better place.'

'Where?' Ahmed asks. 'That's all over, the dinos flew away. And – here they come again, in disguise! Flying lizards of the Antilles! It's like capital. You think you know it can't go on. There's something in it makes it fail – eventually. But – on it goes. How long? Where is the flaw? People become machines: – if they don't, the machines will drive them out. But – how will capital reproduce itself? It's done it through exploitation, creation of the proletariat which, for the time being, seeks itself in fetishes, in what it produces, produces itself as fetishes.'

'I know,' says Nico. 'The flaw is when it is so large, it doesn't need the people, nor a ruling class, still less a proletariat. It is an atmosphere, our nature, a smiling gas, destroying all the animals, the plants, so we eat burgers made of worms grown in laboratories, and in the end – or the beginning – we too disappear. We have no function, no use, even playing the guitar – it makes no difference, no sound among the sounds....'

'How long, Nico, does it take? To get so big it's a huge mushroom, bigger than the world?' Ahmed asks, playing the game.

'Two hundred thousand years,' says Nico. 'You can check. That's called the principle of verification. It doesn't work so well, but it's still the best. Of course, there's lots we know that can't be verified at all....'

'That brings me to a problem, Nico,' Ahmed says, tormented, 'that I have with you. No probing, just sharing; an adventure, we said. But, understood: – we don't tell lies, not to each other. And, Nico – you're a liar, not the normal kind. You make up yourself, not what's inside, but what your outside's done and does. Armed? On the run? The sickness...?'

'You want truth, Ahmed?' Nico asks, irritated. 'This stone here. That is truth. Not zen – it's what you want, hard truth. Take it to bed, buy it a Mustang – it's exactly what it is. Don't you want something more? Here's another stone – two stones both true, but see – in my hand they don't make a something more: – a bigger truth. For that – you need me, Ahmed.' He squeezes Ahmed's arm, then moves to his waist. 'You see, tales, like my war record – they may be puzzling, but they're not bad.'

'Not yet bad,' says Ahmed. 'It depends what sort of puzzle. If you're with me trying to solve it, or if it's you helped slaughter those alpacas.'

'We may never know either way,' Nico says. 'Nor the wherefore. You should be able to solve all that, the cases are similar. Then what do you do?'

'This place is difficult,' says Ahmed. 'We're not welcome here. We see things differently – we've more compassion, less understanding. So, if we two don't agree, we've brought our own patch of chaos....'

'Which helps us understand, be more distant, and be better understood,' says Nico. 'After a while, we'll both be moving on.'

'I need to know....' Ahmed begins.

'You mean the drugs?' asks Nico: 'Me, dealing? Not many, and only to the children. I tell them. 'Your body is the shrine' – maybe that's the zen you're thinking of? It gives them substance, spirit. This city – drugs is the fuel, without them, it would die, waiting to be exploited from outside, a corporation bringing cargo. They seem like capitalism, drugs – the ones from nature and the ones from labs, like capital in bags, but it's not so. They give a take on all reality – real killing, rape, real cash and debt and cops. They say this is a re-rerun: real crooks and people stoned; a vision not of man the worker, but of man closed in his skull, alone with brains and memory, the best he'll have, new age, old age returning, farded, hopping with a stick.... Apotheosis, Ahmed. This is the furthest anyone will get from world-is-ending; see it as a movie of the start, up from the apes, trading and sharing....'

'I hear you, Nico, but it isn't true,' says Ahmed.

'If you don't want it so, then it's not true,' says Nico. 'We're here to see the sights, and sights we are, we're seen. That's integration, reciprocity – for once, Ahmed, try to be genuine, forget the lines you learned, stand on the stage and look! Improvise. Astound us all....'

\*

It's like snow – the desert's white and guys are cutting blocks of salt, 40 kilos at a time – that's not so much, but if you're small and it goes on all day... If you were a cow – wow! It's paradise. Salt licks – who remembers them? No cows here.

'You're right, Nico,' Ahmed says, appeasing. 'Drugs and booze – you consume them and they're gone. Maybe it is you that they consume – then you're going gone too – but unlike capital, nothing survives, nothing gets bigger, the cash goes round and round: if you use, you don't invest.'

'What? What's this?' Nico rants, and humps a block on to some old lady's back.

'I'm engaging with your thought-line,' Ahmed says. 'You know, your trouble is – you're victim of your goodness. You use goodness to arouse a suffering, and then to have it find a way out for you. That isn't goodness, Nico – it's curiosity. Seeing how the suffering live, trying it for yourself. Then – there's your desire for intimacy. The weak, the vulnerable – they're easy to approach because – they need you, need your help. It isn't you, though, Nico. It's anyone at all, with any kind of armour, any make of gun. They're easy friends – they need a hand, and then the hand that holds some cash, some sympathy, some food.

'It's maybe quite contorted,' he goes on, 'or sensibility must be. But your indifference, your opportunism – it's banal, and risky too. Most teeter on a line between the good and bad ... follow the bad, the raft is counterbalanced by the extra-good, so's we don't all roll in the sea.'

'Oh,' Nico says, losing patience, 'I'll show you Lizeth and Cheyenne. They need a friend, a friend with friends, and powerful ones, who know the numbers on the street.'

*

Lizeth is short and happy – just right for Ahmed, who's much taken with Cheyenne, who's tall and pale and melancholy. Nico pats them both, the same, indifferently. They're needy, both want to be friendly, but don't want to be a friend, it's a burden to take on, a block of salt which is the nourishment of life, but on your back it gives you sores and dries you out, bends you in two, like a bamboo wand from a grove of them, that bends but seldom breaks, they say....

'We can go dance with them,' says Nico. 'Dance is life, as Matisse said, it's rare you find a couple without prejudice who'll dance with strangers, no ties except from the goodness you know all about, my friend,' and he joins Ahmed's hand with tall

Cheyenne's. 'No fuss,' he says. 'If you want one of those, you should die and see them carry you off in style.'

'It's my cousin's house,' says Cheyenne, when they have done their dance. A poor house, crooked, poorly kept. No chairs, a mattress that you both stand by, not looking at it, nor at anything.

'I like to be helpful,' Ahmed says. 'Other people, how you approach them – it's a delicate affair.'

'Cash is always handy, yes,' says Cheyenne, as Ahmed pulls out some wrinkled notes and little roundels – where to put them? On the bed?

'Those drinks,' says Ahmed. 'They cost! And the music, my! it was good and loud.'

'Other people,' says Cheyenne. 'Maybe you should give them up. They're an addiction, and it kills you.'

'Yes,' says Ahmed. 'And there's other people get involved in that – not just the carrying out, there's laying in, and digging, singing, firecrackers, all that.'

It's summed up well. Firecrackers – maybe forever.

'It keeps bad influences away,' says Cheyenne – 'Sparks and bangs. Pepper and salt. My favourites.'

'But you can't believe in those,' says Ahmed. 'Besides, there's too much salt. The city's built on it.'

'If you don't believe, there's nothing, just the flat and you must start again. But – where's the destination?' Cheyenne asks.

'It's a good point,' says Ahmed, leaning on the wall. 'You think a destination's given by the track, where it trends, people taking it in strides – but really, destinations are in your head. You know where they are, far off, but in your head they're abstracts, so you can never reach them, nor can a brain attempt a single step. Destinations have beginning but no end, no movement.'

'That's it,' Cheyenne says. 'Living here, it's where you end, right where you start.'

'It's true for everyone,' says Ahmed. 'Except some people wear goatskin slippers, feed peacocks with a silver spoon.'

'White ones,' Cheyenne says. 'Those ordinary metallic birds are everywhere, they're overrated – and the noise!'

'You're right,' says Ahmed, wondering if to leave's indelicate, or to stay is worse, and who sleeps on the mattress.... 'There's many things, maybe, I could do to make your life a better place. But ... I'm naive, and shallow too. Nico – has depth, he sees what everything is made of – even those silver spoons for peacocks – that's his trade, an assayer....'

'Oh, it's Lizeth's too,' Cheyenne says: 'She has the eye. She had it given her, the eye of God. There's clever like her, and there are ingenuous like me. They say we foolish ones – we'll inherit ... everything. The earth. But to inherit, somebody must die. The prophet? Everybody else, the fraudsters? In the end, the earth – it's not worth anything, it has no price, no value. It's fortuitous, a rock with weeds, that swirls in depths so dark there's no way out, no back to go to nowhere worse or better it can go, except – on, on! *Davai, davai!* Forget the fortune, Ahmed, it's a product of a death – it's illusory when you come to spend....'

'You must have listened well, Cheyenne,' says Ahmed. 'That's what all the prophets say. And when you see it's not worthwhile, going to mosque and temple, sacred grove, uplifting gallery,' and Ahmed pauses – what comes next? The void? The disenchantment, truth too arid to behold.... 'The earth, Cheyenne,' he says. 'I gift it to you. It isn't mine, it's not a thing of value, and it can't belong. But here you are. It's everything.'

'I know,' she says, 'that's what they say. Down on your knees and wait. Go to the manif, suffer and march. But thanks, Ahmed, more than that you cannot do, more than give me everything. More than the nothing that's not yours, you cannot give. I think only of myself – but Lizeth, she thinks of partners, conning someone as a team. She's generous, she's given her soul for that. We're commodities, Ahmed, and it's capitalism. That's for now. It's defined, who has some capital can make much more, as much as possible, convert it into our resources and make more and more. And are we able to change back, to something new, or something pristine? We're commodities, like tufty animals for sale, with tusks and claws, the stuff in mines, in air, in nuts on trees, back in nature, rocks and trees. In themselves, no value.'

'No, of course,' says Ahmed. 'Your being poor isn't part of it. Anybody can be noble – as for degradation, I'll agree, it's worse among the rich....'

'Yes, they know,' says Cheyenne. 'They try to give some away. Who has more tries to be generous: – they're rich, and it's all relative. My relatives – I've tried them all. Take an example,' and she gathers the small change, waves it at him, and laughs. ' – is that all you have left, Ahmed?'

'The drinks,' says Ahmed, 'you need them, lots of them. Stuff from several bottles too... But of course, I'm rich. Back where I came from....'

'I know,' Cheyenne says. 'Don't try that one. There's tiled villas, birds with little crowns and water sweet as milk....'

'The world, Cheyenne,' Ahmed says, 'or our brief occupation of it, is run by fraudsters and the rest are victims. Monkey business. But – can I trust you, Cheyenne? You say Lizeth is an accomplice, I know Nico is part of any dominance, any system that will bear him up. Sure, he can be compassionate. He's an entity, all the emotions, tricks and treats. Are you and I, Cheyenne, those twisted trees that lean aslant? Strength or distortion? Is it a seeking goodness, or is it the prevailing wind? Are there good trees?'

'Yes, Ahmed,' she says. 'I'm a good tree. It's late. It's early – I'll think of you, as you wander off to your poor house....'

*

'Lizeth is a find,' says Nico. 'If you don't chime with Cheyenne, she has a friend, Leidy's her name.'

*

It's not the fault of capitalism. The book says it rises from religion, freed from it, by it – away with rote and hierarchy, authority and graft, away with custom – now it's individuals and conscience: freedom, except from yourself. It's religion makes authority, like laws makes criminals. Only if you have believed can you believe in nothing, and nothing but yourself – and it is good. It's the good that makes the bad – but it's not the fault of capital. That's abstract and a freedom too....

*

The city from above – it's brown – tiles terracotta, roofs that rust. Ornamented by white glazed parapets, white pigeons. There's the brown river, then the houses tumble up the hill, once where the wind blew, desirable, now overgrown by tiny houses, as they say, 'of fortune', improvised. Statues and towers – up high enough, you can't see people, remember the aiming guide – two hundred metres and the features are a blur, three hundred and the head is like a sulphur match, four hundred and you're sure to miss what you are aiming at ... the little autos, scarablike; bikes with motors weaving like complicated ants.... There's trains, running on a pencil-line, a link that you can see, there's planes that lift with nothing, like the pigeons, but they don't circle, go straight into their disappearance.

'Don't try recruiting, Ahmed,' Nico says. 'They're party girls. They have a trade.'

'The room....' Ahmed starts.

'The stage,' says Nico, 'where you forgot your line. I like you, Ahmed, you think; you're a curiosity. The time is past for falling down before immensities – the Stendhal syndrome of the humanist. Find ways of survival that succeed, solve what you can and leave what you can't resolve to future genius.'

He lights a long cheroot, and thumbs some poems, fresh fallen from a circle of his friends – a sheet unfolded big as a double-bed; when tucked away, a lozenge: – stow it in your hatband, a tiny diamond like those Tuva stamps, with the eagles....

'Read this,' he says. 'It's light, de-light, burns like an arc, then leaves you in the dark –

*"Down the arcades under the skylarks,*
*swift lights grapple and shatter to emeralds...."*

'Poor boy! He went out like a weld....'

'You've got into the stream, Nico,' says Ahmed, admiring. 'Young talent. That's what people from outside seek.... Without it, places like this are in a twilight.'

'I'm something of a heretic,' says Nico, watching his bitter smoke float up, 'Power comes from architecture. Form, not words, not transformation: – what *is*.'

'The hippopotamus,' says Ahmed, bringing out the reference timidly.

'Yes,' says Nico. 'The poor buggers. Where will they end up? If there's any left.'

*

'Doctor Haas!' shouts Nico, jovial, from the bar: 'Off to rob more tombs? Kali awaits us all, goddess of death – a terror – but meanwhile you take the tidbits for yourself.'

'Not Kali,' says Haas, severely. 'Everyone talks of her here, thinks they see her ... but she fleets. The city's full of goddesses, doing their spin – all cities are like that. I serve, of course –

something from the same mountain top, you're right. Death is complex – there's an industry – the grieving and the hiding, judgments and alibis... Without these exhumations, the tourists will not come. Gods and goddesses: they give lustre. The living here are sad to see. The splendour past – the strangers pay for that.'

Doctor Haas has grit or frit in every fold, naval duds, a trenching tool; a rhomboid on his face tattooed, defends against all hex.

'My dig is culture, Nico and Ahmed,' austerely, he tells them. 'You talk so much about what that might be – come, lend a hand, help dig it up!' the good doctor says, and so they do.

*

The three climb up the hill, their breaths quite uncoordinated. They pant, the words – impressive, but stumbled over, out of time.

'Without a Kali, life would be much the same,' says Nico. 'Birth and death, death and birth. In between there's instinct, what Ahmed calls love, I'd say attachment – that often leads to birth, and so to death. The circle...'

'Of course,' says Haas. 'A goddess, of death like Kali, doesn't stop a thing, but neither hurries it along. The calendar says that often there's more deaths than you expect. What gives significance is ritual – what Ahmed calls beauty. Terror too, and awe and dread – all the time. I ask myself – the rich – did they get a better trip, or were there places reserved somewhere up high, so's they could spy? Maybe they'd need a sacrifice, their roast of popcorn.'

'Your digs,' says Ahmed, 'they don't introduce the metaphysics. For you it's how high up the ladder are the bones, bedecked: civilised? The funeral rites? Clap hands and stamp those feet! Are we up there, tops in the ladder of the civilised, we quick – because we bury, burn, and cry?'

'If you ignore what is inevitable and how it finishes – your end, the end of everything – you are a higher kind,' says Nico. 'It seems. The early ones, all had a calculator, told them when it ends – with pomp and reckoning, stars mustered, waiting, sun and moon aligned.... Arithmetic foretells, and then – it too will disappear. All leads to this, transcendence, judgment, happy and unhappy ends, the humans – where then? Post mortem. Where did they go? The good ones just extinguished, the bad ones – eternal punishment? Better be bad, immortally, I'd say.'

'Not like that at all,' says Haas. 'Just accept what you are told, the best story that there is. Don't quiz the past, don't mock credulity. Peep behind the scenery – and you'll end up bad. Watch the actors, not the play.'

*

As they go up, a little band straggles down past them. A trumpet, whose bobbly notes make him sound like an animal, stops playing long notes as the scientists push past.

'Hey, Lizeth,' Ahmed shouts, 'where's Cheyenne?'

'That's no way to greet,' says Lizeth, though she doesn't laugh. There's no coffin. 'It was our teacher – he's not here.' She wears white flowers, a little sweaty, in her hair. 'They coked him in the town,' she says. It's not meant funny like it sounds.

'Was he a good teacher?' Nico asks.

That doesn't mean a lot; to Lizeth, it means nothing.

'Philosophy,' she says. 'Repose, and names. That was his class.'

'I'm sorry,' Ahmed says. Haas is already far above them.

'But you didn't know him,' Lizeth says.

Nico hugs her – for the past, in anticipation, maybe the present's decorum. He's a formalist – you'd probably not have guessed.

'You love to talk to strangers, Lizeth,' Nico says: 'Most everybody here. School? It was phenomenology, I bet. Maps and pictures.'

Nico and Ahmed follow Doctor Haas – at the top, they can see everything – the town, the whole expanse.

'Talking of hippos,' Nico says, 'the tourists – come here for a wallow. To do the little dirty things they'd never do at home. Rejoice! – the poor are easy to satisfy, and that they're not, and hope not to be poor. The hippo in the mud – the church of the confessions. That mud is ash and tears – what a concoction, Ahmed! It's all profane....'

The stop at a wide dusty hole. There's bones scattered around.

*

'Feathers keep their colour,' says Haas. 'It's a wonder. Like the fire in pots – it must be memory – they cohere after centuries; you'd think they'd be dust like us.'

'You'll polish this up,' says Nico. 'The Ministry will be satisfied. If you've not created any jealousies or asked for a reward, they'll let you open the next tomb.'

'It's so difficult,' Ahmed says. 'You have to make friends – often they're not friendly, or then – they're enemies. There's pressure, like making opals, you must persevere, but it flattens you.'

'Oh,' says Haas, 'I never encountered that. I get on well with everyone.'

'It's not like that,' says Nico. 'If it was we'd all be free and equal. Where's Cheyenne? Made some bad friends, I guess....' and he stares at Ahmed.

'I didn't get to friendship,' Ahmed says, quite troubled.

'Maybe then you should,' says Nico, 'Before you start, you must know everything.'

'Perhaps she left school early, never got to phenomenology,' says Haas, making a peace.

*

'We were set up like in Paris,' Ahmed says. 'I was a *coryphée*, promoted from the *corps*. I must have aimed too high. They said – "His dancing gives great pleasure – but one feels our pleasure's never quite as great as his. It's brilliance for its own sake – and brilliance has no sake, only he does. It's pomp and infallibility." It finished me.'

'Rubbish!' Nico says. 'If it got to you – fall on your face. They'll change their view – they always do. That is their job – you knew yours, it seems. No tears – people like to see tall guys fall down. That's why old statues lose their penises.'

'I thought "a pause",' says Ahmed. 'But I've gone to flab: it's obscene – wanting to raise people up, and I've the physique of a bean.'

'You had a judgment, Ahmed,' Nico says. 'Shows you had a presence. I was in security, then the market – no one knows why one is thrown out, it's secret anyway – and so, no testimonial. It's good, it's very good. No critique you puzzle over all your days. As the poet said, only our heart knows what we are.'

'I've heard you say that before,' says Haas, fascinated. 'It's a good get-out. Me – I publish. But much of what I find – it's true. It's stolen.'

'You find, you rob, you're robbed,' says Nico. 'A moral tale.'

'Oh no,' says Haas. 'What's dead and buried – doesn't have an owner.'

'Anyway,' says Ahmed, 'it shouldn't be about people and rewards.'

'Rewards for accomplishment,' says Haas. 'Even for what shouldn't have been done.'

'I slipped,' says Ahmed. 'I was the best, perfection. Now – I flounder.'

'It's good too,' says Nico. 'I took the risk, I was the Master who faced down death, in battle with the other Masters. I survived. It's good here, and you take the risk. They've been poor here since they're not an empire – when they were great, they went to war or human sacrifice – and it was good for everyone.'

'Exactly so,' says Doctor Haas. 'Everyone digs up the past as best they can – the lucky ones find things that they can polish up, obsidian, feathers, gold. It's never yours, but you enjoy, and that's the best there is.'

'My abiding guide,' says Nico. 'Talking of masters – is this: "The absolute change that threatens us from birth to death remains unpredictable and incomprehensible." Not just for me, but for us all. We choose freedom, and so we choose the perpetual threat. That is our being.'

'Yes,' says Haas. 'We did it at school. It's penetrating, but there is no content. Accept! That's what it says, wherever, whatever you are. Call what you have choice, then freedom. It's a con. You know, my trade's in coffins, hoping there won't be one that's sealed, or lead. To find all the juices there, a kind of mortal hanging on – for millennia, the body, which is all we know we have – entrapped, preserved. Off to the lab? No thanks! That's the threat inherent in my trade – so far, it's been only bones, that would make marimbas.'

*

Cheyenne stays away – she's had a threat, not from philosophy, or ganglia, but a real criminal, her friend, her brother, her hope and her despair. Strangers are fine – but they bring strange things, procedures, connections that you don't want plugged into you.

'You want company?' Cheyenne asks, looking up and down the street. 'There's Leidy. Yenni. They're a bit like me and Lizeth.'

'And you all read Husserl together?' Ahmed asks.

'Don't be snide, Ahmed,' says Cheyenne, pinching her mouth. 'It isn't you.'

'I'll stay on my own,' says Ahmed. 'I'm learning other people may not be so great. It's from when we were in bands. Hunting, specially.'

'They could hurt me,' Cheyenne says. 'Talking philosophy and not having sex – it could mean death.'

'I need to be sure,' says Ahmed, confused. 'Promise me – that's the outcome. Death or mutilation. Then, perhaps I'll help you. You've to be suspicious in this place – you are, Cheyenne, I'm learning to be the same.'

'Talk to Nico,' Cheyenne says, and hurries off.

*

'I'm in a good crowd,' Nico says. 'If I want to go to hospital or not go into jail – I've help on hand. Friends. For them, I am a hunter. They're all gatherers, like you, Ahmed. Incidentally – that joke about confession – the hippopotamus – Augustine. The church in the river mud while angels fly above, like in a Fragonard – they roared. They want a memoir from me. Lies and elisions. Adventures in your armchair. But – I don't have the urge – not poetry, not painting walls. I'm enough in myself. I have no creatures inside waiting to be freed, and think it's me that's having the escape. I'm just a spare wheel, Ahmed.'

'There's Cheyenne, Nico,' Ahmed says. 'In danger, she needs help.'

'It's you,' says Nico. 'Your mission, you're the help we all call on, without exception. Not me – I'm not a diplomat, pressing my pants while soldiers thumb their magazines. I'm not a mercenary, still less a volunteer. A conscript? No more than we all are – enrolled in someone's army, by birth or by cartographers. Who's to be eliminated anyway, to ease your conscience? Who's not respecting human rights and womankind? The family, clan, cartel? Or jealous cousin? Where do you think to hide the corpse? – beneath the judge's chair?'

'Help, Nico, not mayhem,' Ahmed says.

'So she will flee with you? Another betrothal in San Domingo – yes! An opera – the slave redeemed, the black blanched and ripped from context ... but singing like a Trojan, naturalised, a Helen, grubby but restored.....'

'No help, Nico,' says Ahmed. 'Just company – and you can write it up.'

'Hmmm,' says Nico, 'Cheyenne's long bones – like mammoth tusks. A false burial, perhaps? Doctor Haas – a naval man who's lost his sea – but maybe, the rocking swell ... he's stowed it all inside, that is his character. A joker, Ahmed: the little imp whose quips enlighten every agony, the pimple on the death's head. The black hole, the priest, we two mechanicals leaning on our spades – and "thar she goes, me hearties", into the bosom of the deep, the empty tomb ... and then – a miracle! and there she is, pale and walking on the tarmac, you scoop her up – the eagle Ahmed and his timid dove, saved from the lusty body's putrefaction, its liquifaction ... ah! Ahmed! I'm out of list and roll, and ramping up and down in lilting prose....' and Nico laughs and laughs.

'It's an idea,' says Ahmed. 'A death, but without suffering, all keeping mum and holding tight our souls, lest they fly out our nose and we're undone.'

'That's it,' says Nico, settling into someone's feuilleton. 'That night we dragged their own harrows ... over the tessellated pavements....' Oh dear! Could be Dowson!'

*

Lizeth – her scorn like brose, nourishing and raging, flat on her plate – says, 'Always the compromise. Sounding like warriors – save the weaker, never a collectivity! You pretend you've principles – but never the struggle, the contest. Save poor Cheyenne! Patronising and paternal.'

'In our balloon, Lizeth,' Nico says, 'there's room for just one more – not you! It's so: Cheyenne would be the lighter load. Your teacher had it right, gender's a category without the lift-off quality we need....

'They-orientation, Lizeth. There's the sticking point, "it has a high degree of remoteness from direct experience". You'll remember the quotation. You're right, of course: we should pledge to liberate the prisoners of starvation, but.... Let's start with one, well-fed but under threat – Cheyenne. To free the mass, ah, what a fine sound – so long postponed – with us the liberators, bigger, better than dear Bolívar... but there are levels, strata, heights *and* turbulence.... Spirals. Two of you – we would not rise. A million – we would need a battleship – and there is no sea....'

'Come, Lizeth,' says Doctor Haas, 'there's no balloon. It's another of those metaphors you see in the night sky. You're too heavy. You stay here, devise a different battle plan.'

'Different?' Lizeth shouts. 'Hers is a noble rescue, not a battle plan.'

'Well,' says Haas, trying to calm the upset of his gaffe, 'you can't stop people being nasty.'

'But I'm not,' says Lizeth. 'Not nasty, not a bit. So it means that I'll be getting beat, I guess.'

'Do as I do,' says the doctor. 'Gaze upon the dead. There is no face. They're mute. Resign yourself. Your place is here. Violence and retribution – the good books are full of it. It's us, us all. Our history.'

'So, I have a place? Everybody does?' Lizeth asks, a slice of nastiness sliding out. There's no response.

The place – it's a peasant room – a few chairs round the walls, a table, venerable, an altar where the coffin goes, or something else to celebrate, perhaps. All is white, but not exactly bright, the window's small and tight, a mouth crimped to hide no teeth – it's the only feature that could speak. Windows, though – they don't.

*

'Resentment – it will eat you up, Lizeth,' says Nico, coddling her: 'Seek justice – that will blunt the edge – a perfection that contains its compromise. That "doing unto others" – it won't work in our club, our litterateurs, our patrons, buyers, readers, elocutors....'

'Your literary pals....' Ahmed starts -

'Oh, we're into all the arts,' says Nico. 'You should drop in, Ahmed, give us some fouettés. My friends are officers – then, gentlemen, perhaps. Officers are many types – some hard with their men and softer on the enemy, and vice versa. Some in the army – but then in all the other trades: state punishers, and then the curers, reformers, analysts chemists, doctors, zoomen, producers and reproducers, directors and surgeons – keeping everyone in line, in happiness, in want and hope. Manage and entertain, from birth and beauty, Ahmed; to death, resurrection, and forensic archaeology, good Doctor Haas! Succour and inspect – women and men, the gnarled and scarred, the hairy and the shiny.... In the club, the talk is moderated; youth – tolerated, fertilised and pruned. It's all relax, accept: moments of elegance, strata of fine lives, of "was it so?" and "will it, can it be?" It's not executive, rather – reflective. Senatorial.

'You gave up on perfection, Ahmed – so did they. Poetry's like that. Nostalgia and a dictionary. The novel – poor feeble dear – walking on air, my friends....'

'My perfection,' Ahmed says, 'was only about me. Mere solipsism. I was the star that wasn't born – although I kept my vanity. Even as *coryphée* – the top brick on a pyramid of dwarves ... alas, on top you need to be the lightest weight.... Shallow, shallow, Doctor Haas, my past....'

And Doctor Haas – he nods and laughs, and laughs and nods.


## THE CIRCLE

'I shan't dance,' says Ahmed. Nico has invited him and Haas to the artistic circle. Lizeth wouldn't go – she's not invited anyway.

The theme's the moon.

One of the members, a zooman, conservator – presents a project: – a flock of vicunas, first colonists, a flock settled down there, on the moon:

'It's white, airless, like a high plain. The beasts are used to adaptation – they live cheap, on grass and ice. It will be a home. Before we plant ourselves up there – let the animals suss it out. We'll have to learn to live again – it's all so difficult – to breathe, to hear sense through overpowering noise.... There's no reverberation, no echo. A sound travels round and round – probably, it never disappears – the first colonials bequeathe their footsteps, wondering rhetoric, even their farts, the tinkle of hairs that drop from pate to dust.... It never decays, the harmony ... experimental notes, éclairs de lune, les sons éternels – imagine, 'a silver horn/plucks at the silver air' – no more! No breath, no atmosphere ... round and round for ever. No air. Absent declaimers all around: when we colonise – hear the perpetual soughing of the forest of eternal chat....'

Nico's impressed, but still he jokes about 'the Patalunatics', 'Is it so, that every word, the flap of every flag, ring-snaps of every can of beer, resounds for ever? How to make a conversation, when all has been already said, stratified, layers like silica, black forest cake?' and he ogles in pretend despair.

'I'm so uncomfortable,' whispers Ahmed to his Doctor friend, dear Haas. 'It's not my place at all ...' although the Doctor's fascinated. 'No decay,' he says. 'The astronauts can lie around, puff-suited, falling as they are, no tomb, no putrefaction. On the surface, white, silkworm coccoons. For me – there'll be nothing, nothing for my skills, no remains, though all remains....'

'Who goes down there,' the zooman says. 'Will fall into a crevice or a pit, will not last long, not put brick on brick – but every sentence ... immortalised.'

*

'Even if he's wrong,' says Haas, 'and surely he must be – it is the future of our empire, the empire of the moon.....An empire that belongs to everyone, where all are masters, and there are no slaves....'

*

'I don't want to move,' says Cheyenne: 'I shan't leave. If I must leave....'

'There's always a deal to make,' says Lizeth. 'A compromise. It's only mistakes that end up bad.'

'Going anywhere with Ahmed,' says Cheyenne, 'is like a trip to another world. Dark and airless, full of crevasses.'

Lizeth agrees, 'They'd be stealing you, Cheyenne. To satisfy themselves – then, there's the law. Try to keep that out.'

'Oh yes!' Cheyenne says. 'Law! He's a terrible intruder, like death dealing out food and eating most himself. Alejo went to jail, and suffered terrible. Some camps – you die, and that's an end. Others – you starve and scheme, but they have kept a score, and when your work is done – they let you out to live somewhere, somehow. But here, his jail – it's with him always, a chain, commitments, friends and enemies – for ever. No, Lizeth, I'll not let them use law on me – a death that's worse than death....'

'Do you have anyone you trust, Cheyenne?' asks Lizeth. 'I don't. Alejo – your brother? Lover? Boss? In jail? All or some of those? It's not like they say it is, all on the same side. The thing is

not to appear an edible – this makeup helps –' and she shows
Cheyenne some mustard colour, used for smearing on a face.

*

'Well,' Nico says, 'here we are, Ahmed, in turmoil. Hardly arrived,
and now we're in the Helen saga – stealing a woman who belongs
to someone else, having to scuttle off we don't know where, do
battle, risk everything because the top guy in our gang feels
disrespected.. Cut short the saga, Ahmed – that is my advice. Stay
here, don't trip or fight. If Circe calls – you entertain her. No
endless treks, they're not for you: – our Dutchman, Haas, he
doesn't fly, he's anchored to his cemetery. That's right. Don't
whisper to the Trojan Horse, no pat, no apple.... Let women sort
things for themselves – no jealousy, no husbands – grow, Ahmed,
grow up! Forget Helen, forget Penelope – they'll get together, sell
homespun woollens on a stall.

'Meantime – let's you and I go on the razzle, find some
prostitutes, ignore the hardness of their lives, have fun and hope a
gang or brother doesn't cut off our male prerogative and stick it in
our mouth.... Death, Ahmed – that's the speciality here, it's Grand
Guignol, and you must join the cast. Stay with the metaphors – if
fiction isn't stranger than the truth, it isn't interesting....'

'Oh Nico,' Ahmed says. 'Your arrogance! Rhodomontade,
strutting fierce! I envy you! And.... I should confess, my dancing....
Maybe I exaggerated.... Perhaps, though I sought perfection, the
outcome was less perfect than I said: a chorus line more shaky,
uncoordinated than the one I claimed....'

'It's obvious,' says Nico. 'We all do that; we exiles all tell lies
about the height we fell from, how we landed here distraught....'

'A revelation,' Ahmed shouts. 'Of course! The horse is full of
hoplites – what a name! I could design and choreograph, and with a
line, a swarm – HopLites: a cosmic act....'

He is in ecstasy. 'You're frilly, Ahmed,' Nico says. 'You'd be
welcomed in our club. Besides, a dancer's a mere figure – a
mechanism, hammer on a string.... But – choreography ... that's
architecture.'

'You may be right,' says Nico. 'You'd be protection for
Cheyenne. A name, a visibility, a reputation. Cash!

'I'll introduce you to some generals – they're all fans of
Petipa.... It's the drill excites; the uniforms – and then the stalks,

ghost walks and leopard crawls – ah, soldiers! So delicate and balanced when they're not out causing bangs.'

'Have your laugh, dear Nico,' Ahmed says, surfing on his inspiration. 'I could make my name – and yours. You're without qualities, without the talents too. As your creative friend, some of my stardust maybe drops on you, my tinsel dazzles – my genius! – putting the desperate in a troupe.... Exposure, that's the good that trumps the misery. Flashes of fashion, big smiles, everyone....'

'Suppose they can't,' says Nico, 'The dance. Not interested or not capable.'

'Then all the worse for them,' says Ahmed, undeterred.

\*

An idea like that: to seize in all the viscosity of its being, requires creative genius.... Beware, it's slippery, if you don't hold on the bar you'll fall!

Ahmed's project – brilliant!

It doesn't work.

It doesn't work a bit.

It's a pain. No one wants it.

\*

Nico says, 'Your horse – it isn't full of soldiers, it's all horse-shit.'

'Helen the heroine,' Ahmed agrees, quite glum. 'She must be full of horse, of heroin. Superfluity. Over-determination. It must be her, opening the gate – in comes the horse, death's steed, a tank. They lumber in, she scampers out ... rape, abduction, enforced adultery – who would blame her for anything she does?

'No wonder, that she's passive, hallucinates the heroes and the goddesses, the shields, the swords – ah yes, those swords....

'The flesh invites....'

'No,' says Nico. 'Remember, "the eye cannot see itself". Ideas bounce off reality – like peas off a wall, they said. You're not cut out for life, Ahmed. You are a genius – and so, forget the Greeks, they are not in your league. Your plan was excellent, it didn't fit reality.

'Reality – a part of life that's complicated, and you are doubled up in anguish, bedevilled by the inside and the outside that never meet, cohere.... We are a blind man in a maze, Ahmed, or in a tunnel blocked by doors where you must find the tiny key for each, the darkness going on for ever till – oh no! It stops – a wall of rock, you're finished; over. Death, Ahmed. That's what you're waiting for, uniqueness, paradoxically finds what everybody has – the wall, the end.'

'All right, Nico,' says Ahmed. 'The HopLites finish, something else begins. Your pata-poetaster generals – they hold the power. Let's concentrate on that. That is the key, so heavy – to lift it takes the two of us ... and Cheyenne too, and Lizeth....'

*

Alas, he cannot think of anything.

*

Doctor Haas – he doesn't tumble in a tomb. He goes from dig to dig.

He thrives, he lives, immaculate.

Cheyenne is threatened, so is everyone – but no one dies, here in the city of the dead – they're all alive for now.

The flesh invites – and Cheyenne's invites Ahmed's. It's quite enjoyable.

Nico tries out some *terza rima*, in friendly competition with a minister.

'Maybe Cheyenne is threatened because she has a gang,' says Nico. 'Or, she has some power.'

'I only know her non-speaking parts,' says Ahmed. 'The sex is wonderful, but....'

'No doubt she likes her food, Ahmed,' says Nico. 'It doesn't mean you are a farmer.'

'Her gang,' says Ahmed. 'It's a mystery. Is our adventure about that, or is it about phenomenology?'

Nico takes some pocket billiard balls from his pants, and tries to juggle them. 'Phenomenology or gangs? Yes, that's the question, Ahmed. I can't be of much use, I fear. Nothing can be hurried up. You know – that capitalism is the highest we can reach, and it's become the species' default scheme. The rest is titivation... anything more radical – is guerrillas. Everyone has sympathy with guerrillas, at the beginning – even the generals. Of course, yes, there's some who fight who're not at all *sympa*. Then comes a degrade, corruption and ferocity. The generals turn to poetry. Surrealism, dear Ahmed, is the last resort of sensibility.... The rhyming dictionary, or Finnegan – select a word at random, do your riff....'

'You're fantasising, Nico,' Ahmed says. 'The poor ... beneath our nose ... the mass exploited ... anguish and unhappiness – what...?'

'All of us, waiting to be folded in,' says Nico. 'To the system, that determines everything.'

'Then it's not this city, Nico,' Ahmed says. 'It's every city. Cages, wild territories. Where you wait for death? Some pills to sweeten...?'

They swallow this discourse, try to digest – what? Is it dry food? Liquid gold? A farmakon?

'That's drastic, Ahmed,' Nico says. 'Maybe it's true. The countryside – it used to be a place of birth – but now, it's an antechamber to the abattoir.... Anyway – there's always a system – if you're not in one, you starve.'

'Those alpacas,' Ahmed says. 'Now, there's a crowd of them that needs protecting.... They don't pester, don't interrogate.'

\*

'Kali, the goddess,' Cheyenne says, 'She's terrifying, but I'm sure she's on our side.'

'I think she's quite irrelevant,' says Doctor Haas. 'She's everywhere, presiding over happenstance, without a say.'

'It's so,' says Lizeth. 'She is mute. What matters is our families – the fathers falling on our heads and smothering like noxious pancakes; our debts, our friends and enemies, our passions and illusions: the air and water dark and gritty. New young ones hidden underfoot – they're man-and woman-traps. It's life, they say – expecting the great change.... Or not.'

'I dig it up,' says Haas. 'My future. It starts as metaphor, ends as empty pits.' He laughs. That's what you do, it doesn't signify, but everyone feels good.'

'What if there's fresh? asks Lizeth. 'People you know, people from jail. People disassembled, disjointed and decapitated, people – to be forgot.'

'Come, Lizeth,' Cheyenne says, turning away and leaving. 'What a thought! You don't do anything that's to end just left to forgetfulness. Every scrap – it has its use, its meaning....'

Haas holds back – he'd follow Cheyenne – it isn't wise ... her body's fine, in place, in form: don't going trotting after, Haas – just use your eyes....

'My mother said, "You're a naughty naughty boy. But however bad you are – don't finish up a corpse in jail – they'll have to improvise a place – you could end up in a museum, in a case",' he says. 'I don't discriminate, Lizeth. I'm discreet. If it's not artistic, and antique, what is the point...?'

'They use you!' Lizeth says. 'So, you resurrect, but also hide....'

'Salvation doesn't come as ready-made. There's fits. And starts. And stops. I used to be a naughty boy,' says Haas. 'Now I'm a scientist. I can't do bad. I classify, erase. The nameless are of no interest, not to anyone. Besides, I hate processions: and people shouldn't cry real tears on stage – it makes them less convincing. Then there's the flummery: questions and orations ... oh, what a bore.'

'It's true,' says Lizeth, reluctant. 'We're animals – we bury what we don't eat. So long as we don't hunt each other....'

'Oh, we do, we shall, we do,' laughs the good doctor. 'That's not the point. The point's the fuss. The wake, memorial stones, *ex votos* on the wall.... Time wasted, however much you search – time lost. What you can't revive ... you dig a hole.'

'I tremble,' Lizeth says. 'I'm not an enterprise, not like Cheyenne. She's a geometer, she has lines, she knows the angles. I wait – like, wait on tables, count the chairs. I notice if one's empty. And then, dear Haas – I weep.'

'That's good,' the doctor says. 'It makes no difference anyway. We're all the last, the little tsar – it's too big for us, what we are in. A world war? Revolutions, millions conscripted, lost, never counted or enrolled, under the snow somewhere – killed for something or for nothing, always up against the universe, immense, uncertain and indifferent....'

'Yes,' says Lizeth, 'but ... there is being, and there's not.'

'We're chorus, dear,' says Haas. 'If you fall down, we all go with you, into the pit. If you want to do a solo – think again. Don't try to be Cheyenne.'

*

'You're right, Ahmed,' says Nico. 'Be content with that. Take it further – you'll be in trouble, so will everyone around you – even me. I know I'm wrong, thinking wrong things, half-rhymes and borrowings. Wrong usually wins – but I'm not a monster. I want a peace elastic, full of bonhomie. I'll go on being wrong, opposing you.... I shan't write poetry, I promise you – that's a confusion. It's second and third thoughts, sometimes just thoughts. Be simple, Ahmed, be like me – accept that reality is always more wrong than right.'

'What you say, Nico, it isn't so,' says Ahmed. 'Except – for getting into trouble. We all know that. And Cheyenne says I should move out from you. Then she'll move in. Except – you are protection, Nico – she is, she has, none....'

'It isn't so,' says Nico. 'And besides – if it were, she's more protected on her own, obedient. Or secretive. Cheyenne can venture into many lives – repent, grow big or small or reproduce – you can't. Your cash is staked on doing good, the wheel spins once, then you're outside – laden with cash, a prey for the whole street – or destitute.'

'Doing right,' says Ahmed, 'when history tells you you are in the wrong, beyond all reparation, backward where you come from, backward where you go ... it can't go well. Cheyenne and Lizeth, sense and sensibility, and you, Nico, probably a Gauguin without the colour ... we must expect them to be farouche. Cheyenne to be a boss. Not everyone, not every woman, usurping that long evolving line of men can be a prof, adventurer, guide.... The good though – we were told it's obvious, the bad was complicated – maybe it isn't so.... When there's no philosophy, you have to make it up, it's difficult, no one helps, it's quite the contrary ... Cheyenne is troubled, maybe she should leave pheneomenology, it's superficial, existentialism too....'

'No,' says Nico, irritated. 'Let's agree – she has a gang, and Lizeth is her counsellor. Have done with speculation, and prepare.'

\*

'Your vision's generous, Ahmed,' says Nico. 'But you'll find it's limited. Cheyenne won't leave unless you take the family – it makes things less romantic. Besides – where will you go? Who'll take you?'

'It's complicated,' Ahmed says. 'Maybe before we go, we ought not to have come.'

'Well put,' says Nico. 'But I'm happy here – with poetry and powerful guys.'

*

Poor Doctor Haas.... One dig too much – maybe the verbal kind. He'd make a fine exhibit, but the dead – before they can be cleaned, displayed, some time must pass.

'Poor Doctor Haas,' says Lizeth, and she weeps. 'A chronicler. His precious notebooks, flourishes and slurs – so bright and sharp – like brazen horns.... Here are dragons, here are blurs – the smoke, the steam, the happy smoke, the wonder dust – already we are in the clouds, halfway to nowhere, but it's trade, the business ... must go on, it's appetite and *volupté*, you can't renounce and can't rejoice, heaven and hell, and we are briefly in between....'

'How was it for him?' asks Nico.

'Oh,' says Lizeth, brightening. 'A *scalpello*. It's what you use to break the stucco off a wall – that's what he was, poor Haas – like on the synagogue in Cordova – Muslim plaster, foliage on those Jewish walls.'

'I dare say there was horror too,' says Cheyenne, without a tear. 'It doesn't last. It's the tribute that we pay to Kali. Haas faced down the corporation. He didn't do their job, burying the victim in an ancient tomb, and thought that tourism would bring the money in and make us sweat....'

'Oh yes,' says Lizeth, 'the tourists bring it in, but after comes security – the generals ... Does Kali rejoice when we go into rehab? Or just wait?'

*

You fill your lungs with nothing, on the plain – the little flock, the alpacas, moves away from Ahmed.... Protection, predation – prosperity and then a cull.

What to do? A fence? Push them higher? Grow their coats – armed guards? It's trade. Don't eat them, don't fleece them? Find something else to wear and eat....

*

'I've no difficulty with Doctor Haas,' says Cheyenne. 'He's always present. His death is just a hiccup. Alejo – he's not himself, but for me, he's always here, when I want, when I think. Like when they were alive. All of them. It doesn't matter – not to them, and not to me.'

'A goddess is so useful,' Lizeth agrees. 'But you must give her something. I cry – when I feel it serves.'

'That's sentimental,' Cheyenne says, given Lizeth a pretend slap. 'Life is trade, Lizeth, for us, for everyone, and certainly for Kali. It's her business, like it is for generals. It's rhythm – they don't count, the numbers – it's on paper, but you only ever see a sample – if you're in charge, that is. Maybe that explains your tears, Lizeth. It isn't serious, it's the story that you think you're in.'

'You're right,' says Nico. 'It's all trade. The regular guys, they take your cash, they don't help much, but keep you in the line. The gangs – they're fierce – so if you do the deal, they'll protect you to the death. If you don't like the game, Lizeth, write down your thoughts and put them in a drawer. Blue flowers – they'll grow inside your head, and in the end, that's all you'll see – blue flowers inside and out. That's my aspiration.'

*

A party! That's the answer – those leaving, those staying. A party – Ahmed hates them, so silence! No music, no processions, no brides, no corpses.

Yet – they must talk – that's voice, half the music. The rest is heart and feet. 'There's all sorts here,' says Nico. 'We'll have percussion, almost inaudible – scrape, shake and thrum, the bush, the forest and the plain, slither and stamp and thrash – qabak and quiryk, safail and tabla, the guaracharaca and the berimbau, the ganza and the zerbaghali. Whistles too – for lovers, spectres and vicunas, jackals and jack tars....'

'Maybe inaudible,' says Ahmed. 'But alert. A stick poised if one of us – a heart that stops, a fading pulse....'

'There's Alejo,' Cheyenne says. 'He beats cut time – like it speeds up your years in jail. He'll be the wind – the trees are so high, you can't hear a thing, and on the plain, you can't hear anything but air.' The lad, Alejo, forever three years old, is threshing with his little stick: he has the beat, if nothing else, and Nico says,

'Alejo doesn't speak, it's good. His tongue is tied. If I ask generals and cops, he won't have comments they'd not like to hear. Go to, Alejo, *alla breve*!'

'Poor Alejo,' Lizeth says. 'He was the lucky one – he went to jail: the other, well.... Alejo was naughty, not like Doctor Haas, the naughtiness you forgive....' She sobs.

'Music ho!' shouts Nico. 'At least a whisper, a stridulation – cockchafers, and cicadas – the music of forlorn love, a background to our solemn discourse....'

'Where's the generals?' Cheyenne asks.

'After uppity guys, for sure,' says Nico. 'The force of order'll need to sort them out.'

'Exactly where?' Cheyenne asks. 'A name or two? If there's a drama, they send out the boys, don't go themselves – maybe there's a pleasure trip, they feel an urge and thrust it on to someone else....'

'An aria,' Nico insists. 'Give us an air, Cheyenne! "*Ah, fuggi rapido*," "Fly, fly away from this impious realm" ...Come, Lizeth, "We're ships abandoned on the icy waves."'

The ladies are abstracted. Where'd the cops and squaddies go...? And Alejo clucks and warbles.

'Charades!' says Ahmed. 'Bring good cheer.'

'Brilliant!' says Lizeth. 'Transformation. That's the only way for us. Once done – you can't change back.'

'But you can transform still further,' Nico says. 'It's a big enterprise. "Fire", the flame. The mind, the power! – remember what they said about the lamp, it "wimpers like a baby", it has a child's distress, so it shows, "all the world's unhappy". The flame – is alive, a verticality inhabited.... "Light my fire!"' Nico chants, 'Real and unreal, both being and non-being. Light up, everyone!'

'It's true,' says Ahmed. 'We're all stereotypes here. I'm blocked completely. So's Cheyenne. We can't do anything for Haas, but for the rest of us – the flame! As a fly, or as a moth – we are consumed – the flame waits and watches over. We're burned up, every one of us. The lamp, though, waits, illuminates our task. It *is* our task.'

'You make it sound too simple, Ahmed,' Nico says. 'I think you don't remember what our real possibility might be. But we can't stick here, waiting for the end, killing and being killed, selling false consciousness in paper twists – ending like Alejo, another one we can't do something for.'

'What's it to be, then?' Lizeth asks. 'Our charade? Don't say Proust or Strindberg – I can't imagine playing in those gardens, not again.'

'No, Lizeth,' Ahmed says. 'That's quite another game. That's guessing titles. Charades means being people that have never been before.'

'Let's not quibble about rules and goals,' says Nico. 'Charades, not "adverbs" – I myself try not to use those. Let's start, and see how far we get. So, no one need decide if they want to go or stay, who with, all that.'

'Have the musicians go,' says Cheyenne. 'They haven't played a note that you could hear. We'll call them later, when we want some noise.'

*

'I don't think what you want is called charades,' says Lizeth. 'But – in any case, I shall be a journalist, write what I like, go where I want. Have many pseudonyms, so no one knows who or what I am.'

*

The alpacas seek a refuge – higher and higher up they go. It's safer, but there's less and less to eat.

Ahmed discovers you can be elected judge. There's all sorts try – he's from outside, unknown, he has a chance. He's the new number on the wheel, not red or black. Brown – like everybody here. He wins. Everyone has won....

The first thing that he wants – is tribute, a memorial that celebrates the doctor. 'Haas light' it's called, known as the Light Haas.

'The Eiffel Tower – a hazard,' Nico says. 'A red light on four legs. In Rome, there's obelisks – in the evening, God sees the lights on top spell FIAT.'

Ahmed says, 'We'll have a light of justice, high above the city....' The only place in all the universe – thousands come to snap and wonder....

It's set up, lit – though it's a closed lamp, not a flame. A flame pollutes, besides, nobody can understand the book that Nico got the idea from.

## JUSTICE

Cheyenne is told about the tsarist chief, the top cop who after revolution said he'd not been impartial so much as being on both sides. 'On the whole,' he told a Bolshevik, 'I was on the Bolshevik side.' There's no Bolsheviks around just now, so Cheyenne pursues justice – fits and starts and stops. She runs a gang in uniform, and one, or even more, who do the commerce, trade the info, help the judges and the journalist, threaten them, and flit, in grey, through Nico's stories.

Nico is the great success – the stories in the end will find a champion, be published, made into a movie, be part of puzzles on TV.... He doesn't join modernity – he writes, he needs no friends, no other scribblers, besides ... there's all the generals and ministers he's always known. The club – that smells of booze and smoke and men: – he drops in for a drink or two, and sometimes stays all day – there's tric-trac, and every other kind of game. He almost has it made.

'Alejo has his band,' says Lizeth. 'He's done best out of our feast. A percussion band – it shouldn't need conducting, but he beats his time, and sometimes sings along, in his particular voice....'

The sound creeps in – you may not like the city, even be scared by it, but the band makes it momentarily like a home town ought to be, if your idea is that it should have part of everywhere and be unique, with a call-sign spread around the region ... hear it on the bus.

Everything is changed, everywhere, everyone in cities is quite anxious, you'd be stupid not to be, not only people you don't know hurrying, doing things you don't know anything about, millions of them, some just come to gawp – but where Kali's dancing on the hill, you've a good idea that law and crime and vice in lockstep have you in their sights, they're sizing you, seeing if you have protection, maybe you're hiding something like we all do.... So, everyone is scared, and waiting, so the band ... even makes you pause and smile, as you scurry up and down, though you'd not think to stop and listen. It's just clacks and shuffs, in any case.

*

The door's marked 'broom'. Inside, there is Cheyenne. 'I won't wear uniform,' she says, 'it scratches, and besides, it is a giveaway. I'm cleaning up, I sweep the dirt....' It's a big room, on the walls, there's every kind of bird – stone-turners, dippers, waders, storks and stalkers, nightingales in farthingales, thrushes in bushes, robins who steal, starlings who fight their patriotic wars....

'A veritable parliament,' says Lizeth.

'It's in a magazine,' says Cheyenne. 'Your workplace – make it a cabinet of curiosities, a window that you beat against and casually, one day – it's open. Out you fly....'

'You keep an equilibrium,' says Lizeth, in admiration. 'Arrest too many – you are unemployed. Too few – they fire you ... you have it right, Cheyenne.'

'Oh, how banal you are, Lizeth,' shouts Cheyenne, slapping down a pistol on her desk. 'A ruling class is being formed. We'll find a compromise – the good and bad – the idea's from Nico's club – the sentimental and the tough. You see, Lizeth, *I*'m the balance, the good and bad, the tolerant and the bigot. It isn't difficult, but – ' and she opens a closet – there's every grade of uniform, with feathers and with shades, pips and stripes, with AKs and with crossbows, puffy-pants and jerkins, frogs and epaulettes ... 'See, you must be everything, every role there is – good cop and bad, corrupt and puritan.'

'There's more, Cheyenne,' says Lizeth, trying on some feather capes, smoking the meerschaums, trying sappers' hats. 'The great idea.'

'I even fear,' Cheyenne says, 'it is too late for that. The empire. What you need's consolidation. Uniting territory, integrating – monopolising, facilitating trade and traffic. But ... maybe it's true, that now the empire is the world, we can't repeat the primitive, although it's worth a try. There's a ruling class, and all the rest applaud, and vote them in and out, they work till death, are paid in cowrie shells and coconuts.... You see – our food is trucked, the people move to cities, there's no need for canals and mountain tracks. To get our soldiers – we'd need well-built slaves – those Zangids! – or better still, the nomads militarised. Mongols on ponies, Lizeth.... Those – we do not have.'

'Your aim, Cheyenne – it's brilliant: a class imperial! But – nothing of the rest exists. That time is past, Cheyenne: mere despotism. That's what's left,' Lizeth says, amused.

'Yes, there's a lack,' says Cheyenne, with infinite regret. 'Priests, soldiers. Soldier-priests. The goddess – still up there, dear Kali, but.... To pull it all together, make a sack containing trade and traffic, my charisma and my mates.... However small....'

'You can't mean, Cheyenne,' says Lizeth, breaking off to laugh. 'You see yourself as top!'

Cheyenne takes it bad. 'Don't mess with me, Lizeth,' she says. 'I'm affable. Don't be deceived – that closet and the uniforms – not mine. Just guys, way down through the ranks, who messed with me.'

She leans on her desk – an empty top, no cactus even. She spreads her hands.

'What's this?' she asks Lizeth.

'Claws, Cheyenne,' says Lizeth.

'We're friends, Lizeth,' Cheyenne says, 'but no little articles, please, playful or whimsical. My thoughts – they roam. Like alpacas, Lizeth, our trophy animal, in cold and airless places where you wouldn't want to go.'

\*

'What's this?' Cheyenne asks Ahmed.

'A map, Cheyenne,' Ahmed says.

'Yes, exactly so,' she says. 'We're pleased you don't get cases where you'd have to send some guys to jail. The more they send, the worse the punishment becomes. Rejoice, Ahmed: your sensibility's intact. Behind the scenes – just stay there, and be content.'

'The map: it is the city, all neat and held in lines,' he says.

'It is a step,' Cheyenne says, taking the map and stashing it. 'We met with all the guys and sorted out their territories. Each to their own space, and order reigns.'

'The next step, Cheyenne?' Ahmed asks.

'I hope we shan't need another step,' she says. 'Each boss takes the responsibility. It's history made. Kali can take a break. We've sorted out the structure: – structures of the life-world – remember, we did it all at school.'

They stare at each other. 'So,' Cheyenne goes on. 'If there's a case we give you – so long as someone stays within the bounds, it means there's peace. All done, all perfect. Like the beasts: in innocence.'

'And otherwise?' asks Ahmed.

'The case – it goes to someone else,' she says. 'Another life-world. It's instructive. Your alpacas – they need peace as well, and, maybe even more, they need some food.'

'They're like my father thought,' says Ahmed. 'He was for the peasants, believed they had a deal. Then there was that Chinese Square – he knew: the prisoners of starvation, he called them; they could expect despotism, no choice, and that was all. States are like that, Cheyenne, warriors and gods, their retinues, or accountants, cops.... you have to settle, grow crops and pay the tax. Rain and no rain, snow and sun.... If you have beasts, you take them where there's food. Oats and barley – they only languish and grow weeds.'

'I bet your father didn't make it to the crest,' says Cheyenne, laughing. 'Up to the acropolis!'

'He followed illusions,' Ahmed says. 'Disenchantment followed every journey. Every empty mausoleum discovered – he shouted, said the names, and left. What else is there in life?'

Cheyenne doesn't know: school memories – don't help with that. 'We have everything here,' she says. 'The light. It's fixed, no question of its guiding anywhere. Good *feu* Doctor Haas – the greatest tomb artist of all time, a friend of Kali – a man of infinite curiosity. Always searching the surface of the earth – mica, an obsidian chip, a scuff, a swirl – something underneath? And of course, yes, there always is – go far enough, down past the prayers, the varnished boxes, cutaway suits, the tears, the lilies, the widows and their weeds ... the priests – and you will find: the fire! Eternal fire, infinity, the burning heart, Ahmed.

'Patience – it won't come easily, you have to persevere, to find the company – follow the drumming, the solemn crowd – into the volcano. That's the trick. Don't dig, just fall. Drop with your comrades, your *semblables*.... Into the crater.

'In the end – he joined the pale procession, into the white sea, the billowing rock, maybe white flowers in his hair, his Van Dyke beard flourishing and bushing out, death like a desert rain flowering the sand, red, grey, white, lava ... flowing out in death – a grey river, Ahmed, that beard, a Styx, braided rapids, tiny knots like scullers on the spate – caught in the moment, Brueghelled, their oars – spoonbills' beaks, horn spoons a-digging in the molten porridge.... When you go to the uplands, where the little animals are turning stones – you see the grey walls of the mountains, so high, so tall.... And, you wonder – why? What use are they, mountains, what purpose now the fire has died and left them; out of place, tall and silly....'

'I know, Cheyenne,' says Ahmed, quite entranced. 'It's like – what do you do with arms, your arms, when you're in bed? How do you accommodate them? Where do they fit? Where can they be stowed? Maybe we were made without, and they just grew, like buboes.'

'I always thought,' says Cheyenne, 'It showed God had no arms. I'm sure He spends some time in bed – a pine tree trimmed, spinning and tossing free ... always alone....'

'Yes,' says Ahmed, 'disarmed.'

'Shhhh,' says Cheyenne, pressing her lips on his. 'That, you must not say. It is a truth, but truth doesn't enter in a life-world, not any one of them. Volcanoes,' she says dreamily. 'Orgasms. Always when you're on your own. Over and over, always unexpected – and what for?'

'Oh,' Ahmed says, losing patience, thinking of alpacas, 'just for the fun of it, I guess. Like digging up princesses.'

'Where did our fire go, Ahmed?' Cheyenne asks, loosening her crossbelts, unleashing a hard breast, nickel-tipped – a dum-dum dummy – hitching up her skirt to show ... thick felt pants with thick red stripes, and thick tall boots with belts, brass buckles.... 'Did you forget – I was your reluctant lover, remember? The fear – always on me, on us, when we traded sex, like a knocking on the chamber door....'

'It's all so complicated,' Ahmed says, backing off. 'Between us – first, there's custom. Now – it is the law.'

'You're right,' says Cheyenne, buttoning up. 'But – without the thought – the deed is outside perception. It might exist – we'll never know. The thought is everything, Ahmed. Remember, when the criminals come and stand before you – they've thought of death a hundred times ... their death, in prison, on street corners, the garotte, that nail, a rusty finger in your spine.... That is enough! Leave it, leave it there. There's nothing more, no punishment you can inflict.'

*

Lizeth's article – she says it's about schools. 'We're all stereotypes,' she writes. 'All that phenomenology – making a puzzle from the evident.... Detection of guilt, by the guilty....'

'No, Lizeth,' Cheyenne says. 'I told you. No tail-twisting, no mocking *chirichirichii* sounds! – no monkey calls – I know your sort, Lizeth. A joker. Down at the club – my! what a giggle they'll all have.'

'No, no, really, Cheyenne,' Lizeth pleads. 'It's not at all about you, not at all.' Her knees shake, she stands up brusquely. 'Cramp!' she says, her legs shake, she sits down.

'I need to ask, Cheyenne – the bandits....' Lizeth asks.

'Guerrillas?' Cheyenne shouts, so loud some guys pile in, with guns. 'You don't know how cops work, Lizeth. Bandits – is politics. You draw lines even broader than for gangs, for them and you – the difference is: they draw theirs too. The aim's not peace, it's truce. You, me – we could disappear if those lines move too far.... If you're in luck, you'll finish in a wooden pencil-case. If not – the dump. Or printers' pie....!' She laughs.

'Yes, I do see that, Cheyenne,' says Lizeth, calming down.

'Then there's corruption, Lizeth,' Cheyenne says. 'The press is free, and so I don't quiz you. But – do you see me as corrupt?'

'No, no,' says Lizeth. 'You live poor, Cheyenne.'

'It's not just cash,' Cheyenne says. 'It's sympathies. Favours. Trade, and taking sides with people who have stayed outside, and feigned indifference.... Ambitions too, and treachery.... Serious stuff, Lizeth.'

'We've read the books, Cheyenne,' says Lizeth.

'The fear, Lizeth,' Cheyenne says. 'Can you imagine? Fear of being taken, being killed, by one side or the other, and all the sides not on the map....'

'Yes, yes,' says Lizeth. 'Fear, fear. I write my little articles and sweat....'

'I'm not sure, Lizeth,' Cheyenne says, doodling 'Lizeth' on a pad. 'That you can control your pen. We have no Switzerland, no place to keep a foot in while you write your witty stuff. Above the fight, you think? A nod, a wink, a Zadig or Candide? It comes to mind – that notion of the shadow, "sweet shadow", the one you're under, present from birth to death: death "which reduplicates the world like the peeling of a fruit". Which world is yours, what fruit are you Lizeth? A Chinese gooseberry? A *figue de barbarie?Fico d'India?*'

'No, Cheyenne, I don't remember anything,' says Lizeth. 'Maybe I missed school that day – I'd suitors.… Pushy ones. The quote though – maybe you have the meaning wrong....'

'Oh, it was poetry we did,' says Cheyenne. 'Not philosophy, no! A philosophical no! In poetry the words don't count. It's the tread it has, not words. A poem makes you think of death, of ending, quick, misunderstood, unmourned, often – not buried either. Reminds me too of Nico – his "walking on the ceiling" – and how the bandits have a point: start with equivalence, a "me and you", and then there's teeter-totter, and you're out there in the bush, dirty fatigues oiled up – or dropping leaflets like the autumn trees.... Be very very prudent, Lizeth!'

'Anyway,' says Lizeth, 'it's not your thing, the *foco*. I understand. Believe me – it's not mine. It's not who's right, it's politics. Besides, I only cover fashion and extreme sports, philosophy and food....'

*

'A soldier's training – always works,' says Nico. 'Eating cow and drinking milk, or alpaca fritters and maté.... It's staying alive. Only tiny suckers drink our blood, not many monsters lurk and eat us. We won, Leidy: our species beats the rest. Now we get back to civil war. Beating God was not so hard – we have to deal with body, sex – then what's left is the dominion, first the world, then the centuries that we'll need to send immortal guys to stepping stones out there, down under, spinning round.... The universe. It's a weak shot, though. The to and fro is draining, we're emptied out. Our day exhausts us.'

'A real soldier....' she says doubtfully. 'Can't back off. But ahead, there's only dust.... And you, your dust ... so, what are you, Nico...?'

'A real slave, Leidy,' Nico says. 'And of the rest, I must make poetry.'

'Ridiculous,' she says. 'Besides being fat, for a soldier.'

'I've eaten flocks,' he says. 'Never say no. Peace or war, you wield the scythe....'

'You'd be dead,' she says. 'If it's no peace, no war. I think you only trained, and maybe flunked. Learned the lesson, fell off the rope.'

'You're a sylph, Leidy,' Nico says. 'An undergrown wisp. Don't patronise, don't guess.'

'Exactly, Nico,' Leidy says. 'Hands off. I'm eleven, never fantasised.'

'That's the way,' says Nico. 'Don't wait for adolescence, move on to senility, save your innocence till then.'

'No one will hurt me,' Leidy says. 'Except by accident, perhaps. How do you make money, Nico? How'll you hold on to it?'

'Import,' says Nico. 'Stay away from export, forget double-entry bookkeeping. If you don't see it, it's not there. They want stuff in the club; behind each thing, there's an idea. Import ideas – they're light, and there's no duties.'

\*

'Nico,' Lizeth tells Leidy, when they are alone together, 'is corrupt. He's a writer. He listens. He gives you what you want. Mostly you want what's bad for you or other people. Sweet stuff.'

'We went to see the animals, but they'd gone high, high up, we couldn't breathe. He says he'll warn me, if bad is imminent,' says Leidy, 'to me, that's good.'

'It's always happening,' says Lizeth. 'Driving you from home, knocking the houses down, poisoning the wells. With clubs, with fire, with law or defamation: it's like those rich and tolerant peoples – sometimes they fight at home, and sometimes overseas or over rivers, mountains. Whatever's in their way. Here, we only fight each other: when you're poor it's what you can afford. It doesn't stop, Leidy. It's why there's always fear....'

'Oh you're so caustic, Lizeth,' says Leidy, and she laughs. 'I love it!'

\*

'But I thought I had a friend in Nico,' says Leidy.

Lizeth cuddles her, waiting to get to speak. 'I'm too trusting. I took him at face value,' Leidy says. 'His value, and his face.'

'They should have taught you,' says Lizeth. 'It was charades. It's cultural veneer, a profession, the dissimulation, boasting. Don't call it lying. Certainly, it complicates your life, when you think it should be honest and direct. Neat, one-dimensional.'

'Oh, charades!' says Leidy, in full wonder. 'You were playing *that!* I came in, surrendered my best feelings, didn't realise. But the conflict? The guerrillas that at first we can respect, and then we lose the hope....? Or else we're part of it....'

'A part?' asks Lizeth. 'We didn't think of one for you. Nico – he's in a paper cell, he's written it, it's suspended, like a wasps' nest. What are wasps for? Hard to know: they sting, get swatted. There must be something more. A buzzing, many winds, driving to and fro. Sharp but inconclusive, a threat, but leave them be, they don't impinge, and you don't matter to them, not a bit.

'Ahmed – must sit quietly on his judge's chair, hour after hour, even if he has to pee. When he's brought here every day, he must climb the stairs up from the corridor with the pens – holding all the people he will see, cowed, expectant before him. You could only leave your chair if you can take their place. If you're accused, you'd have to prove the unprovable, but no one's listening: only you, and you don't count. There's no document says you were here or there. Nico might have seen you, but his poems aren't a camera: – they don't give benefits to doubt. Behind Ahmed's law there's a shadow of another law that sets you free and makes him guilty, so don't expect it will step out into the light....

'Cheyenne? That's easy. She rents a big house now, that has gardens round, like the circles on a target. She is an eye, the golden one: an eagle or an alpaca; all is gold until it's not. The gold is where the arrow points.'

'I've read it's like this, Lizeth,' Leidy says. 'There's the fear, then the sentence, the dénouement....'

'It sounds easy.' Lizeth says. 'Maybe for a day, it will be. But the big fear, you try to make it tiny so you don't shake and cramp. After a day's relax, when the scene is changed – the little things are huge. They stay that way, they're concentrated, and when you dilute them with your sweat – immense. They are your body, your hunger, your expectancy.... You; being inside.'

'If you're wounded, or you're sentenced – that's it,' says Leidy. 'You *know*. Nothing more can happen....'

'No, it doesn't end. Everything, Leidy,' Lizeth says. 'Anything at all, can go on happening, but you've lost the first encounter.... *There's* the weakness, *there* it starts – don't believe you can tough it out....'

*

'You two, you and Nico,' Cheyenne tells Ahmed, 'you're anomalous. Acting rich, but being poor. Having some instruction – but acting stupid. What can you offer, Ahmed? If I ran a band of monkeys or a pack of wolves – you'd be thrown out, disgraced....'

'You must love us as we are' says Ahmed. 'If a lone goose, a flamingo, say, is blown on to your roof – you must have patience. It will pine or fly away.'

'That's not so. A person: that's who's blown on to the roof,' Cheyenne says.

'You – all of us – we know how things should be,' says Ahmed. 'If you have a part of that, you cling to it. You don't feel guilty for having what you have, because you know – tomorrow it could end, it's ended so, sudden or slow, for millions just like you. Are things better? A little? Best say they are, they might be, shows you're not defeatist nor a schemer. The trouble is – you are not loyal. You don't doubt – you know. The worst – is written in the books and on the monuments. If you tell it – maybe you're a hero. Maybe you'll get a following, a megaphone. Or – you'll disappear. It's the big risk. Some places – you disappear but you're still there, visible in your chair. In other places – the chair is empty. No one's around to feed the cat. You've really gone....'

'That's paranoid,' says Cheyenne. 'Or else you're precious. One of the privileged who sicks it up.'

*

'We're snow,' says Nico: 'Our loves. Not even sand, that blows and settles back. Here, we're free, we don't have the faith. Over there, there's mountains too – but if you're chained, you stay down on the plain. It is a choice – what choice have we, Ahmed, where would we go?'

'Oh, anywhere,' says Ahmed. 'That's the worst.'

They contemplate the past – it gives directions – that's why you're here.

'Leidy,' Nico says. 'We're all in love with her. That house she lives in – it's full of spies: that's how they keep the children clean. You scoff, Ahmed, at poetry – it's the best alibi. If I have to leave the club ... disaster.'

'People leave the mountains for the city,' Ahmed says. 'The city people leave, and others come – everywhere's a little world, you live everywhere, anywhere you can. It's good, a refuge. Some

places, more, you can't live at all, you cannot be a nomad, those
barracks where you stayed for years – now, they're robot sheds. It's
good, of course, but, Nico, where shall we go? Which city quarter
here – India, China or Japan? Who'll keep quiet if there's a
search....'

'We could take Leidy' Nico says. 'A kind of hostage – make her
a cosmopolitan. Tzara and Stein, dancing till late on table-tops,
betting machines full of those unpeeled fruit, remember? 'The
world is not a hypothesis', said Cheyenne's master: it's on us like a
flock of geese, they honk and crap – oh no! It's storks or eagles,
making the sun go red with dust they've raised.... What do we have
as a defence, against them all, the worlds? Leidy, Lizeth? We're
vulnerable, Ahmed – true, they're more at risk than us, but still –
what weapon do we have? Reason? No – it must obey science.
Science? No – it leaps ahead and doubles back, it gives us a decade
more, living in wheelchairs, it takes our breath, we suffocate. It is a
clown, Ahmed – it puts caramels into our hands – then with the
rubber hammer, on our head – it knocks us out. The migraine,
Ahmed! The laughter. They know we're guilty – your bad justice
got from books you cannot read; my imports – when you've gone
high enough, you hallucinate, a larva in the snow. Then they
cluster, shades – I don't think those are your animals, my dear:
those "creatures of one ethereal substance met, in consistory, like a
crown of burning seraphs". Who are they, who shall we meet on the
uplands? Do they have an origin? They must: intentions too. It's all
beyond me, it's a relief to face the cops, their homely tricks – "oh,
hang me higher" you cry out, "shock me, beat me – any way you
want me for I have sinned" and so do you, and so – it doesn't
count. It's bland as junket – our bodies, Ahmed, we make them
strong, pound them like horseshoes, to last .... have them nailed on,
then trot and gallop in the grit...fire from the cobblestones ... but not
for long.'

'We must take Cheyenne,' says Ahmed. 'She could earn for us.
She runs, she'll run interference – lead the dogs on, then double on
them. I loved her, but she's betrayed – even before we came, and
many times since then.... All evens out, even stevens; profit and
loss comes with the trade. Customs? Professional risk. Sometimes a
crate is opened, Kali steps out, maybe its your sister – usually it's
not. Most opened, empty.'

*

'We don't say "moving house",' Cheynne says, 'we say you're "moving fire".'

'Fire? The potter? Or the smith?' asks Nico. 'No, not those! No fire. It's already in the street. And when Lizeth's justice, the guerrillas, come down from the heights – I'll be there, cheering. I want to see the victory – but not be there the following day.... Do I want to live with justice, even if it came? Faith? Order? Not for me! Are those what revolution means? As for the alternatives – equality, fraternity – there's questions long before the flags are furled away...'

'There must be fire,' Cheyenne says. 'It's the sun that's burns – see, I'm covered in it. You said it was honey, but it's not, our colour comes from being smoked as if we're turkeys, hung up and twisting. We're cooked, there's no secret. The cops know everything we know, and vice versa.'

'That's why I don't trust you,' Nico says. 'Everybody knows, knows everything. Sometimes you turn into soldiers, sometimes you give beggars something, sometimes you wait for everything to change, or hope it never does.'

*

'We're here because....' Ahmed says. 'Although it's like this everywhere, still lots of us, we try to get away and find the place where something can be done, shaped, or else you find you're where it can't be changed at all. It's not for justice that we came, Cheyenne – Nico wanted happiness. I wanted peace ... him to do nothing except have the scene set out and coloured up, and nothing's expected of him, nothing at all, except what little that he wants to do. I came for peace – whatever I did, would show I was on the right side ... and no one cared, it made no difference, it made no difference to me.... I could do nothing, except pervert the course of injustice,' and he laughs.

*

'The world's like that, and it's not like that,' says Lizeth: 'The air is heavy on the plain, it's so light up high, it can't even feed a fire.... there's sand and salt and swamp. And jungles. There's places where you hug your enemy and places where she burns you up....'

'Of course, it's so,' says Nico. 'The more the world is one, the more the planes and hollows come out into the light.... Every place I'm in, I think I'm dying there – the procession to the dump – the troupe of hurdy-gurdies with their single legs, charred in the fire, goes hopping on ahead, faster, faster, watch out! – no distorting mirrors, just thin ice ... each stump, each skate, helps draw the pentagram, turn the handle, black olive notes drop into the snow, and music ho! – my turn at last! My, what a fruity voice! .... then at last, the apple, precious fruit of ignorance, forget the good and bad you could never tell apart – rolls into the garden, rests in the soft grass ... and there's your hole! tumble you in, stopper you up, a stone on top.... The voice? ... Who distinguishes the words?'

'It's not much like that, Nico,' Lizeth says. 'You came here by chance, or because of Kali. We're poor, exploited, but it's not about the personal cash – it's about how it gets to you, and before all that, how it's all decided.'

'What revelation, Lizeth! What an insight! Is it worth your life?' asks Nico, sarcastically. 'You can't leave the city, Lizeth. The city's Kali's. She has you, like she has us all. If you're a soldier – there's no battle: the finger of destiny, Lizeth, aims down from the sky. Buzz-buzz. Assassination one by one – and if you're an irregular, there's sects and deals to manage too....'

*

'No mules,' says Ahmed. 'We want donkeys, they're more manageable.'

It isn't so – they're smaller, that is all.

'Mules,' says Nico. 'For tall mountains. This way, we leave no trace. Only, we shall perforce leave mules.'

The way out is vertical – the mules are used to that; Ahmed, though – he is appalled....

'Think!' says Nico. 'The beast is vertical – you're flat, like lying down and looking at a star.'

'The other side...' says Ahmed.

'Why, then you're looking, looking for pussy in the well,' says Nico laughing. 'Those women! When we think of them, we know – there's only one sex needed. We are useless, even our cohabitation's suspect.

'Travelling with you, Ahmed – a ride, two rides, of danger – that's equality. I know you like I know myself, you are my other side. But Cheyenne, and the rest, there is – a subtlety... conviction... true guerrillas. I try with my poetry – being two-sided, a little subversive, not enough to go on someone's list....'

'Where's the food for mules, Nico?' Ahmed asks.

'This envelope,' says Nico. 'Not a letter. They take it head on – coca. Easy to carry, easy to digest. They're true Americans. Renowned for beauty too – like Lizeth. That was a rich place we just left, Ahmed – beccause we're poor. The light – dear Doctor Haas, aloft, and shining. The wealth we underestimated – I ate a fish, a beauty, all the way from Java.'

'The height,' says Ahmed, quite alarmed. 'Maybe it's got in your head.... There's songs – "La Java Martienne", or "Des Bombes Atomiques"'.... Those are heights: no fish. Now, Nico! Get out my head! I miss them all – the diner, Surabaya Johnny's ... the Vian songs – enough! Your poetry is finished, the story separates, each to his own – if they thought that we were gay, we'd end up dead. Reflect!'

'Every city,' Nico says. 'Has its fun side, its funny side. Hedonism. It reverts to Calvinism, the deeper pleasure. Purity – the trimming of the margins, the marginals. That's where the wealth comes from, that's what attracts the tourists: danger and fear – they can't get enough of it. We got too much. So – where next? If there was everywhere, and Kali was nowhere – anywhere would do, would be the same. "Everything" contains the "no", the *non*. Like they say, every birth contains the death. So, what's left? We might feel it's all the same – but it won't *be* the same. It all ends in America? It used to, but maybe not now, because the future, Ahmed, is contained in the past, just like I said. The future's death, my dear.'

This is the crest. It exalts, you can't breathe. 'Feed him,' says Nico. 'Your mule. Get it right in, be careful he doesn't bite.'

'You can see right down, right over,' Ahmed says.

'The States,' says Nico, 'we could go there. Why'd we want to? We could take a plane – everybody does down there. We could be reserved, on a reservation, that's what it's for, and Ahmed, you could pass, pass for an Indian....'

'What'll Lizeth do?' Ahmed wonders. 'There's no guerrillas now.'

'There'll always be guerrillas,' Nico says.

'Leidy's an interesting type,' says Ahmed, pushing coca into the mule.

'Careful,' says Nico, 'his heart could burst with all that stuff....'

'I could send for Cheyenne,' says Ahmed. 'If we go somewhere we could settle.'

'Settle what?' Nico says. 'I thought that's why we left, nothing got settled. We weren't rich or poor, we didn't fit where we wanted. We were naive, I'm sure – nothing gets fixed, not anywhere.'

'It's good I don't want the States,' says Ahmed. 'There's so many reasons there for keeping us all out.'

'You can't stay on the crest,' says Nico. 'The air's too thin. Your alpacas, Ahmed, how'd they manage? They're so delicate – when you deal with heights, you need a sturdy animal,' and he pats the mules, indifferent to him, but revving up, keen on the descent.

'Alpacas thin out,' says Ahmed. 'Slip through your fingers.'

'You know,' says Nico, gazing over at the light, the Haas memorial, the grid of streets, then down to the other side, some trees, guys working at them, buzz-saws early, like a nest of wasps. 'Maybe we're superficial. They say it's cretinism, this obsession with the goddess, Kali. Vendettas, scores and scoring.... Of course, there's always the Americans, customers, complainants, until there's someone else who takes their place. Suppose they sober up, there's no more coca, only folklore – who enters, who comes on stage? – the people, "yes, the people"? The poet said it, "the people, yes!" Where did that go? Remember – they can't have disappeared, there's people, lots and lots, trying to get in, get out.... Where do they go? and us? Where shall we land, Ahmed?'

'The empires on this side,' Ahmed says, pointing down. 'They weren't tender with anyone. Then they got beat, and Doctor Haas – he dug them up. Empires everywhere – wherever we touch down, Nico – France, Italy, China too, and India... Bactria and Chechnya.... Did the good doctor theorise? It seems the norm is empire – each one different, except it has a centre and periphery. The centre: living in symbols for the masters, praying and virgins soothsaying.... Mining and weeding for the outlyers.... There's nomad empires too, but all their animals are dead and eaten.... What is the aim, Nico? A perfect union, or accumulation and processions? What's the grand design....? The species' aim – enslavement or transcendence?'

'It's pillage, Ahmed,' Nico says. 'And profit.'

'You're right,' says Ahmed. 'The urge to empire – even though the empires are diverse, there is a common aim. The opposites unite

– nativism, the indigenes, on one side – diversity, the other. We thought them a contradiction – no, they co-exist.'

'Maybe there's a way for us, Ahmed,' Nico says, mounting his mule and galloping on down. 'Exit from the species. Start another one, maybe – of specimens already rare, so special that the humans put us in a special cage....'

'Oh Nico,' Ahmed shouts. 'That's precious. And it's prison too. We're not exotics – we should be in control, in charge. We're cowboys on the lam....'

And he too goes skittering down.

\*

The air thickens. The descent is over – a new old empire's reached. There'll be another, maybe many, Doctor Haases. The mules seem grumpy, but instead – they're happy, satisfied. A perfect job.

'Your trouble, Ahmed,' Nico says. 'Is you live in a broken frame. Step out! But, of course, you can't. The judge who wouldn't judge. The air too thin to save his animals.'

'Forget it, Nico,' Ahmed says. 'We're uncommon people. No one feels comfortable with us. No judgement works with us, we're unexpected.'

'I hope so,' Nico says. 'You're wrong, Ahmed. If I'd to destroy all my clubmates – I'd do it, for a song, a mumble. Forget the poems – I can't wait for metres to form their fours and fives. It tumbles out of me, runs off my forking tongue.... The poetry? – nothing happens there, though I'm ready for the cleansing, the *chistka*. Away with the corrupt, on with the new....'

'Yes, Nico,' Ahmed says. 'You're versatile, your reflections are mothwings. They never stay and rest, so we'll never grasp your genius.'

'Cheyenne – she had a guess,' says Nico. 'She knew exactly how it worked, when there was shooting, which bars stayed open, and all that. Lizeth and Leidy – they were full up with themselves and what they wanted to accomplish. Naive. Cheyenne had roamed the atlas.'

'Bolívar, Zetkin, Toussaint Louverture – Cheyenne's up there with them,' says Ahmed. 'She knows – people live in poverty there because there's others free: to exploit, protected by repression and the state: behind that state, there's Yankees doodling out their edicts....'

'Don't nip at me,' says Nico. 'Those alpacas – they were a resource. You helped make them ephemeral. People are poor because they've nothing worth to trade....'

The mules move off, the envelope is trashed, adventures over – there will undoubtedly be more for them, they are for hire.

Ahmed and Nico argue – which of them's more reactionary, who more complicit, who's deluded.

'I don't recognise Cheyenne,' says Nico.

'No one recognises their own life,' says Ahmed. 'A first line of defence.'

Here's the mountain wall. 'We'll carve our monument,' says Nico. 'As we want, our lives and how we see them. Engrave all the rock there is – then cover it with moss, and when another empire falls, penury! The beasts will eat the moss – and there we are!'

So, they set to: kilometres of chiselling, till the whole mountain range is graven to exactly what each thinks worth recording of themselves. 'I'm recognisable,' says Nico. 'Ahmed – you are not.'

'I need go higher up....' says Ahmed, already on a ladder.

'You think you're revolutionary, Ahmed,' Nico says. 'But you don't like the noise. I love it. There's no food? – *you* suffer. *I* go to the club, where the fascists are – there, they make Club Sandwiches. Then the revolutionaries take it all over and alpaca steaks are served. What an exalting scene – it's me.

'Some places have politics that's either hope or despair,' Nico goes on, sucking at his blistered hands. 'Just that – no plan, no project. Cheyenne has family, so she can't have either. Ahmed and me, we stood on the platform that's briefly set up, between hope and despair. When I'm despair, he's hope. The platform disappears – and we're off together, hope, despair, no family, all in one.'

There's no response to that – Ahmed doesn't try.

'You came to Kali, Ahmed,' Nico says. 'Everything was on your side – humanity, logic, science. The next step awaited, the evolutionary pirouette, then – the higher kick! Instead – you've lost. Everywhere, we're back to what will suit us best – despotism and conformity. People love being ruled, it brings profitability and security. People hate being ruled – anything, to resist. They look for ways to have love and hate together, probably long ago you could live hard like that. Not now. You're my antique, Ahmed. I know you're not worth much – but what a patina! Craftsmanship, what care in making up your mind, a person wholly against the current.... A whole box of curiosities in one....'

'Put together, Nico,' Ahmed says. 'We have four legs. We could be a dingo dog – a trotting dobbin or a dragon – ideas received, philosophised, explored and contradictory.... Expect nothing new, how could there be – but.... here's the tail, each has one, just one, the critical part, the tell-tale, that gives it all away. Limited and unpredictable.'

'Those beasts of yours,' says Nico. 'They are a mess. They've different kinds of gait and goal. The dragon's chained to guard some riches. The dingo dog – has nothing but the search. They chafe, they walk – the dobbin ... looks for someone who will climb upon its back. That's what it's made for, but imagine! A sack of bones that tells you where to go ... how fast, for ever.'

So, locked in argument, they proceed across the plain, where the next city lies beneath its cap of mist and fog....

\* \* \*

'When I was in difficulty,' Ahmed says, 'I'd take a contract, help to rig a stage, then strut and jive along. *Metall* at Rammstein. What a show, the fire, the spume, the purgatorial songs...!'

'Then flew away the last shred of your innocence?' asks Nico. 'All the living world was there, that day. I'm certain – I was present, singing... or thereabouts....'

'I wore a glitter suit,' says Ahmed, his eyes dimming. 'A newt, a salamander. Bits of business with the lead. No illusions then: you paid – or crashed – for what you got. The crest of being, Nico....'

They walk down the dusty street, its dusty trees, the little pyramid of pears for sale, tough ados rearing up on trail motos, the beauties linked in threes and fours a-giggle – 'I know this place,' says Ahmed.

'So do I,' says Nico. 'I was born here. We all were. I sometimes hoped I'd die here. We all came from a tiny planet, a gob of mud, in a morning you could walk all round. A lake with white birds, a burial ground with black.... There's sheds and shuttered houses – you don't give those weight until you've left. That is not for us. Here, is Kali: before we've had our say, tried out, got the contract – this is rehearsal, Ahmed – watch out, that it's not our end.'

'Leave light, change your voice, modify your colour – sell that guitar, use the cash to buy your first people,' Ahmed says.

'Yes,' says Nico. 'Too bad neither of us had the guitar.'

\*

'That hole in the road back there,' says Nico. 'Full of spiders. Every sad colour. I twisted my leg. It will pass, the pain....'

'You're right,' Ahmed says. 'A nest of spinners and twisters. Now, Nico, be a brave little soldier – as you are. Stride on.'

But Nico can't.

'The clinic's closed,' says the doctor. 'But, since you're foreigners.... It's not free....'

'I've no comment,' Nico says. 'It might affect the treatment.'

The doctor waits. There's people come and go. Some eat those pears. Some check Nico out.

'Really,' the doctor says, 'my speciality is death. You don't come in, my friend, not yet.'

He checks Nico, Nico's arms, for tracks. 'I've not been bitten,' Nico says. 'It's mechanical. Gyre the leg the reverse way, and I'll be off.'

'We wait,' the doctor says. 'A soldier comes. If you're a soldier, we must see whose side you're on. The marks....'

'I can't wait,' faintly Nico says. 'I wasn't regular. There are no marks.' He goes a bluey-white. He's fresh and primal as new-pulled leeks.

'I fear – I cannot stay,' says Ahmed, anxiously, pushing past some squat people, their shopping, their standing firm; not trusting him or anyone.

'It could be chemical,' the soldier says. 'He won't last the hour.'

Nico squirms – 'I feel I'm rotting all inside,' he says.

'We should have offered something up,' says Ahmed, 'to Kali. Those spiders – must be on her side.'

At Kali's name, there is a rustle.

The doctor sticks a horse syringe in Nico's bum, and with his foot he works a stirrup pump to suck it full, and fill a pail.

'We living, we see Kali, when it's done,' a lady says. 'You won't.'

'He's clean,' the soldier says. 'Too clean. He must have known and tidied up.'

'Let's go,' says Ahmed. 'Pay and go.'

'They're not insured,' the lady says. 'There'll be no comeback if they drop.'

'The cure is excellent,' says Ahmed. 'The dialogue's been poor, but no one could do better, quicker, not anywhere. A diagnosis....'

'Won't make a difference,' the doctor says. 'We've seen what we want. This guy, Nico – could go at any time. He is a fatalist – so, his end is immaterial. To him, to us. He's full of common sense and moderate judgement – one more or less of him, won't tip the balance, whoever's holding it.'

'There is no cure,' the soldier says, 'Not yet. Not that you can afford. This is a new disease you have. These portals, Nico, that you see before you – experimental medicine lies beyond. Abandon yourself ... hope's shimmering before you.'

'You've heard,' the doctor says, 'of those "elective affinities".'

'Vaguely,' says Nico, 'at school. But then I found my muse. I left behind the childish things....'

'Don't mention Lizeth,' Ahmed whispers, 'or Cheyenne. You'll get them into troubled times....'

'Spiders here – they bite,' the doctor says. 'But sparingly, selectively. They spin, they make a network of fine wires, stronger than silver, silk or tin. Those are a mattress, coils of spring, underneath our soil, our tarmac and cement. They are our circuits of communication. Everyone is wired, these days – the mechanisms pass beneath our feet and through the webs that lie forever re-channelled, reinforced.... It keeps us safe, but naturally, there is a price – it's poison, Nico. It enters through your boots, and circulates....' and he shows Nico the horse syringe, full of a greyish fatty stuff, a gunk that sparkles, nodes that could be flies or ladybirds, or melted paste, tinsel, or crunched-up Lalique glass....

'I don't believe a word!' shouts Nico – trying to stand, he twists and cramps. 'It isn't so,' he says. 'I never put a premium on what is plausible. I'm an original. Not all I say is literally so. I've guys who slip me cash behind the scenes, who pay me for coining triolets, sestines.... I'm steeped in *années folles.*... You have before you,' and he gestures to include the room, the modest and the arrogant – 'an artists' artist.'

'You must be sick, or maybe – you're extinct,' the soldier says. 'A spy, embezzler – informer, sniper, dynamiter....'

'The problem is,' the doctor tells Ahmed. 'The sickness touches all of us, we've all a trace, and everyone around, hallucinates.... We need to cancel all we hear, but there's no means, it all goes on the record, quite indelible....' and he points to a corner.... There's an old ticker-tape machine, spooling out the interchanges, completed records from when the heroes enter in the clinic and take off their clothes, and see – yes, Ahmed too – a shaded spot of skin, a dainty bite, like Nico's too – right on the ankle, just above their workboot's line....

'There's wards full of guys like you,' the lady says. 'I've sons and daughters there myself – all moribund, with logorrhea, moonstruck, sunstroked, black widow syndrome.... They say it takes some years to cure,' – she weeps, comes back to herself, says, forcefully, 'Like being commies, paedos, misbelievers – all those sorts.'

'We can't wait,' says Nico, rudely. 'We don't believe in science and disease. We're certain only of Kali. She's always there, but never intervenes. Free will, it's called. Belief's no strain – she's imminent! Put on your boots, Ahmed, and take me on your back, and off we go!'

*

Between them, they've two working legs. Ahmed hops, while Nico is malingering, enjoying the piggy-back, then – they stop, make compresses from a fever-tree. They're cured, they think – could be a respite, a regress.

'Maybe the spiders' webs won't work if we climb rocks,' says Ahmed. 'Our friends – Cheyenne, Lizeth and Leidy – they can be compromised by careless words. Keep silent if you see a web....'

'It's useless, Ahmed,' Nico says. 'Kali's messengers – they're everywhere; the stoop, the hearth, the beams, the tiles – silent and provident, heads ornamented with a chaplet of bright eyes ... we were the latest to bear her marks. I was her outrider, a soldier. You, Ahmed: her chancellor and judge. Now – we're two warriors, the Achilles' ankle our memento mori, the hazard that will come in battle or in bed, at the bar or on the bastion.... Courage, my dear friend – nothing has changed, except – our hope of immortality has lapsed.'

*

'Things are becoming smaller,' says Ahmed. 'The cities – towns. Then, they'll be villages. We lived in ideas, an accompaniment of friends: now, it's bodies we're reduced to. The spiders – they know everything, every spider: – that's all they know: just spiders, and what spiders know.'

'Well, Ahmed,' Nico says. 'We're together. What do you want with me? Children? The magic of our first meeting, re-lived, maybe? I'm still the magician, the escapist, the cabinet-maker making desks with secret drawers; he's forgotten how to open them....'

'That escapist – they forget to put the key inside his wet-suit,' Ahmed says. 'When he tries to unlock the chains – there's emptiness. So, he drowns. If I can have what I want, Nico, then I want fun. Lots of it; and you aren't fun. Your joke's not the kind that makes you smile – it makes you think of when you were so young, then it might have made you laugh – and so, out comes a tear....'

'No, Ahmed,' Nico says. 'That salt you taste – it isn't yours, doesn't come from inside – it's the Mediterranean. Monotheism, Ahmed, in every stripe, that brings the melancholy, the tale's been told, beginning-end, nothing left to chance, imagination ... the game is beggar-my-neighbour, off-with-his-head. A culture threatening, written in blood and in a book.'

*

'Maybe it's so,' says Ahmed. 'Truth and a map of where you're going to end. I spit on those.'

They pause.

'I don't drown,' says Nico. 'I never snap those padlocks shut, and I don't trust my crew. All I do's above board – like the movie guy who always wins; his tart, Jackie, she wins too when she's with him....'

'I know the story,' Ahmed says. 'Nothing to do with people – it's that she keeps smoking Lucky Strikes. Besides – you're vulnerable, Nico. A spider got you.'

'A tragedy,' says Nico. 'Not for me, for them. Every web and every thread – identical. A waste of time to watch their holes and hope for something new. They have enmeshed the world – and every one of them's the same, and every one of them is mute.'

*

'A bad end,' Cheyenne says, spotting Ahmed and Nico staring down a hole in the ground....

'The mountains,' Ahmed asks. 'The mules? The fighting. Now, the spiders ... how could you travel, Cheyenne, our muse, who left us arguing and perverse...? How could you find us...?'

'There's a tunnel under everything, the mountains – the bus fare is quite reasonable,' Cheyenne says, quite undisturbed, imposing in her black and white, bombazine and calico, dressed old, much older, as status might require: 'They need to build a city here where you can make enough to live without disturbances.... It's flat – like a slice of ham. No need to climb up high.... No light. No Doctor Haas.'

'Then how'd we see Kali dance?' asks Nico, enraptured. 'Who pays to build the city – even on the plain...?'

'Oh,' says Cheyenne, 'it's villages that cost – they get paid for: in kale and carrots. A city pays for itself – in the first week – with Kali dancing in the bars.... I could stand in for her.'

'No building on the hill, then, Cheyenne?' asks Nico. 'Nothing remote? No Mount Atheos, visitors basketed up the rock into their cell? It's good you're always up for starting something new, even if it looks exactly like the old....'

'I know how things work,' Cheyenne says. 'You don't. You see Kali. I see guys with hods, and Indians doing cartwheels on the girders.'

'Not here, Cheyenne,' says Nico. 'Here's all draining lake, and marsh. Besides – all cities, up or down – they all have districts called "the plain" where you can wear your skin and be a dirty dog, the swan, or golden rain....'

She seems to ignore him. She pats down Ahmed, slides her hands ... 'My, you do love dirty clothes. Ease yourself, my dear.'

She never spoke like this before – 'You see,' she says. 'Between the cities of the plain and on the hill – there is another way. Beneath....'

'Oh, there's a problem, dear Cheyenne,' says Ahmed.... 'In the water....'

'You must have seen,' says Cheyenne, taking off Ahmed's clothes and stroking him. 'That oboists have learned the trick – circular breathing, don't exhale.... True, your face goes baggy, red, an octopus's body-sack, but there are better ways. Think dolphins, seals, and whales – you must relax and suck in oxygen, the birds breathe in and out, and both ways they're refreshed – you need the juice to go down deep, down in the safe dark place where you were once, when your brain was bigger than the rest, your tadpole tail; where you had the dreams that slow, confused, will seep out in your sleep for all your life....'

'It sounds too good for me,' says Ahmed. 'Maybe Nico is a better bet....'

'No, no, you're smooth, Ahmed,' says Cheyenne, soothing him. 'Nico has hair, and he's a dueller, full of holes. He'd saturate. I see your only fault is what all have – the tiny spider bite, Achilles ankle – and remember, Ahmed, no catching fish and tossing them to suffocate – they are our comrades, they have learned survival earlier than us. At first, you may look odd, Ahmed. You'll seem a seal, goggly professorial, quite vague and naive-looking, but then, when you see the woodwinds in their row, all engorged, absorbed, you don't think "penises" – we learned this life so's to resist the torture ... those Americans, they use the waterboard, as if they had invented it. Come down with me – move slow, and don't ejaculate, we don't want to rear whatever might come forth....'

'Those oboists,' says Ahmed, as she draws him down. 'It's not my kind of music...' but they're immersed – tranquil and chirping: fantasy creatures wander up to peer.... Cheyenne's body's long, so long she's round him twice and slowly throbs in rhythm with his heart, not cold, not warm, a bed – like when you are asleep and dream that you are free and all your entrails, cockles, work, in lockstep with desire....

Cheyenne is greyish-blue, her shoulders lightly phosphorescent, cool flames.... She takes in krill, suckles Ahmed. It's black down here – at times a neighbour hurries past, lit up but sober, self-generating, a neon glow, a small electric moon....

\*

'Yes!' says Ahmed. 'If we could, we'd build the city here..... The sex....' He stops – 'would bring the tourists.'

'That's the point,' says Cheyenne, drying them both off. 'It's to resist the torture, not have fun. Keep quiet, Ahmed. Learn an instrument, shut your craw... stopper it, a double-reed, of course....'

'I'm not sure,' says Nico. 'Maybe for you and I, Ahmed, there's not so much. Construction palls.'

'Don't get ideas, you two,' says Cheyenne, hitching a ride towards the mountains, 'I'm not in the building trade. The experience, Ahmed – what you had is neither beauty, nor truth. Just an experience.'

'My favourite, Lizeth?' Nico asks. 'What trots?'

'*Comandante* Lizeth?' Cheyenne asks. 'Who knows? Maybe she drowned. Or – if you go underground,' and she chuckles, 'Usually, that's it. You don't come up.'

'She wrote,' says Ahmed....

'Then she'll be shelved,' says Cheyenne, nonchalantly. 'What do you expect? Transformation? Power that skims across a pond, like pebbles – one skip, two or three – and disappears? Reaches the other shore? No, Ahmed, what you call power, the rock, it may go under, under the surface. Try again, and again! Power – is not in stone or water, nor in some flatness that defies the depth – no. It's not a trick, appearances.

'The throwing arm! Is that the force that counts, the rest just a display? The throw, like throwing dice? No! It's all in the meniscus. It's a law, that you can't break, and so there is no sanction.... There's a rule instead....'

'Well,' Nico asks, losing patience and the thread. 'Is she the pebble, the water or the throw? None of those – just how things are?'

But Cheyenne's gone. For her, building her city is the point.

'She's talking about power, deep power,' Ahmed says waving till Cheyenne's out of sight. 'She means it's not putsches, takeovers. Not water and force.... She's addressing deep power. You don't need deep water. Pebbles on top don't count. The point is, Nico: surface tension. The meniscus always has the same resistance, however much the water-level changes. It's a law.'

'I understand all that,' says Nico, 'Doesn't interest. I want to know where Lizeth is.'

'Cheyenne told you, Nico,' Ahmed says. 'She's drowned or buried.'

'We're finished, then,' says Nico. 'You and I. Cheyenne will build her city – a new kind, partly underwater, in apnoea. Or she won't. Lizeth – won't reach deep power. She may disturb the surface – or may not. Leidy – may follow Lizeth – but she's timid and intelligent – so she won't.... There's no other place for us; we can't drum – Alejo is no guide, and we're not dead, so Doctor Haas has gone his separate way....'

'We're still here,' Nico says. 'I'm mortal, you're a lungfish – anything is possible, Ahmed. An apologus, perhaps.'

It's the end, the beginning. The next step's difficult in either case.

'Cheyenne told me about Leidy,' Nico says. 'A sad tale. She was kidnapped. The family won't pay. They're sceptical – and mean. The bandits took off Leidy's ears. Then out came every tooth.'

'That's terrible,' says Ahmed. 'She had a lovely mouth.'

'Fingers, and then toes,' Nico goes on. 'You can show that now – not in the mail, but on a screen. A piece a day – I'd say one step, but then it was a foot. A hand, and then an eye. Another eye. Her clothes. It's what the capitalists would call a disinvestment. Of course, I mean no insult – capitalism, along with socialism – my favoured systems. But it's turned out bad, the economics, for poor Leidy. Of course – it could be fake. Someone else – or lots of them, piecemeal, slow pruning.'

'Maybe they can graft another person on,' says Ahmed. 'When payment's done; and she'll grow out again. It works with peach-trees – she was no less beautiful than them.'

*

'There's fear,' says Nico, 'And there's profit. If you like – accomplishment. That you can measure, not just in your head. Cheyenne has learned to live with fear – and so – she metamorphoses, sparkles. I don't trust her, knowing what she has to face to be the monster she aspires to be.

'I admit – I choked. I never made my poem, though I had the shape. Spinning discs, Ahmed, discs of obsidian. Or singing tops, all in motion, in full voice, touching – and flying far apart. The empires: how they rose and fell, their songs, their instruments, their metric schemes.... Enormous, Ahmed, the enterprise ... one of my protagonists – a youth who tends the fire that makes the alcohol ... collects the peyotes, turns the aquavit into a trade, a religion, mystic dew ... but that's just one of them – the wrestlers, gardeners, warriors, perfumiers and popes.... The world! – those lop-eared monsters, the dominions and the slaves, the tedious tending of the rye, crabapples, fish-sauce ... and crushing of the fragrances, the musk, the roses and the asphodels ... caging the animals by night that eat you, and by day they sing to you and comb your hair....'

'I have the idea, Nico,' Ahmed says. 'A real pity you didn't feel like finishing it.'

'No, it's worse,' says Nico, turning away to hide distress. 'I finished it but didn't write it down. I know you, and your comrades – I tell the outline, you're enthused – and it's enough for you. You wouldn't read. It's bigger than your life – a continent where you can live and say – "I'd never dare ... sculpt that...." No courage – that's your problem. My creation is a life longer, deeper, more instructive, than your own – you'd watch and marvel, impotent.'

'And all those empires fell, and left a mass of bones,' Ahmed says.

'That's true of dinosaurs as well,' says Nico, irritated. 'That's not the point. You can't have history without the thorns. And snakes.'

'They fall, for reasons recondite and evident,' says Ahmed. 'But – I'm a visionary. They aim, proceed, towards a final state, a triumph – the realisation of the great design....'

'No, no,' Nico interrupts. 'Each one falls, then – cinders, tailings, metal lugs and foundry dross from all the rest – rains down.... We were among the first, Ahmed, the conquerors, and now, on us, down comes the soot, the clinkers, clunkers, from the rest. On our heads, my friend. Is that the lesson we should learn?'

'We disagree,' says Ahmed. 'But our quest's the same....'

'That doesn't mean a thing, Ahmed,' says Nico. 'We're not on the same side. When there's a battle, you and I ... we swing, we chant, parry and thrust ... we cut each other down; drawn words, Ahmed, and pointed slogans. Besides, Cheyenne has drawn you in. Closer than family, or lover. She's protected you from danger, so you think. She is your soul, your mentor, cicerone, the mapmaker....

'You depend on her, on your belief in her good will – she is the brain, and you the hand. It's perilous, Ahmed – you don't know her, not at all, you know yourself only through her. It's an illusion, fatal, perhaps. You know what happens to the young, my friend – the parents regurgitate their nourishment.... It's not a metaphor, it's life, Ahmed. Sometimes, when the food is scarce, the little ones become a snack ... or, if there's rivalry, chick on chick.... Prepare, beware: mistrust! People end up inside their families, their parents, some – they're addled, others roll down the cliff, still in the shell.... Tell me, where's it all supposed to end? Those crows – they're bright, so they get shot. If a link is broken – it all falls down, it disassembles, like good Doctor Haas discovered – rings, in heaps.... Not chains, just links. A mystery. How can you arrive at that? A rite, no doubt – breaking the connections – no eat-be-eaten, so – no chain. And what is it all for? There's a design, an arrangement, but it isn't good for anything, except itself, until it fails – then it's just flocculence. It has no mind, no purpose, it plods slow, obsessively, like waves. decomposed, a tone row, a scale ... wordless, with no melody....'

'Of course, you can't ask questions,' Ahmed says, 'that everybody else has asked, without discovering a novelty. Some little melody, a catch. What's the sea for? If it's not there, there's something else. Survival? But we don't survive, we disappear, we judge, or else we slaughter, and the bugs – eat you when you breathe, and when you stop.'

'This place we are at,' says Nico, tiring of Ahmed's roundelay, 'It's really old. They've not built anything that's new for centuries – they love the old, but they don't stop it falling down.... They don't believe, but there are temples everywhere, mosques and churches, it's all the colour of stale blood, the sacrifices plentiful, routine....'

'Don't ask, Nico,' says Ahmed. 'I don't know what they'll do with it, antiquity. They'll show it off, I guess. Enough that people come, gawp and pay, and nobody asks why.'

'You monetise the past,' says Nico, as they stumble on – past the huge expensive ruins – pilgrims and aesthetes moving with them, stopping off to take a snap, 'But then you have to live in it. It goes on, but is transformed. It's all about the architects and artisans – not what it was all for: celebration of empire and its rulers, and their hobnob with the gods.'

'Now, who's left, they have to live from it,' says Ahmed. 'The legacy. They're bombsites ... arches squinting on to absent panoramas – the buildings coloured ochre, rusty pink, the spirits bought ... the gods all wafted off, the river buried, deep in a rut. The racing factions reverted into football thugs....'

'Oh, Ahmed, you're too delicate!' shouts Nico, irritated. 'Gods into poems, the nymphs – morphed into aloes, yucca trees: really, my old, my dearest friend, I can't afford to carry you, your trills and frills. The games is all that's left worth following. It's life, a crow and snarl, a throw of knuckle-bones. A rig with two is faster, but a quadriga's more fun – more spills! You look for beauty – that's just the odour that remains, it's incense, sweet sewer smell. What you miss, and what there was, is purpose, intention, arrogance and show!

'Without you, I'd have found my niche – instead we have to wander up and down – this endless cemetery, the caverns stacked with bishops' skulls ... the people here – they are pariah dogs, they gnaw each other, chase the vultures off their necessary work.... Empire, Ahmed, that's where the blood comes from, it's endless – barbarians, decadents, easterners and southerners, slaves and flatterers, clients, bootlickers, fixers and taxers, cutpurses, cutthroats, gladiators, high priests, low priests, priests who seduce, priests who traduce ... bags and sacks of blood each one, cash for the boatman – *folles* and *solidi* – all grist, Ahmed, fast food, farro and cowtails, snails and snakes, peacock tongues and river pearls – down it goes, around, around – and then it's blood, anoint the mosaic floors with gore, make crosses on the babies' heads – their destiny ... Kali! she's here, the silent goddess, who's cool lodging is beside you in your skin....'

'Everybody knows, Nico,' Ahmed says, hoping his friend won't leave him all alone. 'The city on the hill, even lots of hills – they're heaped up broken crocks, and the slaves too, who toted them as amphora. It's a city of the flood-plain, growing boils, carbuncular.'

'Don't moralise, Ahmed,' Nico says, unreconciled to his friend's high mind. 'That always comes too late. Do what you like to anyone – only a death can't be undone. Those gladiators – unless there is a grudge – they don't do anything for real. They're like Leidy – lose a limb for money and you'll find that it grows back. Encores are for that.'

*

They'd been forgetting about Leidy. Nothing to be done. You mustn't pay a ransom, and besides, they have no cash.

*

'This place – a city of the plain, reared up on mounds of junk to make it seem it's built upon a hill – it reminds me of an other place, a picture ... some museum? There must be an original.... A pontifex ... some old gent with a pruning knife, a chopping block, making human sacrifices, castrating, washing away the lymph and gore with tears.... I remember, maybe, a whole expanse, given to temples, galleries and barracks – prisons and tombs ... the cenotaphs and catacombs ... a holy capital, shared between Kali and Mars,' says Ahmed, in fear and wonder at the thought.

'You're right, Ahmed,' says Nico. 'That adventure – belief in the invisible to keep you straight – was not a tender dream. Now, you awake. What now? You are the liberator, saviour now. What's the priority? First – the planet. Then, the species. All the rest will follow – but those are big enterprises, and you'd need a Hercules, or maybe two or more. Don't look back. The past – is not a tutor, but a culprit. If your city's on a hill, you'll tumble down, maybe fly off the Tarpeian rock. And on the plain – there's ditches everywhere, bad guys who lurk behind the palms. Let's seek some company, my friend, and... share our task.'

'Oh no, Nico,' says Ahmed. 'We could wait till Cheyenne comes again....'

'She bewitches, Ahmed,' Nico says. 'She wants no pledge, and leaves no gift. Let's hope she's found another patsy....'

*

'I was sleeping,' says Viktor, 'under that leaf,' and he points to a jagged plantain.... 'and your quarrelling woke me. You're both wrong. Those cities, the people who lived in them, dug the holes and raised the towers, divided into classes, faiths, sexes and sizes, tastes and smells – that is no more.'

Nico points, silent, to a forest of tall misshapen domes and spires, to a ripple-wall of tenements, a project.... 'All empty,' says Viktor. 'Some condemned and cleared by force. Some too expensive, never occupied. That civilisation that you both deplore and seek to flee, transform – or climb on, survive like a band of capuchins, a canopy that hosts a choice of beasts – that cling and slither, glide and hide ... it's gone. We've changed behaviour. We don't seek out our similars, for gain or company.... We sit alone, we work in isolation, inexistent friends and once or twice a year we couple, then back to our lairs. We're like the lions – the ladies do the hunting, the males – they screw and eat the cubs. It's a complex – the rivalry, the territory – a space where nothing else exists but us....'

'Yes, yes,' says Ahmed, quite impatiently. 'We know all that, we're penny-anteing with worn-out coins. We would conform, live on our own, except – how'd we get paid?'

'That is the nub,' says Viktor, pulling on some snakeskin moccasins, taking a fine bracelet off his leg, hidden by his pants to resist a theft, and clasping it upon a wrist.... 'It looks to me as if – Ahmed? – you never started looking appetising. For you, critique came first, before ingratiating. A mistake. You – Nico? – I hear the names shouted out in argument – it seems you've finished. You've done everything, and now it's meditation left. You too – mistaken, thoroughly.'

'We're old-style guys,' says Nico, patronising. 'We deal with face-to-face. Gangs and bands, manifs and cops, guerrillas, ransoms – old-style values, everything.'

From another plantain leaf – out comes Amaelle. She has an old-style look, but – 'I'm not an experimental sort,' she says. 'Forget conventions. You don't need physically describe me, give me a family, beginning and an end. It's hot here, and I shared a nap with Viktor. We aren't science-fiction – it's you two, from the deep or height – who need....'

'An explanation? Context?' Ahmed interrupts. 'We are the norm. The world, its empires, and its end – that is our universe. You are ephemeral, rafting on problems unresolved, and futures you can't write...'

'What do you do, exactly, Viktor?' Nico asks.

'I fix,' says Viktor. 'I find things for you. Spare legs and pills, identity, an audience, or trips in rockets or in bathyspheres....'

'And Amaelle?' asks Ahmed.

'Oh,' says Viktor, 'My lover? Amaelle begs. She can't do like me – she's tried it all, they never pay her, so all that's left is loving me, and loving her herself in every possible way.... One seeks perfection, so being a mendicant is another opportunity....'

'All work is noble,' she interrupts. 'I do what there is.'

'I see you sleep beneath a plant. Convenience, exhaustion ... cuddling with nature? But, Viktor,' Ahmed says, 'the city. Don't you live in that as well?'

'It's noble too,' says Viktor, 'but it's turned rustic. We live in it to make us well.'

'We're lions,' says Amaelle. 'I roar. And Viktor hunts. And turnabout. No animals get hurt.'

'There's versatility. It sounds ideal,' says Nico. 'What should we do to join?'

'Choose a behaviour that you think will suit,' says Amaelle.

'Perhaps that's what Cheyenne has done,' Ahmed whispers to his friend. 'She's flexible. Though in all she does – she doesn't bend: it's not done sitting down.'

'That's snide,' says Nico. 'My journey's done. I slump. I do my poetry that way, it's all I know.'

'I don't do poetry,' Viktor says, 'or rather, everybody does, so there's no call....'

'Don't show us round,' says Nico. 'I know exactly how it is – the countryside, just like it was in books when we were very young – all was to enjoy.... The talking animals – pelouches; cows giving up their juice, pigs in cummerbunds and brogues....'

'Oh no,' says Amaelle. 'Once it was so, but now – we know that everybody dies. The world dies too. It doesn't bother us – until it ends, something goes on – the chain of being. Till it breaks, and there are rings, and links – that maybe join up again – but what we have's....'

'The chain of fixing,' Viktor says, and laughs. 'Except it isn't things, it's abstracts that I fix – your personality, your beliefs and happiness ... an infinity of contexts, references to check....'

'Amaelle – she doesn't look the happy one,' says Ahmed, and she hugs him.

'It's all in the saying, Ahmed,' says Amaelle.

'And Kali?' Nico asks. 'It seems she's here and prospering.'

The response is obvious – they turn it over, each of them, like turnstones on a beach.

'Am I Columbus or Crusoe?' Ahmed asks. 'There's all those cities waiting, to be knocked down and built up in my image.'

'For sure, if Crusoe'd had more hands to hire, he'd have walked upon the lake and built the city: – immense,' says Nico. 'Columbus couldn't nail two sticks. Crusoe was an architect – no contract, but he'd redesigned a world. He was the Master, lord of nothing, no one: a fierce god, a Moloch. His savages weren't noble ... they were slaves, no Rousseau he. He – the big God, sailed in a silver box, a cross of gold to nail the FuzzieWuzzies on.... Imagine – if he'd remained alone, and had not written, bottled up that note, and summoned up the rescue team – he could have been immortal, easing out his long bones, becoming a medusa on the beach, then flowering to millions, tiny parachutes, like they were dropped from a Bikini bomber. New life! Nuked life, with six Siva arms, or like poor Leidy – none at all....'

'Crusoe, jiving, ripping up a cliff – screaming to his God to have Him end it all, every experiment, new worlds, a trip to Pluto – that rubbery mutt than maybe never lived save on your screen – the first, the last Man: impotent, the whitey calling for his mate, the Lorelei, a Liebestod – and here he comes! – first, last black – and Crusoe makes a slave of him....'

They stare at Nico, his gestures.... The fear, the exaltation, the red sweaty face. How he recalls the massacres that only one, or two, survive....

*

'Oh yes,' says Viktor. 'On our screen we can be anyone, do anything, at any time, dimension, but ... *our* time, ineluctably, is up! We know the answer, the big ask's no mystery: – we didn't make it! *Genüg*! Too – arduous? Too naff. Convention says – a story has to end, or it's unfinished. So – we ended it. This is the final chapter, murderer revealed – another Roger Ackroyd – the murderer, always, is who knows it all, who writes, narrates....'

'Yes!' shouts Nico. 'That's what my poem says.'

'There!' says Amaelle. 'You see! The puzzle's solved. Why we are we, you you!'

'It doesn't seem a puzzle, though,' says Ahmed. 'Tracks in the sand.... There's lots, all trudge round, look for water. If there is....'

*

'There!' says Nico. 'We've laid out the heavy stuff. There is a question, though – Viktor: I drop "spiders" in your ear. How do you react?'

'You mean the civil war?' asks Viktor. 'Mortality? Intelligence? That goes on, of course. There'll be a fix. Worse – there's the earthquakes. Those are overdue. We're hot, if there were spiders underground – they'll have been fried.'

It's sandy here – quite the wrong kind of sand. Here, it's been rounded, every grain has blown around, smacked into other mottled comrades and can't be made to stick to other grains. Travellers' sand, that you can't build with.

'Spiders,' says Viktor. 'We don't have problems with mortality. We're blown glass. Amaelle – in bed, she's thin as a voice. She tells you all you want, and the body's what you want – but maybe it's not a body that you want? I give you – the something else. That too – perhaps it isn't what you want, but what's to do?'

'Respect,' Amaelle chimes in. 'A body you can hone and tune: it's still quite gross. When overheated – it will overflow and flood the room, like an old electric boiler.'

'This civil war,' says Nico, 'that's more my thing. Thing to avoid. Floods and earthquakes – even harder to evade. Evolution's moving fast – the monsters....and the heat.'

'Oh, they're sweet!' says Amaelle. She's right – they have a quizzical air, they wander round – how to use those limbs, and what to eat? How long do we live, how many pups or chicks to keep our numbers up ... and do we domesticate?

\*

'Here, you're laid back,' Ahmed says. 'Where we were, maybe it's what we're escaping from, except you need to know where to go that might be different ... where we were, you don't relax ... you seek a place that's....'

'Safe,' says Amaelle.

'Yes, safe, but that's just a thing you say,' Ahmed goes on. 'Where we were, they used to say – if you're bad, you will be punished. Or – punishment will come, or should. Now – that's said when there's a mass of guys, of good and bad – or maybe, lots of bad and lots who's job is to seek them out. It's not clear why goodness was so emphasised: we weren't a city on a hill. There's lots of bad – maybe not meant,' and he laughs. 'Here, instead, I don't see ways you can do bad.'

'Well,' says Viktor, 'bad actions – much reduced. There might be a suggestion – even a prod ... an inducement – but I'm not good or bad – don't want to be, don't see the sense.... I might push people to be good or bad – it's up to them. There is no punishment – or if there is, it falls on everyone. It's rain. Once people prayed for that, but now – it falls on sand. We water window-boxes from a tap.'

'This is moralism,' Nico says. 'It's hypothetical. I don't see myself in this – it's all philosophy, maybe psychology, and law and custom too – class, gender and necessity....'

'They'll think of killing Lizeth,' Ahmed says. 'The immaculate. Leidy did nothing to deserve her destiny.... Good, bad, the chop, the waterboard – all grist ...'

'It's to be avoided, all this stuff,' says Amaelle. 'The judgement, principle. And I can see what Viktor cannot do, or doesn't want.... Commitment, any kind....'

'Amaelle – she's been through the test,' says Viktor, laughing, 'She's neither good nor bad. Now, the only punishment that's worth – is what you do to hurt yourself – or, maybe satisfy yourself....

'I give a prod, that's all, if you feel in need of one ... and if you don't, it's quite the same. Justice – is quite another thing. No one knows exactly what it is, or if they do – how does it work? Through punishment? It doesn't change a thing. It doesn't stop a repetition, and in any case – prevention avoids the punishment but not the bad. Your friends, Ahmed – some were punished, but for sure it wasn't just. The guys who punished them – who punishes that lot?'

'I know all that,' says Ahmed. 'It's old stuff – we left, where that is still the talk....'

'Ahmed loves Cheyenne,' says Nico. 'But it's quite irrelevant. She does everything: she hunts, from the savannah to the jungle – an omnivore. Love – doesn't enter in. What matters is we've got away from that place, the city on the plain, and met you guys from quite another world – a city stranded on the sand. Not plain nor hill.'

'It's true, we're different,' says Amaelle. 'But, we'll disappear, whether we are good or bad, punished or the punishers.'

'We're clean,' says Viktor. 'You two – have the fear. It must be terrible.'

'We did nothing, nothing of any consequence,' says Ahmed. 'I was a judge – but only as pretend. Nico did nothing – just had lots of friends.'

\*

'You see,' says Viktor, 'you two – you're an odd assortment. I suppose me and Amaelle strike you that way too. But we're quite intimate, we four: already, we could spend our time together.'

'I don't think so,' says Ahmed. 'About the intimacy.'

'Look!' says Amaelle, pointing. 'Up there – we live there. Down here, there's a kind of dancing bar. Viktor doesn't, but he likes to watch.'

Nico says, 'I don't dance. But I do. What dance do they do here?'

'Any. Or none,' Amaelle says. 'It's as you please. Follow the music.'

'Ahmed likes watching too,' says Nico.

Amaelle and Nico – wave their arms and shuffle with their feet. There's a crowd, not much room. They follow the music, where it goes.

'I hear there's civil war here too,' says Nico.

You have to shout, but even then, no one can hear.

'Marx was right,' says Nico. 'Marx was wrong. His war never happens. It never happened. Will we be here when it does, and how does it end? Will we survive? Be on the right side?'

Amaelle can't answer. No one can.

'It's good!' says Nico. 'It's good there's war, and everyone is in it or pretending nothing happens. Go to! Keep going, on to the end and even further ... no one will be left to write it down. It's always so – it's written down before it happens and when it's over, there is no one left.'

Amaelle can't respond to that. It doesn't need a comment.

Nico says, 'You've sealed your ears, Amaelle, and stoppered up your mouth – you're mummified. Your stupid trivial sentiments, for a stupid trivial man. You don't live in the discomfort of a life. You're the divan guys sit on while they talk about discomfort. You're an animal, Amaelle, remember. Where we come from, they're all animals, they know they have no future, it's all in their cubs.'

They dance on – the music doesn't stop, why should it, the guys aren't unionised, and they don't have what you'd call a contract. They're there to play, and they do, loud, too.

'The fight starts in the hills,' says Nico. 'Then it goes down to the plain. It'll come here too, which you say is neither hill nor plain – maybe when you're old, demented, and you won't remember what I told you to remember, and yet, it will be true. Notwithstanding.'

Viktor and Ahmed sit silent and as much apart as possible – the situation's quite embarrassing. They don't have rhythm. They're fixed on Nico, Amaelle, bumping up and down.

Amaelle's used to people being angry when they dance instead of being intimate, and Nico – is by far too intimate ... his civil wars – it's plausible, but not the place.

It is the place, but that entails no consequence.

Ahmed knows the good life, but has never lived it. He and Nico know the bad life, but so do most guys, and it doesn't make a difference. Viktor lives life sitting down – quite like import, export, except you don't need say what's in the boxes. Maybe you don't have real clients and suppliers – so you make it up. Improvise. A few bars sets the mood, they settle in your head and make a nest.

Amaelle's the easiest – you ask for cash, some give, some don't. The ethics probably comes in, but no one knows how, or if it matters. Most people don't give anything. It's human, like free will.

\*

'You know, Amaelle,' says Nico, sliding a hand round her buttocks as if protecting her from a collision, 'you could come with us. You'd learn a lot, you'd carry on your trade, have a new clientele....'

'Why should I?' asks Amaelle. 'You've chosen to be poor and tramp the world. I'm stuck with Viktor – today he's rich, tomorrow – probably he's poor, or destitute. What I want's a little house. A garden. Your world is headless, irresponsible. No one's in charge, we are all poor.... Moving around – it's an illusion that there's something you can find....'

'Freedom. Culture,' Nico says, holding Amaelle close. 'What you'll see – draining the marshes, building byres and felling trees, ageing jeans and hunting elks – after you, it could all disappear.'

'Exactly,' says Amaelle. 'Too intrusive. Plotless. Trying it on without desire – a running on the spot.'

'You're right,' says Nico. 'But you've not changed – your insight leaves you less happy than before.'

'I don't trust you, Nico,' Amaelle says. He holds her very tight. It's not how they do the dancing here.

'Ahmed and I,' says Nico, 'put together – we are Faust – builder and destroyer, gambler and savant.'

Amaelle frees herself, sits on Viktor's knee, 'The devil I know,' she says, kissing him.

'Can we two crash in your place tonight?' Nico asks.

'No,' says Viktor, 'I don't think so. We have a routine.'

'Our routine is we leave tomorrow,' Ahmed says. Nothing decided – Viktor's place is small, not cheap. There are no pictures on the wall. 'Voices of silence,' Viktor says, 'The museum is in here,' and he taps a flat case, wired up.

'We shan't take anything,' Nico says, to reassure. There's not much they could.

'We left everything behind,' says Ahmed. They sit on the floor, Nico and Ahmed. The spider marks on their ankles – those are visible, and they itch, perhaps they swell....

\*

'It's at low levels,' Nico says. He stands like Bonaparte on a mound. There's fog around, and empty bangs.

'The burning stuff is good for trade,' he says. 'The gas, the smoke – that goes deep inside.'

There's a city ahead, but the gas hides it, if it's lofty or low, even built on water – on causeways.

Nico laughs. 'Amaelle didn't respond to me at all,' he says.

'You're an idiot,' says Ahmed. 'She meant nothing to you. Neither of them did. They're different, they live entirely in fantasy, but in them there's not the slightest fantasy. Everything they do – it seems it's the first time, that they've invented everything.'

'Perfected everything,' says Nico. 'And yet they know what's there – they didn't make it, and it's wrong for them, and getting worse, and they can't do anything about it, except go in the streets and try to tear it down. Smash everything, like slaves trying to sink the slavers' ship they're on.'

'I can't see Amaelle helping the alpacas out,' Ahmed says. 'That's the test for me.'

'I guess we all beg,' says Nico. 'Everybody begs, wants something back, even when they're giving charity – but Amaelle ... it was just work, not the worst, but the most precarious the stigma didn't worry her. Society. she knew that's how it works. It's a good point, not having illusions, doing what you need to do. She's like Cheyenne....'

'You're supposed to think no one's like Cheyenne,' Nico says. 'She was just hard, so much harder than you are, Ahmed. A rock you fall on, and it hurts.'

'It's not a defect,' Ahmed says. 'Not being carapaced. That slows you down. The stupid ones need armour – they can't dodge, negotiate, or run.'

'Those guys are really going at each other,' Nico says – there's deep lines of cops, kitted up, like black beetles facing soldier ants –

fire ants, perhaps. Some – leaf-cutters. The ants are throwing rocks and stuff.

'The beetles win at first,' says Ahmed, 'but there's more ants; if they decide they're in danger, more and more come out their holes. Or they think that they might win.'

'Us? It's a mistake to go in at the start,' says Nico. 'On either side. I'm a cicada, too – where do our interests lie? In other cicadas, I expect.'

'Is this the revolution?'Ahmed asks: 'Is it for this we've wandered so long, so far? Can we settle here and prosper, Nico? If we go in the street, how shall we live?'

'Oh, as we always have,' says Nico. 'You haven't noticed – I trade currencies.... Every place we go, they have an instrument – it makes no music, it's finance, but you play on it, you shave off something, enough for the day. For both of us. It's truth, Ahmed. Maybe not honesty.'

'I know nothing, Nico, of how we live,' says Ahmed, hurrying along, 'There's always war, it's always civil. And you know, Revolution's not about your cash. Ennobling work – that's what it involves. These guys here – they're left and right, and neither too – we're all against the system, and here we see the system's against us. Later, maybe, we'll all be sorted out....'

'This fragrance, Ahmed,' Nico says. 'Coconut oil! I love it. Maybe they put it in the gas....'

'We join the struggle, Nico? Or we wait and see?' asks Ahmed, boiling with uncertainty.

'These guys,' Nico says, 'have no idea what you are for, my friend, still less what you're against. They don't understand a word of yours, and they don't listen.' He gazes at the embattled crowd: 'Isn't that Viktor there? In the throng? See? He wants stability and cash, a better version of Amaelle....'

'Here, Nico,' Ahmed says, 'put this biscuit tin over your face – they're using flashballs – bullets go through you, but these are worse, they hit and cannon off, they're used again, an infinity of times.... I'll tell you what goes on.' And so he covers Nico's head, and takes his hand and leads him here and there, to safety or to this side, then to that, poor Nico, voiceless but protected, sightless and trusting....

'When there was nature, you grew food,' says Nico from within his tin. 'Then there was gold – a scrabble deep, warm in the ground. When you had a leader with a battle-plan, a *strategos* – you won or lost. Famine and drought – that turned your mind to other things – but plenty, now it is to hand, but it's invisible ... ephemeral ... where is the source? The wealth? Do you inherit something? A faith, a coloured eye – your granny bequeaths? A coloured skin? Did she leave you a genetic charm that makes you rich...?'

'I can't answer all that,' says Ahmed. 'I'm overwhelmed. This city – not like the other ones – it stretches ... it's a country, an island, a continent ... hills and plains, hibiscus and fuchsia, lobelia, love-lies-bleeding – how'd they water them.... It never rains, how pale the sun....'

'Spare me the atmosphere, Ahmed,' says Nico. 'I'm stifling in this can.'

Even coca plants need watering – you could make something better in a lab. The original's no answer. The derivative – that's nature too, brings gold, old-style as well.

Nico could speak, of course, but it's not required. A guy comes up to them, shepherds them aside – he looks like Viktor, but more intrusive, more interested in suggesting his own alternatives, so as to impress. He doesn't care about being right, it wouldn't matter anyway. 'He's fine,' says Ahmed. 'I'm protecting Nico, him, in the box. His life is workaday. It's work. Mine too.'

'You don't look like us,' says the guy, Ludis. 'We have to build our nation, us alone. Our city....'

'No,' says Ahmed, 'you're right. It isn't me, but I'm fine with what you do.'

'Ahmed's an idiot,' says Nico from within the tin. 'Though I agree with him.'

'You want nothing for yourself,' the guy, Ludis, tells Ahmed. 'But you accept whatever you're given. You're not interesting. Nico wants everything, but if a flashball hits him, in the front of his helmet, it could knock an eye out. From the side – he could go deaf.'

'I'd still be here to pull him along,' says Ahmed. He loves Nico like he loves Cheyenne – neither are present, both can spend years not needing anyone, not thinking for a minute about Ahmed.

'You don't like things being told plain,' says the guy. 'I can give you shelter – you're two slow horses: those swollen ankles won't take you far.'

He lives high up – the gas is stifling, rising – Nico keeps the tin on his head, it reduces the fug, the coconut oil, that starts to cloy.

'What exactly do you do?' Ahmed asks the guy, Ludis.

'I made the city,' says the guy, Ludis. 'I designed it, someone built part of it. The rest will follow. See – it's extending as far as you can see – though that's a tiny part of it, because your sight is limited. You'd need to travel out – another day, it's clear.'

'Are you a nat or a separatist, my friend?' asks Nico.

'You'll find,' Ludis says, 'there's less difference. The bigger the city gets, it will merge with others. Everything will come about. All will be true. The workers will become the rich, the nationalists will rule the world, be globals and everything over and above and in between. The city-world, it will be new, and separate from all the old, the gobs and blobs of muddy fields and dusty village squares ... the backwaters and the tailing ponds, the beaver dams, the coots, the waterfalls – all these can be put on your roof – if you're a miner, or you fancy birds, or otter fur to trim your hat.... Or any combination of all that. And don't go back – the towns and villages there were – it's useless looking. They have disappeared.'

'I sense,' says Ahmed, staring at Ludis, 'a wryness, touch of mockery, of something incomplete.'

'Of course,' Ludis says, 'there always needs to be a second act.'

That doesn't mean so much.

'You see,' Ludis says, sitting down at a desk and looking at the treetops opposite. 'It's a question of tying it together. These masses who want to come here, who must, and who settle in and find they don't want it, in a little while, not at all, but nothing else, which isn't in any case available. People wishing they weren't here, in their situation, without the means to change it, not at all, not enough – those with a sufficiency, those with nothing, with their own ideas they got from someone, somewhere else....'

'Well,' says Nico, 'they're out there now, wanting those means. Throwing stuff.'

'It's obvious,' says Ludis. '"The means to change what is the product of a change?" I can't do that. If they don't want what I've designed, they must find means, those means, searching for themselves.'

'Maybe those means – we're talking about quite different things,' says Ahmed. 'A means to settle is one: and then a means to change, change utterly, escape. You've made a centre, with a periphery. It all hangs together, like a sentence with a meaning, a subordinate clause.'

There's shouting from below. Ahmed goes on, 'You can stay at home, or go to the manif. Not much choice. Living here – would surely blunt Cheyenne's claws.'

'This,' says Ludis, 'is the best there is. I know. I've studied. If they're not satisfied – it's good. It's still the best anyone can devise. If it isn't to your taste – there's always reason to expect it will all change.'

'It's not much,' says Nico, 'but it's true. You can't do better, Ludis.'

\*

'What do you two wanderers expect?' asks Ludis, dropping his friendly approach: 'There's nothing here for you. Or rather, there is provision here for you, but probably it's not what you would want.'

'We're looking, that is all, says Ahmed. 'The best there is – is not enough. We don't know what we want to find, how long we might be satisfied. The best there is – is not a satisfactory end. It might be we're satisfied with much less than the best, much less. Or maybe nothing, nothing at all, will satisfy. Just looking. Angry sometimes – can't be ruled out – we're not patsies, Ludis.'

'Of course you aren't,' says Ludis, pushing them towards the stairs. 'But – one last thing. Your friend, the soldier – have him leave his helmet here. It's the right size for storing plans. You won't need it – all is quiet outside,' and Nico leaves his tin.

It's not quiet. The boulevard's ablaze.

'"His helmet now a nest for bees",' says Nico. 'Disarmoured and demobilised. What are we doing here, Ahmed? We're back, back at the start of something – building the anthill that collapses, with us within, or strolling past.... Who were those islanders, Ahmed, in the book – not termites...?'

'You're thinking of the penguins, Nico,' Ahmed says. 'The people here are flightless too – they don't take kindly to your poems, all about the past and how you'd do things different....'

'Without my armour,' Nico says, 'my coconut exposed, someone making plans and storing them in my protection – it comes to mind – to go back where we were, in the first city. There's Cheyenne. And absences. That's what you do at school. You learn, poetry's all about it.'

\*

'The big empires – they coexist,' says Ahmed. 'While they rise and fall together, they may skirmish – they don't fight.

'If we went back, where Kali dances – you can see her, morning and at sunset: there's civil war, it's true, but those are everywhere.

'Big empires – they have clients, and they've bugbear states. But, the empires are jockeys in the same race, with the same ambition – to keep on the saddle, their mount straining, galloping. Best not live in the empire, the mega-cities, as a foreigner. No complicated belief – enthusiasm when required. All denizens, and nothing more. Made afresh, no origins to bother with.

'There's wars, but not the final one. In this city, we'd survive, but we don't belong, don't want to understand. When it becomes the world, we'd be on the edge. Unhappy, not respected....'

'I don't choose sides,' says Nico. 'But I don't want to wear that biscuit-tin.'

'We have to think we are significant,' says Ahmed. 'Are you convinced we are, Nico?'

'Absolutely,' Nico says: 'We are the most important people here. We, and our companion, Cheyenne, who did you the favour, Ahmed – appearing in affectionate form ... a feel. There's nothing more.'

'I'm convinced.' says Ahmed. 'You know, I'd ride into the abyss with you – you wouldn't save me, and you'd leap right out – showing you have the qualities you say....'

'It's all agreed,' says Nico. 'If we can leave this immense city, and the suburbs where the people think they have escaped – we'll trek back, back where we came from, if our feet support us....'

'History....' Ahmed begins.

'No problem,' Nico says. 'I shall write the history.'

\*

'This is wrong,' says Ahmed, pausing. 'We don't want where the signs say – City of the Sun. Besides – see, there's a column trudging away from there.'

'No, no,' Nico agrees. 'Not our destination. There's a problem with the sun. Reflect, Ahmed: Cheyenne. She's overwhelming, and she's given you her best. Nothing for me. Then, we're compromised with Lizeth, the *Comandante* ... and there's poor Leidy, saddens everything. "Back" means a replay of all that. Not forward, but not back, we'll go. Climb a hill and scout around. Find someone like good Doctor Haas who'll cure our spider bites....

'Another place, there'll be for sure, where everything is sorted out – see, the condors have come back, sedate upon their spirals....'

Walking is good for you – even though you go in circles – the good's the same. The bad is – standing still. Ahmed, his philosophy – it comes down to circulation.

The doctor's very young. He looks up 'ankle' in his book. 'Alas,' he says, 'you're not secure. You could last just one day. Once set out along the road – avoid the hills and plains, unless you want to fight or demonstrate.... Ignore Descartes – he said that when he spoke of Nature, no goddess came to mind. I prescribe – a sacrifice to Kali – that's the best trick to keep her off.... Although – it may attract her, who can tell. No one knows what good it does, even a hecatomb.... An alpaca, maybe, the choice bit; you can eat the rest.'

'We'd fight, of course,' says Nico, hurrying over. 'But this sickness, our mortality – it tells us "no", and "wait". We believe, of course. Whatever's plausible. My friend, Ahmed, his lost love – she disbelieved in everything. We are in her net, her field, like iron filings magnetised....'

'Cheyenne,' says Ahmed, glazing up. 'She is a furnace – a scaly brown outside, within – pink, red, orange, white – she changes, everything inside, it liquifies, it runs, it flows and cannot move, makes every thing into a flux, she seethes ... hotter and hotter ... there's no moulds, nothing to pour the metals in, it goes on, incandescent, forbidding – wonder: and forever you withdraw, stand further off....'

He is transformed, exalted, altered ... he says:

'She's life that changes and destroys, loosens the forms, merges them, and on and on – until....'

'No, Ahmed,' says Nico. 'Don't think of it. Don't go in the crucible, you're purified there, but disappear. Right now, there is no trace of you to leave: you're aspiration in a pair of worn-out boots. *Connubio* with Cheyenne – forget it: your epithalamium won't leave a cinder or a cone of ash... *I*'ll set your epitaph – "the last good man, the last for sure; the good, maybe"....'

'It's true, I didn't do so much,' says Ahmed. 'Sought, and did not find. But unlike you, I didn't court the bad and flirt with her.'

'Well,' says the youthful quack, quite young, and so exempted from the oath not to do bad. 'Kali's the judge, of course. Of both of you.'

'I don't trust you, doctor,' Nico says. 'Nothing personal. Point us to where we'll be happy, satisfied, even if it might be only for an hour, a day....'

'Oh,' says the white-coated youth. 'I don't do deals. Deals did for good Doctor Haas! He reached no conclusions about his princesses – were they happy? Sad? Falsely conscious? Unconscious? And the servant class they buried with them? Perhaps that's an easier guess.... Why not go straight, when you depart my room?'

'That is the hardest way,' says Ahmed. 'Going straight, when your ankles fail.'

'You've moved around,' says the youth. 'Don't tell me if you suffered. Go separately, if you're desperate. Together, you've three good legs, like a milking stool. If you've nothing left to give, then take.'

'Columbus,' Ahmed says, 'wasn't like the modern sort. He didn't think about what would happen to all the people he discovered. We're like him. That interest in a consequence – it's what historians have. Did anybody anywhere have a single thought about them? Crusoe – he did poor: discovered just one person, or was discovered by only one – a foreigner both! And yet the colony was founded, it has his name, the city too – just like Columbus. He was interested in himself, like us – it's not that he was white, just was half the population, enslaving the other half. Now – there's a story! It inspires me! Music too!'

'You mean, Ahmed,' the doctor asks. 'Your puzzle is – why are you as you are, and why doesn't it interest someone else?'

'No,' says Nico. 'He's interested in being something else. He's gone beyond, far beyond. He is a conscience, way high up; you see a wavering shape, challenging the wind, like a paper aeroplane. Then down he floats – a blackening shape – and "GAWK" he goes. He's still the same old ill-omening crow....!' And Nico hugs Ahmed, laughing, says – 'He drops to where I am. And – I'm changed.'

'You're finished, Nico, that's the change,' says Ahmed, pulling away, quite irritated.

'That makes me take you in my charge,' says Nico. 'Don't mistake that black shape, the conscience, for Cheyenne. She's not a bird, but if she were, birds often incarnate a someone, something, else – those swans! ... and then there's more; they cannot tote a load. They drop things – accidental, you might think, but they've good aim. The tortoise on the coconut – it's not a joke from Paul Gauguin.

'No birds, Ahmed! And no Cheyenne. I know you're drawn to nullity – the furnace, oceans, and the mud. Your death wish is no sacrifice – it doesn't signify. Kali can wait, there's always other dances she can do. She'll have you in the end. So, mistrust the air. Breathe, exhale – don't use it as a stair. It does not hold. Birds use it for its slipperiness – they loose their brakes and there's no gravity.... It's earth that gets them when they lose their masts, their slender sticks....'

'A nullity into nothingness,' says Ahmed, gloomily, scratching his ankle. 'Disappearing – into a molten mass. I didn't ride the elements, nor yet drove myself; I didn't change a thing...'

'No one can, or does,' the doctor says. 'Except for people you don't want to be. Chinggis: the example I shall always give; the other names – might give offence.'

*

'We've done the round of cities,' Nico says. 'We didn't stick. It's time to summarise, find the last place: combine the future and the past, and where we'll wait those out....'

'I'm stifling, Nico,' Ahmed says, pulling at his clothes, his neck. 'It's the toxicity. Of everything – your gold certificates – they killed the trees to make the paper, but behind – there's arsenic and cyanide, rivers, lakes and seas of orange slur. Cheyenne the worst of all – suborning the plants. The honest coca – and the rest, enlightened chemistry turned into bullets and garottes. Lizeth too, down from her hill and trading toxins to pay her squaddies....'

Nico laughs – 'We know all that, we've always known. We're not born innocent, we die of shame.'

It's only an aphorism. Nico corrects himself, 'We live, survive, by hardening our shells. The nacre grows around our eyes and up our nose, and in the end – we croak, blind, choked.'

He does the variations:

'Mercury's our big god, and we are golden figurines – back in the earth we go – dug up, refined, then melted down – bullion and coin – look! My hump – it's pure ... all these years of tramping round, I've grown into a camel, Ahmed – the envy of alpacas.... I'm three curled nines, only a thousandth part's impure, I have an extra hump .... an authentic beast from Bactria!'

'What's this crap, Nico,' Ahmed asks, annoyed. 'About gold? You carry it, it's poisonous, but it's legal, you can do it all your life. If your hump was drugs, you'd have used it, or sold it in a lump. Gold teaches patience, littling... But it's true – you are deformed, my friend – you're pot-bellied, legs like thorn-trees, and you reek....

'This "ecology", this rhetoric ... it's perverse: we have our reasons; we consume, we mine, we scour and pillage, hunt and eat, we milk and flay – we have our locust nature; it is ours, the world, to finish off, complete the epic. Come! the last blow-out, the big *bouffe*! Nature is Kali, Nico. The sun will swallow us, and no one's left to hear the belch....'

'I'm finished, like I said,' says Nico. 'Like you – except a soldier's more useful than a guy like you – ascetic, aesthete. No, we need a warrior, who'll fight and gouge for any side, drop the bomb, cut off your head – it's all the same except for scale.... Nothing's been asked in the right way, nothing resolved, no plan that doesn't gyre and eat its tail and then the kneecaps, like stale scones: the feet – deep-fried flippers, brown as snuff, with nails of snot-green jade....'

He groans. He slumps.

'Courage, Nico,' Ahmed says. 'The standing, erect and travelling – that wears the feet and legs out first. But – this is not the time, and not your time. Our hopeful life – it's all been broached, and fingered thoroughly. *Timor mortis....* that's our supreme wisdom, otherwise – there's nothing, no accomplishment has come to term, nor's worth a commentary ....'

'Too bad,' says Nico, weakly. 'I spit on you, my feeble friend, your clumsy epitaphing. It's always so. The heroes die, the cowards dig the hole, carry the bier and cry, and tear their clothes – there's millions of them, and they never fade. You're one of them, Ahmed. Your task is burying the carrion that someone else exists to eat. My knotty life is done, lived with such care and delicacy, each word quite lexically correct ... and so.... And so it goes, Ahmed.'

'You end, old friend,' says Ahmed, 'but – it's neutral. Not a criticism of our civil life, still less our civilisation, its varieties....'

'You are the humanist,' says Nico, seeming not to hear – or maybe he agrees:

'So, carry me.' he goes on. 'I'll put my legs like so, around your neck – consider me a chippendale. I don't ask you to run – I am a chair, and when you tire, you'll sit on me and look around – at truth, or beauty. ... And I'll bear your weight.'

'You can't die here,' says Ahmed struggling to shrug him off. 'Though when you do, I'll need to excavate for you ....That's not my thing....'

*

'I've news for you,' says Maxence. 'But – the guy, moribund, up on your back...?'

'He's like me,' says Ahmed. 'He was looking to take a side, not thinking of a history, or where the enemy came from, or what a victory meant. Useless, I'd say – and so he took to verse....'

'A puzzle.' says Maxence. 'I understand. There's many mysteries around. Though we don't any more believe in anything, it seems there are exceptions. There's superpeople – those who sing, and throw their spears. There's money, and there's drugs. Cheyenne – she knew what misery the money brings. Having too much, or none at all – it's like the drugs. Drugs – shit, they say, stopped us having revolution, it causes death, without them we would all be free, immortal, sisters, brothers. And all the trade around! It's true – she didn't sing or throw her javelin. She was discreet. Where you have crowds, and traffic, the people flee, or they are chained. It seems there's no way in between. The competition: if you read the Scottish texts, the Glasgow and the Edinburgh schools – for some, it's permanent. Essential. For others – it produces a monopoly – its destiny: its contrary. It seems – you all strive towards monopoly – but you must overcome the other businesses, the cops, the soldiers too – the guerrilla ... Arms. Judges. Monopoly's achieved. And then – competition: up it comes, like teeth.

'It's all trade, it all reverts to that.'

Ahmed knows how these meanderings end: in longer expositions.... 'Cheyenne....' he prompts ....

'It's good,' says Nico, perking up. 'It's good not to have a faith implausible and military – now, perhaps, we can enjoy ourselves ... And do our trade. Me – I'm for the competition, but it's true, the guys get overheated, it's so hard not to seek monopoly, and then it doesn't last.... Back to competition....'

'Your friend's a fine economist,' says Maxence. 'But he's a breaking glass....'

Maxence and Ahmed stare at Nico. 'He's dying,' Maxence says. 'But it seems there's nothing wrong with him.'

Nico stares back.

'The suffering,' says Maxence. 'It never ends. Poor Cheyenne – her destiny, where did it lie? In competition or monopoly? We – she – will never know. Not just because she died, but because the answer changes as time runs by. Remember – clothes. To break those Indians, their workshops, families, you needed factories; the little kids caught in transmission belts – then slaves, cotton versus wool. And on it goes, my friends. Around the world they go – our flimsy togs: Dakka, China, back to Paris, Prato and the States – the fires, collapse of sweat-shops, exploitation – wool's beaten by the cotton and the radiator. On goes the slavery, even to your own desires, fashion, accidie, punk: brains curled up, like rosy chains – the opium yields to little pills made in a lab.... The wars, the suffering – ah, my dear friends! The road to riches – lined with crosses for the slaves.... Maybe your dying friend, a warrior, knows all this – tried to prevent, instead contributed.... Or needed cash....'

'I'm sure,' says Ahmed, 'where there was suffering, he was too.'

'Cheyenne,' says Maxence. 'I'm sure she has found peace. Though that was the last thing that she wanted, the last thing that she gave.... Not that I knew her, but I empathise....'

'You've studied, Maxence,' says Ahmed. 'I wish I'd had the time. Now, if Nico and I had had a bank. They're anodyne. No sweat.'

'It's true,' says Maxence. 'You're fluff, Ahmed. When Nico's gone it seems to me you'll lack street skills. You can't just go out and rob.'

'Oh, a bank's too complex,' Nico says. 'Ambitious. Lots of trades are just too finicky: copying the *griffes* ... making antiques.'

They laugh.

'You hear the one about the prostitute and blowing glass?' asks Maxence, red in the face with jovial anticipation.

'It's not the time. It's not the place, Maxence,' says Ahmed, 'Not with Nico in his condition. Besides, we know about archaeology. That Syrian glass – there's lots of fakes; fakes in the stories the good doctors make up about what it is they find.'

'This doesn't end,' says Nico angrily. 'We're getting into patents, who invented what. Syncretism would keep us here for weeks. The Silk Roads – they were made for spinning tales, singing interminable lengths of song....'

'You should know,' says Ahmed, 'Being a camel....'

'My old friend! What laughs!' says Nico, laughing, then serious – 'They say I'll die and leave you all alone – it's not like that. I die and *I*'m alone.'

\*

'I shall go back,' says Ahmed. 'Now Nico has joined Cheyenne. Those two – a-jittering with Kali . I'll do the requiem for both, or maybe it's a bachanal....'

Maxence comes too – Ahmed can't shake him off. Life is a Greyhound bus – it races on but takes in passengers, quite indiscriminate.

Here's the stockade. The basalt blocks have inserts of obsidian; blades and phaeons – people were here before the volcanoes, or before they erupted like an acne: stabbing, chiselling weapons and living safe. Good to be a warrior, the death is grim, but women are diminished, as alpacas to the racing camel.

Rows of low houses, a partition makes two rooms – one for birthing and one for dying. Cheyenne carried her house with her, inside.

'If we'd known Nico better....' Maxence starts.

'Enough!' says Ahmed. 'He left us valuables – mistrust, anger, prudence. Those are best.'

\*

The first people – they were terrified, but had the best, the fresh of everything.

The arithmetic games, you'd need be quick. Those told the future, how many years there were to go in everything. Not cinema, no pictures. Grim too: when you landed on a snake, you needed sacrifices to push your counter, your life, along. On to the ladder – Cheyenne climbed them, pulling her sisters after.

\*

'My dear friends,' says Ahmed. 'My friends – now out of reach ... we used to meet here, or something similar. The walls, so high, and "thick as thieves", they said. Dear friends – some going down, and others reaching upward ... all reduced now – some hidden in the maquis, some mere stubs, others buried in another's tomb, and – dearest of them all – not entombed at all. Poor Nico – we had no pick. No spade, no sword – to break his ground....'

'I see,' the guide, Josette, says, 'You're full of it: – it's called a "topology of being". I can take you where you didn't go, where the ground had not been opened up, signed off ... sold.'

'Maxence can wait,' says Ahmed, but oh no! – Maxence comes too, to break the symmetry of two, Ahmed, Josette: the guide, the led.

Ahmed takes Josette's hand: it's dry. Silent, unyielding. He squeezes it and lets it go.

'There's always been people here,' says Josette, 'since there was anything. Come with me – down inside the cone....'

'They say,' says Ahmed, pulling back, 'the core of the volcano is molten. A heat impossible –'

'Oh, it's been exaggerated,' says Josette. 'Everywhere is hot these days. Slide down this slope – you'll find it opens out – a pleasant orange light, down where civilisation lived....'

So, down they go. It's not a labyrinth. Here, nothing lives now, there's roots from up above that dangle down – but no trees here. It's much too deep for spiders.

'The lizards,' Josette says. 'The people farmed them. Think "iguanas": the flesh is not at all like chicken – I'd say "restagouche", or tuna.... Remember "in a ragout it would taste like duck" – we must honour, emulate that celebrated explorer, his hypothetical shots into the ruck of little monkeys, the cooking, sweet and sour, the us and them – all hypothetical. Dare we say "a metaphor"?'

'They were large, those dinos,' Maxence says. 'They must have been so cumbersome – the milking. Harnessing. Riding to battle on....'

'Now we have elephants,' Josette says. 'It's the same. Don't speculate. Without the humans, there's no history. A future without us – makes no sense.'

'I'm sure I've seen a proof that says it isn't so,' says Maxence – and Josette laughs – 'Poor doctor Haas – he had a proof for almost everything. He said the further you go back, you'd always find a civilisation. In ours – he suffered terribly ... I'm sure your friends did too...' and she takes Ahmed's hand at last. 'Look, I shan't hurt

you,' says Josette. 'And there's no one here – this level's been
deserted. Everything has died. It's like what a mirror reflects when
there is nothing it can do.'

'Music and dance, those go on,' Maxence says.

Maybe they do. They're not to Ahmed's taste. He sits them out.

'Smugglers,' says Josette mischievously. 'Buried in spice. The
calendar that stops before today. What should I show you, Ahmed?'
and she kisses him on his dry unyielding mouth. 'Come on!' she
cries, 'You old stickleback!'

'We used to hide down here. Store stuff. Tell our secrets,'
Ahmed says. He can't remember if it was with Cheyenne, Lizeth
and Leidy ... or only with Nico, and perhaps not with him. It's just
a cavern, after all, empty, for stashing things you'll never use again.

'I thought of doing something,' Ahmed says, 'that would rouse
up the spirits of the young...'

'A movie? An event, a party, happening? There's so much room!'
says Josette: 'There's no record of that taking place ....A band, a
plot? The Black Hand? Young Turks? Something like that?'

'"Forcible and direct speech", they said was wanted,' Ahmed
says: 'We use the rhetoric of power to make thin blankets on our
cots. Those good doctors – always accomplices. A class that's
leisured, pumped up with the past, its exploitation – invents a
classicism, a tangle of false dreams. "Celebrate civilisation" –
always there, at whatever cost, on whoever's head it falls.'

'You're both skittering away,' says Maxence. 'Draw a lesson, or
let's all go up into the sun.'

'It might not be shining,' Ahmed says.

'It could be night up there,' says Josette. 'And surely you have
learnt the lessons, Ahmed? Or Maxence? You've had time, your
friends are dead, or fugitives in the jungle, or in a ward for those
incurables. Some dumb guy – maybe he drums on.... The rest,
silence is not the half of it. Then there's the agnostics, wanting a
sign – but signs change like traffic-lights. What you don't believe,
Maxence, is worth nothing – a new phenomenon sprouts up, and
everything you've thought, believed, is swept away; null, stupid,
primitive and superstitious.'

'Mine is the scientific bent,' says Maxence, proudly. 'Away with
every certainty!'

'I can't believe this is the old civilisation,' Ahmed says. He
holds Josette tight, both arms around her. 'It's like the old lean-to,
where we planned the revolution. Under the volcano, but Cheyenne

never came here. The volcano never blew, not while I was here. They spoke of it – but everything was dead flat and cool.The plain – was level. Sodom didn't make a ripple. There was gambling: primitive accumulation. The hill, the goal for the high-minded: there's corporations. Absolutely stable, an earthwork.'

'I'm just a street child,' Josette says, stroking Ahmed's dreadlocks. 'Into substances and cataloguing strata.'

'That's just fine, Josette,' says Ahmed, patting her skinny backside, extending his arm out to its full, 'I don't expect anything original: the new costs millions, plain or hill. In any genre you need write contracts. With you and me – that's quite anomalous. I wouldn't call myself a public – you convince me. No need for robot power, Dune, *jeunes filles en fleurs, los Olvidados*: – you're fine just as you are, my dear.'

'That's enough!' Josette shouts pulling away. 'You don't love me. You don't want to make an honest woman of me.'

'That would be a flaw in my philosophy,' Ahmed agrees. 'The making and the honesty – even the woman: – those are heavy loads, Josette.'

It's time for making up.

'Let's agree,' says Maxence. 'They're aliens here, those frescoes and the slicing on the walls ... and so are we.'

Josette and Ahmed scoff.

'You facho types,' Josette says. 'Maxence: you're all empires and monarchy. Princesses – they all have to be. Like Doctor Haas – he, the tomb-robber and gravedigger – said: "All who die come from the royal courts." Fell out with a band.... the good Doctor Haas!'

Maxence lingers round them.

*

'You've always had doubts, reservations, about everyone you met, Ahmed,' says Josette. 'I'm good. I have only needs. I shan't make you suffer, but all the same, you'll suffer because of me. Do you know how much? You want an estimate? In years, in tears?'

'My plan is quite another one,' says Ahmed. 'Civilisation. What is it here? Forget the strata and the substances. Ignore these rows of low waterless houses.... Remember, "The position nearest the fireplace or stove is that of greatest honour." That's what I mean: I want statements like that....'

'I'm sure Josette will help,' says Maxence, and laughs. 'Her family teaches her about the hills, but she lives on the plain.'

*

This space is not a room, a gallery, there's no pictures – no guard, of course. But it's not a space – not one you're not in, or you travel to and fill, momentarily. It's full of what you cannot see, don't know what it could be for, or was. 'It's all mine,' Josette says. 'It's all yours. There's nothing here at all, but I know it's mine. And yours – but that makes no difference.'

'It's like wind,' says Maxence.

'I'm sure, if there's no people, there is pottery,' says Ahmed, trying to pierce the light. 'Dolls, flutes. And wicker shields. A stone abacus, I'll bet, carved somewhere we can't see.'

'Maybe it's like last year,' says Maxence. 'That was full, stuffed, with everything, people, drawings, fruit, flowers as they were, in bud, in bloom and withered. That's what she means. We had last year, and it's gone but we still have it.'

'No,' says Josette. 'I see that fits – it's not what I meant. I have things in my special way.'

Maxence shrugs.

'That's Madam Butterflies,' says Ahmed. 'I want to know how things work, and so how I can make similars, but that function better. Much better. I could write it down – but that's the catch: what you write down is just the furniture, stuff that's stashed that you won't use. Or maybe take it out once – a picnic by the river. Then it's here until it's eaten, or off! to the dump.'

'We could have a picnic,' Josette says. 'That's not written down or taken back to anywhere. People drop in. Your friends won't, Ahmed, they've gone, you won't find other ones – but you'll have me.'

'Not to offend, Josette,' says Ahmed, 'but that's rather, well ... nothing at all. My friends – if they were that – they made a world, no one played an instrument or had machines – they all suffered terribly, of course. I don't mean my friends made my world – they made a large one, though, one that ran around the earth picking up ... dust, and elements.'

'Josette explains it best,' says Maxence, not impressed.

'They were tiles,' Ahmed goes on. 'Tiles make the picture. Without one picture, you can't make another one.'

'I'm a museum of them, Ahmed,' Maxence says. 'All different, but since the genus is "pictures" – they are all the same.'

'I don't see one in the fortress,' says Josette says. 'Or maybe each of us is one.'

'It's a fortress, after all,' says Ahmed. 'Military: made to have an enemy, risking its own life, and everybody else's. Besides, pictures, mosaics – it's an analogy – I told you; not a labyrinth. You live in what you do not see.'

'It all links in,' says Maxence. 'Bigger and bigger, the imaginary museum. Import-export. Tourists, Josette. That's how Cheyenne started – they're curious, the danger will attract, and they bring danger with them. Tourists. Everybody, anybody who can move around, to gawp, to work, to lurk and hide. They're the clients, you're the bargain.'

'The question is,' says Ahmed, 'who owns reality round here? You think it's you, Josette – it's a good beginning, though it isn't true.'

'Forget civilisation,' Josette says, not heeding anyone. 'Leave it. You won't get anywhere with that. No folklore, artefacts, gods with bloody teeth. I am your guide – I didn't make this space. If you prefer – 'I made this space, it's mine, and you've no title here, not to anything, even if you're genuine'. We're all genuine, Ahmed – rays pass through all of us; bury us – we do not rise. That's all you need to know.'

'You'll rise, Josette,' says Ahmed. 'I'm sure. Light! A star, brighter than Cheyenne, whatever she may have done, or wanted....'

'Stars come and go,' says Josette wisely. 'That is their job. It doesn't signify – "plop" they go and centuries, millennia, thereafter – it comes to us: their death, the light. It's not political. It's like the dinosaurs, the early people, their intelligence, coming to us, always too late by centuries. I'm ready for all that. It's not about an individual – the star – she doesn't give a fuck. She can't embrace. What drives her life? You were her friend, Ahmed – Cheyenne: the morning star. What do you know, what can you tell?'

'To be frank, Josette,' says Ahmed, pinned in an awkward place – 'It's not about her, or you. It's all about myself.'

\*

'The problem is resolved,' says Maxence.

He thinks all problems are resolved, or nearly – so, there are no problems.

'Here in this emptiness you have a city – not of the plain,' he says. 'No Sodom. Not on a hill – no Jerusalem. We shan't need look at the fading sun, the black nights. Stable and administered. A poets' corner.... I shan't be there, nor you, Ahmed – Josette will do the things that people want.'

'Where shall I be, Maxence?' Ahmed asks.

'Avoiding people. Looking for a Nico you can sponge off, who'll ingratiate with all the powerful guys, and let you patronise him. Animals aren't grateful, Ahmed: they have to save their own lives.'

Josette drifts away – looking at the little figures and symbols carved on the walls – that basalt, not an easy medium. You can hear a 'screech' as she cleans off the encrustations with a blade, perhaps she draws.

'You have a project, Ahmed,' says Maxence. 'I can't imagine what it is, since clearly you've not got far with it. Around you, people disappear and aggregate – nothing to do with you, I'm sure. Deaths. It's not exceptional.'

'I have no secrets, Maxence. No one has,' says Ahmed.... 'The world is disenchanted. We've had that written down for years. We know everything, including what we do not know. We can do impossible things. People have always invented: that is nothing new. We're as we were, running in the sun, fearing the dark, killing the animals, picking the flowers.

'But – the disenchantment's incomplete. Not that we want a new enchantment – we may toy with one: it doesn't work. It is contrived. After the disenchantment – so what? What does that mean? The first discovery is – time is short, we can end the world; our species – it is finite. What does this entail? It isn't what we want. It is exactly what we want. We didn't cause it. We're responsible.

'All this – is curious, Maxence. I'd say – it's fun,' says Ahmed. 'What's the conclusion? Does there need be one? The point is this – to end the disenchantment properly, you need not aother fantasy – you need a *mago*. Someone who understands the purport of the ending of the enchanter's tarradiddles, his fanfaronades. Who finds a meaning where there's none.

'I start with Kali – goddess of death. She's real – the earth shakes with her dancing. There are many cities where she rules,

like the one we're underneath: the wealth is poison: poison, "shit",
we send to all the world. Our capital. It pools into all the other
capital in all the other capitals, like mercury. And for the poison,
they send customers – arriving in their thousands. In millions. So
many, that we're envied – we need protection, soldiers ... Maybe
we'll be bombed, for being bad and rich and popular. For selling
fantasy. For our presumption.

'Cheyenne – maybe she's the *maga*, the shaman – now,
somewhere in the underworld. For sure, this too is an underworld:
Josette's the guide. But we're the only ones who follow her, faces
upturned, concentrated, as if we saw the sun in her. Dead or alive?
What are we? It's not that I want company – and yet, if there is
company, shaman or not,' and he changes register, hugs the guide
who pulls away – 'Josette is what I'd choose.'

'Good,' says Maxence. 'I understand. We search, how do we
know what there's to find, and when we have it? There isn't much
to grasp in what you say. It's taken all this time to get to nothing
much.'

'Yes,' Ahmed says. 'That's true for me. And all the rest.'

# FAME

## ANCESTORS: FOLLOWING THE TRACE

'Move out the light, so I can see you.'

He's ancient. He's a walnut in its shell, a netsuke falsely aged with tobacco juice. Smell it from here.

'Sort it all out today,' he says. He's hopeful.

A long precious wood table, before and between us.

Soldiers have notched it. The wood the wood came from no longer exists, neither carpentered or freely floating.

'You're very small. I didn't specify, but I had hoped.... Print crafts you, I suppose, even your suit and briefcase; every *ado* identical. I invented New Age – it didn't last: then old age got me,' he says, all in a rush: and he laughs. 'No one thanks you that they are young, still less that they are rich. All time based on the intestine takes its rhythm from the stars.'

He starts the offers –

'Something in aspic? A kipper? I had one. They're good. This? They call it plumcake here – there are no plums.'

Monsters manoeuvring outside – tiny drivers – probably a day off from school.

'Are you ready for adventure?' he asks. 'Think twice before you say "yes and no". You don't know anything – so, the truth is only what you intend. You are God in here. I listen, I'm your prophet. I have the money you'll need to make it big, maybe reach the top. Ask the "why, who, where" questions they used to ask in nurseries, have a shot at the answers – no one bothers now. Everyone is hugger-mugger in the one big nursery, with the one big momma.' He laughs a lot, but the work is taking shape. Very demanding, probably beyond your reach – anyone's.

'You can spend a lifetime learning to be a woman, so they can write it on your tomb,' he says. 'What do you want to spend a lifetime doing?'

93

Alas, that's not an easy one. Whole countries fall down or dry up, completely and for ever. A lifetime's too long to do much in.

Take it slow and easy, it'll all quite soon be done.

'I want you to do my life,' the old man says. 'Be authentic. Live me.'

'Write your life?' I ask.

'Write? I fancy dance!' he says. 'The medium's essential, but it must be something I enjoy.'

'Vanity!' I say. 'To what end?'

'I've no letters, had no work, diplomas – nothing, I hope, that left a trace. Check foreign jails. I've always tried to reach an anonymity. And "seek without a find" is sentimental. Something you must find, in multiple examples; try for that.... No records, no regrets,' he says.

'It's stark,' I say. 'I'd take a lifetime, breathing an uninhabited air and hoping when I'm opened up they'll find a manifesto, warrant, gristle scrap – something of a clue to what you were, or what you did or hid....'

'That's it!' he says. 'Look, find, and justify. The life – it will be buried with me. All you find – is without presence, no lymph, no projection. Press the button as I disappear – "delete"!'

'What's my reward?' I ask.

'It's the idea,' he says. 'Those are scarce beasts. Repeat it for yourself. Reproduce. Devise an ad; someone like you, almost identical, to sit there; so you'd say – exactly what I say to you!'

'I'll do it,' I say. 'It's not at all what I wanted.'

'I'd be amazed if it was,' he says. 'But you're a writer. I'm your material.'

'I'm not a writer,' I say, 'more a wanderer. Bring justice, finding comrades, deploring treachery, denouncing the great....'

'You'll find,' he says, 'it's all forgotten. The goodness of the oppressed and vanquished, of humanity betrayed, good causes traduced and persecuted – we love it. Love to hear it. We know we'll suffer terribly because they're right, the wretched, and they will suffer more and disappear. But – both of us – we'll disappear too. We'll eat healthy, though. We'll last, think of aphorisms, coin anecdotes and funny ways. Coin weighs the same; the heads, the invocations – don't add a pennyweight.'

## TRACKING THE WOMEN

Does it matter where one starts? 'Sex?' I say.

'You're in luck,' he says. 'Amandine. Follow the shape. When I was very young – no one was unclothed – you had to find a secret place. Homosex, of course. Then came the trudge. Those days, for women it was their only capital. A tumble – in those days there was hay, you could roll in it. You never did. Conventions changed – a rainbow came and went, those golden pots, set out for the rain – they disappeared. Tristesse – before and after the coitus, and for ages after.

'Emotions? I could give you the plant, in a vase: rosemary.'

'A clue,' I say. 'What did you do? Climb mountains thousands had already scaled, sailed seas furrowed with earlier keels, drowned sailors staring up with eyes as blue as yours, and knowing more. Much more...'

'That's a chord,' he says. 'We're pestered by obsolescence. Family, if we have one, same for school – another older crew – tells you what's what, the past still lives, you suck it in and in you it's dead twigs you can't cough up. Stuck in your throat, your voice comes from your grave... It's laughable – you never see your failures come from failing long ago, not even yours, the failures that give existence and stifle you.... You're here because the despots and the conquerors – they were never quite as thorough as they said. Those babies hidden underneath the bed – they didn't see. It's you....'

'No, no,' I shout. 'Not me! Forget me! It's you I need to know about. Lover, criminal, boozer, trader of drugs and paladin of the oppressed....'

'Of course,' he says. 'Something like that: depends. You must set down the dates.'

'A place....' I ask.

'A place is never on a map,' he says. 'It's a mistake the literalists make – crass positivism.'

I have no more questions. I have every question.

'Ignore some paths,' he says. 'They lead to gardens you will tend, quite uselessly. Weed, weed, all your life, and in a day they'll overgrow your tomb. Sculpture? – embrace your love, join with them in clay – it doesn't feel a bit like flesh. A movie? All those people, smoking, peering from your eye ... Every art's a dolmen treading on some intimacy. Your insight – transformed into outsight. The precious – shared and licked away like sticks of sugary rock ... an old stamp now soaked off an envelope, the letter disappeared.... That market's died....'

'To be honest,' I say, 'looking for nothing: I could defraud you. Easy. And waste my time.'

'I'm not explaining right,' he says. 'On people – you can leave a mark: on skin. On memory, in pizza cans. Maybe they forget the links, suspend their scepticism – sit back, enjoy, a pack of six.... But, something remains unsaid, untold – and you won't find it, unless you find the person, then it's all interpretation. Or on a wall – a date, a name, complaint, assertion. But you'll never know – they're never signed; or texts and signatures – don't fit together. Children – what do they resemble? Have some, a sign of your great love, they say. They're like books or songs – they're trickled out of you, outside, like tears or spit. I'm talking of the something that is me, what's been left, and shows I was. Not that I cried or spat. *Was.* Did something, acted. Doesn't matter what – that's all gone by. No legacies of dusty things, no interpretations.'

'No,' I say. 'I agree. Marks are on the past, like scratches on a disc. Fly marks on a pane. You want a present that's survived the past. Useless! Time's not like that – it's like an old fly-paper – in some places the poison's been rubbed off, the bodies of the little ones as well.

'You must remember ... the strips were sticky-brown, you hung them from the light – they caught whatever in the room could fly and buzz and sting. What you want, though – it doesn't live, it doesn't stick to time.'

I convince myself. 'Time's supposed to be elastic, to be the same, infinite, or nearly so, stretching up to the stars and down, and if it bulges, or it slackens – it's a tiny bulge, declivity. You want a present that's eternal, that says – "here I was, I did, I am, that's what I left and leave, I lived, I live.... I'm visible – nothing else, nothing I've touched or bodged."

'It isn't so. Get used to it, to nothing and to nothingness, and to the corpse left on the paper. A line or two, recording what I might find or more likely will invent. That is yours ... you.'

His mouth gapes. He stares at me, inscrutable.

'I'll take the cash,' I say. 'But you'll get nothing back.'

'Come inside,' he says. 'There's room.'

'You're too small,' I say. I go inside him, in the shell.

There's emptiness, much room.

'When I was on the sled,' he says, and I hear his voice boom like the bell – 'No,' he says, 'not that bell. The horse – had just the one, not festive. A big bell. Brass. I gave the wolves what delicacies I'd brought. Herrings and sausages – of liver and of meaty bread and scraps … and shins of pork, tails of cow, sheep guts, jellies from renderings, brains and dried tongues, deers' penises.... The wolves – they had them all, and as they scoffed, we pulled away.... Once we were like monkeys, tough but just. Now, we're like the wolves – familial, opportunist: but our songs! A wonder. Noble carrion-eaters.'

'Where were you headed?' I ask, muffled, from inside his twiggy carcase.

'Oh,' he squeaks. 'A frozen sea. It was a path from Riga to Tallinn … ah – the unnamed dead. All looking up, under the ice.'

'It'll all be similar,' I say. 'Sand or ice. Those who travel leave a wake of trouble, when they arrive, they make a sacrifice...'

\*

'Amandine,' I say, 'that was the only clue. What he wants is a life. Of himself, but without the deeds – no intentions, their interpretation. Chance? None of that. No place, no time – those always change, they're our transmission belts, what we want, what we get, what we see from our window, if we have one. No sex – it doesn't leave a trace, he says. It's better so. Cut all that out!

'It's interesting,' says Odette. 'I'd come with you, when you search for life. It's nothing, that's for sure. I can say now – the life, the living – it's all that he regards as trivial and meaningless. It's all there is – it's everything! ... a simple string of happening, of wishes bent to material shapes, a presence, shadow, that moves with the light ... it *is* light, light on light, a smudge on illumination's purity.... You'll fail, my dear – but still, it fascinates. And how much cash....?'

I've no idea. It's not my way.

'Leaves and washers, I dare say,' shaking the carpet bag: 'Forints and dongs, fanams and dinars.'

'We all asked his question,' says Odette. 'When we were tots. We'd not begun to keep a score. Now, we've trodden in the dirt.

'"Only consider – what I am ..." It's an exoneration. After all the blots we make – there stands the white untouched page. It's infantile.'

'Nothing is true because it's in a book,' I say. 'Nothing is true, if it's in a book, unless it's somewhere else as well. If you have the truth, Odette, why put it in a book? Our patron – when I find his quiddity – that is the end. Into the tomb it goes.'

'I'm sure Amandine is literary,' says Odette. 'With themes. A tortoise. Or a shipwreck. A reader might find it quite a thrill – normal people, obviously not.'

'I think we'll take the savings, go and look,' I say. 'This country – on it trundles. The rulers – haven't changed for centuries. The base, the popular – they're always moulded where there's profit – they lose their tools, their factories, they're given sex and mental health, some cash each month to keep you swimming on.... Then that stops, and you must improvise again. It's not for us, Odette. We're not the patient types, we don't invent a future we won't make, that won't come....'

'Ask Felipe,' Odette says, 'Before you spend my cash.'

## FELIPE: THE TRICKSTER

'Forget Odette,' Felipe says. 'A lover who becomes best friend – it's poison. There's no trust where there's no bond, no chains ... If it's her cash – that's worse. She has an interest to hoist her sails and off she goes!'

'Why do I stay, Felipe, in this saddening place?' I ask, cast down.

'You must!' he shouts, his little reef of beard seeming to darken round his sallow face. 'The rulers, my dear friend – they must be discredited, bogged in crises they can't manage, and they're blamed for causing.... At that point, when there is collapse – the aim we both have struggled for is in our grasp....'

'I can't dissent,' I say. 'It's only when they can't go on, rule in the old way, that the barred window opens, just a finger-breadth....'

'And there's your hand!' Felipe shouts. 'That's what it's for.'

'I know,' I say. 'The great change, the transformation – rising from disaster to salvation ... that is the scene. But – what I want – I'm sure it will not be like this ... won't happen ... will collapse in turn, become a farce, a war, a compromise....'

'You must commit,' he says.

He's right to find me flexible. Or weak.

'My good life, Felipe,' I say reluctantly. 'It's a dream, a picture. Shows I'm good, having hope and being sceptical.'

*

'People who want to leave a clean page,' says Odette. 'They must have left a fortune, an invention, somewhere they might even have forgot. Or else there was a massacre – so complete, no one was left to tell or even find it. Felipe would love that: a scandal, to finance the new regime, or to castigate the old.'

'No matter, Odette,' I say. 'Let's slide away. We can be ourselves, be anonymous. Like migrants have to, but it is our chosen plan, our goal.'

'I don't want that,' says Odette. 'All the things I've learnt, religion and scepticism, nationality and not, gender and something else – all that is me, hard won. I'm not anonymous. What you want's to be what your ancient mentor says he is. Eternal presence. You leech on his illusion.'

'On his mystery,' I say. 'That's just a story. People aren't interested in those, everybody has one – it's how you tell them, one of them must be the special one.... He's a hypothesis, another of them....'

'That's how you express your fear of being wrong,' she says. 'That you've been following a primal dream, one that's always swept away and disenchanted by the innovations that you hate. Mind science, plugs in your ears, full of moondust. Your ancient friend – he's awake, for now. No surprise he'd hope he could go on.... Others go on; create, enslave, they make their poetry, build the camps.... Life! The Chinese bourgeoisie, they drive the horses now....'

'Enough!' I say. 'Maybe it's so. I knap my flints, while the world trades lasers, and makes a plan to stop the universal blinding of us all....'

'I know,' she says. 'You are incorrigible. You'll die believing, how in the cane brake there are nymphs, with prickly demons keeping you away....'

I say, 'And in the end they kill you, they kill everyone. It's blasphemy that does for us. Hope: it breaks the spell, we sleepers in the witches' wood, we wake and step across their threshold, once is enough....'

I quite believe it, believe everything. I never concocted anything.

I'm a throwback.

I'm a visionary: when the good life comes, born from the horrors, I find it bland and dull and patronising....

We create nothing – we love its smell. The smell of God: turps and marble chips and spit and shit. There's no One there – it just comes, just happens. It would be good if we could make it happen, but we can't. We screw, we throw pots, carve a pleasantry on cockleshells – nothing is created. There are processes – the gestation, the turning wheel, the words there's no one there to say them to, and they make sense only when you chisel them and ponder ... invent a meaning of the meaning.

Intermediaries. The world is full of them – an industry. Sniffers of creation – impresarios and dealers, auctioneers and syllogists: money comes from diffusion, an audience! paying and gawping.... A public – stupid and superficial – like us when we're not scraping on our shell....

Shadows. 'Shadows,' I tell Odette. 'We make shadows.'

'Your old man,' she says, 'wants to *be*, cast no shadow, no imitation. Make him – make him your god. Only gods don't have a shadow. Mind you don't end up his shadow....'

## RED LIGHTS

We find Amandine quite easily.

'I do a little show,' she says. 'Paco will come too, if you want something appropriate.'

'We'd need to know,' I say. 'What you'd require. And how far in we'd need to go.'

'Decide,' says Amandine. 'Paco will leave at midnight – he collects,' and she giggles. 'Paco's *pacco*. It's a source, you understand, we can't do without. The question is, are we to be three or four. It makes all the difference. I have a friend. With her – we could be five or four....

Amandine takes off her blouse. Her nipples have flat tops, like scarlet pills for something.

'I used to have an idea,' I say, 'of the end. Where it was leading, and where I wanted it to go. That's fading, but something of it still remains. A cheshire cat, a grin, a natural rictus, smile – cheese! Cheshire cheese! – but that stood in for the goal, the thing, the place, you wanted there to be. A sign of almost nothing, but the hope there would be something, after rather than the nothing you'd expect. Depending on the rest; the cat, of course.'

'I'll put on something,' Amandine says, pulling out a disc. 'to put you in the mood.'

'Oh no,' says Odette, laughing, 'Not "Sorcerer" – that's way too naff!'

Amandine puts it on anyway, it's vinyl. She has Bethania too, I see, some Fado – Amalia? ... I can't guess what her show is like, and do we participate, or watch and get in the mood? Is it like an old-style play, everything worked out on stage, or like the pantomime where kids go up and sing and kiss, or just jump up and down, enjoy the lights?

'It's the meanders, Amandine,' I say. 'In theory, every river ends up in the sea. But these meanders – they're immense, they're continental. Round and round, no issue, – I'm in a skiff, and that too, if you don't watch out, that goes round and round as well.'

'I think I'll start out with a dance,' says Amandine. 'When I have fixed the light.'

I take Odette's hand – I feel it's right, a stop or start. She pushes me away. Amandine does the dance: it seems to me, quite well. Even very well. Too long. Quite embarrassing, all told. The room is small, we can see parts of Paco as he takes a shower, close to us, doubling and stretching, in the alcove. There's steam – it doesn't interrupt the shimmying, the rolling – I remember 'jelly rolls'.

He's very hairy. Hair seems to fill the room.

It's up to me, and up to Odette, what we do, joining in, or following Amandine, her beat – who doesn't give instructions. We sit and contemplate – at least, I do. Odette is stirred – maybe she knows how to proceed. Maybe it's something she's never seen before, nor thought of, like going to a country where they pray, don't drink – and go to belly-dancing now and then, when they can pay the price. It's properly the *danse du ventre*, of course, the other phrasing's patronising, racist even.

When it ends, Amandine asks Odette, 'So, is he satisfied?'

'Oh yes,' she says. 'I doubt that he could be more.'

'You could be a pro, Amandine,' I say, and we all laugh. 'The old man,' I ask. 'How did he seem? Was he himself?'

'Yes,' says Amandine. 'Yes, himself – that he was, and much much more, which is the point.'

\*

'I was satisfied,' Odette says when we're outside. 'I'd like to see the show with five of us – two of Amandine's friends – that way there's more cross-currents.'

'I found Paco was obtrusive,' I tell Odette.

'Oh, I was told he's nervous, waiting for his *pacco*,' Odette says. 'He's on the street till late.'

'People are very nuanced now,' I say. 'About the history of emotions – how they're represented. If there were more and different – or if it's just style. History. Class; getting paid for what you write. Making a show.'

'Basic ones,' says Odette. 'High energy – you can let them out, emotions. Then there's all the classifications, the naming, and getting other people to put up with you.'

'Deep and heavy, Odette,' I say.

She sees it as sarcastic.

'Go away. Get lost,' she says. 'Live your life, don't prowl round rich old guys and then they want you to analyse them, as if they're varnished and been framed.'


## MONASTIC FOOD

There's a hostelry, a castle, up on the rock. 'No bell,' says a sign, 'Watch out for rocks.'

'When it's full,' says Odette, 'they stone you if you try to climb.'

I'm not hungry anyway. 'It's customs, I expect,' I say.

'Natural justice,' Odette says. 'You bring that up. It's genius! Sin – that went, a few decades and no one speaks of it. Natural justice too – where's that? I'd thought to be a judge – they failed me. It's a problem of equivalence: nothing can be equal to another thing. I insisted. They said a lawyer shouldn't do a favour to a client – I was unaware.... Lying. I thought that was the aim....'

'I believe in responsibility, but without a punishment,' I say. 'I guess that's literary.'

'I was a lawyer,' Odette says, 'without a client, though. It's hard. No cash, but you know everything. Who pays the judges?'

'It must be the lawyers,' I tell her. 'I love to work, but not the paying kind. Would judging suit me? I could study law like you.... But then – where's the judgement? What's the point?'

'Oh,' she says, 'there's lots of unsolved murders, random ones, it seems. It stems from the ethics paper they make judges do. It is the nutshell question in exams: "Who, how, why – and after?" You – the judges – choose a target, strike – then ponder consequences. Now,' she turns to me. 'What is your crime?'

'And yours?' I ask. 'And Paco's parcel, what can that be?'

'Tailors work late,' she says. 'It could be twist. I bet he's good at buttonholes. I never was.'

'My patron's crime?' I say. 'There must be one, or else he'd not want to strip away the past and step out nude.'

'It's odd,' she says. 'If you're a lawyer, to want to be a judge. It's like a locksmith, who wants to be a burglar.... Shall we climb the rock? Maybe they serve eagles' eggs? I love these faddish places, where they think you must be rich....'

It takes us hours. The stones have points, there's plants that smell – valerian, it makes you doze, and some that make you sneeze. At the top, 'We're closed,' they say. 'Preparing food and no one comes. It's an exhausting day. Sleep here. There is a truckle bed that's free. Fornicate, and then – boiled eagles' eggs, and down you go. Into the basket....'

'Can we trust them?' I ask Odette.

'This is the path "he" took, for sure,' she says. 'They're all brothers here – he'll have brought Roxanne.... This must be the prophet's rock....'

And at once she sleeps.

The basket bumps us down. 'How they miss their country, Africa,' says Odette, belching loudly. 'Those eggs are far too large,' she says. 'They love it so, Africa. Brothers, in aprons.Would we miss our country like they must? Europe's so slick, and then the nether and the upper parts just fray off, like old sacks. Sand, water, debris, like a flooded water-colour box....'

'Amandine told you about Roxanne?' I ask. 'It's not a pattern, I hope. A caravan of women. Roxanne – comes from the steppe. I expect she was coveted for the gold she wore. But – there's no story, no revelation there. They're ancestors to all of us. We're staid. Amandine's room, remember – so small – she can't charge more, it's evident. Stuck – that's us. The good times, the blooming – over long ago. Now, we've shut our shop. That's all we had – a shop. Not even a store – that sounds as if there's mounds of stuff piled up below.... Our country, Europe ... a butchery.'

She seems not to be listening. I say:

'You and I, Odette. What keeps us close together is not having intimacy.'

'There's always more,' she says. 'He must have been a traveller, the last explorer. Bringing back some shrunken heads. Put them in water, they revive – women with shows, with installations, manifestoes. Roxanne asks "what next?", she doesn't explain what she has done before, "Oh, I'm unemployed," she says, so's you don't ask. The future is materials – things not used before, like Belgian linen or black clay, wormy wood, ships' empty holds ... Roxanne makes empires, crumples them up by night and puts them in the morning's trash.'

'She's an artist?' I ask. 'Sorting stuff? The visual? All "objects found", hummed melodies. Music, pictures: – you'll never beat the black and white. The depth, the detail lost and gone.... Our brains in pickle to a broth of precedents. Tunes in your head. Sing to the cat, then wow! there's thousands out there cheering you. I prefer words: – true, they're there, in different languages, in drawers, each with a label round its neck, but you can stand them on a shelf, in new rows....'

'No,' says Odette. 'You didn't see – where we were in the dormitory, all the others, some unfed, others waiting for their seconds.... They told me about Roxanne....'

'She? Planted the flowers on the rock and chiselled out the points?' I ask, 'I thought we were alone – I slept at once....'

'Oh,' she says, irritated, 'you're eat and sleep. Don't see how everything in a life changes, like skins you grow out of, and you leave the old ones hanging on a bush.'

\*

Silence. I wish I was elsewhere, but where I wish to be – once there, I wish I were elsewhere.

'Roxanne – there's a Roxanne, but "Roxanne"'s a collective,' says Odette. 'They do anything you need – pics or movies, or a group, a band. And contraband, and documents, and walking down the street in fives, so tall and strong. Causes and insults and complaints, and minors doing awful things but they can't go to jail.'

'And there's a Roxanne, fronts all this?' I ask. We all need one of these.

Roxanne – we find her easily: she sits, you stand. 'My hands,' I say. 'Look! Climbing the wall to get the food they wouldn't give – those marlin spikes ... you ruined me.'

'I had in mind,' she says, shifting one golden leg, thick, marine – like those curly columns in the Vatican, black, bling and strass – onto its partner, similar, 'How it would be to climb the masts. The crows' nest – of course, the grown-ups fly away, but there are eggs. You eat them all – there's no more crows, not ever. Rejoice!' she laughs. 'You can't escape your destiny, they say: oh yes, you can. That's my work, me and my pirate crew. Slaves freed, bad omens turned around, entrails analysed, love philters brewed.... Maybe you two,' and she holds out a maté gourd, 'Would profit? Of course, it's like all libations, liberations – on the day, it works. Then there's the recoil. Centuries to walk through flint and tar....'

'We had eagles' eggs,' Odette says.

'Those Yankee boats,' Roxanne laughs. 'That crew from Africa – hmmm, I'm not sure that they get on....'

'You have a massive enterprise,' I say, flattering. 'The extinctions, the cohabitations – all in the name of progress....'

'No, no, silly boy!' says Roxanna. 'I sort things out, I do not cure.'

'That ancient narcissist,' Odette says. 'He must have used your crew....'

'He wanted scrubbing clean,' says Roxanne. 'I told him, once the sea-worms penetrate, there's little to be done. They don't give up what they have ate.'

'So it's pointless,' I say. 'Strip off the expedients and happenstance to find the essence – doesn't mean a thing.'

'I signed him on,' she says. 'Like I could you two.'

'And we could do nothing, like the guys on the rock? Eat the food, not sell it on?' asks Odette.

'Well,' says Roxanne, sighting along her fat left arm, as though it were an arquebus. 'I saved them from drowning, not from the bombs and lightning strikes....'

'You have the inventiveness,' says Odette, 'but not the force. It doesn't work.'

'I know how things work,' says Roxanne. 'In the end – it's loss and suffering. That you must accept. We were not called, we were not the ones. I expect that no one, nothing, is.'

'It's all too reasonable for me,' I say. 'In the end, people associate to have more force. Your little squads....'

'Umbrellas don't stop the rain,' says Roxanne, briskly, stretching out her legs so one sharp shoe pinks me on my shin.

'Tell me,' Odette starts. 'I'm losing something – the sense of the plot – the rock, the slave ship and the dormitory.... The prison, and the barracks....'

'Remember,' says Roxanne, mounting a black Russian in a chalcedony holder, puffing away, 'I have many secrets. And, I'm not your friend. I'm today's news: I know everything about the past, but you know nothing of today.'

I smile.

Her left hand – she has on a glove, Greek boxer's, to the elbow, full of studs. She hits me with her knuckles, on my nose. It hardly hurts – then comes the backhand – that hurts lots, from ear through jaw....

'There!' she says. 'That was unexpected, you're insufferable. Reaction is instant, your condition must have lasted years.... How'd you parse it, genius, my blow?'

Odette laughs. 'He's been a pain,' she says. 'And now he feels it. Brilliant, Roxanne – were you a grammarian or a judge? – the gesture's to the point....'

'Now, maybe you'll understand,' Roxanne says. 'My opinion of you hasn't changed, but now you know it scientifically....'

'I've told him,' Odette says. 'He needs another mother tongue, another colour, gender – something that would fit, a brain more understanding – better climbing skills....'

'And you, Odette,' Roxanne says, 'are trivial and malcontent. The squad I've put you in will sugar you and spice him too,' and she pushes us out her room into the dusty street ... she's no bigger standing up than sitting down, but has a mighty rump that lets her loose a combination of those swift blows that shake you up....

'You pig!' Odette says to me. 'Obsessed with body size and violence....'

'It's so,' I say. 'I'm slender, and a coward. Accept me as I am.' Odette does not respond. 'I enjoyed the climb,' I say. 'But not the incoherence at the top.'

It seems Roxanne enrols you in a squad whenever you encounter her. My ancient sponsor – he must have followed her awhile, then split away, Roxanne's crampons hammered in his brain, a pathway to some place he wasn't worthy of, a twilit garden, never revealed but it makes you weep to think you had to leave..... Another harbour beckoned, a haven – turned out just a postcard tacked over the captain's porthole....

'Be serious, Odette,' I say. 'Roxanne is just a boss, a would-be leader. She's sat deep in her destiny – if you follow her, there'll be confusion, partial satisfactions....'

'Like she says, you idiot,' says Odette, 'that is the best. You'll end up looking for yourself, like your old man.... The rock! You have to climb, to scramble up, follow the tracks, hold on! Even a fall – you hardly have a blink to recognise – and then there's nothing left – it's better than abortion or the injection you gave your ailing cat....'

'The world, Odette,' I say, appalled. 'The history we shall not live to see.... Is that the choice? – false prophets followed, or time run out, as you're curled foetal in your shell...?'

'Don't start from there,' she says. 'Start from the species. You're a speck, a smut on the lens. Existence isn't guaranteed – not to the immense, nor to the miniscule. Find your lookalikes, coagulate, cohere. Hold on. But not to me.' She adds, 'Roxanne. A great presence. You find those very rarely.'

'I don't consent to anything,' I say. 'To nothing that exists. I don't recognise anyone who fills a space. Anything that exists will not be there tomorrow. It's me too – so it isn't individualist.'

'That's it, then,' Odette says – she seems regretful.

It's the end – usually you should regret.

'The end. Only in a sense,' I say.

## APPROACHING THE UKRAINIAN STEPPE

*'We express ourselves necessarily in words, and most often we think in space.'* H. Bergson

'I'm in space, Felipe,' I say. I mean I want him and Isolda to fill the space – with what? Solid space?

They stare at me, sympathetically.

I say, 'Nothing fits, it all makes a picture, but it doesn't adhere, cohere.'

'We all feel that,' Felipe says. 'Don't let it go pathological. The composition you want, it doesn't mean symmetry applies to everything.'

'... and I have money,' I say. 'Imagine life without.'

'You don't have much money,' says Isolda. 'You've so little, it's not worth struggling over, like you do.'

'I have a patron,' I say.'But of course, that makes it quite uncertain. It's up to him, but then – he's dead. Now, everywhere I go, the people! I don't have tolerance – their spud faces, grimy *doudounes*, those quilted jackets....'

It's revealing, and demeaning, I suppose, this exchange.

'Do you really want symmetry,' Felipe asks. 'Wherever that leaves you? You could be a crone gazing at an anunciation, struggling to stay within the frame.... The wrong kind of child, pushed out the shack to beg alone – but still rule-bound and accepting.'

'No,' I say, 'I wouldn't want that, but I don't want what I can't make sense of either.'

'It's good to fall out of the frame,' Isolda says. 'You never really drop – after all, you're paint or gilded wood, and you're style. I'm a painter of evil, I've nothing in common with the painters of the good – but that's a customary rule. It grips you, though it's just a local twist. Those Italians – they made no distinction, good and evil all the same to them – look where they ended up...'

We laugh. The Carpathians are far behind us, there's a marshy plain – can't think what to do with itself, its great expanse. Woods with elks ... dust long ago made into rocks....

'Symmetry is wrong....' says Isolda. 'The wrong idea.'

'It's anything you can contain within a frame, a disc of sound, however wild those are, or held in covers, a body, a village, city, or an island,' I say, sensing they think I'm trivial and ignorant.

We're passing villas, extravagant, even overblown, deserted ... Rom chiefs, who've worked out how to be rich, and live mostly somewhere else. We're the wise nomads now, bumping past, reclining in the pick-up's shell, we're magic beans expectant in a rusty pod.

'*L'amour-la mort*,' Isolda says. 'A man's desire blocks the woman's search for pleasure.... Then Honour, with his scythe, takes over. The quest is vain, the satisfaction – it's all inside. Pleasure, desire – we know them for ourself – for others we can only guess.'

'That's what my sponsor, my patron, meant to say,' I say, but Felipe says:

'It's not about that at all, although it's symptomatic; men and women – there's a symmetry!' He laughs, it's sarcasm. 'But who cares,' he says. 'Seek! Maybe it's more fun than finding....'

We bounce along, we show some documents, we're not believed, who cares....

'We're all Jewish, and we all die for being what we are,' I say. I often say it, but the landscape, jiggly black and white, brings back those pits, those people lining up....

'It seems to me a pleonasm,' Isolda says.

'Don't stay with that,' Felipe says. 'You'll not be understood. You'll go into dangerous fields ....'

'Oh,' I say. 'I'm secular – the bible too, a terrible tale, a warning, the story of the species. You have to love your nature, I suppose, gruesome though it is. It's still the nature of the species, of everybody.... Be pleased it's obsolescent....'

'That woman didn't think you were a good acquisition,' Isolda says. She means Odette. 'Watch yourself. Why are you coming here, Ukraine? Do you speak Ukrainian?'

'Russian,' I say. 'That ought to do. I love them; my friends, the *dusha*, the spirit – what I should have been. An immensity, always under threat, enemies within, just like my soul and yours, a struggle with the demons – agglomerate and decompose, there's never rest from threat and spiky imps, never a peace, a bosky languour, never sufficiency, always the poet pinching your behind....'

'It's not like that,' Felipe says. 'There's lots go off to Poland, no time for fantasies....'

'What will you do here?' I ask.

'We're scouting out a movie,' says Felipe. 'That's our fantasy.'

'There should be more than two of you,' I say. 'I've seen movies, that when the guy is humping the big star, there's scores around, holding their meters, gesturing a "sshhh"....'

'Sex can be done quite tastefully,' Isolda says.

'So, it all comes back to what I said,' I say. 'The species, battles towards a civil show-down, a shout-out: no survivors. We started various – then we strove for unity. That's a dream! You're Moguls! Fold upon fold, it all makes sense, it chimes – but there's no reason to it, just coincidence. When the Mongols – just like you – turned to being Mughals, they carried it all down, down South, the story of mankind, the warning, and they showed how the single law, the unifying principle, however strictly it's enforced – it fades away ... transmuted.'

Isolda, Felipe – they draw away from me. 'I'd go further,' I go on. 'I told you my credo. We're all Jews, all communists – it's the simplest, most illumined thing to be – otherwise, you're fachos and illusionists – remember that street, how shameful, the *via delle Convertite*, quite unspeakable the whole affair, centre of civilisation, what a joke....!'

*

I started wrong with them. We book in – a marble building, immense and pompous, fat guys and spies, not many. But there's bugs. Around the light and in the beds.

Isolda asks – 'How far do you expect to go with us?'

'I want to reach the steppe,' I say. 'Sarmatians. The life, the gold...'

'You're speculating?' Felipe laughs. 'Buying, or digging stuff? It's all Greek or Iranian, or both. Guys on those horses – interested in the bling and being mercenaries – not building kilns and hammering.'

'It's my idea,' I say. 'Nothing more. I have a name too – Ayesha ... easy to find, perhaps.'

'Think!' says Felipe. 'They were tribes, families, gangs – they spoke what people near them understood, they made families with who could stand them. Ayesha's a name that crops up everywhere – in comic books....'

'Exactly so!' I say. 'My patron – I forgot to ask his name ... he travelled round. He knew the world, enjoyed himself....'

'Enjoyed Ayesha too, you think?' asks Isolda, acidly. 'I know your sort. You're another "last man". You think, like Cicero, your amanuensis, that you can sum it up, the world, that after you it ends, declines, will leave a space your size, that can't be filled.... We all think that – but when we're very very young. When we are grown, we know we are not worth a toss.... The world spins round – it's all it knows, with or without us on its back, unreflecting, whether we are dinosaurs, beetles or Petrarchs....'

'And what's your movie maybe all about?' I ask.

'Great art is not like that,' Felipe says. 'Besides – we may write sonnets in spare time, but I am proud to say: forget the flickering image. That's our cover. We're investors. Spies. Contractors. What we find – we sell. Gold, horsemen – even movie extras, battalions –

even stars. Indeed, the tourists love the sun – our star: we'll sell that too....'

'Then why this travelling poor?' I ask.

'We've no money, just like you,' Isolda says.

'We couldn't sell you,' says Felipe. 'Not even as an actor, someone you are not. Maybe –' and he waves a silver fork. 'We could open you. Have you a pearl inside? Of wisdom, or heavy, to hang around a neck? Dissolve in resinated wine, have the big chief drink, then cut his head off? The Sarmatians – buried in a mass of oyster shells. Those snicker-snees – maybe their world was oysters....' Isolda jounces on my chest: she says:

'Maybe the cossacks stole the Scythian horses, taking the lead, always under orders, massacring, opening the world, all you oysters, waving your little arms and legs....' She leers over me, a wicked daughter.

'I'm no profit, Isolda,' I cry out – no use, she's pulling off my boot, the one I keep my cash, my gold, in.

'Aha!' she shouts. 'You runt! Nature makes an extra pup in case there is a good year – normally, you don't survive.... It's the same with people – take the capital, they're shadows in the birch wood, they melt into other peoples, like they don't exist and never have....'

She's very strong. Her weight – it is her strength. 'Now,' she shouts at me. 'You know how slaves are made. Why there's so many slavs around – now, how'll you walk where you are told without your boots?'

'I know,' I say. 'Bark. There's the bark.'

'There's room for guard-dogs too,' Felipe says. 'I've infinite sympathy for you, your soul. It's all been doubled up – you and your soul, your different paths, how the souls wander off, accelerate! – the autos that aren't motor-cars, they're *autos-sacramentales*, the penitence for sins you've yet to be accused of, the tests – held over fires that smelt the gold in bones, your skeleton.... Bequeathe your body, let your soul arise....'

'I know,' I say. 'It's big, bigger by far than I can comprehend.'

'We get things done,' Felipe says. 'Look at the Krim – Mongols shipped in, shipped out, up and down the steps, on and off the big grey ships ... all in for the great adventure.'

'Look,' I gasp out, 'I'm your friend, whoever's side you're on. Maybe – Isolda was the name, and not Ayesha. I searched for you instead....'

'And here I am,' Isolda says. 'I am your incubus.'

I'm terrified. If I'd stayed with Odette – she was alarming, not frightening. No one will identify with me: – fear's not associated with someone else's story – it ought to be.

'I don't fight,' I tell Isolda. 'I surrender. I'm afraid of losing.'

'You could be useful,' Felipe says. 'Driving the car we are about to steal.'

'Useful? How?' I say. 'Remember, I have my own plot to follow....'

'Usefulness, by definition,' says Isolda. 'Doesn't say how deep, how long. Just – useful. Rejoice!'

*

Driving is like they say, easier than riding bicycles.

This is a cellar – you have to pay to go inside. Does the sign say 'Mahagony'? There's music, loud and pushy.

'There's a guy,' Felipe tells me, putting his face up very close, 'Knows this guy who made some pills, they make you think you are a lizard!' and he laughs. 'Everybody's trying them! The latest thing...!'

'No,' I say, 'I won't buy one of those,' and he laughs some more.

I'm in the gang.

## AYESHA

'That's Ayesha,' says Isolda. 'Maybe not the right one,' and she points to a short girl dancing like a nest of snakes. 'She's not Jewish, and I'm sure she's not a communist: what are you, dear?' she shouts across to Ayesha.

'I believe we can all be born again,' Ayesha shouts back. 'I follow the Buddha.'

'That's the best deal,' says Isolda. 'You can do bad things and start again. There's a margin. There are many chances, and there's ropes let down you can climb up. Or fly, if you have wings.'

'My old mentor....' I begin. Ayesha drops a pill into my drink.

'The first is always free,' she says. 'That is the revelation. The next ones – you try to return, to find the revelation. It is never so...

There's only slither and humiliation... The exit's bricked, the tunnel has collapsed, over and over you re-breathe stale breath....'

'Remember, Ayesha....' I start again.

'Oh yes,' she says. 'I bind up wounds. Your jaw – I could tie it up and send you to the front again ... you wouldn't speak, it's better so. Language is a giveaway....'

'I'd forgot,' I say. 'It's true. Someone had hit me – no reason, or maybe there's a thousand ... but if I'm dumb, I cannot ask the way, or trace my predecessor, forerunner, as you like....'

'There was a guy,' she says. 'Looked much like you, without the wound. The blow was yet to come, and so I packaged him, I bandaged everything that might be hurt ... I gave him all my care – then, off he went....'

'That's ridiculous, Ayesha – a story has an end, or else....' I say.

'For sure, it had an end,' she says, 'and here you are!'

There goes another pill.

St George deserted, saw the steppe – a place of constant movement, took his short sword and 'Hey guys! I'm off to find some dragons ... ' They laughed, he looked for me, to put another wound upon my wound ... he'd be repaid with sex – those captive maidens, saved from the roasting.... Tramping on against the flow, at night curled on his oyster shell, a cultured pearl, impostor – stripped of his sainthood, his existence, his name for sure, joining anonymous people, Kushans probably, darkening like a gallstone, grit in the penis – an irritation, an anomaly, travelling down the maze of entrails, hoping for a soft expulsion – a missionary for second lives, a second birth the most immortality you can take, until to walk and eat becomes a drag, death or oblivion, down to Cambodia, or a discreet retreat into Mongolia....

'Where have you been?' Isolda asks me. 'We've not yet started using you.'

'Oh, whatever form I take, I'm sure I'm destined for a martyrdom,' I say, trying to keep it light.

'Which is it to be?' Ayesha asks. 'Me or Isolda? I bandage wounds, she inflicts them, so's you can go on and do the same to all the rest....'

'It looks like both of you,' I say, longing for another lizard pill – the strength, the guile – you need those on the steppe....

'You criminals,' Ayesha laughs. 'You don't respect a name. I'll call you Gyorgy, like the other one, your inspiration, the transparent Master....'

'Pills, Ayesha,' I say. 'More pills! My cash – Isolda and Felipe have it all.... Call your dealer on your little pad....'

She laughs. 'My pad, yes, I live on it. Look – histories: the US, the USSR, two lines is all the space they need. Every language and all history – nutshells. One message brings my dealer, another it can kill you.... They know exactly where you are, whether you're dragon or a saint....'

'So what?' I say. 'I only asked for pills. Not where they came from, or who trades – as for your phone, I bet no one knows about Sarmatians....'

'No, but there's insults and obscenities,' says Ayesha, quite shocked. 'Ancient Ukrainians – it seems a sensitive theme! Those guys, their theories! The ladies do not have a guess, and they are right. Things of more consequence, though – you can't read about them, they come flying through the air....'

'Everybody knows all that,' I say. 'Things wear out, the price drops and they're simplified until you're just a character, a single, a stroke.... Pills, Ayesha!'

'Money, Gyorgy,' Ayesha says ... and 'Time to hit the road again,' Isolda says.

'Drive!' says Felipe. 'Sober up, Gyorgy!'

It's a new one, a big Toyota, nobody's bothered to lock up. 'Crime,' says Felipe. 'To be successful, must not obsess. Think about it all the time, and it's an office, enforced work. You must steal, and all the rest is interludes that leave you free ... Free for hours a day, forget your arty consciousness, the history, the animals that lurk within your skin – look up through that windshield, the trees flicker like a movie and we're three new unexplored and verdant continents, untouched by exploitation ... being our natural selves....'

I try to object, 'This place – there was so much imagination, even when the guys were running, they thought of making things, wearing them, then leaving them, passing on.... We're just symbols on the run....'

'Oh no,' says Isolda. 'We're all imagination. It's just – you mustn't leave a trace. A word punched in – that's you done, finished – insults and interdiction. Useless.'

Trees – like enormous chrysanthemums above – 'The road!' Isolda shouts. 'Watch the road, we're not in Japan now!'

'Well,' I say. 'This car – for sure it's not reported – belongs to crooks or cops, or somewhere in between.... Besides – I'm not a scholar. I don't study where I'm in, mostly it feels I'm in nowhere, and I'm sure that's luck.... Of course, I'm on the right side; for the people, against the law, it's complicated, naturally, as without the law you're fucked, and mostly it's enough to mention rich and poor, you're molten, cast, and assayed where you're born, your colour and your grannie stay indelible, and you repeat what you are told....'

'And hope the peasants get to keep their land and scrabble on it: you follow the big voice.... You're a classic, Gyorgy,' says Felipe. 'A warrior. Don't unload your gun.' He laughs, I watch the road.

I begin, 'Ayesha....'

'You'll find another Ayesha,' says Isolda. 'If we don't run across the other one. Ayeshas – they have soul. It doesn't always do you good. Those pills ... beware! Lizards and cicadas, seem inoffensive, immortal even – each winter they have disappeared, then, in the spring, here they come again! Those are inoffensive, but, mostly, animals are not. They eat each other, we eat them, the pigs and dogs especially: it is quite a fight. Some pills – they do the same. Now you're a lizard, then you're the ibex, savaged by the ocelot.... It doesn't matter if you think you live just once, and then it's done with, written in the book: or if you think it's circular, and need not ever end. Everywhere there's room for savagery. You'll see, that when we've killed the animals we go back to the start – we are the animals there's always been. Mostly we don't taste so good, but....'

'I don't see Ayesha in all this,' I say. 'She feeds you; bandages you, gives a shot....'

'Isolda's being mischievous,' Felipe interrupts. 'Ayesha is fun: she prepares you for the next day's stage. You wish you needn't move, would stay with her, but onward you must trudge....'

We drive and drive. 'We're good guys, Gyorgy,' says Felipe. 'We steal only from the rich. True, we don't donate stuff to the poor, but this way it's more profitable, and it gives us class.'

'Don't try to leave, Gyorgy,' says Isolda. 'Or we shall hand you in. Your story: – like everyone's, once lived, it's fiction, fantasy.'

'Gyorgy,' Felipe says, as we bump along, 'You think this is a shabby kind of place. You think in terms of countries, a hierarchy of fairylands – a place that's sweeter than another place, you get a document, then they can't throw you out. It isn't so. It's going to be one world, with trade and traffic everywhere, and everybody moving round and trying not to hit a snake and falling though the

boards, you're hoping you can clean the floors and not look down –
a climber on the vertical, your arms are tired, there's lumps of ice
and crumbly rock upon your skull.... This here, dear Gyorgy, is not
so bad, it's middling.... Don't get sick, or caught; learn languages
and maybe take your scrubbing skills abroad – and why expect to
live too long, you've seen it once, those re-runs, re-makes – always
crass.... And don't expect to find those guys on ponies racing
through the grass....'

'Every place,' Isolda says. 'Is the best place there is, so long as it
and you are temporary.... Every patron shows the way: is Rama –
but you're not in the script....'

There's explosions. 'Take no notice,' says Felipe. 'It's
boundaries – not up to you. Or maybe you would like to fight?
There's causes everywhere, you have a choice.... It could be your
best way out of the situation we have put you in. Go! You're free,
Gyorgy! Fight the good fight – there's one for every opinion and
conviction....'

'I understand,' I say. 'I just need stop the car. And after all –
these loyalties, they seem ephemeral – a faith, an origin, a
principle, we hold them, they're inked on our skin, we inherit, we
despair, we soften, we forget.... I have a second thought about
Roxanne ... a self-inflicted blow, deserved: a trap? Amandine – a
victim? It may be – following my old man ... who knows where that
will take me? To myself? To him? A homage to the continuity, the
history, the deference to what has been and here we are...? To
someone I'd not thought to be, and what would that mean anyway,
me, or someone else? Ephemeral, my dear...!'

'Oh well,' Isolda says. 'If you're convinced you see what's right,
or good, or not so bad, and what's for you ... act, take the
consequences....'

'Yes,' I say. 'It's consequences. And starting places – I am a
bug, Isolda, I metamorphise, to my final state: life for a day. I fade,
wings lose their powder. I'm snapped up....'

'So!' she says. 'You say you're on our side. Somehow we must
suck you in, whatever you turn out to be. Or nonetheless, you're
guilty, complicit – and we shall hand you in, and you will thank us
and repent. So, then – you'll be a penitent. Your calling, Gyorgy –
a voice, a horn-call, air shakes across the snow: "dragon-slayer ...
non-existent tamer of wild unicorns..."'

'I know what you mean, Isolda,' I say. 'There isn't always a
right side. If you spend time thinking, there's a less bad one,

perhaps? ... but who'd take a risk for that? You must leave reality behind – it becomes a poor indicator, it's always on the move. So should you be. Trust the unknown, it's not something that will bear your weight.'

'Relax, Gyorgy,' Felipe says. 'You're not asked to sacrifice. You're a follower, not a good person.'

*

Felipe goes inside the ministry. 'He has us stay outside,' Isolda says. 'For safety – but so's we don't know what's in the deal.'

'How did you partner up with him?' I ask.

'He took me. Off the street. Like we took you,' she says.

It's not an explanation, probably.

Felipe doesn't reappear.

'Let's leave the car,' I say. 'And walk.'

'And run, discretely,' says Isolda. 'We shall read about Felipe in a book.'

Of course, there's other doors. A tunnel, too. All ministries have lots of them: for sure, Felipe finds an exit, joins another gang.

*

'I should tell you, Isolda,' I say, as we trot along. 'I don't know Russian. I speak three, maybe four words, plus all the borrowings. I fear nothing, I know the worst, I'm not inferior or superior, everything happens to everyone. I've had sex, I don't want any more. I care who rules who – but not what colour they are, their language, or the history.... I will accommodate you, Isolda, to the limit....' and she turns and smiles, not invitingly. 'I'm not contemptuous, I'm not afraid....' I add.

'I know,' says Isolda. 'It's good to be like you. But – what do we do next? Can you find us anonymity – a nook without illusions, and stories round a cold fire?'

'Of course,' I say. 'They might even find *us*, take us in....'

'You must forget history and reason,' Isolda says. 'This idea of survival – Jews know we don't survive, communists are learning fast. There's no centre to anything, has never been. Forget all that – it's poetry. It will bring you touble here. And wherever else we go. Even on the steppe – especially....'

'You're right, Isolda,' I tell her. 'We don't have bus fare between us. I write nothing down, of course. Why provide a future no one wants? The present – it's a wall, a wall of bricks we'll have to put in place, sharp, extra heavy. Besides, I'm sure you gave my cash you stole to Felipe....'

'Yes,' Isolda says. 'That is the rule.'

'This is strange territory to me – and I don't mean Ukraine,' I say.

'You must learn,' Isolda says. 'Go a step down, and you can say anything you like, rant, not too loud, no fists. Go a step up, it's quieter, but the same. The step we're on – be very very careful about everything, even stuff you find, and especiually loose stuff you find in your mouth.' She pinches my arm. 'Because I say "steps" doesn't mean you'll get to climb them up.'

'Who will feed us, Isolda?' I ask. 'Will it be from altruism? Religious duty, or some secular charge, maybe even something in geopolitics that only some bosses understand – or politicos, or anarchists....?'

'It's all as useless as your wanderings into cosmology,' Isolda says, slumping down. 'We should have gone up and joined Felipe – we were useless moralists and cowards – we assumed he got caught, doing something negative....'

'Or maybe getting the negotiations wrong,' I add. 'Food, Isolda. I don't want to help some state by eating off its fingers ... still less religious satisfaction by pigging down, or maybe humanism, enlightenment, the species ... its pathos.'

'Maybe we'll fall in with cannibals,' she says, gasping. 'Who'll want to fatten us. Or maybe there's a surplus of potato skins, irradiated corn, experiments in pesticides, mass killers ....'

'Yes, best stay clear of easy eats,' I say. Her desperation sharpens my appetitie – I salivate, I gripe, I fill with methane gas, to ease myself I crap – all over; who will love me now? I wonder. It started off so well. These steps – a church? Nothing to eat in there – I crawl in.

'The materials,' I say aloud, though Isolda's not here to hear. 'The silver. And the icons – not great free-standing art, maybe, but illustrations to a book – a book of tortures and those passionate for death, their vestments tacked with crosses, torture instruments, the waxy faces stapled on to suffering.

'It's magnificent. Product of an overriding mind, a mind that rides onward like a horde, driven by the heat, the sickness, population collapse, shortage of women, escaping smallpox and the measles, a one-time wonder....'

## LEARNING A TRADE: GIVING ADVICE

'The original idea was good,' I say. 'Needing a project, the whole world becomes a hunting-ground, a treasure hunt – a chase, a quest ... that sly old man, sending me off to find immortal life for him, so he could start again, avoid apocalypse, live forever in my skin, or his.... What every one of us would want, but he was plausible and unafraid and unrestrained....'

'This is modernity,' Odette says. 'There's always some way of getting out of where you don't want. Even in jail – there's tunnels, lawyers, charities and regime change ... never give up, you're right!' She looks at me with interest. 'Your story,' she says, 'sounds like vampire comix.'

'No, nothing to do with religion,' I say. 'Nothing remotely – except people say some questions swim around like pilot fish, it's forever religion, during and after, whatever religion is, it's like birthmarks, you never get to scrub them off....'

'It was good of you to search me out,' Odette says. 'But – I still don't like you. You change continually, and yet you're fixated on continuity. I guess logic is like that, things following each other. I've been having lots of sex and conversations – there seems no link between them – the orifices differ, but that's all. The case for "nothing follows" is the same as that for "everything is linked".'

'I'd not considered that,' I say. 'It doesn't upset me, one way or the other.'

'I'm off to see a picture show,' she says. 'It must mean I've lots of cash. Your theories are constricting – I don't want you with me....'

'Materials,' I say. 'Their mastery precedes a theory. That's what I think. Tinsmithing, then silver, gold, and cutting diamonds. My disciplines.'

'I don't see your point,' Odette says: 'What did you learn? What did you teach?'

'I wasn't there to do good,' I say. 'I went along. I knew nothing. There's no confusion with materials; no judgements, no making things what they don't have in themselves.'

'Exploitation, that's why you were there,' Odette says. 'You say you were constrained – it doesn't sound like that to me. Just imagine, if you'd gone somewhere to do good! What a disaster!'

'Oh, I dare say my old man went all over. He was an idealist, going into the forbidden places, that's for sure,' I say.

'They'll say – it was a church; you vomited, it was a revelation. A punishment – your devil. Overwhelmed, you sought illumination, you were unworthy.... You wanted light....' she says, inspired.

'No, Odette,' I say. 'Not light. I wanted food. I'd no resource. It was the end, as we've foreseen – we'll go and rob each other, then there'll be nothing left, our patrimony consumed – then nothing more at all. Those huge near-Soviet cities, a monument to revolution, the path that petered out, the vision that we couldn't match, our legs sucked from under us.... An end requires an objectivity, it isn't just for you ... except, you react, you're terrified – a subject off the edge.'

'Find yourself a Kazakh friend,' she says. 'Like I have. There's food and camel milk. They're great in bed as well. Invent!'

'I'm stuck, Odette,' I say. 'I can't get through the thorns, the thicket, I'm caught fast ... my horns....'

'Here,' Odette says. 'I must be off. Take this....' She's gone.

It's a piece of bread, on top, a pink slice: somewhere a soul cries out – it grunts, poor piggy. I put it in the bin....

*

Crises pass quietly here.

'I wanted to be free,' I tell Violanta. 'But the best I could do was go where they had not been free, the horsemen, but were a symbol of a free place, a free life.'

'You didn't want to work,' Violanta says, more sternly than is good for her – she's frivolous.... 'But you didn't want what comes with it – being poor. Most people work and they are poor. They can't always trip to places like you saw, where the horsemen were not free, but they fit a fantasy....'

'It's true,' I say. 'True but gloomy.'

'You can do without being free,' she goes on. 'That desire – it has a history. Correct that, you see the impulse is antique, a piece of blackened silver fallen off a something else. And then you're cured – you seek what's attainable, and if you will, you label it, like in an art collection.'

'Freedom was an extra,' I insist, '... really, my task was to live out my life just as myself, it seemed – but "an other" intervened. Model, ghost, and destination. I didn't know him well, my predecessor, the old old man. If there hadn't been the cash involved, I'd have preferred a woman, or a sharper, more articulate soul instead....

'We follow what's already there and fast it disappears, like the ploughman stumbles after the horse ... the ox. The woman. Or there's nothing there at all, no traction. That way leads to freedom, do you think?'

'I've an idea,' she says. 'Counselling the prisoners. I know one ancient con – in as an ignorant youth; out soon, an ignorant old man. He thinks in years: they pay you by the hour. Advise him – how to spend his last few months....'

'Oh,' I say, 'it'll take time. How many hours can I hope to earn...?'

'Just one,' she says. 'Most of us don't get that long.'

'Will he have gone mad?' I ask. 'It makes it difficult....'

'Oh no,' she says. 'By the law, you're only mad in your behaviour. Language doesn't count – there is no sanity in tongues or brains.'

'Then,' I say, 'if he set no store in youth by being free – being confined is beyond a philosophy. You do a thing, and then there is another thing, with wigs and gowns, and handcuffs too. You don't lose anything ... even by death.'

'Nor do you gain,' she says. 'It's hypothetical, of course.'

\*

He's pink, unused and sunless. 'I'm the bottle,' he says, sitting like a snail snug in his shell. 'Buried underneath the ancient palace; now that's ruined – open me.'

'Usually,' I say, 'it's vinegar. Or insipid. Vodka would be better – tequila with a worm. In Ukraine, koumiss ... gone rancid or to stone....'

'Open me,' he says. 'And taste. But don't get pissed, or they won't pay you. I've been everywhere – in these years I've flown: the moon, the stony slivers – no mystery at all to me, and I'm not chipped and scuffed like you; your tripes – a nest of rattling snakes....'

'Tell me first,' I say. 'What is a life for, what is it worth? What did you do to take this path....? Staking your life, losing, suspending it....'

'You tell me,' he says, 'and I'll say if I agree.'

'My time – by law, is paid, by the hour,' I say. 'My time, my counsel for you – is worth a bottle – of vodka, or of wine – fair to mediocre. Did you spend time counselling yourself? And what did you do, to be set along this stretch of road?'

'All these years, I advised myself.' he says: 'I've earned a cellar. I don't drink – besides – the cellar's locked. What did I do? Suppose I have forgotten it. Or remember only blows I took....'

'I did nothing bad,' I say. 'Not ever. Someone slugged me in the jaw, for my education. I don't think she went to jail.'

'I have been fortunate,' says the old con. 'I have had a life as a caterpillar. What are they for? To be a butterfly. What are they for? Why – to flutter and be eaten. Come to term – they make you full of joy, my friend.'

'And is it good to feel you have been fortunate?' I ask, hoping for the reward, his transcendance, his perfection, his bright wings....

'No,' he says, sadly. 'The bottle says "drink me" – but it's hypothetical. Maybe no one will, or I give them hangovers. I don't care. It's not my scene, and not my worry. Today – I'm happy. It's wonderful, and all the things they say were bad I did – they're here inside....' and he taps his big ostrich-egglike head.

*

'They won't pay you for that,' says Violanta. 'You didn't orientate – not to Mecca or Jerusalem, nor to the Buddha, or to gardening. You drank him, and he ran you. You're under the influence.'

'I'll try again,' I say. 'Maybe he'll turn out to be a larva, a mulberry grub – his answer's always changing shape.'

'You evade the truth,' she says. 'That's wrong! You're not in jail – we don't yet know your crime. Nor your intent. You let him steer you, because all you know is you yourself.'

'I know who eats caterpillars and who eats butterflies,' I say. 'And so what each is for....'

'The butterflies – they are for joy,' she says. 'Enlightenment. Jugglers of shape and time. Some say – they're ladies who've cast off their *niqab*.... They paint themselves, and everywhere they go.... They die to make birds' nocturnes and aubades....'

'You're right,' I say. 'The cell – it holds a special case: a queen, with workers clustered round to keep her living while they die ... except, she doesn't procreate ... so, nor does he.'

'What would his child be like?' she asks. 'Unlike him – so unlike you'd wonder what birth, genetic links, might mean. A spider? A lawyer with a web that catches spirits, parcels them for afters.... The judge who sends his father down, like they all do, and down all fathers go....' She drifts.

'He knows the compounds,' I say, 'the corridors – better than I've known anywhere, better than chamberlains, than butlers, knows where you mustn't stay, or must avoid; who seeks to harm, and who to love.... I've been in cities, and know nothing of them, or the people there ... I know nowhere ... the voyages he's made – successive earths, fold upon fold of fantasy, of animals that are other animals, of boiling seas and solid lakes, of days that flicker past like clouds and clouds lined with villanelles....'

'Next time,' Violanta asks, 'suppose he jumps on you, attacks?'

'I don't see why....'

'Oh,' she says, 'you're so provocative, Gyorgy. You ask, you answer – who can follow you? So exasperating –'

And she hits me on the ear – her cane, perhaps a sword-stick she has not deployed. It stings and bleeds. 'There!' she says. 'Look what you made me do!'

'Maybe you were born for this,' I say. 'It should console us both.'

I think – suppose I beat up the old man, the convict – show him what they think of him ... then I reflect, maybe I was born for that. And change my mind.

\*

'I know you,' Violanta says. 'Your type – seeks excuses, mitigation. Pulls time over everything like a tarpaulin. You'll say – "Killing in the service of a state? What does that entail? Even for a clan? A family? – vendetta, *faida*, to avenge or save ... A regime? the rules get bent. Always. Do your performance – lament the bad ends they make, the poor, the dead, the innocent, the shady ones... Quite casually the end may come, in spying. In a game, in gaming, over money, over a woman, for a woman, for science or a lie, for more room and for less, whole families or men of military age, women and children, everyone you see – frustration, provocation, raptus, jealousy. Rough company, one word, one blow, many words and many blows. Or random. A dare, initiation, boredom, a hot afternoon, an insult given or received, a gang, or someone who won't join a gang, a rival or his little brother, love, hatred, nothing much at all....'"

'No, no,' I say, 'I'm sure there's no excuse. Futile – a sense of duty or no sense at all. Sheep-stealing often starts it off.... There's steps – I imagine you go up them: bad or stupid put them there, or laws of hazard – there's not much at the top....'

*

'Don't travel, don't do gardening,' I tell the con. 'They'll disappoint.'

'When I get out,' he says, 'the ones I knew – they'll all be dead. I guess that is the point.'

'You're an old man,' I say. 'Am I supposed to follow you, to learn? You're nothing, a blot, a smudge, I despise you, you're of no account, if you're redeemed I know a thousand people who are good, better, don't need converting, don't cause pain.... You're sediment, a floating scum.'

'I know your sort,' he says. 'You're quite indifferent. It's good, you're right. I don't want your counselling. I'll tell them not to pay you, like last time. I don't want your money anyway, even if you think to share it.'

'Forget natural justice, old man,' I say. 'I've no time for it. And you're the one they caught. Incompetent!'

'Yes,' he says. 'That's good. You know what life is for.'

*

'You don't go deep,' says Violanta. 'You talk around it all, avoid a judgement. It won't do – your guy – is he a *facho*? Don't you care, with all the chattering about the metamorphoses?'

'That's not the only point,' I say. 'I'm like my inspiration – we avoid the potholes in our path.'

'I work,' she says. 'I tell lies for money in a store. And for amusement, I took lessons to teach me how to paint. Look – here's a parrot – I took its outline from a book. I have no talent, though. I ask friends to help me finish it. It's like you, exotic, endangered, painted on by many hands, not like the life, its squawk left behind somewhere in a tree.... Here, paint a feather on,' and she hands me a brush.

'You're a good person, Violanta,' I say. 'You take some care of me.'

'The message is "don't come again, don't pester me",' she says.

*

I tell the lifer, 'They let you out to die. My advice is – take painting lessons. If you've no talent, you will still have friends. The keepers don't want you dying here, inside – it spoils the punishment, the show, if you are dead.'

'That's just what I had hoped to hear,' he says. 'Thanks – no one could do more....'

This time they pay me. I don't ask Violanta how she knew you could get cash by offering advice, in jail.

## LEARNING ANOTHER TRADE: GOLDSMITHING

I have a stool. Hammers. Much trouble with *repoussé*. My teacher says it all comes naturally, the substance guides you, suggests the form, the shape. It isn't true. You don't sign it, not gold or silver, tin's low down the scale, there isn't room on diamonds. You'll watch my hands; my face remains a private territory. Sarmatian work is always evidently just like that, just what it is. The same with mine – I innovate, and I conserve, worship and desecrate. Hammer and stickle. It's rusty soupcans full of musty soup.

The rich guys stole designs from everywhere that's near – except ... it wasn't them. They bought, accepted: – didn't need to steal. Stealing came in, I'm sure, somewhere along the line that didn't lead to me but here I am. Copying – not reproducing. I can't, in any case. Don't want to. I go a way with images, and then they fade, drop, droop, reassamble – every pixel is original but from a different pic.... I'm a bird, my eggs, my chicks – don't look like .... copies of anything. Copy the good – that should be the goal. Over there – maybe. Here – it's not. The good is not the good – it's just a copy. To copy is to cheat. Break the chains – what's left is broken links... What we see a second time – surely, is a copy. The original, of any style, is what you see, hear, read first time. there's no aura, no repeating origin – copy, copy, copy. That is our world –

'We, everybody else. A copy. Does it matter, Violanta?' I ask her.

'All your women,' Violanta says, and laughs. 'Men too! And were they similar?'

'The model for them was Odette,' I say, 'Though you're not at all like her. But there's nothing special that unites them, or divides – chance and change. The words are near identical.'

'And that stuff you're chiselling?' she asks. 'A pot?'

'It was one animal, but I may change it to what it's more alike,' I say. 'You have to see the soul. You start from there – it's best if they're alive and watching you.'

'Yes,' she says. 'So varied, place to place they change and disappear and come back in different colours, shapes, and mostly watch their families and eat some dreadful stuff.... We human ones are all the same, or nearly so, but some are shits, and on the whole I'd want to start it all again, and bet on animals – not achieving anything at all, just keeping to their plot, going along, orderly and modest.'

'You could be a genius, Violanta, or full of whimsy – even both,' I say. 'But I've had enough of following examples, being picked up off the street....' I'm calm, but quite determined.

'Oh Gyorgy,' Violanta says. 'I hope I haven't hurt you: I want nothing close with you.'

*

*'A cloud of large blocks of stone is much more transparent than air of the same average density.'* (J. C. Maxwell, 1868)

'Well, Violanta,' I say, 'intimacy can be established in and for a second – cohabitation last for an eternity. Are there to be adventures? Your work – does not inspire you, and, especially, not me. You're an Ayesha – lost somewhere, a solid, like Felipe in the ministry, both in and out revolving doors, and I, like all your acquaintances and friends, I visit you, unpredictably, I'm your dead-alive cat, revolving round your little rock, as it too revolves – Isolda, maybe she joined up with you, all three fingertipping, gripping on, as the revolutions go – round and round, Violanta. I hope they never stop, I love them, they're my seasons, my flux....'

'"September Song",' says Violanta. 'That can't reach an end either – the next time you sing it – it stops so you can start again. If only it was so ... life, death! Philosophy – it has no ends, Gyorgy! That's my finding – it's my genius. It's the best and worst about it, a story that must have a resolution and so an end, but doesn't – the song, I feel, goes beyond that by ignoring the consequence of what it leads to – entirely.'

'I'd like to go to the Ferghana Valley – not now,' I say. 'As it was; a legend. The water's changed, changed utterly. The flow's transformed, what was precarious becomes impossible. It was rich and now it's poor.'

'That's quite another thing,' says Violanta. 'There's "little time" that's ours within; and then there's "time immense", outside, like sheets of sand and scrub you can't do much about – time that belongs to hydraulic engineers..... I'd like to go to Arakan long ago – a rich place. But now – it's a killing ground. Those Buddhist bigots – their bigotry creates a land of suffering. You'd only go to make it different, if you imagined that you could. Ayesha – a Buddhist, took it quiet and green, you said. Those pills – she took them all, turned into a lizard, couldn't turn back again. You must be very very careful what goes in....'

'Soup,' I say. 'We drink it down, and like they say, it comes out words, necessarily. That's the reality....'

'They don't make alphabet soup,' says Violanta. 'We got too intelligent, too smart. We wanted something cute – animal shapes, like the animals in Turkestan – something to hold us: imagination. Then, our brains slowed down, green with soot ... that's what they say. We're not up to it, Gyorgy. We travel, and we gawp and gape. We make the story, and it doesn't end, resolve. it's in a loop, but it can't last. It's like your contacts, like mine, all the men, the women – they walk in and out, sit at our table, eat off our plate, play their mandolin and beg, run out without paying, or go work off what they owe in the kitchen....'

'I know exactly where you are,' I say. 'We'd never afford it, dinner at the Tour d'Or. I'll straighten out an empty can and whittle it. Something new, not the golden tower. It won't chime, not like the garden bell at Combray. The restaurant we can't afford to visit ... they leave a bell on every table – you ring and hope it wakes a waiter. Those royal sturgeons – they've not been served for a hundred years. A favourite of the tsar. Ting-ting.... No one will come. You have to hunt the food yourself – try to avoid what's

natural, avoid the suffering, the rights – concentrate upon your own
– your rights, the suffering – you don't know why, why you, it
must be pesticides don't let you understand – your reality, and
everybody else's – it isn't good enough. It slides away, it trudges
past, people in columns, long marches, in tennis shoes. Take heed!
Break away!'

'Free will,' says Violanta. 'When they test for it – it's random or
perverse. Not at all a good. You can't blame the reality you make –
you're not responsible for it, or anything, unless you join up, wear
the armband.'

'Do you think I'm up to any of the tasks I've set myself?' I ask.
'I've wondered.'

'Of course you are, you must be up to it. We both must,' says
Violanta, encouraging. 'You've not chosen anything difficult. Or
unusual.'

*

'Where shall we go?' I ask.

'First, we must establish where we've been,' says Violanta.
'And – by the way: on the way – no sex, no peeping, no hints;
forget it.'

'That's Tlemcen,' I say. 'A postcard. White boxes for living in,
pink streets....'

'They lay down pink sand on the cobbles,' she says. 'But if
you're not rich, don't live there.'

'We don't need live....' I say.

'Oh,' she says, 'I believe in living somewhere. They did me
wrong. Below the waist, you see – I am a different thing, a beast, a
jackal type of thing. It's a defence, a handicap. Nothing bad can
happen to me, if I get sick, no one can cure me, I'm unique. You,
Gyorgy, you will travel closer to society as you start to wane, your
legs curve out, your lungs die slowly, and they stare up at you, the
bucking bronchials, the shredded throat that sang the *vincerò!*,
chawed by cubs or grubs too small to walk, their mother butchered
by machines, put in the pot, like mine, and seethed: they creak,
those lungs abandoned – it gives them comfort.... You've been
newborn, you cry, you're fed. But not this time, like all good
things, or nearly good – you gutter out, Gyorgy, like a rubber ball
that's lost direction and its bounce. Its destination.

'I – I've always been there, in someone else's world, a half and half....'

'I bet ... those legs, you can run fast,' I say. It's pretty flat to say, but there's no protocol....

'The clothes constrain,' she says. 'And limbs anomalous – aren't made to fit, are not a pair. Besides – I have no lair, no savings, no hole – that's all you need – a dash, and down you go, it's not a marathon....'

'I respect it, Violanta. It's your wish....' I say.

'No,' she says. 'You weren't listening. It's not. Your mother, I am sure, let you grow fat – a cuckoo, fratricide, the greed, the mourning, nothing to be done, no reparation, just resentment. In your eyes she spat, so's she could bugger off to somewhere. You'd aspiration, a patron too: no use! You couldn't sing. Two notes! Your life – it's not good luck! Me?' She wonders. I can't prompt. She says:

'I'd like to be ... lodged in a white room. Inside an egg.'

'A white uniform,' I say, 'like someone who cures for living, for their work. There was a guy in white in the snow – sniping, he shot four hundred Russians, some must have been Ukrainian – picked them out on their first date, daguerrotypes, in summer feathers. Finnish. A good name for what he did. But, Violanta, I'll protect you if I can, and if it seems the right, although – I'm not cut out for it. I should have been in opera – the one where they're all men, and sing falsetto, higher, higher than the wren....'

'I'm not convinced,' she says. 'You're a slack jack. If you work, and show up on time, you'll find your legs grow to the same length, and no one notices you, not anything about you, not even that you're there. If I need picking up, or brushing down – I'll find a way to contact you ... You're not a bore, everywhere is new. That's good, I guess. You're not much use, though.'

'I'm lucky, though,' I say, looking at the postcards. 'Look – here's Arakan.'

It's tinny grey, from far above, with fecal mud. 'There's places really tarted up,' she says. 'With taste, nostalgia. If you ride a bike, and have some savings, or can work machines ... they take you on. Pay you, and who you live with, or you fuck on Friday nights – they don't give a toss what happens to the cash, it all flows back when they type out zeroes on a piece of glass. And on it goes. They love the history, can't get too much of that....'

*

'They're animals,' says Violanta. 'People who cause things. Animals. It doesn't matter which beast it is. Now, pack up your hammers and your flame – I want to talk to Silke, my good friend, a sharp blade – if we're to travel. How should I describe you?'

'I'm a materialist, of course,' I say. 'It's my work. I could make you chaplets: – tin missed being precious. I can't think why....'

There's Silke – I can see her eyes, undulating as they frolic, she and Violanta – through the big window of the thé dansant. She rests her head on Violanta, watches me ... the taxis up and down, their sulphur colours and the black. Beyond me and the street – she might see the sea, sulphurous and tarry. Round and round she goes, on and on goes the sea – the gyring couples wrestle rhythmically: the dominants, sea-eagles with a petrel, driving their partner up and down the sky.

My two are accomplices, they cling together like two skins of paint, two ermines.

*

'Well, Violanta,' I ask, 'what does Silke think of me?'

'Oh,' she says, 'I forgot to ask. She's very trenchant, don't you think?'

'I only saw her eyes,' I say.

After a day when we're together, Violanta and I – it's clear, it's a great mistake. She scarcely speaks again. She wants to see everything, but she has no reaction, she's a wall, all makes a thud and bounces off.

'Here!' she says. 'You deal with all our cash – you understand all that.'

It isn't so, not so at all. She reproaches, and she's eloquent: nothing suits and nothing fits. The colour of the world – it's hohum. Maybe I agree. The rich are vulgar, the poor perspire too much. She isn't wrong, but tomorrow we shall all be gone.

'People. Scenery,' says Violanta. 'I can't take them in. I can only speak when I have my space around me. You, Gyorgy – you love wallpaper, there must be a panorama, you need to watch the revolving drum, painted with legs and manes that flicker up and down. I need the silence of myself....'

'That's an ultimate condition, Violanta,' I tell her. 'Like my old man – what's left when all the rest has passed, been seen and catalogued.'

'I'm saddened, Gyorgy,' Violanta says. 'You're not authentic. You're a bee without a hive. You don't avail, cast no shadow, make no image on the silvered glass.... You tap away, make things that maybe look like other things, but you yourself – you don't appear in them. They're grave goods, anonymous – even if we knew who'd made them, it would be a name, no more.'

'You mean, to have a weight, a presence ... I must be in jail?' I say. I'm quite appalled: 'Surely, I'd disappear, be like an alloy, copper dissolving into brass – but invisible, confined for ever there.... Suffering, isolation, punishment: is it possible that you, Violanta, who've worked and lied, kept mum and schtum, think creation comes from prisons...?'

'Yes,' she says, 'that's what confinement means. Birth. You have another, another one, who's you and yours but not at all resembles you.'

Here in Agadir – it looks exactly like The Hague, tall low-rises, bins along the streets, a water cart moves slowly up one side and down the other.... I talk and talk, greet the good folk we meet....

She's gone. She's disappeared. This is a place – you can't look for anyone – there's thousands here, like birchtrees in a wood: there is no in and out.

## VIOLANTA'S SAVINGS

'Instinct,' she said. 'Spontaneous – do something! Violence – not that dreary stuff about the struggle. Here, whether you talk or not, you won't accomplish anything. Even reflections on violence ... useless. There's no pure Syndicalists – no more! High ethical values? Socialism? Salvation? It's the void, Gyorgy! Annihilation calls! Do it! run with it! There's always plenty to complain about – injustice before and during, then after, when they've imprisoned you – quiet torture, or the noisy kind. Suffer, sacrifice – measure your power against the crows.... Shut your eyes, the black birds love to pick those out....'

I said, 'It sounds best not to get caught.'

I'm not so sure doing what comes naturally is best – most animals find it's not, they're down the chain, then down the hole....

'The rich allow themselves their anarchy,' I said. 'It's the mountain top they've reached ... It's clear, in jail, the other cons will wonder why you're there – won't understand. You've nothing much to sell them.... My old patron – I bet he went to jail in many lands – but he had years to fill. I'd rather be anonymous somewhere....'

'Don't try it!' Violanta said. 'They'll see you in the street – you'll have to prove you're someone, even someone else. Anonymity would help you not pay tax – but you've no cash. That doesn't work. You'll have to 'fess you're someone, with a name, a past, and then you'll get a document. And that is you.'

'It's hypothetical,' I said.

'Well,' she said, 'that cash – it was my savings.'

'I know,' I said. 'There's lots left.'

'There never was lots,' she said.

\*

'All those adventures,' she says. 'Women – attracted to your story. Then they drift – it's all gravity. Tides, moon-talk. You know – I could denounce you. Stealing. Plotting. If they've no case, the cops'll beat you – you're not a desert Arab, but you're worse – a city type. Pale as a peeled mushroom, black moles burrowed in your face. That way – you'll think of violence, and how you'll lose. Break a window, you idiot – steal something that'll last you years and pay to dig your grave – last all your life, better than a pension. Choose my shop – there's gold and diamonds, and I'll smash your twiggy fingers with my club....'

She has a flat voice, but it's alarming – 'Let's find somewhere we can drink and wash our face,' I say.

'Why?' she asks, truculent. 'I want to see you beaten up and beating back. Where does washing come in?'

'Your face is dirty, Violanta,' I say. 'You're letting go, just because we're on the road ... It isn't done, until you can't avoid it. Besides, we're doing intellectual stuff. Spiritual. You need finish it before you get the pay.'

'Love I can do myself, for myself, by myself,' she says boldly. 'Vengeance: anger, pay off scores – I need you for that. Be my weapon, assert yourself. You must be trimmed and sharpened, though.'

'No vengeance, Violanta,' I say. 'It's all been done, every brutal ending, you can't imagine worse – adding to it's just repeating.'

# TRAVELLING AROUND – SOME MORE

'You have to go inside the houses,' Violanta says. 'Everywhere outside is dirty, peeling off. Only inside do you see how things can be different.'

She throws open a door – there's a mass of faces, bodies on the floor on flattened mattresses.

'Oh shit!' she shouts. 'They're from the Maghreb – so we must be in Holland. Things are various here – but the Dutch aren't – they're throaty. Silke gets excited, chatters, and it's like she suffocates.'

'It's tragic,' I say. 'No one knows why they're here and what they're supposed to do. Everything done, good and bad, is cancelled when we die. And you, Violanta – I can't believe you are a destination, or a destiny, a fate. Fates sit and knit – you're leggy, flirty too.... We roam, and *where* we are is not at all the *what* we are....'

'Oh fuddy-duddy,' Volanta shouts again. 'There's Jade Mountain, Monkey Island – we've not seen those. You buy the tickets, I'll put up with you... There's always novelty – no one can help it, you must give birth, can't hold it all inside....'

'I know,' I say. 'Something unexpected always comes. Hope. See – my metal-works – all on the screen, frozen on, straight from the steppe. A marvel – my hands shake, so I print them, designs, patterns, the brooches and the clasps and torques. A homage, tribute....'

Violanta drifts away. 'I'm curious,' she says. 'Everything. I watch the river – not the banks ... we're destitute.'

And she laughs.

'We've no money, Violanta,' I say. 'But we're not poor. The poor – they die. Hunger and thirst, with hands outstretched for charity, greater than love.

'We've played our part in violence, greater than ever, salvation more banal. We didn't wear our swords – it would have looked ridiculous. But when we had the cash, we paid our whack: it went on bangs and banks....'

She's not impressed. 'They all say that,' she says. 'So what? What next? A new twist, Gyorgy, a grin, a distance.... It's not about poverty – if it were, they'd help us, arm us, say we're lazy, voted wrong, make us spend, give us a tent, a cheque. We've none of that. Maybe – we're wastrels.'

'I dare say it's that,' I say. 'You have no end, Violanta. Go see what Silke says....'

## SILKE: SHEARING TIN

I split with Violanta – but – we've set up a philosophy by talking through. Not is and ought, real and the rest – but how the universe is set up for us two.

Polished tin – it doesn't look like silver, but will do. I cut the shapes with shears, with lighting and Sarmatian pictures – it resembles an original...

So, I make some cash.

Silke is calm. I ask her what she does – 'Publicity,' she says.

'For famous people?' I ask her.

'Of course not. For the unknown. There is a mass....' she says.

'What will you have them do?' I ask.

'You haven't understood,' she says. 'It's all hypothesis. But – I could bounce you up ... except ... you cut sheet tin. You have many precious things: you know the world, you've seen everything, and nothing stuck, the same with men and women. Your father or grandfather, explored time everywhere, every floor and wall, with nothing happening at all, two meals a day; a dreadful crime, indescribable. Or was he framed? He knows time, from within. You need not: in fact, it doesn't serve you, knowing it, at all. Without time, there is no punishment ... but – he's done it, lifetime, industrial, for all of us.'

I cannot weep for him. She says:

'Forget the jewelry. Be a pot, a vase, Ming or Pandora ... all done, and emptied out.'

'And you would bounce me up?' I ask. 'I don't see why. Except for cash.'

'Suppose we put you in a shell and land you somewhere populous,' she says, '– with millions clustered round. Maybe they're tiny, could all fit in your shoe. You'd tell them everything, I'm sure – all that there is to know, in outline ... All that could matter to them, not to you. Forget your expedients. Be naked, be a Gulliver. A Crusoe. You might fit in their shoe, and they could have you multiply – identicals, like microbes. They're ingenious, skilful, they can reel in your astral rock as it travels up and down. Just – forget the steppe, my friend....'

'It wasn't at all fun, out there,' I say, ingratiating, 'even to gallop up and down.'

She doesn't know. Nor do I.

I ask her, 'Do you have clients, Silke?'

'Many thousands,' Silke says. 'And thousands have me too as theirs.' She laughs. 'And – my compliments! – those tin tiaras show you're nearly there. You should be poor, but you've hooked on to dangling ropes. They'll pull you up. Make a new culture, invent new demons, new tattoos and runes. Annexe the world, like me, and play it like a shaman's drum. It needs be entirely yours....'

'You must have wings,' I say, and laugh. 'I bet you spend days in Lanzhou, and then Caracas before dark, and on to Santa Rosa for a steak....'

'Oh,' she says, 'I'm not a carnivore. But, yes, I do have wings. Not like a butterfly.... More like a moth....'

It's true. 'And may I touch?' I ask. 'Maybe the dust, the powdered colour, would come off....'

'No, no,' she says. 'They're sturdy. They are for hovering, while the world turns beneath. Then – if it's attractive, I alight.'

We're very close ... her wings, they're warm and soft.... 'That's enough,' she says. 'Now you know what's real. That'll do.'

*

'You think you've sorted somethings out,' says Silke. 'But all the people you have known – they are destroyed. Some dead for certain – Isolda, Felipe – in filing cabinets, maybe somewhere, don't look for shallow graves. Odette ... the madam maso – I feel their anxiety, and how you do hallucinate! – you have to wait, ask the doctor "Do I have something?" "Will you cure it?" "Must I pay?" "Will it hurt and kill me, when?" Is this a doctor, or my pain, doubled up, a near-life dancer made of resin pepped with pigments, the flesh fat-colour, de-boned, smashing his antlers on his drooping feet, see him arched there, just legs, a deck-chair folded, a proclamation of creamy tripe hung on a rope, his arsehole unashamed pointing at the sky, a mouth – "Ahoy! Is anyone up there, on the lookout" – slave-ships and galleys hove-to preparing for a fruity broadside – plums that bruise, are bruises, ready to bleed, with red veins and brown crusts of the fallen – no hope, "you've got it, Pontiac" – the nurses laughing, know anatomies inside out – nurses in motley knitting through the night and casting you off at dawn. Did they suffer, everyone you knew? It's all over now, done and forgotten waiting for the next...'

'It's not me, Silke,' I say, dismayed, 'I never want ... I watch people who are hurting, I'm not responsible for anything.'

'Well, who?' she asks. 'Who else is there? Your mate? Your double? There must be will, to break down wills, the old murderer, they let him out, gave him a nickel so he'd call if they could help.... Into business as a tree surgeon, lopping and polling: decapitations and grubbing out a speciality.... Don't tell me you didn't applaud him, and snitched the nickel off him, not that it buys anything for anyone.... "Here comes the pruner to cut off your plums –"'

'You must be right,' I say. 'In all beginnings there's a painful end. Maybe with me, the middle hurts as well ... We could unfold the dancer, in the vertical he can swing the lights, clash those stars....'

'No, no,' says Silke, 'when he stands, you see his dangling breasts – remind you? Not every me can hold a yours....'

'I'm not interested in this,' I say. 'Shapes, forms, growth and paralysis, sickness, the flicking tongue's contagions – my concern....'

'Is getting to the end,' says Silke, laughing. 'You disappear, leave your dump of dead boxed meat ... but all the rest? Where do those rocks end up, how can they fall to no finish, no bottom – round and round like young flies circling the switched-off light?'

'Yes, Silke,' I say. 'I think it is like that. No glue, no gravity: nowhere to drop out. An infinity, eternity, of dust.'

She alights. She's near me, not on a branch, there is expanse, no branch, no tree, not even metaphorical.

'I believe in history,' Silke says. 'Where it came from, where it goes. That is where the suffering arises. You don't believe in it, because you'd rather not. It's too slow for you, you can't erase or add when it has had a say. We're at one with ephemera, though. With ourselves, and the people who float by.'

'It's not much, Silke,' I say. I don't want any more.

'That's so,' she says. I wait for her to start – 'But, we two....' She doesn't say it. It's a relief.

'Where to go, it's a problem,' she says. 'My friends are where they are. I need be the same. Europe – it's so full. Asia – worse. You can't take it all in – all those lives, going on, like spillikins, or the magician's box – you're inside and he thrusts swords through you.'

'There's Kentucky,' I say: 'Blue Grass.'

'Goats would surely thrive,' she says. 'By law, they are inedible there. A place that there is only music fads around. That suits. It would be soft, falling strains by now. I don't know of anybody there. Maybe it's deserted.... No family stories, complaining of hard times – we could have our own hard time, pristine...'

'I feel we're almost there already,' I say, hoping we needn't go. and maybe find it not there after all, but us, looking, vainly.

'Your trouble, Gyorgy,' Silke says, 'is you're still too binary. Desire rules you – you see roads as going this way, that – because the people want to go there, maybe in time to both. Rich and poor, good and bad – it's an obsession.'

'It's that I'm lazy, Silke. Of course life is a cake, not cherries in a bowl. The oven means there are no dinosaurs, they had their cake.... And blue ridge mountains – you can see them in museums,' I defend myself. 'Landseer saw them, they are in the distance – the Rinascimento put them behind the scenes in paradise that ended with the execution....'

'*That's* where you get your symbols from,' she says. 'That's your museum, the big book with the talking animals, the giantkiller, the magic beans, the beast, the lamb. Forget it, friend. We shall have goats. If they all die because we're ignorant – we'll go on. With nothing at all. Only worms and ticks, tick-tocking but we'll never know the time – except that it runs out. Runs on. Runs.'

'I'd no idea you were articulated so,' I say. 'When you danced with Violanta – you looked like two cloth dolls, hands and feet sewn together so you didn't flop – held up, I'd guess, by wires above.'

'I love the dance,' says Silke. 'It's what keeps two people separate.'

'It didn't look like that,' I say. 'You were fulfilled – as nothing. Something not there at all.'

'Well,' she says. 'If they let us in, we'll soon find out who's right. Those Mountains, for a start – not in Kentucky. The Grass – you got that right. Bullseye.'

\*

'You're wrong,' she tells some guy, administering a quiz. 'We're not monotheists, even of the wrong variety – we're animists, lapsed, I think.'

'That phase has passed,' says the guy. 'We are full up. No room, even the deserts – filled with striving and resentment. Go away!' He's a gatekeeper for the continent.

I'm much relieved. We shall not be admitted. No goats, no grass.

'The thing is, Gyorgy,' Silke says. 'I have talent. I'm quite sure – it's big, bigger than I am. But – it's priceless. I don't earn. Help me!'

'You're not the only one,' I say. 'Yours is the paradox that plagues our time, merit ensuring poverty. Myself – I'm a designer, smith – I too have talent, but I'm clumsy with my hands. The pictures in my head – they don't transmit to precious stuff. I thought of taking lessons at the source....'

'Don't be an apprentice,' Silke says. 'There's no kennel, so your master can't make you sleep in one. It's worse....'

## LEARNING A TRADE: PLUMBING

She's right. My master is a wondrous smith, no doubt, but he's a plumber too. The pipes are lead and terracotta. They walk off in the desert, and they leak. It is my task – to make them fast, and have them wait – a draining up and down, whatever comes, whoever reverses gravity.... They're ancient, these old conduits, Mamalukes or lookalikes – planted the marble cisterns....

'This is the basis of our work,' he says. 'Go to! Like it or not – water is our life, and we are water in the pipe....'

'There's no water, Master,' I say, 'except when there are floods. Let me skip the pipes – go to the gold....'

'That's a family affair,' he says, 'for sons. I've only daughters. Your woman – not daughter, and not sister. No one would adopt her....'

'I'm already son to several,' I say. 'Acknowledge me, and let me learn. Silke – she's with me, but it ends there. Not kin to metals, nor to me.'

'Wait!' he says. 'As a son, you'd have to go to war ... we'd lie about your age, but in the end, you're all conscripted. Goldsmith and warrior, those are two trades I see you least adapted for.'

'There's still a choice,' I say. 'Being a bastard. You're cursed with me, a clumsy coward. Now, do your best ... Silke – she's not subversive, but she's independent, loves no one, but she wants all other to be just the same.'

There's larger, more immediate things. There's enemies, and there's the state – a pirate's tricorn over us – a thunder cloud that brings no rain, with severed arms and legs – you see them, up there in the black and silver, not deposited for empire, civilisation, or for much at all ...

'Then, there's Silke,' says the man who's not my father. 'She doesn't fit.'

'She's talented,' I say. 'But not here – it's too hot to have her digging up the pipes, and there's the drought....'

'That is irrelevant,' he says. 'This is a place it doesn't rain. The drought brings change quicker than any other plan....'

On my last day, he takes me in – his workshop. There are wonders – gold and silver parrakeets – their tongues are lead, the gold and silver feathers rise and fall – the breeze we make, strolling up and down, is quite enough....

'I'd like to make a golden man, but it might bring conquistadores,' he says. 'Advise me. A golden woman – what message might that send? A man – is naff. A woman – suggestive of a process I don't intend. Gold fixes you – the earth, and value; shining. Subjects, objects – all mustered in a drawer, there's nothing I can add except my twist. I create, I don't concoct creations....'

'An ostrich,' Silke says, and adds. 'That lays those Russian golden eggs.'

'I see this isn't to my taste,' I say. 'Fantasy movies – not for me.'

'It's where the market is,' the Master says. 'If I were free, I'd try some other thing, adventurous unpopular.... But as you're leaving, unfulfilled and uninstructed – take this cage....'

It's full of gold and silver birds.

'But – I am not your son,' I say.

'I'm generous,' the Master says. 'It's just the way I am.'

\*

'Failure instructs more than success,' I say.

'He made you look mean,' says Silke. 'It didn't rain, and he gave you a patrimony. And kept his secrets and his clients. A genius.'

'Rilke spoke of the depth of the Ukrainian steppe – of course, it was bigger then,' I say. 'Must be a metaphor, but it's meant for me: another patrimony.'

'I saw that movie too,' says Silke. 'He rhymes with me. I found the desert full of lightness. I looked into the houses. I talked to people and drank tea – I was creative, while you were learning that you weren't.'

'We lived like bad dogs,' I say. 'But I didn't feel like stealing. I would have, not long ago.'

'"Tell the swift water: I exist": – they had rain then. And winter,' Silke says. 'Those ancients – it's no use them or us repeating it. What isn't there – it's gone, it isn't waiting round the corner.'

'I'm ready to try something else,' I say. 'Authenticity is out. Quiddity – no one believes in it. Water comes in bottles, not in pipes – it's all quite changed. When the bottle's finished, you can blow against the neck – out comes your name.... Airy creatures are called from the bushes, round they frolic, bending like plasticine. "The Dance" – you must have seen the pic.... The bottle – used to hold absinthe, now it may be coke....'

'If you'd talked more,' says Silke. 'You'd have known that, ages back. It's fantasy – an origin, a perfect figure, a Vitruvian – reproducing for eternity, a skin that you can enter in and wear, pass on. You wasted all that time seeking the perfect dancer – piles and piles of time, stacked up and alien, like they say. Unusable in that form.'

'I could Hollywood it, Silke,' I say, 'make it all a mystery, no answers except what's known from the beginning. Eternal return, but in a circle tiny as a ring. A fake rock hidden among real ones – maybe it doesn't hold the heat. You locate it when the others have a mountain lion at dusk lain there and warming up. The false one is deserted....'

'That's dull,' says Silke. 'So, art can't do hot rock. Though it's true, Gyorgy – you re trapped inside a genre. Guys start young, bum around, face what they say is danger, end up old and write a book. Or pay for someone else to invent it all. Stop looking, Gyorgy. Maybe you can't do anything, so why go on searching for an everything? Everything is always there and has been, nothing to find that we don't know already where it is.'

'We had a plan,' I say. 'It's past. Though, we could settle those goats down, and see how they do, farming themselves. We could step back ... '

*

'I didn't believe in spending too much,' I say, 'On the emotional side.'

'Oh,' Silke says. 'It's not real, not real money. You can splash! There's no bill. Not if you start off poor, at least.'

'I love gambling, Silke,' I say, 'but horses – they're almost always willing. They line up, they run ... but people....'

'You must have known people,' Silke says. 'Before you started looking: following. Besides, I like gambling too.'

'Genius,' I say. 'I've known them; it was not contagious, so it seems. One drove me distances – there was a course, another genius set up: analysis. We reached page sixteen of Kapital, but there were problems with the car. The time. He started working nights. No, I forget.... Another bought a harpsichord – it came by mail. A box. She had to reassemble it. An hour – and it was hopping. Grasshopper songs. Another: "contemporary thought", each piece of it. A genius too – all of them. I stole the Tractatus from one, and I have it still. I wonder what happened to all that. And all of them.'

'You're rather stony, Gyorgy,' Silke says. 'I like it, naturally, but – those pebbles get in my shoe, then in my knee, my kidneys and my eyes.'

'Think carefully of all I said, Silke,' I say. 'You'll see why the Tractatus was a start. You move on from that; the steps, the grades, shedding a life with each one upward, onward, a flute broken for each month spent in splendour, till you reach the place of sacrifice. This is the goal. No ruins, no more steps, no palaces with desks, no office hours, nothing to plug in, no batteries supplied. You and the sun, tongue-tied under the knife, the priest. Then – pouf! Away, all of it! Numbered propositions is the least. Nakedness, only a start; alas, you have to say the word, to know the language, so's to stop it all. To stop the language and the word. It melts: the meaning that you give – is butter-icing. Away the hierarchy, all order, everywhere! The boss guys ... off with them, the lexicons! In any case, you work quite well without all those, don't even try to read a book, or paint by numbers.... You start from here. This is the beginning. Is it the end? I think it doesn't matter much ... not to life. Or stories.'

'The Master,' Silke says. 'Do you recall? There was a war, over the hill. You could have helped stop that – given him peace.'

'He knew, he heard – he's lived in that place for ever. The wrong side always wins, that's what he says;' I say. 'It's energy that wins, not peace. Wanting to be boss. You can't step in to that, Silke. He knows: in his trade, the secret's in the hammering.

'Remember, everything I say – it's a philosophy. All the answers. If you want, you can back off down the tunnel, find the questions – but what would be the point?'

'You patronise,' says Slike. 'I have my own, answers, questions, just like yours but different. Attained without your help, and quite quite different from yours – from words to things – and then you find the things have gone. Maybe there's a pile of stones. Is that them, or are they underneath? The words? You string them any way you want. You'll find they bang together, or they squeak – there's many uses – even I have not discovered every shape and sound, and, yes, the thought is there: maybe they're things as well, or partly so, to finish as a heap of stones. Fake stones, cooler than the real....'

'You haven't understood,' I say. 'Clear it away, the clutter and the theorising – you're left with you yourself, then you must clear that too – away, away!'

'You're a movie, Gyorgy,' Silke says, drawing back. 'You're Jacques Demy's garage – people bring their vehicles, get fixed, go off – and you make a song of it. Nothing stays in the workshop except broken parts....'

'A movie's too complicated, Silke,' I say. 'I'd like to be – a scroll. Too brittle to unfold.'

'I hope you find a love that loves you like you love yourself,' she says.

'Of course! That's health,' I say, downcast. 'It sounds a solipsism – but it's not. It's the white page they put, after the legalities, the lists; it is the blankness that precedes the text.... And at the end, concludes it.'

'You could put it simply,' Silke says. 'You need to start from emptiness, so you must destroy all cognition that's preceded. Then – where do you go? a void – not being looked at twice, no questions, scepticism towards words – let alone when they are strung to make a necklace or a suit of mail....'

'I think that's it,' I say. 'It doesn't sound familiar, so it might be a morphing of what I've said....'

'We'll sort it out,' says Silke. 'You can address a crowd of savants. If they laugh – that's one thing. Throwing stuff – another. And – so, on and on....'

## ODO AND BEATRICE

I can't refuse. I don't accept. My! There's hundreds, come to hear quite something else ... many have cloths on their heads in different forms – protecting from the lightning, the tortoise-strikes, the wrath of This and That. The Sun – unconquerable companion – at least, for now, must wait outside. Others are bald, no cop-out to unknowns, no metaphysicals among those....

There's a poster – 'a new non-theory of everything'. It's good: my name is written wrong.

Behind the scenes there's firemen, maybe they're Ukrainian police. 'Never explain yourself,' I think. 'It all flows irrespectful....'

I tell them – there's no summary. The truth, if that is their desire – lies in the studying. If I conclude, and everything proceeds indifferent – it shows I'm wrong. So, I don't conclude. But – what is wrong with being wrong, I ask.

There's movement to and fro, and in and out. There's breaks for this and that. The audience – it changes totally, replaces itself, time after time. 'You see!' I say, 'There's no instruction, just a confusion about rooms....'

I finish, I withdraw. There's been some repetition, inspiration, incoherence too. A great success. For what?

'Beatrice', 'Odo' their badges say. The last two in the hall, wanting the last word, ingratiating – 'You speak like shepherds at the start of time, quarrelling about how and if the universe should be set up,' says Odo. 'Before they invent their sheep, their goats. Bim bam birimbam!'

'It's like a nursery of pre-Raphaelites, before a portrayal of ineffability,' says Beatrice. 'And you – a dragonfly, dithering on the lectern's edge.'

'And Tzara entertains,' says Silke. 'I'm disappointed, Gyorgy – you were not intimidated, not at all.'

'You're so serious,' says Beatrice. 'Don't you go sometimes for the rough? Or even tumble?' and she winks at me, quite louche.

'Beatrice has the brain,' says Odo. 'I want to be like you, though – making a fortune. The motivation business. Beatrice pushes ....'

'I want no truck with motivation, Odo,' I tell him. 'There is far too much.'

'We're complementary,' he says. 'We both urge on from different sides. Beatrice says – the middle is the quiet spot. You just pick up cash....'

'Silke didn't ask for any, Odo. She didn't think to. I may need take some crime, a peccadillo – into my hands,' I say. 'You two – you have hedgerow eyes: – like weasels. I don't see you driving a big stolen car.'

'I know your sort,' says Beatrice. 'Once – socialist realism, then true communism. Now – those ancient realities, clean-shaven socialism – not even spoken of. Living in a past that wasn't, a future you won't be here to see – none of us, no one. Circumvent the system, Gyorgy, brush yourself out of the picture gallery – those are the dead, the ancestors. Nevermore! Publicity! Start in it, end in it, ennobling repetition, the nearest anyone can come to immortality....'

'What exactly do you do?' asks Silke.

'Things break, they fall apart,' says Odo. 'You hold them and the seams split, the glue doesn't hold. It's little bits – they stick out, costly, fragile, symbols ... protrusions, spandrels. We're nuisances. What we can break – we do.'

'Jumping off the buildings,' Silke says. 'That's not for us....'

'You're wrong, Beatrice,' I say. 'I don't move with times. Time lets you down. There weren't good times, not ever. Best finish with her, time – though it's true, we'd have no way of going on, no accretion, no secretion. If we're lucky – stasis.

'But if there's time – that's the only way luck can be fitted in. I thought I'd made it clear in my performance: don't want what there won't be, don't want what there never was. That way, if truth interests you – you'd be closer to it. It doesn't interest me much – truth. And I don't think it will be a happy day when it arrives.'

# VINTAGE MOTORS: MY ANCESTOR'S CHOICE

'This motor – too big, too grand, for this old guy,' says Odo, laying us out in splendour in the shell of this venerable red car. 'I said I'd always wanted something similar. That is the truth.'

'The guy,' I ask, 'did he know that he was robbed...?'

'No,' Odo says, 'it was something of himself he was ready to discard. He and his Dodge – scrap in the making – you cry, watching the doc. Those plants and trees, that live for centuries – flowering, then death, rebirth – the seals of Solomon, love lying bleeding, jacks in the pulpit – they'll be around next year, and on and on – he, you, will not.'

Odo doesn't see the world as if one day he'll not be alive in it. He's not attached.

Beatrice and Odo – they're *casseurs,* but independent. Just for themselves – a judgment, then the execution. What has survived, they leave alone, but maybe paint a thought or draw on it. What most concerns is stuff in quantities no one has thought out – the real effects, developments....

'It's all your thoughts,' says Silke, admiring them, the thoughts, Odo, Beatrice. 'Not the symbols of the big, the rich, on display, and asking for a finger in the eye – but a running judgment on the new, a show trial of the ill-considered and the inconsiderate....'

'If it was my mentor who'd been hearing my philosophy,' I say, 'he'd know, taking is no theft, he'd big questions to answer before he croaked, losing his motor didn't enter in....' I'd mostly forgotten him, the old tough nut – they all are tough when they've passed their century, blaming their eyes for the tears that flow when they behold the forests, present and mostly past, the sea, the sea, not starting over, or maybe just one more time....

'We make our choice,' says Beatrice. 'If I wasn't with Odo, but with someone else, more dashing, better read, the objectives, the targets, would be different. Life is not a shopping list, you know,' and she stares at me, accusing.

'We're not vandals,' Odo says, turning his eyes off the road as he veers his head to talk to us, we three, lined like swallows on the back seat, he the chief swift: faster, faster. 'Though the Vandals built. We don't construct....'

'My treasury of birds,' I say, clutching the wires of the cage close, seeing them tremble with the motion of the springs; the hoopoe, the owl, the nightingale, their crusted claws glued on the coral perches, 'will do for cash.'

They're not saleable. I won't sell. 'Are they valueless?' I wonder.

'It's miraculous,' says Silke. 'We won't sell, but we are given more than they'd be worth. It's capital, or loans – I quite forget. We'll spend it, we can't pay it back – and we have the birds as well. There's nothing you can break in that, Beatrice.'

'Of course not,' Beatrice says. 'Like we wouldn't break the car, with all of us inside. It might break down, all by itself. Nothing to be done. Just wait and see.'

'You fit very well with Odo,' Silke says.

'I fit with anyone,' says Beatrice, 'until the end. But – the fitting: it doesn't end. Where does it go, where does it reside? Who rigged it, set it up, compatibility?'

We laugh. It's very neat. She'd leave Odo, that is clear – she likes the thought of Odo. The body, shell, though, it's like all the rest, restless, foxed, freckled and liver-spotted – nothing special. But you can't leave someone while they're driving you quite fast.

*

'Where do we sleep, live, all that?' I ask.

'He took that old thinker's car because it would hold us all – longs in the back, shorts in the front,' says Beatrice. 'How's it done on your planet, Gyorgy?'

'I'm fascinated,' Silke says to me. 'To see them break a thing. What might it be? Might it be us? The world? Things that's never been, or have a natural decadence – or a remedy for everything? Something's invented, a salvation – and those two say "No! We've reached the term. Enough! Off with their heads, the dreary lot, the clinkers buzzing round their star – how drab and cold...."'

'I hope it's not just capitalism they want to break,' she says, wearily. 'That's like a cancer or a field of daffodils – it takes those centuries to make their colonies, and then it's deep implanted ...'

'I've read the books,' I say. 'Maybe it's organic, capitalism; dies when its time arrives ... or else it takes some millions, subscribers, not just with a hohum, but plans and fighter planes ... to knock it down, and then....'

Without that sleep, though it's uncomfortable, I'd not have had my dream.

## MY DREAM

We roll along – the suspension – not like a Pontiac, quite firm; there's cows – their breath comes in, it's udders and mucking out – a smell of trampled soil. I lie with Beatrice, who is long, we're top to toe – those toes in my mouth – a touch of sub-marine, wriggling like five-armed starstruck creatures at low tide, they waft and stir, oh! – to be submerged. 'These toes,' I say, I recognise. 'They're Odette's – she need not have bothered, there's so many, women: all with toes – Ayesha, Violanta....'

'Yes,' says Odette. 'But it's much better I am Beatrice – she breaks, I was a bore, talk leads to more talk, that's all: – and she creates, destroys....'

'That's what I need,' I say. 'My mentor – he was good and bad, lived in a Manila drain, a penthouse in Trois Rivières – and none of it was his, he wanted movement, that way to find the answers, stripping off the circumstance, and what was left, after the penury, the glut ... lean years and fat.... That was the worth. The nugget, pearl.'

'Now, Gyorgy,' says Odette. 'You must be brave. What I'm about to say: your Cicero, he died, not a question asked; like all of us, he barely saw what he should ask – then death ... it's sad. Though – he, Cicero – he was a fucking lawyer, crow. You could have had a Virgil – ends the same, five feet or six, toes galore ... Resign yourself. We have no hope ... it ends before we start, we hope there is a chapter two, a sequel, but it isn't so, it's dark, too dark to see, you're just a head that's full of tears, deflating football, yellow as a jonquil, the last air squeaks out – the balloon's neck pinched like your arsehole that you can't control, a puckered cat's arse – oh yes, Gyorgy, it's awful sad....'

It is. The tears – they flow over Odette's toes, a puddle, then a lake – we swim, we animals, we drown before we're born – rescued into air, we gasp, it's not our element, we suffer, love the dying and the moribund....

\*

'Hey!' Beatrice shouts, 'you're drowning me – I can denounce – you're not born to violence, not like me, my lover Odo – we can show you how to break and make: – a fortress where you can't get in, no window and no orifice....'

It's so. I don't know how: Beatrice can take a rock, hollow it out, make mica windows, and a rack for pickled things – sea cucumbers, overstuffed puff-fish, clowns with scarlet snouts.... It's a marvel, a tiny pyramid, a tomb proof against all raids.

'If you can't paddle, Beatrice,' I say, 'then try to swim, and dolphins come around, watch for those orcs that no one sees, but terrorise....'

'No, no,' she says. 'No swim! No tears! I'll burn it down – those jewellers: and make a calf, a cow of gold, a totem for old savants, sat round, conciliar, with their agate eyes and staves of tin.... I'll burn the richness and the fake and make an ingot – it will be my child, I'll nurse it, my udders – see, they're wet with milk, we're swimming in it ... suck, Gyorgy: how you suck...!'

What a joke! I laugh and laugh – my tears have made a sea, but I am dry, my aged ancestor died ignorant, a child who'd managed massacres, learnt nothing, but cried 'more, more', it moves, it moves! until he died ... they buried him in me, there's room, I'm a dried raisin skin – drive on, drive on! Hooray for Mr Dodge, whoever he might be, who gave us space and speed and told us they were both the same, were time, a timing chain....'

'You drool,' says Beatrice, 'all over me. When you are senile you will be a flood – not Noah drunk, but Gyorgy dribbling.... Salt, too, salt and cold – the White Sea ... the river Ob....'

'Life destroys,' I say. 'It's sad, it's terrible.' A spit, a spate – it's nothing. Beatrice, though, she's not appeased.

## THE WONDERFUL BIRDS: A FORTUNE IN A CAGE

'The next big place,' says Silke, 'we'll stop, and you two can break some things, and let's see if you know your trade and if it's worth for us another chance with you....' There's no response.

'You're dated,' Silke says, 'like celluloid.'

'"They use guns. It's timeless,"' Odo says. 'Remember *Driver.*' Again, there's no response: the rest of us – we haven't seen those movies. We are dated too.

'I don't like burnt things,' Beatrice says. 'I have an allergy. Too many people round me – it's the same. As for attacking guys who're trained, frustrated – those night-sticks – they hit out.'

'I understand all that,' Silke says. 'But if you hate crowds and burning stuff – you're not real *casseurs*. What's left is hammers and anarchy. We're all into that. Especially hammers,' and she nudges me – a little joke, like movies no one else has seen.

She keeps the Sarmatians to herself – Odo and Beatrice are smart, more intelligent than us, but I don't see them into Medes or Gargars, ancient peoples who're immortalised.....

Beatrice is 'long' – she goes to sit with Odo as he drives. He drives like the giraffes run – never mind the distances, and here it's flat as the Ukraine, all cement roads, little cities on the hill, like in the paintings of a paradise.

'Windows,' Beatrice says. 'When they were plate, a smash, and they could take an arm off quick as wink. Now, there's just a white star left. A new galaxy, perhaps. The window doesn't break – just a starburst, on the way to start or finish. You don't get in, besides, it isn't done to steal – and anyway, you can't.'

'I'll sell one of the birds,' I say.

'Beautiful,' says the guy, 'Fantastic. I wouldn't sell if it were me.'

'There's more,' I say, but he is right. He takes a hammer: tap tap tap.

'White metal,' he says. 'Copper on the wings. And life! See them, cockyollies, how they beak each other!'

## ANOTHER HEIST

Beatrice, a 'long', puts her arm around her 'short', Odo. We move away, the street is empty, and they take two long ice-picks from the Dodge.

'Trotsky's Orphans,' Silke says, but no, it doesn't fit.

They hammer on the armoured glass. Like miners at a face, alternating blows. Thunk thunk thunk. Then they walk away, quite slow, no one comes out. They don't look back at us, drive off, quite slow.

My old man's motor, and his story, go off down the road.

The window's patterned with white stars – nothing has penetrated. The upper constellations – must be Beatrice's – 'The giraffe,' says Silke. 'And the bear.'

Lower down, there's Odo's: Orion. Then an expanse – the White Sea, or maybe it's another universe, the milky udders, and as a parting shot – that really is a 'Parthian shot', but people make mistakes when there's no bows or cavalry – he leaves a Venus, solitary.

It looks like ice, the glass – like someone's tried to make a fishing-hole.... 'There's no one there,' says Silke. 'Just a machine, no legs, no toes, it can't leap out, protest. People – they don't live here now – those houses are machine sheds where the messages depart, arrive.'

'It's called a hub,' I say. 'It's real, the messages, all that. We're not; we don't intrude. The hammering – it's just symbolic.'

'Banal but true! Odo and Beatrice, they knew we had no cash,' says Silke, 'but they showed us what they did. There isn't any more to them. Too bad – your story, that big Dodge – away, away. Where do we go now?'

'We slept with them, they were so smart and sure,' I say. 'And what is done? What remains? Does Beatrice leave a trace on me?'

*

Down there, there's tall buildings, a labyrinth for birds. 'Those cities are in mafia hands,' says Silke. 'Guys who don't believe in souls, in spirits – not like you do, my friend. There, people disappear – they have no further value. It's true – the state makes people disappear as well – and some in uniform are even paid to march to nullity. But there's a trace ... people mean money for the state, it needs to track them, but the mafia wants the disappearance full, complete. No trace, no questions ... not your place, Gyorgy, not your place.'

'We all disappear,' I say wearily. 'The time and the procedures change.... We cling to tails – the tails of creatures that preceded us – but they are Cheshire cats, only the tail is left....'

## TIME FOR A DRINK

The bar is glass, under and above, the spirits at one with their containers ... '*Le cortège passait, et j'y cherchais mon corps,*' Silke whispers. A woman we know soon as Lauren stares at us, her eyes two stoppers, fishy pearls ... what's within? Blue Bols or vodka? The barman's anxious, hops from long clinging toe to toe, a grey parrot waiting for the gesture that will rouse his squawk....

'I told you,' Silke whispers. 'The hands of the mafia, dead hands, Orlac's hands, hacked off a murderer but full of brains....' We laugh.

'Well done,' says Lauren, standing in her gown, a negligée of sorts, with prissy cuffs and neck, a long boa's body digesting us and other spirits in its rubbery gut.... 'You're stoics. Lapsed, of course, like all of us – the real thing smiles. Laughter is a step over to the other shore....'

'That's where we're swimming to,' I say. 'You hope for currents with a will – the Hellespont, the trip to Hell – but lands you in a grassy garden, nothing more ... where you've always wanted....'

She ignores my flummery. 'You two good folk,' she says, 'are what I'm looking for. I need a ride....'

'Oh we're not centaurs,' Silke says, laughing quite loud. 'We've been unhorsed as well!'

\*

Silke and I – we're both attracted, strongly, to Lauren. Neither of us wants that. Desire is always there, a well, quite often poisoned, full of treacle or of horse-hoof glue, it clings, it makes you gripe, you drink it down, it's bane and then.... It's gone!

'What a parade!' says Silke, thinking like I do.

Lauren joins us. 'Let's think how,' she says, dropping to whispers. 'We leave this glass. We look and all around there's us. We're trapped! We'll drink, and maybe that's release – when we can't see ourselves ... when we don't reflect, when we're poured out.... Oh,' and she laughs, 'It's clear – how it's banal! That is no cure – or else we'd all be blind by choice. Not seeing – it's illusion.'

'You must come from mafia town,' says Silke, lightly as she can.

'Oh, I'd love to be a citizen,' says Lauren, stretching out. 'Where there's mafia – citizen's a thing you cannot be, it hasn't reached that point. Or – maybe it's gone far beyond. The future – an untrustworthy beast, you know.'

She doesn't laugh there, as you mostly do. 'Order: you need that, I suppose,' she says. 'The state, the mafia. A stone head, both faces, looking out beyond each other.... I'd love to be a fisherman – one of Rousseau's, where you gather on the shore and vote and fish for

golden rings. The general will: – I think all fishers know already
what that is, without town meetings.'

There, she laughs: 'I'd not want that for long, of course – I want
to go down caves, write operas, eat leaves and dance in jungles –
no feathers in my hair, of course.... None of this for long – it all
becomes conclusive it you let it, woe to you, to anyone, who turns
it to a trade, life sentences....'

I drop into her mood. 'I thought of the White Sea,' I say. 'No
people – just the climate. Then – my real home is the steppe –
westward, there's enlightenment, eastward....'

'Yes!' says Lauren. 'That is me. Eastward. China! That's where
destiny has space, there's turbulence – those stages of development,
they last a year, a month, a twinkling .... Yes! There – it moves!
You don't get burnt for seeing or for saying that: – it has to be!'

The talk is fine, but false – the truck that ought to take us onward
– doesn't appear.

Lauren wilts, she languishes, she even primps a little in the
glass.

'Goats!' she says. 'The abattoir – there must be one. Just a
tractor-trailer full of goats ... to pick us up.'


## HELP! GET US OUT!

We wait for days. We drink. It costs me birds – two larks. Set up
and perched in their new glass cage, they don't know which way's
up ... no dusk, no dawn. No ceiling and no sky.

At last – a truck ... I'm sat next to Lauren, while Silke has passed
out ... we're fairly drunk.

'Your centrality, Lauren,' I say, nervous she's around me,
tempting as a cliff-edge. 'I don't see it. You're diffuse, the figure in
your carpet swarms like tadpoles, you're at once in flight, at rest....'

'Clever boy!' she says. 'There must be profusion, or there's
nothing that survives. You must do everything, there is no victory
and no defeat, no service and no legacies....'

'You're mafia, Lauren,' I tell her.

'No,' she says, 'but – I'm attracted to your Silke. You're prickly,
she is smooth.'

'I don't have anyone,' I say. 'It's good.'

The desert runs and runs. We have to stop quite frequently to
urinate. I miss the steppe, the frozen sea. The goats – each shouts,

each halt they think's the final one, they have no god – they've been the minor deities themselves, or attributes at least. It's done no good at all.

*

'These are the gates,' the driver says, speaking for the first time. 'You goats,' he says to us. 'Do you go on? Or is this your destination? Not everyone can choose....'

'You do it all yourself?' Silke asks him. 'You must know the rope....'

'Often they do it by themselves,' he says. 'It's in the blood by now. Come,' he turns to me, 'if you've decided, today – no further. Hop down, you tipsy three. Which is my bird?'

'The blackbird. See, it's silvery, but tarnished – you need rub him up,' I say.

I'm down to finches now.

The truck goes on, passes through the gates.

*

'Now,' Lauren says, 'forget the goats. The revolution that you venerate – won't be of use to them, or you. We had one, long ago – it's mafia now. That's me, it's us, the way things are – what isn't that, is me. Maybe that's what you're looking for, Gyorgy – us tortoises without our shells....'

'That's heavy stuff, Lauren,' I say. 'I'm fortunate. Between what I'd want, and what there is to get – there is no link.'

'Exactly, Gyorgy,' Silke says, holding my arm and pulling me away from Lauren. 'You're a goat, like all of us, Lauren is mafia, a goat, or both: there's nothing to be done, nothing to expect from her....'

'My, Gyorgy, you're so hot,' says Lauren, twisting from Silke, holding me. 'Sex? With me? Desire – or wanting just to calm it down? It leaves me – well, a bit indifferent. The mess, the panting, climax, anti-climax – do you really think....? You'd like to see me nude, without my shell, and peek at everyone back where I left: the hierarchy, the oaths ... to keep us all in line by guys like me, who hate to keep a line?'

'Of course, Lauren,' I say. 'It might be just the booze. Intelligence. That is the devil – when it comes to rule, called mafia or the state – we're all like you. Two-faced. Fearing superiors, trampling the unfortunate.... And – whatever side we're on, we run.... And are they after us?'

'You see?' says Silke. 'Lauren's dangerous. An agent or a target, both....'

'We can't leave her here,' I say.

Beyond the gates – the abattoir. Give her a finch, leave her to bargain an escape?

'Don't think of it!' says Silke. 'Those two drab chicks – they are our capital. Let's find a truck that takes us somewhere else. As for Lauren – boss on the run? On the run from bosses? Just on the run and looking for a ride?'

'It's not what I should be thinking of,' I say.

Lauren says, 'The problem is the males. Those goats ... all billies. Nature doesn't take the hint – it churns them out....'

In her way, Lauren's irresistible. 'The answers are starting to come in,' I say. 'Nature, rights: when the new state came in, that's when the questions started. It could do so much, the state, the spirit – but it screwed up. Now, we're waiting for the big new state, the spirit of the age, all time – but maybe there's an end to everything instead.'

'It doesn't seem to bother you,' says Silke. She seems irritated, but she doesn't stamp her foot, 'The state we're in.'

'You're right, Silke,' I say. 'I'm vulnerable. I've made my living from the weak – now, if they don't make theirs from me, there's nothing left....'

'That's new!' says Lauren, resting her chin on my shoulder from behind. 'Living. I don't see signs of living here.'

'I mean,' I say, 'what comes about or stays concealed, in its pod, its prophecy – it's insignificant to me. Thinking is something you can only do alone … in your own time.'

'I think!' says Silke. 'A truck. Without the living stacked inside like goats. Going where we desire.'

'Aha!' says Lauren. 'Back to desire! It's like the furnace packed with pots – one flaw, one bubble of air, a sigh – the lot explodes. Yes, that's desire – you keep the heat, while all the plates and ewers bake. Those are what's useful, have a price....'

'You're wrong, Lauren,' says Silke, sounding mean. 'Your simile is crap. Desire produces nothing valuable any time. It's baked alaska, coldness within....'

\*

We move – gas station, onward to the next. 'I miss carpets,' Lauren says. 'That's the only thing these places lack.'

'How do we get rid of her?' I ask Silke: Lauren hears, she says, 'I don't bring catastrophe, though often it may serve.'

We look over the far-off mafia cities. 'I heard about the fire,' says Lauren. 'It doesn't come. It was designed to torch those sheds – the big machines, the engines that would shoot us up, the pioneers, survivors, persecuted, military ... cowards and heroes – fingers in the universe, tickling the big and little gods, without respect or aim. The whoosh terrains that we could use to live on, build our dumps.... Instead – look, Silke! A great wall of glass, riding forward, on to cover everything. A wave! Wave back, Gyorgy! Who knows who now, where from – you can't blame militias, nor your hairspray....'

Maybe that's true. You can't blame anyone – the water is cathedral glass, rose, Prussian blue, and jonquil yellow, umber, magenta – the flat's submerged, some tufts stand up – some prophets' rocks ... so, you must find your hill, stand there with your bible and your goat, inspiration, sacrifice; and nothing more. Disaster! Biblical.

'You're a petrel, Lauren,' Silke says, admiring, scared. 'You run before the storm, like Rameau's neice.'

'Perhaps those machines were fixed, escaped and blasted off:' says Lauren. 'They, my friends, they could foretell ... this time, the flood, we hadn't planned; next time.... The cunning ones, they will survive.'

'And save us all?' asks Silke, quite amazed.

Lauren smiles, and starts to sing a lilt – it isn't Kaddish, but it's reminiscent.

'It's true,' I say. 'It's all foretold, the plagues: and more, all multiplied, reversed and voided: flood and drought, the locusts and the dearth of flying things.... Disasters come from sins, omissions.... You seem an innocent, Lauren, and now we're in a place where all the sins await catastrophes we've earned ... after the exterminations and the gluts, there'll come the greed, the lust and anger, envy and mistrust.... The water came – we weren't prepared. Are we prepared for tempests ethical...? Lauren, be honest. Do you escape, or do you bring disaster on, it follows you, your friends, they execute....'

'I know,' says Lauren. 'You suspect me. I know the answers. I found out – where I worked, the people are not clean.'

'Punishment is one thing,' I say, 'crime another, Lauren. If the plagues are punishment, it doesn't stop the crime recurring – new crimes, new punishments, and on and on. This time, no big god to blame or bow to – just us ... sin, burn and sin again....'

'Oh, I know,' says Lauren, hugging me. 'I've friends. Friends are eternal, as you know. Mine can fix things – it is just that science, inquisitive and not respectful – is bad for business. Or, let me say, science is a business, and it's one my friends associate with rocketing, thumbs in moon's eye ... not at all their fief, their cup of tea....'

'You see?' says Silke. 'Stasis. Inconclusiveness – except, things are concluding all the time.'

'You're wrong, Gyorgy,' Lauren joins in. 'You want morals, stories, things joined up. Carpets. What you need instead is friends: forget the morals and the tales. Watch out, watch everybody. If the Murano wall comes up the street – don't close your door and hug your cat. Run, Gyorgy, run!'

'She's right,' says Silke. 'The mafia's not in the story, not been invented. The book says it was the raven found its tree, on an island green and fruitful, for the Crusoe and his crew.... Another, rocky islet, sandy, gritty, not so green ... that was for Friday....'

'That's the story, as it's told,' says Lauren, nodding wildly: 'Surely, Gyorgy – that's worth my finch?'

'I've just the one left,' I say. 'The other finch.'

'It's us, Gyorgy,' Silke says. 'That story. Our identity. Culture. Thick: thick as thieves and saints. To be preserved. Unique and irreplaceable.'

'You're odd, you two,' says Lauren. 'Every band, a gang, a couple – has character, it comes from living together, like a village. It's all rubbish. You can't trust! There's tattle, jealousy. What matters, is having friends, no matter what they do or think, that's not your business. It's loyalty. You don't get that in a country, or a street. Seek friends.'

'That's luxury,' I say. 'Here, people can't live. They work, they can't pay for stuff. Work or not work – it's the same; and you can't move, the others don't let you come. We're the lucky ones, Lauren – we don't have much, but we can move around, we don't run, not like you, we don't have friends like yours who burn the science down, its sheds. Those black holes – they're heavy with new stars.

You're afraid of what comes out of them, the heavens pregnant with light, crowding out the galaxies, making gulfs in oceans, killing animals indiscriminately.... Imagine. Lauren, you're a creature that walked round – a meerkat, say, and then new matter's born, you're underwater, the pressure too great to have you sing in it, you're not a whale, you're just a sombre fish. Opening and shutting, silent, in a hole....'

\*

It's true – there's one finch left, and no one to give it to, or sell.

\*

Come to that – the land down there that went beneath the swelling glass, the water, it's all there is.

There's not much choice.

The three of us – we start to walk down, where the water's mostly disappeared.

## THE LAST BIRD

'Now,' Lauren says: 'Remember. I left. There's nothing where I found you two but goats and trucks – so, I return. That way – I'm in credit.

'Here – we're all mafia. There are tops – no top. Don't fuss and don't denounce. Look, live. Help clear the mess the flood has left. The wave – was not to clean, it was to drown. It even drowned a mafia. Mafias – are there to trade and earn. They kill judiciously – they're not made for that, battles and massacres, they want loyalty, legitimacy, and trade. Watch and learn. Hands in pockets, pants buttoned up.'

The people – every kind. Every origin, and every size. Quite charming. Some of them,

'And some are rough,' I say.

'Gruff,' says Lauren.

There's lots to be cleared up. It doesn't make for peace, there's skirmishes.

'One day,' says Lauren, 'maybe all these bands will get together, set up an authority. A frail state. The chiefs'll have their pictures painted, really well, and set them on the walls where these new guys have their desks ... and there'll be unknown ones who briefly come to wear the crowns.... Rather than weak state – beneath, it's an accord.'

'The holy Romans?' Silke asks – she's fascinated by pageantry, she watches all of it, when there's tv....

'Yes, something like,' says Lauren, and she kisses her. 'You're a bright girl,' she says, and kisses her again.

'Silke,' I say, 'you're like me – a weakness for the stories. Lauren's the lucky one – she gets to make them up.'

'We're back before the start, this way,' says Silke. 'Over and over, all begins. I'm amused, but for you: avoid return. It is the end.'

'I'm here,' I say, feeling I could cry. 'What do I do?'

'You could paint the pictures of the great,' says Silke. 'Steppe art was not what you could do. If painting's hard – try photographs.'

'We have to live here, Silke,' I say, remembering too late, I owe her nothing, I'm nothing to her either. 'I suppose it's improvise again. Live with the times. There's no alternative.'

'We're all monkeys,' Silke says. 'We love a story or a pic that speaks to all of us, the species, that we recognise, that fires us up. Add a patch of fur, a warble, or a gift, a condescension – big snarls at little, little charms the big. You seize their attention, give them something new – a bright thing, something that tinkles, a puzzle most can solve, a treasure like a dead man's wallet dropped in a ditch.... Art, Gyorgy: art that brings in food. Remember cookery – a base of homespun, then there's a pinch or two – some cumin of originality, a capsicum of dare, a tabasco splash of rude.... Everyone likes pizza; if they don't, it's couscous.'

'I think it must mean photographs,' I say. 'For me. And frames.'

## SNAPPING

They're all anonymous – the chieftains. My Monas. Some bring frames, some bring animals as pay. I've tapped the fashion seam.

'The live ones,' Silke says. 'Especially the goats – they are a capital. For when we have to leave.'

These guys – if they pay in coin, it's theirs, their heads; some helmeted, some with collars military, pastoral.

One says, 'An instantaneous? A pic, a flash, a twinkling? – yet I'm here for ever in my bones – the "ever", at least, that's yours to live. This is a standing, I'm not even sat. You work in seconds, fractions of them – that's not worth a spit, a sneeze....'

'I know,' I say. 'It's art. You pay what it is worth to you. This way a picture doesn't age, and nor do you. It's you, and it's not you. You leave the studio as you are, eternal, and every step you take, you age. The pic stays like, but you are not. In the picture – you don't move, just your image is transferred.... That's you, and not you, not a part – a whole of nothing: thinner than thin air ... today, for ever. You think it's reproducible. It's not. It's quite original – here, hold today's newspaper, show that you're alive today. Tomorrow will not count ... will not appear, you could be in the hole....'

'It's not so,' says the guy. 'The photographic image has no legal personality, no substance. It can't be stolen, the subject's not involved, is not stirred in.... It isn't you – that's right! You fleet through it, sylph in a mirror, gazing in your pond. Narcissus has no portrait, Gyorgy. He's your unborn ghost, infinity of soul on silvered slippery glass, a mocking, foretelling – snapped to infinity, elastic: you elude him, and your gums recede, brain skips more grooves, blood rusts.... These pics are nobody and nothing. Illusions, Gyorgy. That's what you sell. But not to me!'

He leaves – it's quite irrelevant, he looks like all the rest, like you or me.

'A hint, dear Gyorgy.' Lauren says. 'No quips. And no philosophy.The bosses here, they have coarse tastes, quite physical sometimes.'

*

'I might stay here forever,' I say, quite glum.

'We'd see you were all right,' says Lauren, shining bright. 'Silke could figure your accounts. If it's sex – we'd see to that,' and she nudges Silke, who giggles, does a little prance.

'Your Virgil said you must wait right to the end to see yourself,' says Silke. 'And he surely didn't mean you take a picture then. Revelation is the last, Gyorgy. It doesn't have to mean anything, to serve. It's not something you put away to look at it tomorrow. That's it. Curtain. The rest, the public – they go out, to their

carriages, in the rain. You don't. You have the prize; you can't
have more.'

'Or less,' I say. They don't hear.

I'm on this path....

*

Lauren and Silke – they shack up, I'm on my own. It's good.

Lauren says, 'Remember – I warned you. You know everyone;
who are the chiefs, and those you haven't seen are rivals,
underlings. If you can't run, you'd better hide. I told you....'

'I remember none of that,' I say, appalled. 'I thought this was for
ever, I was sad but calm.'

'These guys,' says Silke, 'protect, and tax, intimidate. Just like a
state. They're organised – in bands of Magyars, Vietnamese – so, a
racist state, it isn't possible. Each marches with their own. Life's
difficult, the territories – they're not fixed, ah! those boundaries....
But all the same, you know the rules; pay up and be polite. Do that,
you're safe, and what of yours is left, you keep.

'Now – you've all the mugshots in a file.... You hold their cards,
Gyorgy, the bosses have just realised.... You hold the spirit of the
place, its portraits, genealogies, who pays, who has emporia, who
coins in gold and who in tin – you've all the bricks to build a state!'

She laughs. I'm downcast, apprehensive too.

'The wave ... Silke?' I ask. 'Whose idea? And state-building –
really not at all my thing....'

'Think of the wave,' says Lauren, 'as the wave of change – a
cleansing catastrophe that brings in mud, a mulch that helps us
change the scene.... Nothing to do with us poor beasts ... a motor of
transition, stage machine ... nature transforming, in its time,
primitive accumulation to finance capital, military feudalism to an
agricultural form and back again.... Militarised nomads, sweeping
everything away, the skulls piled up like empty coconuts.'

'That's it?' I ask. 'It seems old hat ... quadrille of forces, nature
on the march.'

'Take it as I say,' says Lauren. 'Entirely natural, unpredicted and
unpredictable. Think! Imagine getting rid of dinosaurs. They were
too successful – all that time they lingered on, invincible, illiterate,
tone-deaf. Something – a thunderbolt – had to hook them off the
stage.'

'I'm not at all convinced,' I say. 'The wave was dense here, obscuring everything. After – it was much the same.'

'That's your perception, Gyorgy,' Silke says. 'Now, think of your project. Think of avoiding retribution.'

'Should I leave, Silke?' I ask. 'I know all existence must depend on banks, they say, but there's other things as well....'

'You leave as you came in, Gyorgy,' Lauren says. 'With nothing. Emigration means expropriation – sometimes worse.'

My last finch – I put him down my pant front, and sew him in – no one will look there, I think.

'Of course, I'll follow you,' says Silke, 'but I've to settle things with Lauren first....' She doesn't seem so keen.

'Lauren,' I ask, 'when we found you, why had you left here?'

'Oh,' she says, and waves her hands, 'I read the Book. It reveals. Disasters push the show along. They happen – weather, chemistry and finding gold – volcanoes, geysers, everything you see – it's natural. Do not touch, or get too close. Dialectics, Gyorgy, read it, the book: Dialectics of Nature. Forget the human stuff: – it's laws and impulses that pull the cart, determine universes, skies and light.... We read old Engels in the schools – it's nature, matter, that drives everything. Forget old Marx – he's not permitted here. He says it's up to us: it isn't so. Electricity, the genes – they are the continuity, and change. You follow them, the forces, knowing the science. Forget class and exploitation.

'The bosses would have torched the science lab – the whitecoats wanted to have spying eyes, surveillance, focussing on us.... But – then you came along, and snapped the chieftains: art! Now, you must pay, dear Gyorgy. Remember: Nature – does it all. You don't need know the science – that is not the mechanism, the impetus. It's nothing but descriptions....'

She talks on.

It's not believable.

I say, 'And the portraits, Silke: they are poison, so it seems. What'll become of them? And me?'

'Oh,' Silke says, 'they are your fame. We'll maybe wall them up – or – there's the flames. Don Juan, the *Flammen*. Wages of sins, my dear. Or else, it's waves again, more murky glass, and we are flies, stuck in the jelly, ambery, Lalique all over....'

And we contemplate. There's portents everywhere.

But – what's Lauren's story? – 'Hurry, hurry along,' she says, pushing me towards the slope that you must climb to leave when guys have stripped you, taken what they want or must. I hold tightly to my pants, my finch. They let me pass....

## LAUREN, SILKE: LOVE AND THE HISTORY OF THE WORLD

I think of Lauren's judgement. 'You're timid, Gyorgy. It doesn't need to mean you're cowardly – but maybe, being so, you'll not reach your end ... the end you want.'

'Perhaps I don't want an end,' I said. 'The Master, Engels – our Angel – he saw what holds our society together here – it's force. 'What is the cause of force?' he asks. And what's the answer? I forget, Lauren: enough that it is so.

'The peasant war. We peasants fought – the princes won. Three centuries pass, we fight again – who wins this time? *Big* princes, Lauren: nations, states.... Where is my place in that? ... me, timid or a warrior?'

'You're not a peasant, Gyorgy,' Silke said. 'You have no land, you're not a landless peasant or a proletarian – you've nothing, except Lauren's idea: your art. The snap. That made a problem that you didn't mean, and can't resolve. You're not a revolutionary, nor a committed artist who overturns a system with a brush.... You're an accidentalist, an opportunist, chancer, who's on the run....'

'It's not a problem, Silke,' I had said. 'If I run fast enough.'

*

Then Lauren said: 'I've told you everything you need to know about myself. Reflect. Then think of what I've done to you, what you're left with after meeting me, and taking me back here.'

* * *

Giacomina! Fame in sight! Is this the apotheosis of my old man, what went before, so I could have a life, original? My photos – real people. That's my fame!

*

I'm desperate.

Giacomina!

'I recognise you!' she says. 'Come in! This is a refuge – famous people come to rest, no names, invisible; the cops – maybe they lie in wait behind the hedge, they don't come in.'

I see a low-rise open court, in nowhere, desert motel, without the cars.... 'Oh, no motors here,' she says. 'When they are rested, the famous ones are fetched. And – no, this mansion isn't mine. But I'm the good. The *bonne*. I make you comfortable, but of course, no sex, it wouldn't end if once I offered up....' She eyes my finch.

'No, no,' I say. 'It's prickly, rebarbative. It's worth a night or two, the bill. It screeches, chirps – no song ... spiky metal, nothing intimate, but lives forever.... Nothing intimate....'

'Oh,' Giacomina says. 'There is no fee. You're famous – that's enough. And I am good.'

'My fame – my work,' I say, 'No one can see it, it was all the bosses pictured, snapped.... It all has disappeared... '

'That fame is quite the best,' she says. 'The artists with apprentices, writers who could pay their hacks to sit and twirl imaginations ... you never know who had done what, who chiselled and who forged....'

'I know all that,' I say. 'I did steppe art – now, that's all beneath the ground, in shady graves – the permafrost, so long as it holds firm....'

'All that is better, better, best,' she says, and frolics in delight. She looks like Odette, or Violanta, with a touch of Silke, though it is Lauren in my mind, her fame, her trade – uncertain and uncertified.'

'Giacomina, you're a beauty, moreover, you are good,' I say. 'There must be some heavy guy behind you, throwing out the personages unpresentable or stuck – those cut off, no motor, no legitimacy....'

'No, no,' she says. 'I'm good, it's true. The *bonne*. That needs no help, no crutch. I'm better than your dreams – you don't wake here once you are settled in, until your majordomo or your sidekick comes and takes you back to where you fled.... You won't see anyone but me, and I smile all the time. Here, there's no power struggle and no history, no mystery, no Lauren ... only when the world ends do you get the bill....'

\*

I'm all alone. Giacomina goes in the other rooms, there's talk and laughter. With me, she's silent, but she always smiles. There's vehicles at all hours – some guys run, and some are carried, in or out. It's good: at least it isn't bad.

On the wall, it says, 'I am truth. I am God.' That's good too. I concur. I wonder if all the rooms have those words, but there's no way of finding out.

'It looks like no one comes for you,' says Giacomina. 'Don't take it bad – it's rather good, it shows you're not in need, not that I have anything to give, but we're both happy so.

'There's heath and dunes,' she says. 'Cross them as you leave. The landscape's inconclusive. No reason you would linger, and it's clear you've gotten all you can from here.'

'Everything and nothing,' I say. 'And the food's not good.'

'It's me that's good,' says Giacomina. 'I never said I'm good at cookery.'

I keep my finch, and leave during the night.

There's been no bill – I expect it will arrive in time.

*

When I reach the sea, there's a boat, flat-bottomed, waiting. I wade out, and feel my finch drop – I see it, green and silver, winking, twinkling as it floats away, already safe from me, it ducks beneath the wave.

A sailor gives me some seaboots, long and furling over, filling with saltwater, holding me down, on the deck. The nausea begins, the sailors laugh.... I make my way up the beach – it seems I'm on a little island, the boots, too heavy, I waddle like an albatross.... I leave them, and come barefoot to the grand hotel. There's no one on the desk. I have no cash. In the restaurant there's no one, and I sit at the head of the long, the only, table; wait.

'No food!' says Alceste, the waitress. 'Out of season. Nothing! No service.'

'I'll have what you are having,' I tell her. There's the smell – of pheasant stuffed with lark and served with leeks from Andaman, a purée of Drax almonds.

'It's rough stuff,' Alceste shouts, as she goes back to where there's roistering, the clash of glass and silver. Here, it's cold. The bandstand's empty, I climb up and try some riffs on slackened drums; they're damp. I pluck at the lank bass.

The squad of servants, some in tails and some in rags, swarms from the kitchen, 'music ho!' they cry, they partner up, and start to reel around. Two notes – a winding up, that is enough to start them off, like clocks run down too long, and keen to catch the moment. It's a poor show – but it earns me food, and Alceste says, 'The kitchen has the only heat: we all doss down in here – we can be bunkies, if you'd like....'

I have to work. Taming nature? A garden of the primal kind? Down go the bushes – but the birds can't roost, and so I plant and tend.

## TOO BAD – THE FINCH IS LOST. ALCESTE....

'You're useless,' says Alceste. 'Gardening means you have to wait. *You* persecute the green. Now, what are you looking for, Gyorgy, that brings you here?'

'This. Here,' I say, 'You. I don't know.'

'Do you regret anything?' she asks.

'Nothing much. I read the Proust, how it goes on, life and the people on the frieze. And the Russians – how attractive sin is, and excess, and what there is to do afterwards,' I say. 'When you think you've had enough.'

'Suppose I told you, all the meat you eat is boiled up managers?' she asks.

'I know,' I say. 'I'm pleased it isn't field animals. The males are sweet and stringy, the females acid, fat. We pretend we are not used to it – but it's flesh you crave for, we all do, till our species' time comes to an end.'

I suppose I regret the Sarmatians: now, I can't ride, don't have a family, speech is not much use to me.

'Life here is limited,' says Alceste, jollying up. 'But it's good. No strangers, no end, you see another beach, could be another island just like this one. Sailors, on the move. No slavers.'

'Have you thought,' I ask. 'What happens when supplies run out?'

'That's brilliant!' says Alceste, with admiration. 'I suppose ... a landing craft will come for us and take us to another shore, another islet. These empty hydros abandoned – rich tourists swarm around like bees – some places they desert, and others you can't get in, full up!'

'You have fine shoulders, Alceste,' I say, managing to stroke them.

'I know,' she says. 'It's my head. Too small. Arab horses – they are the same. The proportions are got wrong. I'm made for carrying pails.'

'There's more urgent, dramatical themes, I know,' I say. 'Much more than me; that suck you in, give you an experience, not just the eyes and ears. I think, at last, that what I'm looking for, though it seems small, pared to a shaving ... it cannot be attained. Or else it's trivial, ephemeral. Not the truth: – that's all around.... I sought – remember – the quiddity of me myself that might resemble what a horde of sardines has: – its sardinity....'

'Oh, they're there to be put in cans,' says Alceste, moving away. 'I know what you mean. It's like us hoping the aeroplanes won't come, hover, then..... That the boat will dock, and the sailors be kind and point us somewhere new.'

'We're birds, Alceste,' I say. 'Sex: if we have sex, we don't need sing. Or if it's there, available, we could think of it, in silence. Food. Brought in. And us, locked up safe at night. If we fly away – we'll die. And if we stay....'

'Birds have never had anything bad happen to them,' says Alceste. 'Maybe a sly push at an egg – whoops! ... a little greedy brother, sister, over the edge, and that'll teach!.... But – it's nature. Love and peace – they're not in nature, Gyorgy, don't be deluded. We're a mystery. Why are we here, in this dirty cage, untouchable and disagreeable, a company for anyone who passes through?'

'That's a story, Alceste,' I say. 'We make them up all the time. It's chance. That's what we run from, murder for, are pardoned and – the rope breaks, like it did for me .... I lost my finch, my capital – out through my pant leg. If I'd had it, I could have paid the sailors – a long long voyage.'

'Go sit on the shore,' says Alceste, not unkindly. 'Wait and watch, your bird might be washed up on the sand.'

\*

It's cold and windy. No boat comes. Alceste sits beside me.

'Don't think of leaving with me,' I say.

'Oh,' she says, 'I wouldn't. I'm not nurture. I'm just waiting with you. That's all any of us can, us here. They say one day there'll be no more like us, we who don't know where our food comes from. What do you think, Gyorgy? Do you care?'

'I've my troubles, Alceste,' I say. 'Vendetta, mostly; my avengers. Then there's what's to be done, done next.'

'It's imponderable, Gyorgy,' says Alceste. 'Forget it.'

'You guys,' I say. 'You've nothing. But you're not the regular poor that they say do still exist – slums, poor farmers, victims of this and that: and yet you're here, poor, waiting for a shuffle sideways ... re-location.'

'Someone must have thought, one time, that we'd be safe,' she says. 'We are. Why are we here? It's our story, Gyorgy, just consider yours. It's like Odysseus – some guy shows up, recruiting for the Trojan war. Go down in history, he says, your duty calls – sort out your bowstrings, my old friend, or else.... Odysseus, our hero – he resists. Penelope's brand new – he wants a screw....

'There's banter, pages of the tricks and wiles exchanged, Odysseus wins the joust ... but then, anyway! he's off! It's his story, full of monsters, syrens, sailor pigs and polyphemes.... Quite unbelievable, until it's you who bleed out on the sand, stuck like a porker....

'Be wise, Gyorgy. Tell the guy, the spy – you've a condition, can't travel.

'Your old man, the mentor – him with the morals and the quest – forget him. He's a chancer, a romancer. Maybe he runs camel trains and needs to spin a song, a tale, to help them jog along. Don't try to trick him, or beguile or play the pacifist. Waste him. Find a space among the rocks and stuff him in: anonymous and shipwrecked. Go back to your house, amuse the kids....'

'We have to have a story, Alceste, or there'd not be metaphor and simile,' I say. 'Our tongues wag in four-four time. There's no way out. It's story, yes, of course: it will end when there's a climax big enough for someone to remember who we were....'

'Still with the "someone", Gyorgy!' Alceste says, and laughs. 'Farewell, remember me; oh remember me....' she sings, a thin shaky voice....

## THE BOAT: BENEATH THE WAVES

She's gone. And here's a landing craft, a guy with tickets standing by a capstan....

I tell him, 'I can't pay. I'll work the pumps and load the guns....
Skin the dolphins, beat the slaves....'

'Ah,' the sailor says. 'The easy jobs. Everyone wants those....'

Sailors. Some have beards and some have breasts.

'We sailed the Caspian,' says the mate. 'Ayatollahs? What a
joke. Dress codes – oh, what a laugh – you should have seen us
when we docked.... Each has a code, and some have more than
one.... The Revolutionary Guards? Sellers of contraband cigars....
We took the ship and walked. Carried it shoulder high. The Black
Sea – it's indigo, not black, but all depends on clouds – it has no
colour of its own – then through the fiefdoms, little princelings,
chancellors – all pirates of the lowest sort – just stevedores who've
walked the plank and stolen it.... And so – we reached the big one,
the enormous ocean, that one day will wake to hunger, swallow all
the rest, the stones, the sandy lands ... abandoning, at the last – an
ark on Everest, the only rock exposed, impaled ... the drunken boat
with drunken Noahs, the memorial of all you landsmen, scruffing
round your shrubs like dogs, gobbling your nuts and grains ...
eating berries like a starving bear....'

'Well, Armance, here I am,' I say. 'I have no destination, no
credentials. On the shore, I leave dear Alceste who you say will
slide beneath the waves. Her wail remains – "remember me,
Gyorgy; o remember me ...."'

It's so plaintive, that I weep.

'That's right!' says Armance. 'Salt in the salt. You're clearly
one of us. Your *semblables,* the earthmen, heated up the sea until
the countries slid like chocolate puddings 'neath the swell.... Their
souls....'

'Turned into albatross,' I say. 'A wheel, a scatter of
abstruseness, clangour of the avantgarde, of poets, gyring genius –
no soil to walk on, forever in the air, their wings some broken
metres long....'

Armance, the mate, he leads me down to meet the crew, still
chuckling at my shantying – 'Olà,' he shouts. 'Here's one of us ...'
and I see seamen, like this were a submarine, it stretches far and
narrow, a bunkhouse, longjohns out to dry, guys bartering and
wagering, and round the hull I see collections, malappropriated for
sure – there's shrunken heads and pipes of Pan, veranda posts,
silver katars, bronze dings – 'We go everywhere,' says Armance.
'Till there's no one left a-swim, and nothing saved except what's
tacked up on our boiler-plate....'

It's almost credible – I say, 'The island that I left, Armance ... was not submerged....'

'Oh no,' he says. 'It floats. Your Alceste – she is safe. She'll drift.'

'This boat,' I say. 'It looked so small – inside, it's like a whale. The belly of a whale.'

*

The guys are roused! I see them better – rough types in shapkas, girls who could be flappers, wearing granny's clothes – skirts dirty round the hem, cloche hats, or maybe they're caps pulled out of shape on hard round heads – 'The brine, the spume....' says Armance. 'It gives us life!' – pushing me through lines of laughing guys – 'hoo hoo hoo' they go.

All's jolly. 'The worst has come,' says Armance. 'It's over, we've come through, now, we don't need try to do anything. Trying has always been the worst – no one else does, no one would say the wolf tries, or the kiwi bird.... And you, Gyorgy, are you still in love? That's something not for trying willy-nilly....'

'Yes,' I say. 'With some of them, the women, but not all. I was closer to the men, but you don't call that love....'

'Call it anything you like,' says Armance. 'No one's listening, and if they are, it's not philosophy nor culture of the most expensive sort. Your words – is handfuls of runny treacle, don't try to grasp it, and don't believe them when they say all cultures don't belong to you – everything is yours, Gyorgy, and mine, and all the crew's.'

*

'It's a relief,' the lady says.

I'm sure she's from Iraq, but there's a silver label round her neck. 'Sherry' it says.

'You have to dodge the bombs, and then you dodge the camps,' she says. 'There's cowboys, and no cows, and Indians and infidels.... Praise, thanks, be – it's over now, and for the fuckers who brought it on and sold it in their newspapers – I hope it's over too, but where I needn't see them, bones beneath the waves....'

'Oh, that's it exactly, Sherry,' I tell her. 'But – forget the hosts of dead. I walked away from conflict when I could. In Ukraine, we turned our tail ... a noble gesture, we felt they'd troubles of their own....'

'Blame without punishment, injustice without justice – it's a farce,' she says. 'I hope the guilty suffered plenty and – now it's over, over for us all.'

\*

'Right!' shouts Armance. 'Remembrance day is done. Time to get up steam – onward, onwards, my fine lads and lasses, all power to the engines! Heed my knout!'

The motor? I've asked myself, and there they are. This is a huge pedalo. The guys leap in the saddle, feet in stirrups, slow, slow the wheels turn over, and we move!

'Armance,' I ask. 'The eats ...?'

'We are a combine harvester,' he says, proudly. 'The paddles turn up floating stuff – krill and cucumbers, puff and clown – a dish for Neptune ...'

I'm not a gourmet – fish is fish, and all the rest is what fish eat. I take a bowl of stuff that's swimming round to Sherry – 'Chérie,' I say. 'You choose ....'

She dips a long thin arm, deep, deep into the broth. I guess she's suffered hunger, and down she bolts a wriggling thing. Her other arm – it holds my hand, so tight, it leaves a ring of redness when I drag it off. 'Peace!' she says. 'The deep. Eat and be eaten....'

'It starts so,' says Armance. 'You find yourself adapting to the elements. There's salamanders in the fire, and fireflies in the air, and dragonflies in steamy caves – down here we come to seek a place in nature.... Up above – we've suffered, toiling up and down, there's hills and valleys; here – it's level, even-stevens all your life. You find your depth, and, just like on the earth, you dodge the big guys who change their register, frequent the heights, the depths, the shark who swims with seals and kings – then dives among the lowly sort, catches crabs, joins swordfish gangs....' He laughs. 'Of course – it's just my joke, a cod....'

He laughs again, as if it never ends – the jest down here is infinite, I fear, and through the portholes I see bones – forests of them, human struts, stacked up like cuttlefish....

'Where does this end?' I ask.

'Oh,' Armance says. 'We breed. This vessel is leviathan. Until we rust, we're sovereign of the seas. There's no way out. The law is simple, but it's law, forever, unchallengeable: natural law.'

'It's abolutely not my thing,' I say. 'This is infinity. The world has ended, but down here, it just goes on. In time, these sailors will grow gills and breathe beneath the waves. And then....'

'Yes,' says Armance. 'One day, the globe'll be dried out, the sun will rage, some creature feeling curious will lie and pant upon a shore – and off we'll go again!'

*

I feel a pressure, and I quake: is it epiphany? Or panic?

'Help, Armance,' I shout. 'I must get off.'

'There's nothing to get *on*,' he says. 'You might say – therefore, there's no where to get off.'

'Exactly so!' I say. 'That's why I'm terrified. I hate the sea, Armance. It's useless if you're not a fish, a sponge, a star. A squid.'

'Leviathan is all those things,' says Armance. 'You might say – 'the state, the sovereign'. I serve. It is the source, the truth. It's God. Whoever's a reflection of the single God – is God. That's me. It could be you, if you would just submit, use logic, be less arrogant....'

'I know,' I say. 'I'm not a humanist, I don't believe in me as representative of God. I cringe, I crawl, I prepare all life for the one day when I shall die and all of this, this puffery, is vain, my thoughts, imagination – are no more, it disappears, *all* disappears, Armance. There's nothing left, the sovereign, the god you call it – is no more. Belief in It is empty, humming, buzzing in the breeze, an acufene of vanities.... The certainty of death – that is our anchor, all else, all belief – it stems from that. One day, all disappears and so – the pictures that the mind projects – those disappear as well.'

'This is ... heavy stuff, my friend,' says Armance. 'We should somehow send you up....'

'You mean,' I say, 'send up a bird. To look for land.'

'There's Alceste's island, with those liveried pigs,' he says, 'Alceste's a siren who's bewitched you more than most.'

'Crap, Armance,' I say. 'There's a resort, with staff, no guests....' And as I say it, though it's true, it seems improbable. 'Yes,' I say. 'Send up a bird. But which and how?'

'Don't you have one, Gyorgy? Look carefully inside your pants, turn every pocket....' Armance says.

'No, no,' I say. 'A little bird would bring us luck. Instead, we'll have to send an albatross. A soul, a poet's soul. Don't look at me – I don't believe that stuff: one's life is poetry, it makes you weep, but it's quite false, imagination playing tricks as it plays on everything, the neurones and the ganglia, inventing universes, starships, captains courageous and not ...'

'I've lost everything,' Sherry butts in. 'Take my soul too: – have it fly off and find a bush, and we'll get rid of Gyorgy there, marooned and lonely – like I am right now....'

'No, no,' says Armance. 'That's too kind. Maybe there's some subterfuge that saves your soul, Chérie...?'

'Of course,' she says. 'There always is. I keep this pic – it's al-Hallaj, the Sufi poet, hanged, martyred, early in our fourth century. They say his poems are no good – besides, the Sufis are a current under threat, if not anathema.... His soul, his albatross, will be our guide....'

It's genius, and a sacrifice from Sherry quite unsought, unparallelled. Although – she's not a tender sort ... your name's not set in her memory, for sure.

'That bird,' I say, '... the problem is – the poet who apostrophised all poets and their poetry, stressed that the monster bird can't walk. It will not find us land....'

'Oh,' says Armance, opening a hatch, and thrusting Sherry and myself up on the deck. 'Enough! There's always details. Poetry – no exact science there. We shall make do. Maybe the bird will caw some telling way....'

Indeed. The unknown, unfound – it must appear in some unexpected shape.

'Land ho!' the lookout cries. And Armance, his whale ... they spew me out on shore. No mystery, some sand. Sherry waves, turns, and goes below.... Farewell, farewell ... and nothing more.

*

Near the end: the old man, his crimes, his women – mine. I've made a life, and lived through his – the men and women – got what they could from me. It's a success – life: no mystery – someone else will pick it up, and run, run, run....

\*

I scout around ... maybe there's a footprint over there.... A Friday? Or maybe *I* am Friday, destined to brew the glue for Crusoe, his handicrafts. He's relentlessly practising his DIY and singing hymns: my fate quite similar to death....

There's no one. It's a relief. Then – it becomes worrying.

An old man in a cave. Better, almost, than nothing. He's blotched – an old lambskin: what's left when the plump resident has been consumed. He jumps in at once, 'Ah yes,' he says, 'after the flood, we think "apocalypse". You're a smart type – I'll bet you want the secret....' I don't jump at that.

'The secret. Beware!' he says. 'You learn it when it is too late. In the moment you're no more, you see what your being means, has meant.... Until then, it's trudge and drudge....'

'Oh,' I say. 'I've been rowing in your sticky pond for years, battling the meniscus, a water-boatman with oars that bend and fray....'

He's unabashed. 'Death,' he says, 'confirms our physicality. It shows we're real, just as it sweeps away all that we've been and thought we were, and saw from every angle and from none and read in books the truth approximate, concealed, and non-existent. We were not, we are, and we are not. The middle passage, Being: all is cancelled out. The arguments, the science and philosophy, the tests, the probabilities, the books and spools ... the memories and lovers clustered round – it all depends on you, on that one brain, even as it fails and jitters. Once it's gone – no certainty of anything, just the one, the inextinguishable eye that has to register, that paints the fables, the horses, rockets, shrapnel, viruses and golden torques.... When that eye shuts, out goes the light, and leaves ... nothing whatsoever.... The secret comes to everyone – you glimpse it at the end – the pictures stop, the credits are bestowed, and then, the light is fading and you see "The End" – *Fin*. For the fish,' he jokes: '*fine*, if you're a *cafone*, a believer who thinks you'll see your mum, peering through the coffin lid. That's "fine": especially if she has a halo on her head that's made of finest gold.... Ah yes – the Sarmatians.... Got it all from Persia and from Greece. You're no different from all the rest who hope to live from copying. Look! – the only thing that matters is the detail – the metal is irrelevant. The detail – it escaped you and the rest.... Design is everything, it's style, my friend....'

He sits back on his rock. Behind him, the cave looks damp and dark. His rock – is barnacled: no connoisseur's! He proclaims –

'Go, then! Go to the other people.' He makes a gesture, broad, contemptuous. 'Some survived. Those towers are taller than Mount Everest. The hopefuls roistered up above the flood, and strove to procreate quite indiscriminately, in case they're out of luck next time, don't reproduce. That's why the bars were built high up.... Against catastrophe....'

'You know all about me,' I begin.

'Yes,' he says, 'that takes a glance – but it doesn't mean that I know you. I wager you have known lots of people, and nothing, nothing about each one.'

'Yes,' I say. 'Women especially – appreciation: was not for me from them, and not for them from me....'

'And yet,' he says, 'there was your miracle. Deliverance from the whale. In life, you frequented hotels, not the temples. It didn't bring you joy, but then … maybe you weren't made for joy.

'And yet you sought the heights, those bars high in the sky – maybe you thought the gods lived there, unseen and unsupported, in thin air.'

We laugh.

'I have a fishy gene,' I say. 'It must be that that saved me.'

\*

The towers – high up, they shine, snow-white at the peak, the windows gaze without emotion, blue and white, take it all in without a blink or tear. The lower floors are green – the algae leave their colour, but their fronds have been consumed by special insects ... brown heaps of fritillaries; now dead or moribund upon the mud. Bred for the job.

\*

Climbing the stairs – it takes a week. Then – music! Music ho! There's arms waved in the air. Chinese women dancing while in conversation. Alas, no Peking Opera ... I say aloud, 'Those generals with their pheasant plumes, trundling round the stage like floor polishers....'

No one reacts. They don't see me. All long forgotten. I despair.

The old seducer, my seer, my wise man – legitimates my solpsism. All knowable is what we see personally; know, suspect....

'*Viva!*' someone shouts. 'A survivor – toiling upwards from the deeps....'

They gather round me. I feel I ought to speak, although I haven't thought, don't want. It's for them, not me, to speak....

'It's wrong,' I say. 'My way has not been the way. Don't trust old men.'

'Then who?' the guy asks. 'Anyway, we don't trust anyone.'

'It's still wrong,' I say. 'You haven't understood.'

'Well, nor did you,' he says, a triumph in his voice.


## LYUBOV

'There's no booze,' says Lyubov. She looks like Odette, and her face is dirty – I guess the flood cut off the water. 'No pills. How does that fit with you? What do you believe in, Gyorgy?'

'I don't believe in luck. I'm a gambler. It's turning out well for me,' I say. 'You don't need believe in anything to gamble. Natural justice, perhaps? Nothing too obvious? If it's natural, you must believe it's there, but there's nothing you can do about it. I'm for causes, overturning things, but you need millions of people ... it doesn't always work.

'You have to follow fashion, every sort, in disbelief, of course. Bibles, uplifts – warriors and prophets chancing their luck. Poets too. Gamblers all. Luck doesn't come in, but the old guys were superstitious, they didn't know nothing was planned.... Spin the wheel. Trying to pull off the big one – God, President, Victor Hugo.

'I fell in the sea.... Where I was – was running out of food. Then – swallowed by a whale! – you're food! But – it seems you're not. There's bouillabaisse all bubbling, in big bowls. There was Sherry too, her soul all she had left, they'd made her sacrifice everything.

'The people here,' I tell her, '– they're dumkopfs: they wouldn't understand.'

'*You*'re hard to understand,' says Lyubov, looking fascinated and unconvinced. 'Although it's simple stuff. And – here you are, come up the stairs, and find us, we're all sweaty. Warm, safe and smelly. Is that luck?'

'I knew you were here,' I say. 'My Virgil told me. Gambling isn't about luck. It's chance and having good contacts. Unlucky people do it too ... all the time. They don't do too bad, they're the same as anybody.'

'These people,' Lyubov says, gesturing, 'are hopeless. Out of luck. You know – they're waiting to be rescued. What from? Even the Chinese here are all a-tremble – so timid! The Manchus even, can you believe? I'm sorry you toiled pointlessly up the stairs. I need you. I'm going down – I need someone to carry me if I need.

'I can do the first bit to the col, but don't want to slide all the way down on my arse.'

'And then?' I ask.

'You ask?' she laughs and says, 'you of all people! How should I know? A thousand cuts? Addiction, confessing on TV? A terror suspect? That's you. Me – it'll be different, because I have talent, I'm beautiful, but not a stereotype. I can be Russian or Ukrainian, just as I wish. Montenegrin. That's a good thing to be too.'

'This scene....' I start....

'Oh, just scaredy people without the wit to jump into a whale,' she says.

Already we are half-way down.

'I tried to make something of myself,' I say. 'The steppe. But you're always moving on, there's other peoples pressing on your back: so, westward! Once you're settled, you need imagination; and ways to sell them, your designs....'

'Well,' says Lyuobov. 'You want to be something? Be a toboggan –' and she seizes me, squats on my chest and we swoop down to the ground, out over the stir of butterflies: – there's the crabs waving the big warning hand, the frogs considering sex ... And it's dry. A plain, with blue sea-grass.

'You see?' she says. 'Wait here, and there'll be horses coming. All the way from Mongolia. Or the markets – Chach, Balkh, Merv.... One day you'll learn to ride, maybe.'

We're both breathless.

'I'm off,' she says, scrubbing her face with scruffy water from a pool. 'I'm famous already. There'll be more of it, and I won't care.... What do they know? Anyone.'

And she's off, running and skipping, sometimes resting, and then off again.

# CLEANSING

The square is full, more people piling in. We're back to rivalries. Hats versus caps, like olden times: – porkpies, fedoras, not a cap in sight here – those cheesecutters, cutting cheese in musty grottoes....

One part is fashionable, the rest is teetering, between collapse and restoration. 'Fashionable,' I say. 'Does it mean it's in a fashion, or just could be? Ephemera....'

'Don't quibble,' Masha says. 'You're a nuisance, now you've lost that job. The arts – either you create, or you're a bunion, a pain....'

'I did much, accomplished little,' I say. It's true; not good, not beautiful.

More and more, the people congregate – 'This installation we're to see,' I say....

'It's everything,' says Masha. 'Pre-birth – plastic sacks, warm water....'

'I should have worn my even-older clothes,' I say.

'There's no real contact,' Masha says, quite irritated. 'Then you lose your up and down....'

'Those,' I say, to needle her, 'are precious to me....'

There's a crescendo – we turn, there's a camper, old, besieged. There's guys who're trashing it, just beginning – puncture the tires, tear off the mirrors. The white scarred wounded shape – blind and crippled, like a fairy-tale stag, a whale.

'What's the fuss?' I ask. 'Strippers? A brothel?' There's no room ... 'Or foreigners...?'

We see a guy, black-stubbled, frantic, waving from behind the screen, terrified for sure – then someone prises out a bollard, a dissuader, they are called, and smashes at the windshield. 'Now they can't leave....' says Masha, fascinated. 'Maybe they have animals inside. You know, to make bears dance they mutilate their paws....'

More and more, into the square – some for the arts, the show, some, we imagine, for the lynching. Some indifferent or keen on both....

'Are there two crowds, Masha?' I ask in wonder. 'Some guys pause to throw a rock, then join the line we're in, us artistic types....'

'The birth is what we'll feel in death,' says Masha, pushing distracted people to one side, mastering the line, shortening the time to have the new – the old – experience....

'To me, Masha,' I say, 'it's meretricious. It voids all experience. A snook, Masha, cocked. A simplicism. Reality is different. You go round the sacred mountain: the air is thin, then there is none. You climb and climb, prostrate and creeping on, your own length thrown down every time, a tortoise with no shell ... your tennis shoes – you wear them on your hands – your flesh is shredded all the same. You die. You pray. You suffer, Masha, so as to go on. There's fleeting revelation, purity – then, there must be another time, the same quite soon. Unending challenges. This, though – this show – is sugar water. Birth fluid, bagged in plastic.'

She's not listening. I say, resigned, wishing I need not see the scene that rages round – 'so, so so – to the king's ship, invisible as thou art ... some heavenly power, guide us out of this fearful country....'

'Nonsense,' she says. 'This king's ship's a womb. You're absolutely visible. Imagine a play where everyone's invisible: you'd love it. It does not exist. It can't. It must not.'

\*

When we finish, and come out, through the press, the crowd – the van has gone.

'There!' Masha says. 'It was a show. A spectacle. Involvement, participation. If they'd wanted it to end another way – they'd have had the camper set on fire....'

'It's more complicated than it seems,' I say. 'The fire. When they design machines – they start from suppositions there'll be a sabotage: propaganda by the deed. Anger; justice manifest in flame. The design's made to make destruction difficult. It doesn't prove a thing, I know, if it should burn. The guy, though, in the driving seat: he seemed frantic, scared.'

'A show,' Masha repeats. 'Over. Forget.'

'The birth experience,' I say. 'We've seen it, passed through again. Where does it leave us?'

'Think!' says Masha, so loudly we're surrounded. 'Something rather than nothing. Do something! That's what it means. Don't submit, don't excuse. Don't see things through – truncate, my dear! Cut short! Nature's shown the way. Bang goes a beetle – another steps forward, takes its place. We can replace them all. There is no plan, and no design, no "better" and no "worse" – if we become the only living things – let it be so, and prosper. Forward! Write nothing down, do not prescribe, do not proscribe!'

I've had enough. It's true, what Masha says. It's how we act, probably it's Kant – no sentimentalism, no design – that's right.... If you're wrong – there's no more punishment than if you're right.

'Shut up, Masha,' I shout. 'Don't bully, don't hector. And find your own way home.'

I march off, furious. She looks surprised, and then she too marches off.

*

She goes – where I don't know, never went, never asked. She's come to me – we're bears, bears in the wood – sometimes we socialise, have sex, watch the babies grow. Then off alone....

All women wear a veil. Secrets, giving pleasure. Do they get pleasure in receiving, or is giving a trick, a gratifying way to receive? You wear the veil, always, like being carried in a palanquin, a sedan. You peep out.

I don't regret not seeing her. If this were a sacred city, like Qum – we'd stand in the right place, and there we'd meet: design – if we so wished. Qum is paved with gold – not solid bricks, but cartouches. If you're in need, you prise one off ... Or a magic city, Prague, Turin. The same people, acquainted – circulate, like on a carousel.

As it is.... There's sex – not much, but what is much? What you have is what is right. It may bring you trouble – crabs or notoriety – but it's right. Don't read it up in books – you do it right, for you, and everybody does it exactly as they should, in exactly the same way. Forget it.

Men – they gamble, stake their lives. It's suicidal. If you win, you get to make another bet, and if you lose – it is the end. It's not for power men play – it is for death, the excitement of the risk,

oblivion delayed. Those Germans, Nazis: – didn't heed the sum...!
In the end, you're bound to lose. Quite soon. Playing the same
number every time. And who wants territory in foreign lands, with
foreigners around that you don't understand? It seems perverse –
like guys who shoot themselves, but first kill all their innocents. A
scenario. Don't put men on the stage – they'll fuck it up. They'll
corpse.

   Secrets – women. Nasty secrets, evil whispers ... just too bad....

*

'This is an easy job,' the guy says. 'Cleaning the street – it never
starts and never ends. you're in the middle way. If you can catch an
eye – they take you in – a desk, an office. You'll regret you left the
street.... It's like composing music – you grow old, carrying your
stuff around the indifferent universe. At last – it's taken up....
There's fame, with office hours. You miss the street, the solitude –
the music of the stars, my friend – it's yours, it's distant bells
across the cold and dark ... bells, gruff, ephemeral. Tolling for
you....

   'Here – take this broom....'

   It's not my thing. It's temporary – but so is time.

*

'In the street,' says Don, the broom bestower, 'you see everything.
But remember, not everything do you need to tell.'

   'Oh,' I say, 'I'm moderate. I put what I see in pictures – you
can't tell other people about those.'

   'That's not enough,' says Don. 'Not everything is explained by
evidence before your eyes.'

   'I give what's before me every kind of benefit – of doubt, of
point of view,' I say.

   'It's not a joke,' he says. 'It isn't stereotypes, like what you think
of men and women. Remember our ancestors – those monkeys.
They didn't see or hear. Because they cannot speak, we can't
accord them rights. They feel, but they are tufo in the pyramid –
they don't communicate with us, they're merely linkage in the
chain. They can't do wrong, and so – they have no rights. Now,
that's you. When you've been taken, given your job, then you can

speak, have rights. Before – forget what you've been told, or had in other lives....

'And have no fear – we don't eat bushmeat – you monkeys don't recognise the rights of anyone at all, no duties, no sentimental compromise – sweep, sweep, eyes down....'

\*

It's been years. Don's retired. I should be a planner, promoted, in the warm. I should have found a fitting way to talk and feel, not jokey, not pretentious. I can't find the tone.

'You're Masha's friend!' the lady says, 'Like me.'

Tatiana. Fine boots, but scuffed. A hole? Or maybe a tar effect ...

'It's quite a metaphor,' she says. 'Sweeping, where she met her end ... the truck. Masha, her little boy, gone like feathers from migrating geese ... swept, bagged and burned. The trucker didn't see them. Nor did you. No one sees you. You only see my boots.

'If you're hit, they identify you by tattoos – I bet you haven't one. Look at me – beneath this fine old leather coat, penetrate, deep down, I'm naked. Do you see tattoos?'

'Oh yes,' I say. 'The mystic knots. Snakes, dolphins, palmettes, clouds.'

She doesn't tell. Certainly, she doesn't show. 'Tatiana,' I say, 'we're puzzle pieces. We're part of some big picture on a box. Some, people, irregular and lost, jigsawed into life, drop on the floor. Some end in piles of street dust – a head, a hand, a bedstead finial....'

'I'm sure the box is huge,' Tatiana says briskly. 'So big there's no picture on the top. Pieces don't need fit together.'

'The job,' I say. 'Tatiana – I've waited. It is earned. To be a planner....'

'Oh, you'd be bored,' she says. 'Bollards and chains. That's the most you'd do.'

'It starts there,' I say. 'And ends. The affair of the camper – never resolved.... A module – trouble!'

'Do you see?' asks Tatiana. 'Everything? What goes on out here?'

'Of course,' I say. 'Runs on the bank ... runners. Gangs: gangs in trainers, gangs in suits. Accidents and purposes. Coins of potin, fake fanams shaped like laurel leaves, notes inflated, knobbly with zeroes, fat as tractor tires.... No one sees me, I see everyone – all passing, from their past, intent on having futures – and I snap them, in their present – today's moment that they may not leave.... Like Masha – stuck in her existence, like you said, like celluloid fusing in the projector, until the image frizzles....'

'Oh, my dear,' says Tatiana, laughing, with tears, 'You poor idiot, Manuel. It's gone! All – over! The joyless street, a moral tale? No more! You're an exhibit. This pathway's a reconstruction, for the visitors.'

I pause. Yes, it's a surprise – I couldn't know. 'It makes no difference,' I say. 'I'll have to wait some more, that's all – my job in planning, by definition, waits....'

'Cleaning,' says Tatiana. 'With a brush? They go much deeper now. Not cleansing people, but what accumulates by chance, destiny, scuffs of nature, bits fallen off – outdated news, fag ends, the small unmourned and shredded dead. The goal is purity.... Eveything re-used or disappeared. No detritus. The shiny world – all must give lustre, Manuel.... All that is – must disappear.'

'Come, Tatiana, nothing is whole,' I say. 'Nothing is clean. The people see me – maybe I am the scavenger, the beetle omnivorous, gravedigger, vulture – like you say. But – it's just work. Approximate and grudged. That, no one sees.

'The painter grasps the flower, it's hers, fixed, transformed, and doubled up. People see the image framed, think they know the synthesis, of what it came from, what it represents and is, and how a mind has baked it all.... It isn't so, Tatiana. That's a trick, a game. It's merchandise they see. A cake, discarded. Clean streets, mean streets, stuff – dumped. It goes – to somewhere else. Next day its twin is here, guttered, fresh.

'I see before, and after ... then I add in time.

'What you see – I only guess.

'I don't tell you everything I see right now ... the candle flame: "the candle burns tall, its gules – rears up".... Tell, see: therein is the mystery.'

Masha. Over: in the middle, somewhere. A bundle in the street.

'I know you, Manuel, you are the master of what isn't there,' she says, and laughs. 'Masha was furious when you walked away – never forgave. That riot; stone-throwers, boxers thrashing with *le boxe savate*: death. The installation, birth. The start and consequences of all that trouble. So angry that she didn't watch for passing trucks....'

'As they say, Tatiana, there's no end to anything, so probably there's no start,' I say. 'Maybe the rubbish, everything that is, will be, is so ephemeral it needn't register. My philosophy of the broom makes sure it disappears. Philosophy cleans, there's one for everything....'

'You were a promising lad, Manuel,' says Tatiana. 'Your downfall has been anger. Yours, Masha's. Taking things too seriously, as though there was some permanence. Anger, rage – it has no resting place.'

'I'm sorry, Tatiana,' I say, 'but I feel nothing. I regret – yes, I regret time's spinning wheel, regret myself, regret yesterday. They go – emotion doesn't enter in. Or – it's irrelevant. I didn't know about poor Masha, the birth and death – a boy, in uniform perhaps, armed with a knife, on ketamine. I can't regret the unknown, Tatiana. '

'I could help,' she says. 'Help you feel and bury. It's not necessary. Like every trouble – best forget, and if you can't, suffer and in the end, – forget! Think of nature: the seasons – a disappointment. A mind, no brain. A brain – no mind. That's your philosophies.'

\*

Tatiana has a room to rent. 'Why are you so poor?' I ask.

'Oh, I help,' she says. 'Your job – a dead end. Mine – open country. But – you could sell my paintings ... drawing for ads. Scenery ... You know all that.'

'I was humble, Tatiana. Booking halls, setting up a lectern....' I say. 'Though entertainment is a universe....'

'Exactly,' Tatiana says. 'You know everything.'

'Your stuff, Tatiana,' I say. 'It's dreadful, though.'

'It's the expression,' she says. 'I'm an expressionist,' and she laughs.

'No one's interested, Tatiana,' I say. 'People have that all inside, all ready, when they come to you.'

'I help poor people,' she says at last. 'That's why I'm poor. I do it for logic – not love or pity. The economists say where there's greatest need, demand – there you make most money. But – it isn't so.'

'Demand and need are different, Tatiana,' I say. 'Economists know that. You should too.'

'Sell me, Manuel,' she says, so close I could hug her and not need to move my feet. 'It'll help you afford your room, I'll give you ten per cent. It's enormous, the rent – I'm the only one available. I'm fabulous.'

'You are, Tatiana, but economists don't know,' I say, embracing her, as if she had been Masha, and if Masha had been interested.

'Your work, Tatiana,' I say. 'It's not dreadful. After all – there's nothing is. It's worse – it is original. Like everybody else's, it's admired, and you admire what they have done. We'd put it in the street on show....'

'Fuck you,' she shouts. 'A pavement chalker? Crust for a crust? You swine!'

## THE SWEEPERS' BALL

'It's just a joke,' sys Sean. 'We don't dance, Manuel. We're here to say farewell, with Paulie, Liffey and the rest. They closed the street, we're all at liberty. Besides, someone had got you fired ... they said you were so keen, and yet you dreamed....'

'I waited, Sean,' I say. 'Waited for the call. It seemed a logical employ – you get promotion when they spot you, and besides, it all decays. What you find or make, is thrown away, is broken, fades, and passes, it's life, destroyed, it reappears as something else, and so, so, so....'

'Is then recycled, and reborn – it's love, and death,' says Sean, a tear twinkling in one eye. 'Nature would deal with it, as mulch, a slimy pit. Some cities made a fortune from their heaps of dust. Not now. Nature is moribund, slow as a worm. Chewing over and over, excreting loam. Now, see the fires, the smoke, the ash – it's killing us ... camorras live from them, the sweepers and the bags of crap.'

'Is that who paid us?' I ask. 'It's not an honourable thing, to be a camorrista, Sean ....'

'You were like the rest of us,' he says. 'Necessity. You worked well for them, Manuel. You didn't see what you should not – but everything was cleared away. Ready to reappear, all thanks to you.'

\*

It's evident, it's the same for everyone – there's me, and there's my shell, the 'Manuel' I'm forever growing too big for.... I have to watch him, anticipate, coordinate – be very very prudent. Manuel is straight, but tricksy too – watch what he says, his false curiosity, the feelers pulling people on towards him, close and hugging – never to pass the digesting wall, never to an 'in'.

The I is inviolate, of course, like everyone; there's no 'in' to be admitted to....

Tatiana – she's a big big problem.

From now on, I'm not I, I'm Manuel.

'Have you found your place, Manuel?' Liffey asks, with some concern.

'A friend's friend,' Manuel says. 'At night – she shouts. There's something there that won't come out. Something that's grown on her, a symbiosis? Like mistletoe on oak. A crab in someone else's shell? A boil? A tumour? Psychosis? Though – that's superficial. Something we both have – regret. Anger. Not hers alone – it's ours. She screams – it's not a good place to end, nor to begin.'

'She needs the knife,' says Paulie. 'Cut it out. Bottle it – a worm in tequila, an aunt's glass eye, kept in a drawer.'

'In a cigar box,' Paulie says. 'We had one like that.'

'Is she in love?' asks Sean.

'For sure,' says Manuel. 'If you share a house, you have to be. For her, it means punishing, for a friend's sake. A little boy as well – who knows who he belongs to...?'

'No one belongs to someone,' Liffey says. 'They fire you, even if you do your job.'

'I float her up,' says Manuel. 'Everything she does, written on the sky – it comes from me, is mine.'

'Like those aeroplanes, writing in white fluff on the blue?' asks Paulie. 'That's publicity. I'd not be proud of that.'

'Well,' says Manuel. 'If you want to read it, you'd need to bring it down, transcribe. What she crosses out – that's what she feels. There must be somewhere to look at that. The rent – is huge, but all discounted – it's what I think her work would fetch. Of course, you'd have to pay to have it prettied up.'

'Be careful, Manuel,' says Sean. 'It sounds to me that she's a con. Nothing is hers – it's all arm's length – except I bet you wrote it down. You're contracted, my friend! Never sign, Manuel, don't write it where it can be falsified, your generosity become a burden, written in your blood.'

'Oh yes,' says Manuel, and laughs. 'She gets mad! She strikes out – if you don't bruise, you bleed.'

'It doesn't mean it isn't truly meant,' says Sean. 'Emotion – isn't law, or milk. There's no care in writing it, no date it has to sour. You have been spared in life.... You're glass; the dangers struck against you like bewildered birds ... you're free now, nothing to do, nothing to be done.... Life will put you in her cart and take you off.... There! It's a song of farewell. For you, brave Manuel – a life of struggle and obedience.'

The others gape. 'That's frank,' says Paulie.

'Quite political,' says Liffey. 'I have arguments about such things.'

'She must remember her homeland,' says Manuel. 'And not know how it's changed.'

'She'll not be fluent,' Liffey says. 'We are, but so what? This is our homeland, we're just stuck here, and see it all.'

'She may have many homelands,' Paulie says. 'Most people here in jobs like ours – they travelled everywhere before they were let in. It never finishes, it flows until you reach the dam. Or sea.'

'The dam is where you find the fattest fish,' says Sean. 'You snag their mouths, and what a flap as they are suffocating!'

'She must have tramped through civilisations, and when she comes to ours – she's voiceless....' Paulie says. He's scared of strangers. Doesn't know what he should say, or what they mean, chatting to him.

'No,' says Manuel. 'She screams. Like I would, but it would seem I was talking to her. I scream inside. Just for myself.'

*

They brought no booze. We stand around, look each other in the face.

'We're off to do some soldiering,' says Liffey. 'Me and Paulie. Not Africa – it's dangerous. We thought – a garrison, not doing good. Polishing the trucks and counting ammunitions. Sweeping the sand, being on guard, and watching stars and hearing animals. The good life.'

'You're old,' says Sean: 'You've less to lose, if it all blows up.'

'We'll be strategic,' Paulie says. 'Glory, while we bull our boots. A sense of destiny, each moment – it's fulfilled.'

Sean pulls Manuel aside. 'There's money due,' he says. 'Not much – but double, if the destiny of Paulie, Liffey, holds. If they're enchanted warriors – their pay is due to us. They're off, as soldiers

– against the grain, the will – as heroes. We have no future, not
even one in being killed. Did you think baroque, Manuel, while you
piled September leaves? Put curlicues on Satan's tail and cherubs'
locks? Love and desire, dear Manuel, go hand in hand, but when
the cash is handed out – you don't hold on to anyone....'

'It isn't just,' says Manuel. 'But – what does that mean? If we
forget our Kant.... Any cash that comes – will only be a half of
what we have deserved. Economists know that. What disturbs me is
– what did we see, or didn't see, that's worth the gold?'

'Don't ask,' says Sean. 'Monkeys may see – but they can't tell.
Stick to your nature – there's law, a natural law. The future, witty
Wittgenstein averred – moves in a curve. Independent of everything
– quite natural. He might have said that spirit's parasitic upon
nature – and we can proceed much further – admirably, it's said,
from natural law, we have principles in accordance with the actual
positive law – of Germany.'

'Oh come, Sean,' Manuel says, laughing. 'For one, despite the
reference – we're not in Germany. And then – the heritage of
thoughtful stand-up man, us all, erect – it's not a printers' pie, a
gallimaufry. You cannot pick and mix your arguments, to justify....'

'You're wrong,' says Sean. 'Nature – is exactly that. A stew of
seasons, good and bad, of surfeit and of dearth, invasions,
massacres, extinctions. That's where natural law comes from, that
is why we gorge on windfalls while our fellows have to eat their
cubs – while Liffey, Paulie, stalk their brothers – we shall scrump
the haughty pear, the russet apple....'

\*

'Bone ends,' says Manuel. 'I store them as I pick them up. One day
I'll empty out the box, over the floor, and fit them all together. A
new animal, a man, a woman – something: a beast. And *Ecce
homo!*'

'That's how Liffey and Paulie will need to resurrect,' says Sean.
'Their boss'll tire of them – they're too obedient. Some guy will be
elected, and the first thing – down they'll go.'

'If only we could save them,' Manuel says. 'We could have
taken on their mission, done it all for them....'

He flails, high with his fists...

'They'll see the light,' says Sean. 'Somewhere in Syria, on the
road – there is no fighting now, it must have been the firework

show. You can make huge fortunes there, rebuilding, trucking in some food, running clubs, raves, in Damascus City....'

'Don't you believe in betrayal, Sean?' Manuel asks. 'Our mates, traduced? I want none of that – making you feel guilty all your life....'

'It's ours,' says Sean. 'Our lives – all lives – are priceless. Whatever sum we take – is not enough.'

The dope that Liffey brought – it's quite adulterated, it doesn't make you fly, you flop and flap. 'Those guys, our mates – Liffey and Paulie – they don't get revelation – they get shot, somewhere on the road....' says Manuel.

'A road that Manuel was sweeping....' Liffey hears the word, sweep, sweep – he laughs, and riffs. 'The twisty alleyways in Naples; or the grid at Ostia, where Aeneas disembarked. Poor Sean and Manuel try to sweep the streets so Trojan horses can parade in triumph through the Spanish quarter, up the Spanish steps....'

Sean and Manuel – they're convinced: their friends will die somewhere on an unswept road – not heroes, not old soldiers ... aiming their brooms and impotently shouting 'bang!'

*

'Warmth, Tatiana,' says Manuel. 'Show me warmth.'

'That went out with periwigs,' she says. 'Besides – it isn't show you want. You want proximity.... Fluid exchange....'

'They didn't say farewell, Tatiana,' says Manuel. 'Instead, we sent off two old friends. I'll have cash, for sure. It's undercover pay – we'll take it for what we maybe didn't see. We'll steal as much again from those two mates....'

'You're disgusting, Manuel,' says Tatiana. 'In any case – there's cameras that do your work. Technocapitalism is its name.... The camera knows what it has seen. You, it seems, do not.'

'We saw many things, and some passed unobserved. There's knowing, Tatiana, and there's knowing too,' he says. 'There's books written on the theme ... And then there's contradiction in the seeing – a light that strikes another light, another colour sparks ... shadows and ghouls.... All's complex when we humans are involved....'

'Oh,' says Tatiana. 'No doubt it's all banal. A pay-off or a knife-thrust.... Watching creates your capital, Manuel. Use your walled-in eyes to promote my work....'

'What you want, Tatiana, is very hard to find. A casual killing –
has its price, is done or botched. An income – that is difficult. A
reputation – a cod, my dear, it's slippery, its empty mouth entices
you, it wags its tail, it begs and blackmails, it slips from under you
– frolics in the ocean with the shoals....'

'It's vital for us both,' says Tatiana, trying to hide some tears.

'Maybe we tie you naked to a pole and hoist you on a
monument,' he says. 'That could induce the curious, maybe....'

'Slow, slow – *Langsam, Wozzeck* – no epic, I beg you, Manuel,
no spectacle....' she says.

'I've got my rhythm, Tatiana,' Manuel says.

'Sweeping!' she curls her lip. 'You swept away your curiosity.
You don't think what brings it in – only how you can make it
disappear.'

'I'll tell you two secrets, Tatiana,' Manuel says. 'First – we have
a hiding place – everybody in our trade has one. We can lurk there,
let it accumulate, we are unseen, the power that does not intervene,
that does not care. Free will – is ours, Tatiana. The rest, impotent,
must trudge through shit. The second – when there is a bomb, an
accident – you'd think the two are contradictory! But in my world,
the answer to them is to clear away detritus! You can't shift causes,
or a side that someone takes – just the rubbish that is left. Make the
world seem empty once again. To start again, clean, bright....
Order, Tatiana: that is emptiness. Think of what I've said. You –
untidy, a ball of wool with endless ends....'

'When Masha had her lovers, Manuel,' she says. 'That too – was
cleared away. That too was order ... you weren't there, you weren't
aware – there was no rubble, and no promises....'

'And yours, Tatiana?' Manuel asks, disbelieving, needled too.
'Lovers – if you call them that. Under the carpet? Held breathless
in the bread bin?'

'You wanted to be something, something more than you: creator
of creators,' says Tatiana. 'but you have the knack – inflating what
you do, so it rears up, ennobles you ... the cleanser. Polisher of the
street – the sleepers, sneaks and cutpurses, the sly, the slinkers,
wanderers, stars of the peep, massagers without messages ... clean
up the sick and sluice the blood. A lens without a film, eyes that see
and nothing that records.... Can you be sure, Manuel, you're so
much larger than the shabby you you started with? The fear, the
terror ... don't you have a space...?'

'It's there to disappear,' says Manuel. 'It's destiny – if it appears, it has to go. The dead – escape. No one wins for ever – the pieces resurrect, another joust's prepared.'

'I know you don't care,' says Tatiana, angrily. 'But there's history, looking over your shoulder, as you pick the legs and heads out the gutter and put them in your scoop.'

'People are cool about these things,' says Manuel. 'They don't feel ready to make a judgement until it's over. They say "over", they mean "forgotten". Sean has a slant on this – he says "stupid killing – the Americans. Mean killing – the Russians. Murderous killing – the Nazis". It's superficial....'

'It's more, Manuel, it's meaningless,' says Tatiana, more angry still. 'The world is not a nutshell.'

'No,' says Manuel. 'The world has two eyes, lit-up, it stares out at us from its forest. The world leers, Tatiana. It kills you from arrogance and greed and nervousness and vainglory and motor cars and stuff from vapourisers.... Everybody gets a labelled chair and runs to sit in it while the executions run their course – Chinese, British, French, Serbians and Turks ...'

'Flapdedoodle,' shouts Tatiana. 'You talk on ... The media are full of what you think. But you're not responsible for that, and nor are they responsible for you.'

'You mean there's a procedure,' asks Manuel. 'That can be followed, so's to arrive back at a philosophy? I thought it was all just numbers. Ships coming in and out, prices, assaults, cops' wages – all the things I never knew about.'

'You saw it all pass by,' says Tatiana. 'What you didn't see was Masha.'

'Oh, Masha again!' says Manuel. 'I'm certain she avoided where I worked.'

'She was like me,' says Tatiana: 'We're of the people. We have emotions. You wanted to become a boss. Then, you let go, and fell and fell. But still – you want to settle everything. Living in your metaphor – you're intent on clearing, cleaning things. It can't be done – we're at the limit, and we quarrel. It isn't good or bad, it's different, and from now on, things won't change. Everything will change – not for the better or the worse. And everything is dirty, Manuel, it will be, we invent and throw away, and suffocate, and if we clear the garbage there'll be viruses, or bugs, or guys with an infection spitting in your ear....'

'I don't fit,' says Manuel. 'It's true. But – I am right. I've struggled out of history, I'm learned in myself and for myself. Everything will pass, decay, be swept away. All that is left is reason. Not us, not our bones. Who but us is interested in skeletons? Reason – not invented, there it was, on a heap, shining and original.'

'You're out of time,' says Tatiana. 'Collect the dirty cash, and then I'll criticise, condemn. It never is enough, the rent you owe....'

\*

'In case you doubt,' says Manuel. 'There's no one else but you, Tatiana.'

'Push my stuff. Make it famous,' Tatiana says. 'It's me, but much more valuable.'

'I haven't followed markets,' Manuel says. 'You're an unknown world.'

'No!' says Tatiana. 'Forget that "who might you be?" stuff, the genealogy. Dynastic, foundling – children are made of plasticine. I'm forever infant, procreating in the cradle creatures unknown, ethereal. I'm another planet – when the light strikes right, I'm bright as any star.'

'Just one tiny thing, Tatiana,' Manuel says. 'Don't you think it's cruel and pointless, hammering me with Masha? She can't feel, but what I may have felt for her, you've never asked. It's good you keep remembering her, I guess – but in this way, she seems a monster too. Like me. Like you.'

'It's what you did,' says Tatiana. 'Unforgivable. Emotions that you might have had, you two, it doesn't count. Quite unforgivable, what you did, and how it all turned out.'

\*

'To get money,' Sean says, 'you can't just put your paw out, beg.... To make the story, we must break in and steal what we have agreed. All is ready for us, but we have to cover it with secrecy.'

It's an ear. The building, its architect – inspiration, dreamworld, he wakes, takes his pencil, looks in the mirror – yes, it's an ear.

Not an easy shape to build.

'See,' Sean says. 'There's no security. This is the lobe. Look: those divans. you can bounce on them – but don't. We follow round this little gyre, meander, this stretch of pinkish marble, then we're at the desk, and ready to go down, where it all finishes, and thinking starts ... onward! the dark, the shaman's drum, the trip-hammer, ready to signal that we have arrived.... Music, acufene.... And then – the pay-off. In the bag. Our life's work, earns us another life. Adventure, Manuel! Just stoop and gather.... Say – "bless you, invisible lord, captain of the mint – take my love, I give you my devotion – thank you, o Fortuna...."'

'We want to take, not give,' says Manuel. 'An ear's no good for us. It'll hear us jemmying, and tell the brain.'

'You haven't understood,' says Sean. 'The idea is, the building's full of suited crones. They must be made to listen to you. You're the petitioners, postulants....'

'We're earwigs, then,' says Manuel, irritated; but he giggles – they both do. 'There'll be balls of wax in corridors, like in the movies, those bushes, tumbleweed, careering in the desert, sweeping us away ... embracing us, smearing us – like tarbabies...!'

'Like waxworks,' Sean agrees.

They're creased with laughter, scampering and hobbling in the corridors. Incapacitating mirth ... Kick down the door – don't break the glass and use the hammers, those are giveaways.... They find the bag. 'Swag,' says Sean, laughing some more.

*

They don't imagine Liffey, Paulie, stuck in the sand in their besieged Defender, waiting for some zealots who will cut their throats.... Maybe not zealots after all – just guys who see a chance of hostages, a ransom, don't believe in anything at all except the cash, opportunists with a scary label on the news....

'The cash!' says Manuel. 'Count and divide.'

*

'Tell me about Sean,' says Tatiana. 'He must be interesting.'

'His folks were kings of Ireland,' says Manuel. 'The English deported them, all, to India. Over the years, some were trampled, some, tied to cannon mouths – the most humane, the quickest way – were blown through, like reeds.

'He walked till he found the Chinese railway, and here he is.'

'And is he dark?' asks Tatiana. 'Dark as me?'

'I'd have to think,' says Manuel. 'He's quite worn down. A spent cartridge case, quite coppery. And small.'

'The best people often are,' says Tatiana. 'It's a misconception, thinking otherwise.'

'Thinking "best", Tatiana,' says Manuel, censoriously. 'Is a misconception too. Sean doesn't care about his being good. After all, his whole family had their careers, their reputations ruined. They passed laws, wore crowns, touched for evil, or for good.... Their ruination done by others, thinking of something else, taking their money, giving nothing back.'

'Looking at a life like that,' says Tatiana, 'it tells you everything. Why we bother, why we read French philosophy, do calligraphy at school, get tattooed, eat durians, catch an unknown illness touring in Laos.... Refuse astronauts' training, take money from a stranger for quick sex, nearly marry a third time, have bad kidneys....'

'I know,' says Manuel. 'That's what we do. That settles it. Is it what we are as well? I think it must be so.'

*

Paulie and Liffey – they don't know Sean stole their cash, that could be used to pay a ransom. It's good that they don't know – ignorance is usually a blessing. Instead, they offer to change sides – even religions, if that helps. Of course, they hope their comrades come and kill the kidnappers, or send them to hard jails for ever. Meanwhile, they all make friends. It's good. At least, it's not all bad.

*

'Art,' says Manuel. 'The basis of it's money. Or, sometimes, with real harsh regimes, it is obedience. You're an anomaly, Tatiana – your stuff's original, but no one's paid you to outdo the rest. It's useless altriusm. You'd be loyal, too, obedient to a boss – that's the way you're made, you think it is a gift. It's not. It's that you're angry, trying to look soft. Then, there's your defence of Masha. A casualty, not a victim. And who's not here, nor the little boy that no one knows ... who is responsible....'

'Oh, for sure, there's someone knows,' says Tatiana. 'How the boy happened, and the consequence....' as she prepares a rage.

*

'We're attached to you,' the guy says: Liffey calls him 'Moon': 'Not like domestic pets, more like field animals. A sacrifice; though hunger, not religion, is the key.... What do we do? Call in the butcher? That is what they do – but you're not edible, just equipped so poorly by your boss. Lost in the sands....'

Liffey can't answer, Paulie, as usual, turns away. 'It's beautiful, this place,' says Moon. 'Just think – we're almost at the end. You, us, the landscape, continent, the greed, the faith. It's repetition now. Getting machines to carry on our work. Our play. They don't ask for ransoms, don't do anything except what they've been told.... It's sad – no, it's a bitch, this evolution, archaeology, the "nevermores" high in the trees.... Our end. Us hominids – a scramble for the exit. Then – nothing. Crawlies, eruptions, rain. To think there'll be a 'nothing much' for millions of years, and then they'll find my tooth, or yours, poor Liffey. Grind them to dust. Maybe they will speculate on who and why we were.

'Will it start all over? Lunatics with revelations, the rest falling in behind?

'We chose this grove because the birds, if there's some left, will rule the roost until another beast, well-read and armoured, is crowned "king of the world...."'

'Oh, it'll take millennia,' Liffey says. 'And what if they can't read? Or dig?'

'I can't answer,' Moon replies. 'I believe your mate, Paulie – has revelations, maybe he....'

'Revelations for a soldier,' Liffey says, 'are useless. Soldiers already know. We're prepared, for 'eat be eaten'. If you sweep, you know the cleansing's only for one day, the next – all's rubbish once again.'

'We could sell you both,' says Moon. 'Each time you're sold, you're worth much more. It's profitable, it's economics – till you reach the last. Then, you're more expensive than you're worth....'

Liffey doesn't need to ask – 'what happens then', it's economics too.

'The part about the value and the price,' he says, 'I never understood. Even the bosses don't.'

'Well,' says Moon, 'there's not much you can spend it on round here, you'd need to take a trip, though there's a guy who brings stuff round, he has a truck....'

*

'I could buy a pic,' says Manuel. 'One of the Tatianas. A huge price. Then someone else would buy it, paying double. And so and so. Your fame, my fortune. Until it stops. Unsold. Back to zero, stale stock, the kitten no one wants, the runt: you keep it all your life. It's beautiful. The picture? Stack it with the rest....'

'A fraud?' shouts Tatiana, resentful, disappointed too. 'After the theft, the betrayal – you propose a scam....'

'Of course, Tatiana,' Manuel says. 'Your work is priceless, but it's valuable, I'm sure. Maybe, indeed, it's worthless, worthy of infinite esteem. You choose the formula. Like Masha and the little boy: their existence – irreplaceable. Yet – no one has missed them, they leave no space, no figure missing from the clock-face, no caryatid dropped, fragmented – nothing. As though they'd never been. Even the driver of the automobile, didn't see a thing....'

'You're brutal,' Tatiana says. 'A monster, farrowing like a raincloud – making the world fill with lycanthropes.'

'I'm running,' Manuel says. 'I left the envelope, the baggy suit, of "I", behind. I made my way from dirt to riches.... I've a plan for everything....'

'The money.' Tatiana says. 'Anyway, it isn't clean. You're right – it doesn't matter. You're an expert, Manuel, in living in the dark and turning on the light sometimes.'

*

'We must use imagination, Paulie,' Liffey says: 'Think of the missionaries – in the desert, on the islands. Cannibals, head-shrinks: bugs and snakes. Philosophers and bigots. They brought their message – some survived. The message stuck. Somewhat. Enough to let them leave, in many cases. The rest, well – it can't be worse than this. Let's wriggle our way out.'

'We don't want them thinking we believe in it,' says Paulie. 'No one does, no one can ... belief is out, my dear!'

'Be realistic, Paulie,' Liffey says. 'The new, the plural society – doesn't mean we all believe in many things. There's many different people, each believe in one thing, however ridiculous. The point is – you can change. There's no reason behind it all....'

'I'm with you, Liffey says. 'Let's make good Muslims of these guys. I suggest we start with numbers. Nineteen. Seven eight six. The twenty-eight letters, and above all – fourteen seven seven....'

'It's too sophisticated, Liffey,' Paulie says. 'Protection, avoidance of a blasphemy – we don't need get to that. Persuade them that they mustn't kill us – that's enough.'

'No, Paulie,' Liffey says. 'The numbers that protect imply a knowledge of the text. If these guys don't kill us, or sell us so we'll be more at risk – they'll see the system works. For us, at least. Our knowledge has protected us – we pass it on. They'll be convinced....'

'To me, they'll see it's blasphemy,' says Paulie, turning pale. 'Remember too – pass knowledge of a secret on – it isn't secret then. Don't meddle, Liffey, or we'll end up worse.'

'We can't be worse,' says Liffey. 'We could try another way – Christmas day, what does it mean to you?'

'Oh,' Paulie says, 'That's obvious. Three ships went sailing by.'

'Exactly!' Liffey says. 'Three! It's even easier. Attach yourself to curiosity.... And if that fails – there is philosophy. Husserl, now: much neglected, I would say. Remember: the psychology of the life-world – "self-understanding by *a priori* principles ... a self-understanding in the form of a philosophy".'

'Is that right?' asks Paulie. 'Maybe numbers is a better strategy. I'm not sure Husserl works when you are kidnapped, ransomed....'

'Oh Paulie,' Liffey says, and laughs. 'Many things can work. The point is – we're a species who kills its lookalikes for trivialities; not to eat, to eliminate the competition, clear the field for sex, infanticide – all that. Just impulse, raptus, overspill. It must be a tabu that we have to conquer. Bulling boots and ironing uniforms – easing the springs ... those are a magic, that permits you to overcome your sense that killing kin is not the thing – not even if it is for cash....'

'Well,' says Paulie. 'We can try. Our aim is survival, not a blasphemy. I remember – dissimulation is permitted in the Books, if it saves your life. To me, though, your maths ends in idealism. Just like Husserl does.'

'There is a bright light,' Liffey says. 'Even if our mates could find the cash for ransom – they won't be allowed to pay for us.'

'It's worth trying,' Paulie says. 'All of it. The more we mix it up, the easier it'll be to explain to other people, if it works.'

*

'Hey!' shouts Tatiana, banging on Manuel's forehead with her knobby knuckles. 'Is there anyone in there? I've Manuel's shell here, maybe the tortoise that once lived in it went dead.... Give the cash away, Manuel. It isn't yours, money's too round and slippery to belong to anyone. See it falling down the cracks and in the well. Give it away – make other people feel they're rich.'

'No, no,' says Manuel. 'That isn't logical. I don't know what to do with it, the cash. So – if I give it all away – I shan't have solved a thing. There'll be another problem too: poverty. But the cash – the question won't have been resolved. Giving away's a cop-out, Tatiana.'

'Giving away the cash – might keep the cops away,' says Tatiana, laughing at her play. 'Give it to them – and you'll be innocent.'

She knows he won't be innocent. She wants the money too much for herself to think it mayn't be there....

'Not innocence,' says Manuel. 'A moment of confession and renunciation, following a life of guilt, first seeing and not telling, then doing. Full of not fulfilling. Not telling....

'I think – two people make a tangle. Each life – a cat's cradle of ungraspables. There's no classes, no class struggle – just the force, you see them, each one, individual trees stood whispering – in a pine forest, each quite separate from the next. Pushed from beneath, heads whishted by the wind. Each indistinguishable from its mates, but totally unique.'

'I knew someone just like you,' says Tatiana. 'We took heroin together. Horse.'

'I'm surprised,' says Manuel. 'Like me? The same quote from Husserl, then?'

'It's the one everybody knows,' says Tatiana. 'It saves you reading all the rest.

'Horse. A sugar lump. It's called horse, but you don't ride it. You're the horse, naked, in the meadow. Everything comes to you,' and she laughs.

'It sounds disappointing,' says Manuel.

'You pretend, Manuel,' she says. 'There *is* class struggle. You don't want to see, you'd rather run people over with not seeing them. They die quick, hating you. It doesn't matter, they don't know your name, address – they can't come banging on your door.'

'Show me around, Tatiana,' says Manuel. 'I breathe the differences; people – water in a river....'

'I'll take you round,' she says. 'Look: my picture. Image of all the images. I've tacked things on, they move, if you are minded so to give a push....'

It's true. All moves. Islands drift, the wounded put on smiles, erect, they wipe clay off their pants.

'You can't "go in" a painting,' Manuel says. 'It's not a place....'

'Oh yes,' says Tatiana, unrolling metres of her work, much larger than the wall, you have to walk around, 'Take Benin. I want to go, you can go in – but where? Where's the door? I've never been, I've seen the kings, it's not a place like this....' And she shows Manuel a tiptop corner of her pic. 'This is an oyster. It moves, reacts, it opens up its shell, it's mouth is a vagina too ... and see how neatly packed the birds – a creel with hunted ones all dead – the curlews, grebes, shovellers and turners ... let's see if we can put them back in life....

'Here's a dark pond, and there are cliffs, of chalk and clay, with holes for parrakeets, they lob the eggs down on the cars – a line of blue red green yellow Hudsons, De Sotos, Packards – if they were live, you'd think them ducks or souimangas – and here's the guys in uniform to sweep it up – the frogs, the bandoleers, crosses and stars, for valour and for cowardice, for nothing much and vainglory, washing in blood .... move on Manuel!' She points to even more – 'There's stories here, with flying viziers, cows you mustn't touch and wolves that drink their milk ... up there, are stars, the red, the blue, and others too – all shapes, with tiny bloaters looking down through reeds, moley beasts which blow through organ pipes long as a Route 66, it's muzak from a million years away....'

And she unrolls, explains, pokes something to be still or move, and in her chanting voice, she shows Manuel the towns – the rusting ones, some made of toasted bread and some of lobster shells, and people – people grey, or pink, like whey, burnt chestnuts, black as closed cabinets or grey as lungs ....

'It's the world, Tatiana,' Manuel says, marvelling. 'Imagination, seizing and digesting, concepts, art – the world, yes! Is it any good? I'm not so sure....'

'Oh, there are little ones,' she says. 'Oiled oblongs. You roll them up, forget them on the train, they go to auction – some don't sell and others go to banks that lock them up until they turn to jade....'

'It's brilliant,' says Manuel, quite overwhelmed. 'But is it art?'

'Oh foo-de-doo,' says Tatiana, much annoyed. 'I didn't ask you if it was.'

'But no one dies,' Manuel objects. 'Incinerated in their hut or butchered in a hospital, or hanging from a boabab tree.... It's life, but doesn't breathe. The horrors, Tatiana....'

'Go round the back,' she says. 'You'll see all that, if you've the nasty mind....'

'You put it there,' says Manuel, annoyed as well. 'The mind is yours. I am just eyes.'

'I can't do anything for that,' she says. 'You swept, looked, didn't see. You stole. Does any of all that entitle me?' she asks expectantly.

She doesn't mention Masha. How would she come in...?

'You give us a complete world,' says Manuel. 'And what's the point? We've one already. Full of accidents and Mashas by the score....'

'Besides, you're wrong,' Tatiana continues. 'It's not the world: mine is the universe. Didn't you see the little bloater getting sonorities from the *soubasse* pipe that even angels can't? It's in another galaxy. That one's too far – you'll never reach it in your tin space spider....'

She smiles, laughs at him, hands on hips, triumphant.

'I can't imagine who would want this picture,' says Manuel. 'It's, well – scurfy. Like an eczema. It peels away, it jiggers up and down, it might infest your corners ... it smells like rashers of a yellow dog sunbaked on tin sheets....'

'Yes,' says Tatiana. 'It's all of that. I'm surprised you spotted it.'

'It's the price,' says Manuel. 'By size, it costs a fortune. As for value, I'm not sure it's worth anything at all. But what concerns us is the price. If it looks too high, people won't enquire, and too low, they'll think there's a catch, it's broken, someone's brought it back as faulty....'

'How much does anyone need? Fuel, food? You only live a little while,' she says. 'If you can pay the price – then buy it. It'll serve you, leave something too for after. Get for it what I need, need for my life.'

'Your world,' says Manuel, 'is wild. I don't know if I'd take to it.'

'You're in it, Manuel,' says Tatiana. 'You've no street now. You've seen the map, I've drawn one in – they made Benin a thin tall country, squeezed between the rest – not like when there was the trade. Slaves. Raw human meat, worth thousands. Alas – for being a bad Oba, king Ewuakape's wife felt she must atone for him, became another of his sacrifices. That's not for me – not wife nor sacrifice, no matter how many millions feel it is their duty or their destiny. I'm not bound by time or nicety, you know.

'It's just a detail, you'll have missed it – the little king, the Oba, with his servants, a sculpture, though without the slaves. Everyone who could, sold everyone they could.

'We did well, now we only have to sell ourselves. I'd sell myself, Manuel, that's what we do here, but I didn't put myself in, not in the picture.

'Follow the structure, Manuel,' she says, wiping off a blot, a smudge, her coat sleeve black with paint. Choosing a tiny brush she adds a face, procession, a tree-like scroll. 'I'll guide you, have no fear, it's natural, all as it spills out of my hand. There's no light switch anywhere, everything just has the colour that is theirs.'

They pause. A roaming scrutiny....

'No one helps you, not in time or space....' Manuel says, weeping at the thought of loneliness.

'Oh they do,' says Tatiana. 'They help you move on to the next. Mixing perfumes, seeking the Gorgons, designing a plastic oesophagus: you need take the first step. You have no choice. Leave the cash behind....'

'I've looked and looked,' says Manuel, quite alarmed. 'I must have hidden it, forgot exactly where. No one but me and Sean knows it exists, and only I know where I might have hidden it.'

'Nothing *I* do is hidden,' Tatiana says. 'No one paints cash into a picture. Maybe the spiders got it ... or you exchanged it into something – gold into paper. Birch bark. Mulberries. The worms – maybe they sucked it, and then wove, maybe made you a cloak, a tunic that has you look like something you are not, from somewhere you've not been....'

*

It's very dark. Liffey and Paulie try to sleep in holes they've sculpted in the sand, their negatives, counter-figures, mirror-bedmates, as it were. It's very hard.

Moon rouses them. 'I know nothing,' he says. 'What will happen. It's nothing that concerns me. If I knew, I wouldn't tell, but I don't know.'

'Come!' Liffey says. 'There should be happy ending. What would it cost you, or us? Just write one in. A tiny choice....'

'Of course,' says Moon. 'But I don't know ... happy or sad? Maybe there is no ending? Just not yet? Or never.'

'I wonder why you came,' says Paulie.

'Now now!' says Moon. 'There's no use being angry. Especially not with me I know nothing, that's all I can say.'

\*

'If you can't find the cash,' Tatiana says. 'You're out of crime, another story starts.... Go to the police: denounce your friend. Conspiracy, at least. So, you clean your hands.'

'I could confess – to get more cash ... those rabbits, Sean's pets, I had them killed – greed, yes, I confess,' says Manuel, 'To get a bigger share, I made a threat.... True, it was just a dream, but such a shock for Sean....'

Tatiana stares –

'It makes no sense,' she says. 'Besides, rabbits exist to be destroyed. That was no threat, poor friend. Sean will forgive, he's your partner, so, he loves you....'

\*

The sergeant, cop, says, 'Sit down there. Don't change your mind – you're here confessing. Don't move – we're photographing you. Every second there's a snap.'

They both sit quiet. Then, the cop says, 'That's no confession, and no crime – every rabbit we can find is killed, and eaten on the spot.'

'They were his pets,' says Manuel.

'You're here to denounce your friend,' the cop says. 'It only shows you are a shit!'

'Then, there's another case, that carries even more remorse....' says Manuel. 'There's Masha ... and the kid....'

'A crime?' the cop asks.

'No, just negligence,' says Manuel. 'No connection ... except what's in my head, and Tatiana's too....'

'Come on,' the cop says. 'Find more crimes. We can do anything, once you tell....'

'There was Dahomey,' Manuel says. 'Tread softly there, of course.... You don't seem humanists, but even so....'

'What you don't see – you can't be held responsible for,' the cop says, putting down his pen.

'Behind it all there were big guys – I don't know who....' says Manuel.

'Go away!' the cop says. 'You've no cash, and nothing has been stolen. You came here to incriminate your friend, and float a nonsense of a plot. I'd say, everyone is innocent, except you....' And he talks on: 'The people who don't come in here, driven by their fears and whims – don't you see, they're slavers, gangsters, murderers – in their heads is every plot and plan.... It's everyone, quite probably, except for you....'

*

'I don't mix with guilty ones,' says Tatiana, numbering squares upon a board. 'Until you're clean, dear Manuel, you'll live in your squalid world. And mine – I'll turn it to the wall.'

And so she does.

'This is the finish,' Manuel thinks. 'Cleansing has to start afresh each day. It's relative. Under the carpet? Most people don't have one.'

'It's good you feel guilty,' Tatiana says. 'Everybody should. It's better that your friends should hate you – they are right. You made a fool of yourself, trying to face down the state – that's good too, next time the law will beat you till the blood flows free. That's good too. If you disagree with everyone – it's better so. To paint you on my universe you'd need a brush so fine – one hair's too many – no one will see you: when they do, we'll both be dead. That is supreme: you reach a height where you're invisible and no one hears your squeak.'

'Or it could be down, down the hole, Tatiana,' Manuel says. 'I don't trust you, your changing views.'

'You must distinguish, Manuel,' she says, 'between the crimes in history, the things you did, and those you dreamt you might. Find what you stole, the cash – or else it's just a memory....'

*

'I must confess,' says Manuel. 'Sean: your rabbits ... my vindictive dream....'

'They were delicious!' Sean tells him. 'A pie – big as the full moon! I might have asked you in, but you've a tender heart. The cash?'

'Oh,' Manuel says. 'It's been stolen – I suspect by Tatiana – she believes she's owed ... And yours?'

'It's washed,' says Sean. 'Clean, anonymous and running for me like a thoroughbred. Don't let them cheat you, making payments for poor Paulie and his friend. The cash won't help them....'

So, they reminisce, Sean and Manuel. 'There's Tatiana,' Manuel says. 'Her artistry ... her wants....'

'Oh Manuel,' says Sean, 'you're thinking small. A picture's bounded, just some metres square. Think big. Make an offer; you could buy the universe....'

'I'll put the picture up for sale, Sean,' says Manuel. 'A notice – pinned on a venerable tree: 'the UNIVERSE, by Tatiana'.

'Who would want it, buy it, make an offer? The thing is, the universe is wrecked: a mess, a first attempt. Unfinished, abandoned....'

'I think that explosion buggered it for good,' says Sean. 'The idea was to make a pleasant spot – animals to pet, red flowers, and birds that sang. Instead – you'll see – there's deserts, gas, and heaps of empty space, rocks of all kinds – and gold, Manuel. Useless except to start a fight, and have poor devils tunnelling....'

'You're right,' says Manuel, 'but being right's no good. I could ask Tatiana to cut it up – in squares. They teach you that in art school. Sell piecemeal.... Alas, Tatiana paints exactly what there is – a universe that bodgers made....'

'I'm sure,' says Sean. 'She's tough. Her universe, the original, they'll be identical. And yet – everything that is, is full of weak spots, like a cheese. Tatiana'll be the same. She ransoms you with Masha. From what you say, they both had habits, addictions maybe ... and there's a ghostly child.... Your cash? You and her alone with it – and then it's disappeared...?'

'I've no plan except enjoyment,' Manuel says. 'My money. Loving it.'

'What do you want now, Manuel?' Sean asks. 'We could set lawyers on her – but then the cash would all be spent. Torture? You say she's tough....'

'There's guys who paint with brushes on their feet. Hands, feet – then teeth,' says Manuel 'If we had to take them off, she'd be a burden....'

'But not on you!' says Sean. 'From what you say – she is a realist. If she's truncated and can't paint, there'd still be the universe, the original, spread out for her to contemplate ... We could threaten that we'd mutilate that too....'

'It gets too complicated, Sean,' says Manuel. 'But you're a friend indeed.'

\*

'I've found the money,' Tatiana says: 'Look! It's been mostly spent.'

That's so. There's hardly any left. For sure, there's not enough to bring you joy.

'I had debts,' she says. 'People gave me things, things I needed. They must have broken in so as to get paid.'

'I can't undo anything,' says Manuel. 'If you didn't see them, there's nothing to report. Let's call it quits – neither owes anything to anyone. I want nothing from you – and you've nothing that I want. Anyway – I can't live in this dirty place. It's not natural – there's all the stuff you leave, don't clean, Tatiana, then there's mounds of dirt you can't have used, but you've brought in. It heaps up, all around – not human; no one could move it, not with a broom, not with a machine....'

'I know,' says Tatiana. 'It's my project. Subsoil. I've done what you can see, the surfaces. This here is subsoil. Underneath what you can't see – is all the riches. Jewels, precious stones, the silver. I can shift all that.'

'I'm amazed,' says Manuel. 'This is no good, not for anyone. It's dirt, not even pay-dirt. You mess with this, you'll find a devil underneath the pile.'

'I know,' she says. 'But – I didn't take the money. Not for myself. Nor for the devil, not even if he sings for me. This dirty-looking stuff? It's just subsoil. Don't be irritated – it does no good, but it's my project ... What you usually don't see, but you know it's there.'

'I was joking,' Manuel says, 'about the devil. And now you trump my joke with one of yours. Of course it matters; what you don't see always does!'

'You've lost your hopes,' says Tatiana, dreamily. 'Went with your cash. This subsoil's very intimate – my people dug it.'

'Everybody's people dug it,' Manuel says. 'Or made others do it for them. I understand, that after the universe, all those surfaces, you need completeness: the underneath. The pillars, the support. But, a picture of it – that's trivial, I hope you know.'

\*

'I'm not a victim,' Tatioana says, 'and I never steal or cheat. It's that I have rough neighbours. The very best, but any favours have to be repaid....'

'So,' says Manuel, 'you still owe? Maybe they were people that I saw, and didn't register....'

'Yes, you're right,' says Tatiana. 'We should run. I'll pack my war chest....'

And she does. The bullets – little tubes of paint for squiggles and some fancy wisps, the incendiaries, for spraying on the jewels and minerals, and then the heavy shells, maybe they're full of germs and such, atoms for sure – for laying down the landscapes and the sky....

'It's work for six days at the least,' says Tatiana, laughing, as she bundles up some rags. 'My clothes,' she says. 'We have to dress our parts. You are a drifter, Manuel, I see you as a dhow – its sail, pointed like a pigeon's wing, trimming to every breeze, strong on purpose, vague on destination.

'The earth!' she shouts. 'We have to take that. It's my next. And shells – green turban shells, nelloed silver – making a frame, a bed.... We'll need a table – eat! directly from the earth, a table made of minerals and watery beasts ... otherwise, Manuel, how'll we spread out our bread and scrape?'

'We'll take the big picture,' Manuel says. 'Live in it. Sail, float, tramp in it.... Fold it to make a cart. Then – there's the wheels....'

'Potters' wheels,' says Tatiana. 'Each year I took a course, and baked a myriad of figurines – then stole the wheel. There must be four or five. Heap high the soil, Manuel – we'll find seeds and bulbs, and birds.... The parrakeets, escaping, they will hitch a ride.'

'I suspect,' says Manuel. 'It will make a show.'

'People don't look, don't see,' says Tatiana, tipsy with the thought. 'They'll be like you – thinking their inattention will grow

cash. Besides – there'll be our flag. It's tattered – they'll think it is
for prayer....'

'We have no country, Tatiana,' Manuel says. 'Aside from your
armoury, we have no arms, no knives, no dope: a flag....'

'The flag is up, it's over you. It's white,' says Tatiana. 'I
surrender. So should you.'

'The devil,' Manuel says. 'His detail: what will draw the cart? I
had in mind – a horse, obsidian black, iron oxide black.... Or....
White – limewood, alabaster, walrus ivory....'

'And where'd we find one?' Tatiana asks, 'And feed it? No,
Manuel, if we must move – pulling the cart is up to you. Or else –
we'll park it, use our minds to travel there and back again....'

Tatiana's tall and ragged. 'I can beg,' she says. 'With threats. Or
steal. Why not? Where did these guys' money come from? Travel –
if our feet itch, we can pull the universe over us, at last we'll see
the stars, they wheel and squeak like bats, they call us, Manuel,
they call....'

Manuel is silent. 'Your child, Manuel,' Tatiana hectors him, 'is
up there too.'

'No, Tatiana,' Manuel says. 'Not mine. Now, not anywhere.'

'You're so proprietorial,' Tatiana says. '"My" child, "my"
money". When you were in the trees, and just an "I", you were
much more huggable. We must be flexible here, Manuel, for now,
we're in the universe alone – but others may come in....'

They do. The cart fills up and overflows.

There's some are learned in the law, and some are learned in
themselves. Some learned the clarinet, and some didn't make their
second day at school. 'We are the earth,' says Tatiana. 'They are
the salt.'

'The bath is always full of them,' says Manuel.

'Not every cart is so equipped,' says Tatiana.

'Their pets,' he says. 'Some bite.'

'Each is unique and named,' says Tatiana. 'We must remember
nature, though it's evanescent, like the past. Without the pets, our
brain is dead.... Many of these people go way back – to when there
were the steppe, the jungle, the forest. They'd be doing well there.
The pets – even further back, to where you had to dodge big
animals. Think rocks, Manuel, and how we're all encased in them,
pretty as etchings, all together, like in an ossuary, our big eyes,
looking up....'

\*

'If we had sold a picture, Tatiana,' Manuel begins.

'We shan't,' says Tatiana. 'That's good. It's very good. Why should anyone want one, unless they're very rich? My prices! They're immense, there's only some rich guy could think of it – some puff-ball, a streak of died red hair, two balls like conkers left to burn, harden, too long on the fire, belly like a pot-egg, pregnant with sour shards....

'We live in them, Manuel, my pics – and all the others here, the warriors and the corpses, mothers bringing forth their joyful beauties – they don't see what I see, never will, it's good, good, Manuel, let no one think to appropriate, frame a part of me, chirrup banalities to fill their idleness, their empty wall: go! away, away!

'And all you here, my grubby squabbling thoughtless friends – you ignorant beasts, go bray and baa, give milk and wool and cheese ... that's what you've decided you must do! you're wrong, but I don't hassle you: ignore, be blind to everything – rejoice! You're poor, you won't grow old, you'll live by charity, without a care for frauds and markets, work and pensions.... All the good gods live in poverty, they live by offerings from the poor, from scraps and tiny tin replicas of food, compete with snakes and monkeys for a piece of honey-cake. It's good, it's pure.... Have kids galore – they'll bring you joy and tedium, you won't leave anything for them, and when you die, they'll kick you in a rubbish-hole – it's good, Manuel, it's you; it's noble and it's clean.'

She shouts to all the company, stretched out beneath her stars, and curled up on her soil, the laid-down bed: 'If you've spare cash, give, give – and I'll buy quinces from Tell-Halaf, plantains from Gabon....'

'Your triumph, Tatiana,' Manuel says. 'It wakes us, stirs us – it's a hot wire stuck in an eye and in your brain, the ganglia that give you derring-do, except ... there is no battle, no front, no win, no lose....'

'Oh Manuel, you're a child,' says Tatiana. 'You think you can get down from the cart and join the stream, of guys in brogues and gals in bras, the respectable, the savants and the salaried, a place to sleep that's not on wheels.... It's false! That world is gone, it isn't yours, it's like your child, not yours, not anywhere.'

'Your world, Tatiana,' Manuel says, 'is set up here, it lets rain in, contains our smell – is true and false, for ever – or a day.

Millions of years, or seconds – no one has a watch so big so small
to measure its infinity, its cardiac arrest.... I must find ... my
own....'

'Another cart?' says Tatiana. 'It'll be identical, postiche, a copy
or a forgery – can you tell a difference? – and you will be the same
– you'll trail behind you like a tail … 'Masha, the little prince...'

'No, no,' says Manuel. 'You are the past, dear Tatiana, eater of
dynasties, deflowerer of palaces ... and our food! Potato skins and
peapods....'

'All there is,' says Tatiana. 'Use your imagination. Love what
is.'

'Chaos,' says Manuel. 'He, the god who guides and instructs us
– He produced the earth, that we call the gentle Gaia. That's wrong:
– or, better, it's an insurance, to call her sweet. Her brother – he is
Tartarus, the sink of hell. Is that the choice? The dusty sister or the
brother, all afire? And do you cast me out, Tatiana, laying on me –
the mystery of Masha, a homicide, punishable, with eternal
wanderings and casual death? Adding on – the mystery of what I
didn't see, the missing glimmering, among the things I saw, forgot.'

'That's fantastic!' Tatiana says. 'An inspiration, Manuel. The
myth, the image. A subject for a canvas, you'd need a ladder to
reach the top – or you could dig a ditch and start from there....'

'The choice is yours, Tatiana,' Manuel says. 'Mine is not purity,
but a sweeping: constant renewal. Love – must end in separation, or
it will not have been. The end belongs to the beginning....'

'Wise words,' says Tatiana. 'Too late for Masha....'

*

From the cart, there's sound of joy and sorrow – you can hear it
down the street.

'The return of the wild,' a guy stood next to Manuel says: 'But
we don't qualify.'

'We're in between,' his woman – Cydalise – tells Manuel.

Hagan shows him pictures – 'There's blocks – apartments of
eleven hundred, three and even five thousand....'

'Like catacombs,' says Manuel. 'I have large pics – they
wouldn't fit. Bee-hives – all sticky, some exploited queen....'

'Oh no,' says Hagan. 'You must qualify – they're cops and
nurses, gravediggers, janitors and sanitation, teachers, floor
walkers, walkers on wires – hi, low, slack and tight – see those

brown shrubs, there is eternal snow and cold blown down to give illusions of a climate – here come the girls in uniform, their hair bunched high, like for a prom, and clothing uniform, sea-grey, they're off to sing and dance....'

'If you don't qualify, I'm sure I don't,' says Manuel. 'It seems unusual ....'

'Oh, it will come,' says Hagan, and Cydalise says, '...how it was.'

'We don't agree,' says Hagan, laughing, hugging Cydalise. 'We make a compromise, that what has been will come again....'

'You're wrong,' Manuel begins, but stops – maybe these could be his friends, though they may be liabilities as well....

'These dancers, graduands, prom queens or novices – are they real? And all the honeycombs, the projects, machines for living in, set up in the scrub ... all unfinished sometime past, or maybe there's a plan to finish them, before new people come, traffickers, not employees, making a way, not taking wages now and then, selling themselves and dangers too....'

'Oh Manuel,' says Cydalise, 'you spot it all! The parasites, the pirates...! Is it real? Of course it is, it was – you put the scenes together, like a movie, but it's not, the actors are all real, or were, or tomorrow they will be like they are, or they can be.'

'I understand all that,' says Manuel. 'It's rather jesuitry. We humans make a distinction, crude and shifting though it is – between a past and future, and we are in the middle, even though we know the past was not quite like we think, the future lies out there, a map with nothing pencilled in, a blank,you'd say....'

They laugh, Hagan and Cydalise.

'You guys fallen off the cart,' says Hagan, eyes brimming with his mirth. 'Just listen to yourselves! A past that wasn't; future incrutable and blank – and yet you ask me what is real? You must grasp this – it's very hard, for us, for most, to calculate and pin down what there is and what there was. And I suspect we don't, we two, my lover Cydalise and me, don't qualify. Put us together – what do we mean? We aren't the same or even close, when there is sex, each plays a different part and thinks of better pasts and emptier loves, and what's to come, a time when there's no one, and there's nothing, no lust, no prick to make you cosy up to someone else....'

'I see that you don't qualify,' says Manuel, 'not singly, and clearly not if you're a pair. Maybe you have a document? Those in the cart – they don't have one, but now the cart is getting full, there's Tatiana wanting space and solitude, and maybe there will be another cart, or maybe guys will lie around, on the street, a private sort of spot, sleep, dream, party, socialise, just like they did when I swept clean....'

*

Cydalise says to Manuel, 'Don't suffer, not on our behalf, or because of what we say. Don't cry – it makes us suffer so. I confess, for Hagan too.... We often make mistakes, forget quotations, don't verify a thing we cite.... We really do not care at all about the real, what is, is not. We're just like you – we make a judgement on the spot – "it seems ... it's plausible ... we can believe ... there is a precedent...." What we want, really, to know, is "how can we qualify?"'

She hugs him briefly, to show soft feelings. He doesn't move – she hugs again, this time she slips her hand inside his shirt – the people from the cart wear spacious clothes, as if they're wrestlers from Japan, inviting you to take a hold and maybe get thrown down....

'Don't worry if things were or are to come, the repetition – if it comes, and you are lucky so – it all will blur,' she says. 'You can bet, what's the first time something comes to you, it won't at all be something new for someone else. That gives a spin, it takes the edge....'

'Well,' Manuel says, much aroused. 'What happens next?'

'You see?' says Cydalise. 'Nothing at all. You needn't worry, now, future or past. It's nothing, nothing, Manuel. Nothing you don't know, or saw and don't recall.'

He tells her about the scene with Masha, how Tatiana has invented....

'Everything? I don't think so, Manuel,' she says. 'Just think, reflect. There's much much more. It happened, I am sure. Don't fool about with "real or not..."'

'It's true, Cydalise,' says Manuel. 'It all happened. Just – I'm not responsible.'

'Ah yes,' she says. 'Exactly so. It's not about the real at all. The question is a moral one, not memory or real, or what you did or saw. It plagues us all. It shows we are a species, linked each to each, as if we're on the savannah still, the tail of someone else firm in our paw, your own tail gripped by someone you don't know, all in procession, off, striding to a destination.... We're convinced there is one, an objective. When we get there, Manuel, what do we do then? Write travel books? Build a memorial wall, with little pictures of the dead, like you need for passports, or to drive? Don't dismiss it, think it's boring, repetitious – it is the central puzzle that we turn around, like donkeys circling, harnessed to a beam that draws up water from a well or grinds our grain, except....'

'Yes,' says Manuel, 'I know. There is no water, and no flour.'

'Maybe you should get back on the cart,' says Hagan: 'I'm sure you qualify.'

'Oh no,' says Manuel, 'I've done that stretch – Tatiana's first picture; creation, judgement. I'm her admirer, agent: I was there, when she brought forth the universe. Enough! It is inimitable. She doesn't see it so, she would do more. And on and on.'

'Let's not give up on Masha, and the child that certainly's not yours – like all the rest you say you didn't do,' says Cydalise. 'Or didn't see. Tatiana's a fantasist – she could write scripts or do scenarios – except they're fantasies with one foot on the ground. You can't take off that way, Manuel – you must let go, and see the little houses shrink as you fly over them, the walls and watchtowers, the death-pits – you're too high up to see if there are signs of desperation, suffering ... those strings of people, each holding on to one in front, like monkeys, as they cross the desert... Masha – hmmm. It sounds a Russian name – that doesn't mean a thing, of course. True, there were camps for them, but so there were for almost everyone, except the guys who say they're innocent and always on the purer side. It's not Dahomey that Tatiana sees when she sees Masha trudge along the street, thinking of faithless lovers, or her hunger, or can she dump the kid, his snotty nose, his weeping – no, it's just a general scene. Like there's on tv, or on your phone, it could be anyone or anywhere, it could have happened or be in a plan unrealised, weighed in the balance, an artful finger holding down one pan....'

'Oh Cydalise!' says Hagan. 'You're so banal! There's no processions, no one has a tail to hold, except the devil, with his horns, his soft black pelt. Tatiana is a dramatist, she doesn't know what's really Masha and what is in her mind.'

'Oh, let's be fair!' says Manuel, trying to slip his hand in Cydalise's so Hagan doesn't see. 'Tatiana knew, *I* knew, a real Masha, not her child....'

They stare at Manuel. 'Then,' says Cydalise, 'it could all be true.'

'Yes,' Manuel says. 'Except she never actually said what might have been significant.... My part? A death, or two, some blame, responsibility – but could be personal, or wholly chance, without a tie, a link, my innocence....'

'We'll leave it so,' says Hagan, laughing. 'As we move on together, there'll be time to do analysis: set your brain in neutral, Manuel....'

'You see,' says Cydalise. 'Responsibility – our duty, culpability – is limitless. Can you ignore it? Can it ever be discharged, without – what? Repentance? Useless. Tutelage – look out for others? That isn't popular, not written in our brains....'

\*

'She's desirable,' Hagan tells Manuel. 'Cydalise. That – you've spotted. She's not innocent. Deeds. You don't know what, and she won't tell. I am responsible for her, you see.

'Remember, Manuel, if you can – the night they lynched the vanman ... Masha abandoned, maybe raped and clubbed to death. Or coma, eternally ... Perhaps – she'd already lived, survived, another experience like that – a jail, or slavery, or ... you imagine... No child, unless she'd felt responsible and sheltered one....'

'What do you want, you two?' asks Manuel. 'Are you a flim-flam pair? I own nothing more than you can see. I come off the cart, I want to make some headway before I tumble in the ditch.... I've no time for making Kantian cabinets – first twisted, then straightening the timbers, carpentering a single moral law that we shall break, right from the start....'

'Oh, don't be scared,' says Hagan, laughing more. 'Of course, it's written that we fail. And yet we march, make war and peace, accept the risk of being live and ductile – we two, we're not your masters, Manuel. A comradely exploration: that's all we propose. Off you can run, whenever there's a stretch of open road....'

\*

The street is gay, hung about with globes and flags, eternal Eve of festival. There's sex shops, game shops, gaming shops, emporia where one-arm bandits stand in rows, for your inspection, each

holding out the same stiff nazi arm for you to shake and try your
pluck, your steadfastness ... on with the cherry harvest! There's
little cinemas that show short movies with truncated ends – 'no
virgins admitted', says the sign – you watch and pay again, again
the climax never comes, there's peepshows too – 'watch it!' don't
get too close, it ends with curtains dropping like a guillotine.

'I've always wanted,' Manuel says. 'To live high up above this
scene – an attic, a Soho bubbling on all night, a cauldron, a
steelworks, a row of furnaces, smelting frustration, hope: – it's
eyes, Hagan. These people – concentrate, they watch, record, there
is no dark, it's nude, you peer in every crease and fold where you
ought not, at every reel of oranges and pears and pairs of wavering
bodies, thrusting like a Mackie Messer....'

'This is the place,' says Cydalise. 'There's no ground floor – the
first floor is a whore, her maid – you ring the bell, it's Clara in the
day and Karl at night. No one needs venture higher, where we'll
be....'

'It's occupied?' asks Manuel, 'the penthouse?'

'Yes,' Hagan says. 'We've occupied it. Be assured, no one but
us will climb this high....'

So, up they go. 'The everything is fine,' says Manuel. 'The
music, though – not to my taste.'

'Oh, we can shut it out,' says Cydalise. 'There's triple
persiennes, thick glass with fish – look, they can move, and wave
their fins. Maybe, Manuel, when you were young, you had the
game of fish. You hooked a cardboard haddock – who knows why?
Well, these fish aren't real – they move between their sheets of
glass, like in a tank, the sounds kept out. So, you can concentrate
on what comes in your mind....'

'What do we do here?' Manuel asks, pulling the fish shutters up
and down. The others laugh,

'We *live*, my dear,' says Cydalise. 'This place is the best there
is. And it is where you've wanted, all your life. Most people crave
it, like we do.'

'There's peace,' says Hagan. 'When we were in Brazil – there's
gangs with thirty thousand people, armed, all selling drugs! It's
dramatic! Wow!'

'You were living there for drugs?' asks Manuel, quite naive.

'Of course,' says Cydalise. 'You need to. Everybody does. But
it's a myth they make you go inside yourself: you are effaced, a
landscape stretches out, you put on it what you want – pink rocks,

snakes as long as rivers, trees you can live in, faces you can colour, some of them your own. You do not learn a thing.

'There, you can't live high up, not like here – the bullets, Manuel ... they end up high....'

'Yes,' says Hagan, quite solemnly. 'We saw everything. A lot. What did it mean for us, what could we learn. What was to be done; where do we go from there? Everybody's tried to move along from that. The law, the theatre.... poems, prisons. We found so many people, pacing along our path – finding excuses, not for themselves, but for the others. Blame and excuse, they're twins....'

'Oh, that's where you're going?' Manuel asks. 'That's the illumination! It's been hacked over so many times, poetically, angrily – the wars, the famines, deportations, strategic hamlets, re-educating, camps and bantustans. We know it all; there's nothing to be done. The best you dream up, to reason, explain, condemn – is palliative. Everyone is guilty: discriminates, is prejudiced, hauls up some childhood insult, croaks it out, commits some primal murders, invokes a blindness to what is obvious and inadmissable....'

'Yes, Manuel,' says Hagan. 'You're right and wrong. Fortunately, we are not moralists. There's nothing, nothing useful, to be done. It's why we've quizzed you: – you are like the rest. Experience on the cart – is empty. Tatiana – replicates the world. There's only one earth for us, search space for ever, that is all you'll find; in the gigantic mirrors, your distorted face: but always you. Perched on a whirling rock. And us.

'This is your reward: down there in the street is enjoyment, lust and scrabble. It sets you up. Life, its noise, emotion ... everything you swept away. That broom!... And lo! the next day there it was, exactly similar!'

\*

Life in the attic – could not better be. World food downstairs, and booze from every vat and still. Guys who go up to the first floor – will sometimes hesitate, try going higher, chat on the stairs with Manuel, Hagan, Cydalise ... guys spilling secrets of their states, and fiery gossip too.

Manuel is kept at bay by Cydalise, who has him on the boil. Hagan's tolerant, or indifferent. They jog along, lower down the fishy blinds towards the dawn, dream of a miraculous catch. They sleep until the street's swept clean; the trades, the traffic, starts again, identical. It never rains.

'They say going on the stage – carries a strong erotic charge,' Hagan tells Manuel. 'Especially if you wear no clothes.'

'Did Cydalise ever try?' Manuel asks.

'The theatre,' says Hagan, reflecting. 'Is always with us. In us. Is it teacher or tart? The same with music. I believe Cydalise plays the lyre, the *oud* she calls it. Music says nothing but makes us feel as if there's been a message. It's like Benin: sculptor, king or slave – you never know which way the leaf will fall. Heads or tails – or on the edge.'

'I mean,' says Manuel, 'did she perform?'

'You know,' says Hagan, 'the first plays were on a cart. *Mother Courage*. Not that Cydalise is courageous – not yet, at least. The stage here – it's a table top. If you fall – well, if you survive, you'll have breaks and bruises. I don't see any of those anywhere on Cydalise!' And he laughs, patting Manuel on the arm.

'You can go deep here,' says Manuel. 'There's most of the species' attributes so dear to us, that keep us at the top, and it's all priced within a narrow band. And – it's clean, it has to be, not like the scarecrows on the cart....'

It's all exactly true.

Manuel reflects: he says to Hagan, 'I'm wondering ... the bill ... this is an expensive life....'

'Yes,' Hagan says. 'We're expensive people too. You should consider, Manuel, how far you've come. From wanting to be close to artists, and make your cash from what they make – now, you are *it*! You're art, Manuel. No more a hanger-on, bacteria with a broom, who steals and fawns: – you are, inside, just what you want to be. There's nothing more to be achieved.... The motto? Do no good, nor ill.'

'It's true,' says Manuel: 'I'm at the top. But ... sometimes, I wonder, if there is sufficient impetus. In short, if my momentum is enough....'

'The fish?' asks Hagan, laughing. 'Too passive? Philosophical, slow jawing round and round, a spit    a pebble comes out, exgurgitated.... Should we change the scene to rhinos? So timid ... and so slow....'

'I watch you,' Manuel says. 'You do all this for me – and what's for you? Cydalise – unparalleled in world or art: and you, Hagan, a hero. Pacific, a warrior ... All anyone would want to be, you two –

exemplary, a joy – your sympathy, your sentiment, your altruistic acts.... Who has not wished to be like you ... the world, the species, in your image....'

'Well,' says Hagan, blushing, 'on those, your views, you can't expect my commentary....'

They laugh. 'Of course, you think we're spent,' says Hagan. 'To some extent, it's so. But we can help our fellows still ... I feel I am a patron, but not patronising....'

And Manuel embraces him, and pulls in Cydalise as well. They stand, three graces, pure, marmoreal.

*

The street is rocking. Hagan, Cydalise, go down to buy – some leeks from Iceland, *fichi d'India* from Palermo, for their snack – 'Is it just possible,' thinks Manuel. 'That where I am, Cydalise once was? Was she once art, and now she's not, she's something else. And what?'

*

'Nearly everything depends on cash,' says Hagan. 'Tatiana likes to have a court – jokers, lick-spittles. It costs, even living poor – it costs. Maybe she, in cahoots ... maybe your friend? They robbed you. You don't need worry – we have money, Manuel. Lots of it. Let's be precise. We have credit. Even more of that.'

'I know,' says Manuel. 'And I have everything I've ever wanted. Now – I'll have to want some more. But what I miss – is making things. Producing, you could say – not just moving dirt around, and see it all come back.'

'We'll help you, Manuel,' says Cydalise. 'The colours, plangent sounds, the picture books ... those are the easy parts. These will attract, like seeds attract the little birds. That's art: – *on s'engage et puis on voit*. You would be more lustrous if you did all of what they call the arts. Some acting too, even strutting down below. As for your past, the cart, and Tatiana ... Masha: the mystery. None of that is art, my dear, but it is visibility. You might stop there. I had to, naturally.'

She hitches up her pants. 'I'd no idea....' says Manuel, falling back.

Cydalise's legs – they're beautiful, they're after Boulle, a pair of crafted wonders, nacre and ebony, paste jewels and lapis lazuli – 'I fell, dear Manuel,' she says. 'The climax, for a ballerina.... You're frozen in the air, your partner's spent, he can't support – you soar, you hover like a lark.... Down in the pit I went ... the cymbals ... a clean cut, they're terrible sharp discs, sharper than a critic's slash....'

'I could write your tale, Cydalise,' says Manuel. 'Or – there's my sweeper's life. Or Liffey, Paulie – old soldiers dying every way, and every day – and on they go, braving the painted desert, birthing caves, carved rocks, the seers.... Courage, massacring, boredom, racism – anything can happen. There's Masha too – all ripe for fiction, more and more, jam on jam and bread on top....'

'And underneath. Yes, that's wonderful,' says Hagan, unenthused. 'Try your hand. If you find the thread is straining, and the weaving palls – press "delete", no one will know....'

'Now, it's all invention, Manuel,' says Cydalise. 'Perhaps you lived the past and found it really real. It's gone, now, it's time to be creative. Your life – it's shaky ground. Start from here and what goes on below. Us. Who we are, why we have selected you. Remember – you are creation. There must be an ego, hidden below this "Manuel": – bring it out! Let's see it, does it have wings? A tail, scales and gills? The start of something never developed, never left its nest of skin and bone? Or a Balzac, Hugo – a Verrocchio, a dead-eye dick – drawing the mugshots, shooting the mugs.... A genius. What we were told we all are, till we fall....'

'Or we get dropped, Cydalise, like you,' says Hagan, laughing, not quite kindly.

*

'We'll need some photos, Manuel,' says Cydalise. 'Some colour, for publicity.'

Everyone is coloured nowadays, some permanent, and some a fantasy each day anew – the Chinese president has the Long March round him many times. When leaders meet, they find a room and strip off, share the pics, and maybe do a sequence – a Bactrian camel starts off in the sand, and ends in someone else's zoo, for childrens' rides ... equations started on a paunch find their solution on a lady chieftain's bum.... Shared stories, shared tattoos – it's provocation and alliance – see the bosses hug and spar...!

*

'I hope these paints aren't toxic,' Manuel says.

'Your organs too – they enter in the scheme,' says Hagan, using a three-haired brush to figure in still lives on Manuel's knees. 'The colours penetrate, your heart is blue, your liver green....'

'You're art, an artist,' says Cydalise. 'Hold still. I have to place a city on your face, a million people, towers around, a siege, perhaps, a plague with pimples, shrouds beneath the eyes....'

'I'd no idea,' says Manuel. 'You need a presentation so full of life and history, and destiny.... And after all – it's only me. I've not begun to craft my legacy....'

'We must think big,' says Hagan. '*Mappa Mundi.* Your penis, now – the Empty Quarter, maybe? Instead, a glacier...? The popular gaze flies first to that, the member for all and anywhere – that glance, a low flight like a pheasant's....'

They laugh, they set to, Hagan and Cydalise, they transform Manuel, he becomes a codex, illuminated, universal man and woman. 'Now you need a tail,' says Cydalise. 'And maybe hooves, and boxers' thongs around your paws....' They giggle and they fantasise, complain that Manuel's so short, not fat enough for seascapes or a dawn.

*

No one shows.

No one at all. Zero.

No public, no publicity – no one knows that he exists.

'It's a masterpiece,' says Cydalise, covering Manuel with a spotted sheet.

'That's what Tatiana said,' says Manuel. 'About her universe.'

'Maybe they all stopped at the floor below,' says Hagan. 'We are up-market. Top-heavy. Elitist.'

'You could try your luck down in the street,' says Cydalise, hugging Manuel and ushering him out.... 'We wouldn't ask a fee.'

'It wears off,' Hagan says. 'The coloration. Then it's silverplate, very elegant. Then wrinkles.'

'Write on scraps and draw on walls,' says Cydalise. 'It started so. Think: not the first, original man, but probably the last. That should inspire.'

'I never wanted fans,' says Manuel. 'Seven or eight followers ... a recognition.'

'Then you didn't want to be an artist,' says Hagan, 'you just wanted friends. You're lucky to find you're not truly what you'd hoped. Art requires distance, and that excludes a touching on the truth, or on reality. Most don't want that. It chills. You want closeness, an answer for your being, but you have no question: you're a tyro, Manuel. Go hungry, don't borrow – that way you'll discover what you are.'

'Millions are hungry,' says Manuel, crying, 'and they don't find out anything at all.'

'Some will be stars, for sure,' says Cydalise, kissing Manuel. 'We're all creators – some make planets, some a baby, some – a commode. Some made *you*, or tried to: it didn't work out. That's the public! Never within call.... Persevere! Don't climb on another cart, don't fawn on some twister who claims she is a painter! Make your own wheels, doesn't matter if they're not quite round. Almost no one's are....'

*

Ah! The street again – what inspiration! Better than a Yankee pond, or Zen and monks – the buzz!

Manuel's still weeping – so are many more, and stumbling too. He slumps.

'Is your paint dry?' asks the guy. 'I'll sit beside you, not too close. To make your way, you need a dog. A big one – people give cash, not because you're destitute, but because they think you'll feed the dog. It is your hook. They are the slippery fish.... I bet you're here because of people who weren't moralists. Their lives, like yours, are merely vanity. Morals – they don't creep in. You had them, lost them – or don't know what they are. Morals! They bang on the door, the wall, send you to jail, to war: they ask a lot, loudly – but they don't care about you, not a bit. Best ignore them – other people have. You too ... a sceptic born.... A cart, a penthouse – they are nests, and you, dear friend, a bunch of twigs. You can be woven in. Or dropped. From working in the street you pass to street again, but unemployed. Pure Zola, Eugène Sue. Or Booth!

'You never read, you never learn....

'It's not bad luck that brings the wheel around to where you start again, a little further near the ground, deflating, sick and old – but

ready for another spin. You and your wheel... You see –' And the
kind stranger takes a can, says, 'Now, close your eyes ...' and pours
a solvent over Manuel's head.... 'Fate gives you many chances, but
not infinity, because you die, before or after you have seized the
chance....'

'Not luck,' chants Manuel, colourless again.... 'A chance....'

'Off we go,' the guy says. 'You're thrown out the garden – not
your fault. But then – it's your time to start a civilisation,
soldiering, doing the sacrifices, learning lines in plays.... Busy
busy....'

'That solvent,' says Manuel. 'The taste ... let me eat a peach,
something in season here – a pawpaw, giant gooseberry ... clean the
palate....'

'The story everybody knows,' the stranger says, 'is their
granny's religious tale. Forget all that. And all the theories – the
left, the right, collective, individual, of species and of clan –
everything that helped bring us to our present state – eliminate,
forget. Suicide! dear Manuel. A scrabble for survival! That is the
miserable choice....'

'So, we don't discuss philosophy and art, morality and science,
all that stuff?' asks Manuel.

'Of course we shall,' the stranger says, wiping the last pigment
from Manuel's nose. 'We'll have camp fires, tea-dancing with
tickets, brothels and bookmakers – anything you want, that makes
you feel secure. But – we shan't take them seriously.... You'll have
friends, the recognition that you want – and best of all, you've
nothing anyone could want to take! You're too old to be a thief, a
cop, a bully-boy, a father, wife, or captain – army, sea, or industry
– you're too clumsy to drive a dodgem car. No, don't be afraid –
you're not exploitable. No more. You are a simple human....'

'Oh,' says Manuel, fired up, 'I'm more! I am creative.'

'Yes, of course you are,' the stranger says. 'Call me Varnak. I'm
free, I was a prisoner, and now – I have no shame and no
repentance. I am what I am!'

'It's an old trick,' says Manuel. 'Yours. But I've no choice. I'm
beholden to you, Varnak. Thanks for the peach.'

'Don't get excited now,' says Varnak. 'We need to move from
topicality. No messages, no appeals to others, no reverberations.
Sex: you've been everything, I guess ... gender too....'

'No, no,' says Manuel. 'I've tried, not been. Every colour – and now none. All opinions discussed, tried and in the end contested. None of the options attracted me.'

'You fitted none of them, you mean. Perfect,' says Varnak. 'You started off a snail, and now – its shell is left, scoured out, the flesh consumed. You could be porcelain.'

'Wonders,' says Manuel. 'Show me wonders, Varnak. I need wonders.'

\*

'Here's your dog, Manuel,' says Varnak. 'A white dog, very rare. Love it, cherish it, or it will run away, run back.... It will make you rich, just let it take over from you....'

'You stole it, Varnak,' says Manuel, appalled. 'It would run away where it had its home, if I let it. Its love is selfish, or unconscious, a tic, a gene....'

'Nonetheless,' says Varnak, 'it's a better bet than you. It's wise. You aren't. Now, let me tell you what is what. Dictators trump dictators. You're the dentist, Manuel, imagine – dictators are like dragons' teeth, pull one, another grows. Let them fight it out – those twin warriors, remember, they fight their twin, rooted in their furrow like an artichoke, to the death, and then.... They're the Imperial Guard. Stable polities bring humdrum to their people, but their armies bring horrors to those they call the foreigners. Peace – distrust that word. War's simple, peace – hmmm. Democracies crush what's outside, dictators what's inside. A skilful regime can make you drunk: it has you breaking stones for many years, and then, the martial music stops – relax! A wild creativity's born, euphoria, the brain goes spinning round – and then, again, back in the box and making plastic ducks. People love freedom, Manuel, and when they've had it – they have learned submission too. It's all temptation: sacrificing other people or your own, assassinations, dirty dealing – the satisfaction is covert, but assured. You're tempted – do it, don't do it. You hover on your prey. Save or condemn? Eat carrion, or do battle. Maybe – choose a day of hunger, sharpening the appetite ... enjoy the titillation.'

'All that, it seems you've improvised....' says Manuel. 'It's crude and raw. False, I suspect.'

'Oh, I've had power,' says Varnak. 'I could make you skip and crouch! You know what you'd like to be – but I know how it works

– the world, when it gets hot, or cold, and I've been improvising left and right.... Changing landscapes, inscapes – makes you hop and strut, march to my time, stops you stumbling on, milking your goats and eating them.... Sacrifice, Manuel. You have to hand it out. It's not a destiny for me!'

'You were in jail, Varnak,' says Manuel. 'Getting caught – must be a proof of weakness....'

'Rules, Manuel,' says Varnak, laughing. 'You make them; it's your fault if you're found out breaking them!'

'It's too cynical for me,' says Manuel. 'I pull in my arms and legs, you see my prickles, nothing more....'

The white dog lets its tongue hang out, and shows its ribs. Small change comes drizzling down.

'Find a team,' says Varnak. 'That's the key. People with guilt, who want to hide – pull them out, don't heed the slogans – "connect with your inner tree". That stuff's crap. You're desperate, Manuel, you've an imagination, you think you are creative – really, you're a pawn. I – I'm a nest of termites. I pullulate, then I swarm. Projects, schemes. But they don't trust me, no one does... That's good, they're right, but – nothing gets done, nothing's accomplished....'

'I have a secret that I'm not party to,' says Manuel. 'There was a woman – apparently I'm to blame, for what, I can't be sure.'

'That's good,' says Varnak. 'Keep your anxiety on the seethe. Forward, now – with me!'

*

Enlightenment. Renaissance. Heavy things – they fall. Light things – rise. It seems eccentric to investigate what's what, taking years to classify – even making mistakes, explosions, deaths and tumours; balloons and sludge pumps. The scientific revolution. It kept them, keeps them, busy – aeroplanes and rockets, it all follows ... gas and lead.

*

'If you summarise a life,' says Manuel, 'it's bound to seem eccentric – the longer it goes on, it's crazy, if you were to tell it as a tale. Up or down? I've met people who were outré, but I was the normal one. That's why I didn't rise, I got nowhere, nowhere at all.

You, Varnak, are eccentric, probably dishonest, a skyver.... Teller of tales.... And now, that dog....'

'You have to start somewhere,' Varnak says. 'This somewhere is an excellent place. It's visible, like you: you have a secret; fine companions ... ambition, artistry ... a nobody. They're doing well, the nobodies. People from the top drawer – they're finding it is closed, with them shut in to fester....'

'Well, what?' asks Manuel. 'I don't want big money ... I feel I've failed, am being punished – and what for?'

'That's good,' says Varnak. 'Not wanting cash. I or my cousin, we would steal it. Or denounce you for the theft of dogs, take your pitch here on the sidewalk – though even that is metaphor.'

They gaze, gaze at each other, the starting place, the place they have both tumbled into....

The dog – must be a wanderer, its ambition, calculation – off it wanders, by little stages. Round the corner sometimes, always returning, every time until ... it's gone.

*

'No, no,' says Varnak, sobbing, starting to cry uncontrolled. 'Don't say it: failure. Success belongs to you alone – failure is due to other people – I should know. Starting over? How many times, how many promises.... Humiliation, Manuel, dirty deals and dirtier thoughts.'

'I hunger, Varnak,' Manuel says, 'for something of beauty. An altruism. Nothing live or natural – when animals do well, they end up in abundance, and then – there is the cull. Nothing in nature, Varnak....'

'Then, the second peach – is not the cure,' says Varnak. 'I don't know why ... it never works with pleasures – the second's ordinary, the third too much.... It's like: you see – and that is it. A second time of seeing – confirms or not. It's nothing like the first. No revelation. And know: you know, or else you don't. Correct what you knew the first time – it's not better. No wisdom, just a confirmation. Sometimes, of course, an upset. Disaster, loss of faith.... Maybe you only get one try, like shooting apples off your childrens' heads. You see, you know. That's it.'

'You mean – I'm finished, Varnak,' Manuel says. 'They paid me not to know or see.... Except, I know, I saw ... was paid, was robbed. That's it – the end. Life, Varnak. Only my anger and my fear with Masha – that must be what counts.... I could repent, deny....'

'It doesn't work,' says Varnak. 'No, it never does. It's like the money crimes – you go to jail, and yet the crime is nugatory. Only life matters: saved or lost, it's irreplaceable. You ought not go to jail for that. Or else you're always there, locked up, a presence on us all.... The cash – you give it back, or just run off. Money comes and goes – depends on where you are. On trivialities. It shows the world is based on roaming throughout space, not on reason, nor the scientific stuff.'

'You make it worse,' says Manuel, calling the dog.

It doesn't come.

'Maybe what you really seek, my friend,' says Varnak. 'Is a caress. I'd give you one. The first one doesn't count, only a second shows intent. And no! – I don't have second ones of that – no second kiss, caress. Think! We must rise, Manuel. We're down, and so....'

*

'Hell,' says Manuel, 'you show me hell. Now take me out....'

'Oh come!' says Varnak. 'No one believes in hell. Straighten up, smile – your life so far is trivial – some tracking in the dust, is all. More, Manuel: you must ask for more!'

Manuel is silent.

Varnak goes on, 'When your secret, your anxiety, doubt, guilt – when those disappear because there's nothing there, just an experience, finished with – seen, known, of no account – you will have nothing, Manuel. No marker, milestone, document. No credibility, not for yourself, or....'

'Or?' asks Manuel. 'There's no one else. Tell me, Varnak, why you want to boss people, reward some, take credit, making others crawl. It seems a petty thing. Power. A thrill, a bore, a peril.You could do better going to the track, watch the last minute before the off, see where the money goes, follow – and make good. It's easy – we all do it....'

'Oh Manuel,' Varnak says. 'That wouldn't mean a thing. Reward and punish? Not my thing. If you want, you can set up to feed the hungry. If you want, instead, give gold and diamonds to the rich. It's just a choice. There! – that's politics for you. And power. It's a slalom, downhill skating ... then, the supreme! The militarised nomads on their ponies, behind you – the barricades, higher than mansions made of precious chairs and escritoires.... You're history!'

\*

'This is how we live,' says Varnak. 'Our state of nature. In winter, there's the burrow –' and he leads Manuel down an iron stairway. There's warm tubes and rivers, black with soap and shit. Sleepers in alcoves, a catacomb.

'Wear a blanket,' Varnak says, 'and it's better than the home you didn't keep.'

In summer – a green pond, with white flowers, 'You camp out here,' says Varnak, 'on this platform.'

There's shade, a roof held up by teak trees, grey and cracked. 'They floated them down the river, when there was,' says Varnak. 'See! There's every kind of creeping thing up there – lychees too, birds with bright eyes, brighter than yours, and tails a metre long. Sometimes – even longer.'

'It's wonderful,' says Manuel. 'Especially down the ladder. But – what do we do?'

'Yes, you're right,' says Varnak. 'Down there is my space – I get to share it out. Each counts as one, and no one more than one. If the pipe's too hot – you roast. If the river's too miasmic – then you choke. But – it's permanent. They'll never replace the underground, however much they say it's to be eliminated. It serves. Without it – where'd you go?'

'That's true,' says Manuel, overwhelmed. 'Anywhere, you can start again, invent it all. Not difficult. Seek, find – there's flints – and in them saws and files and knives – just tease them out. Swords in rocks, loaves in the grass, cement in the beach.... You're born inventive, knowing it all. A re-run.'

'Exactly,' says Varnak. 'It's like movies. Your Western – as time passes, Indians play themselves, the extras aren't Mexicans any more. Mexicans make Mexican movies instead. The big changes – you can imagine – repeat the Big Bang, the Flood, the Plagues – then it's Game Over,' and he laughs. 'We modest guys who live beneath the feet – we have it hard, but we go on: sheep, up the ladder in the spring, transhumance to the pasture. Then the snow comes. Down the hole you go. If you've been lucky, of course.'

'You are the overlord, Varnak,' says Manuel, with some, a little, admiration. 'The up and down – those are your realm....'

'It's the eyes,' says Varnak, dreamily. 'The sentiment you think – maybe you paint – behind. The trust, suspicion, that we know why they are there, their purpose, destiny, our plan's secure – and yet they want to frolic in their habitus, their own, their family ... and all we spare them is the hooves. Synthetic glue works better – so that's the only part they claim.... Their heritage.... Who knows where they go, those hooves – I guess the horns go down "au fond du bois",' and Varnak laughs.

'Oh no,' says Manuel, finding tears near to brim again. 'We're surely at cross purposes. I don't believe in *facho* talk, even in jest or by hyperbole....'

'We always think there's something higher,' Varnak says. 'We reach – up, up – and so we waver, shake, perhaps the tumble.... That's why we seek out guys like you, Manuel, to help keep order, take off the load, the hatred, from ourselves....'

*

'I'm a sneak,' says Robbie. 'Trust me.' He's clean. 'Varnak put you in charge of fights ... if they ever catch him making order, imposing reason, they'll beat him, put him inside for ever. He's been bad, a sneak, a schemer. An old con. Now he's chief. Watch – that's how it's done.'

'I need a place,' says Manuel, ' however small it is.'

Robbie is a jerk – he wants to run the underground, Black River too.

'Oh,' Robbie says, 'lots of us here have jobs. It costs too much up there. You have to have a woman, kids, the lot. I'm starting over way down here. I'm starting a civilisation, though there's thousands of years still left ... no hurry. The path up there – it meanders. The species is ending, too many short-cuts. I know – it's my job, to make things obsolete – useful things. I'm logical – I eliminate, so down here I can begin again, another way.'

'Wonderful,' says Manuel. 'Though you don't convince. Just – don't give me trouble.'

'Do everything,' says Robbie, trotting after Manuel, pulling at his neck-hairs. 'Let nothing stick. I've walked on the moon, sung Tristan, dredged plastic fish from ocean caves, financed motorcars that run on water, been elected to the Slovak parliament, crossed deserts, been rescued from a cliff. Remember this: don't give your name. Take cash, rent space, leave before the end, don't appear in program notes, keep a foot on the bottom in the pool ... load your carbine yourself, don't try to skin giraffes....'

'I'm with you, Robbie, on all that,' says Manuel. 'Don't rent space down here – it isn't yours. No noisy intercourse. Don't smoke cheroots. Share spliffs.'

'Yes,' Robbie says. 'You're cut out for this job. This is your home. It cancels out whatever you have done before.'

'Free,' says Manuel. 'Very free. A place where freedom can be practised. Great repression, going with it.'

'Exactly,' says Robbie. 'Say and think anything, for sure you'll not be heard. Don't fight. You'll end real bad.'

'I see, I know,' says Manuel. 'I'm free. I'm in bonds. It's good – an inspiration.'

'Just – don't trust Varnak,' says Robbie. 'He sees it all runs smooth. Keep within what he tells you, you'll be fine.'

*

'Life ends in books,' says Manuel. 'The culmination – then the dry ending. There's folkore down here, you could make a fortune writing it all down, paying to have them printed – the tales. My! it's so dull. Everybody has an arse, a prick, a cunt, and everybody farts much of the time, and ponders incest, robbery and fraud. We are all beautiful or ugly, and with magic can do nearly everything until we're found out and have to pay for stronger spells.'

He stands tall, head at the roof.

'The clowning's over,' Manuel says. 'What we do down here is hard-edge, machined thinking. Then it gets hot outside, and we go up, sit outside the temple. Don't go in there! The past, Robbie, imagination: that's all passé!'

They laugh – they're almost mates – at the little play on tales. 'It was all life once,' says Robbie. 'But – yes, it ends in books. Not down here, though – there isn't light ... many can't read, besides....'

'Funny, bold, titillating and transgressive – you need all those just to survive,' says Manuel. 'Though what really drives the show, the band – the rhythm – is quite sober-suited now.'

'We're monks,' says Robbie. 'We don't ask where the birds who feed us find the food, what's expected in return, who Varnak serves and whether we serve him. We pass our days in poverty, we pray for Kurdistan and Mozambique, we do philosophy, and if we feel it – we may do a song and dance.... Modesty, Manuel. Think and move your lips, but not a sound! No doubt we're useful, but the "why" and "how" are not on our horizon.'

Robbie might have a job outside – but no one sees him climb the ladder to the light. He's a mystery, like those all monks must have.

Manuel's idea is – no medieval bawdy, nor the brawls that go along with it. No playing barbary organs in the night.

'Are you quite sure, Manuel?' asks Robbie. 'We know we're animals – but spinning tales raises our morale ... brings a closeness to the pack....'

'I don't believe it brings us closer to the truth,' says Manuel. 'Then there's deaths. We should put cadavers in Black River, that is theirs as well, float them out, where they're seen, not stock them in an alcove like a cheese....'

'Of course,' says Robbie, 'this is Enlightenment. Silence and absence, nothing to mourn or caper to....'

'This is as it will be,' says Manuel. 'Once let it all regress – and it is done and finished. The story. Just repeats.'

\*

'It's good,' says Varnak, 'that you have an eye for order. Remember though, first: order is mine, you just take its fragrance. Then – don't export it. The cadavers – they're yours. Keep them. Finally, if you're straight – find a woman. She'll keep you occupied. Take Anouk. She's fallen, you could be one of her hard times she's falling on: she's had an abundance of everything, you'll be familiar....'

'Where are you headed, Varnak?' Manuel asks.

'The uplands,' says Varnak, laughing. 'Most have been explored. Tonality. Atonality – it just takes time, and you've done it all. I'm building on you and your crew, Manuel, you are my pirates. I make my contacts, and you get charity – charity ties you to good books. That's your destiny – it's all written down, and there's trouble if you go against the preachers. You're unarmed, so you can take the blankets – they're not the ones with smallpox seeded in.'

'If we're pirates,' says Manuel, dizzied by the tale-spinning – 'You're the captain, and you must show us where the prizes are.'

'A radio,' says Varnak, closing the subject. 'It won't bring order and reason, but you won't need dance and risk falling in the river.

Be patient, Manuel, I'll get you out of there, and Robbie can take over....'

\*

Anouk has tramped the world. She's not suitable, but Manuel tells her everything, about Masha too. Nothing more is to be said, no secret's unrevealed.

'I don't see....' she says. 'There's nothing there, no story. If you're in jail, there's people die, you have to play your part, and then it all repeats outside. It's called the learning, Manuel. Parallel. On one track, there's remembering and forget. On the other track, you learn, repeat, then you cross over, and you forget, remember. What's the link?'

'It's what you do, quite locally,' says Manuel. 'The king of Benin, his slaves, the sacrifices.... Everything for art. Or custom, power – a bit of everything. You learn, repeat, you follow – probably, you hope you may forget. You lose your enemies, that's true, but making sacrifices – it means you have to execute your friends. It works in jail, and in the palaces: it hardly matters who it is who holds the knife.'

'I don't think the *Oba* helped make the figurines,' says Anouk. 'Artists: it's better they don't repeat too much, they learn but don't forget. Maybe I mean they'd rather not remember....'

'They don't need to,' Manuel says. 'It comes out new, even the pastiches. It's terrible for them – it doesn't fit what people know. People pretend they recognise originality: it's false. They're ignorant – the unfamiliar amazes them, or irritates. It's all new, the first of anything.... The killing and the flattery, those strike a chord, they never change.'

'You're an original, Manuel,' says Anouk, eating the dried figs Varnak gave him as a favour. 'But it doesn't help us here. It's pointless. It makes you look a dumkopf.'

'Above me, there is Varnak,' Manuel says. 'Below, there's Robbie, wanting to take over. I'm in their sandwich, Anouk. Am I ham?'

'No,' she laughs, 'it's a mash sandwich: you'll get spat out.'

\*

Robbie says, 'Anouk? She's a good sport. Nothing personal, Manuel – I consider her my woman. It makes no difference, of course. Just for info....'

'She's clean,' says Manuel, at a loss. 'That's not easy, down here, with all the moisture.'

'She knits her clothes,' says Robbie, trying to move on.

'I saw,' says Manuel. 'Her personality – it's warm.'

'You know about Descartes,' says Robbie. 'And Bergson too, no doubt. How does it happen, do you think, that first it's the body that's a machine. Now it's the mind becomes mechanical. Wired and glowing?'

'It's science,' Manuel says. 'Statistics, actually. Everything is counted – bodies and minds come out the same....'

'People always counted,' Robbie says. 'Fingers. Goats, and cash. Anouk – you'd not say she was a machine? You wouldn't want a robot made, not exactly like?'

'I hadn't thought,' says Manuel. 'But no, you're right. We could each have one – an Anouk, one knitted and one clockwork. And yet – there's clocks that's all mechanical, but on the hour, there's every kind of bear and fox, and jesters, warriors too ... they circle round and cock a snook....'

'No, Manuel,' says Robbie sharply. 'They're all powered the same. Clockwork. Probably batteries by now.'

'You need the cinema to bring it out,' says Manuel, trying to close off the conversation. 'The ticking and the tock. The near, the far, the now, the then. Though possibly you'd say that was clockwork too.'

'You're the artist, Manuel,' Robbie says. 'You could keep a diary, of what we do. And how it ends.'

*

Robbie has heard – they'll be evacuated, kicked out, rehoused, put on the street, in jail, in agriculture or in industry, or in locked wards.... Or destinies not thought about, selection of the useful and the useless, the absent and the present, favoured and the negligible. It's Varnak's plan, Varnak the saviour, the humanist, the benefactor. A step up. Enough is true and false to give him lustre.... Reforms that nip you like a revolution: the cops, evacuation. New life! Trucks to take you to new places – where you'll have to pay a rent, and look for jobs and not pay all the bills, and then there's trucks, can't take you anywhere, maybe they can, the hidey-holes are closed, in disrepair, and maybe you're on lists, not one, but several, and have your photo in a file, with lies you've told and trying to disguise your phiz with hair and gurning too....

\*

'It's Varnak – he's negotiated cash,' says Robbie. 'A great man, growing greater. You'll have to earn, Manuel, to live somewhere, wherever you are sent. What can you do?'

Manuel wrings his hands. 'Of course, I can do anything. The higher up the tree you go – the easier it is to pick the fruit. But – this means, Robbie, if it all gets better – first, it'll be worse for me. Then – for everyone – including you, Robbie, who'll take my place, then find you take responsibility for all that falls and falters.'

'We don't come from a slum,' says Robbie. 'For us, the slum is next. We come from the underground, that's all. Philosophers – they don't peer that far down. There ought to be ideas that you can settle in a corner of your hut, there's not much room. A big idea, full of wind and gas – you put it there and it deflates. Philosophy – it's hard to find one for your hut – I use the term 'hut' loosely, Manuel. Maybe it's bunkhouses that await.... It may even be, in sympathy with the deprived, there's no philosophy at all, for anyone.... Suspended – belief, conviction – maybe it's a good. I use "philosophy" quite loosely, it's never been of relevance to what I hope awaits me....'

'Yes,' says Manuel. 'The idea is the closer people live, the more they'll make their fellows clean and sober but – it isn't so. There's trade and irritation too. Even rage, cage rage.'

Birds suffer from it.

Military-style trucks come. It's hard for people in damp clothes to climb up. 'How much of your earlier life do you remember, Manuel?' Anouk asks.

'It's not the time,' says Manuel. 'I don't remember much. Nothing happened. I remember everything. No one now must stay below – they'll stopped up the entrances, we'll all see the palaces above, made of marble blocks, those immense horses, rearing up, no sexy parts, that would be *de trop,'* he laughs.

'Is it so, Manuel,' Anouk asks. 'There'd only be one way to leave, when we are all gone up – the dark river, which you don't pass if you don't have the fare, a friend to close your eyes and slip a coin beneath your tongue?'

'Yes, that's exactly right,' says Manuel. 'It's my responsibility, to see you off, without a fight.'

'Oh, if we fought....' says Robbie, eyes dead as a cod's. 'We could hold out, maybe a week. You'd write it down, Manuel. Would it be read?'

'I'd need to organise all that,' says Manuel. 'See! Those guys have come to stopper up the holes....'

And Anouk pushes Robbie down, stamps on his little hands, the fingers scrabble, they are clean, the nails are cropped and – down he goes.

The military-looking guys – they put the cover on, and Anouk says to Manuel. 'You have responsibility for all of us, bar Robbie now.... You can assign the space, the bunkhouse needs a titled guy to say who's near the stove, who's near the door. You could do that, Manuel,' and she hugs him, not for long. 'Now, help me on the truck,' she says. 'My skirt is heavy, long and full of other skirts....'

A favour's done, and Manuel knows it is a manacle, but better that....

'Up here's enlightenment,' says Anouk, as the dust rises from the wheels – chalky and stony dust. 'Poor Robbie, his thin voice, those white legs like one-by-ones, the kilt, the little shiv, stuck blunted in his sock ... another friend and foe: left far behind, like all your women, those who survive! – your comrades too, like – who? the tearful Liffie? Paulie, the wall-eye he had made specially, inserted so he's be a marksman, never miss a shot – if he were armed! – both pegged out on thorns or suspended from a baobob, hoping their plot will twist, turn and drop them....'

'We're dependent on my *capo*,' Manuel says, morosely. 'Varnak....'

'Oh no,' says Anouk. 'True, I am his scout, his bright bird, who soars and sees encampments, ponds where philosophers may ponder, fester, camp.... But, you know, he has no fief, no land or tower, no mill, no keep: he's not a gatekeeper. He seeks a door that he can watch, decide who's in and out – or, at least, a beggar's window, where the charitable leave some worn-out stuff, and in obscurity, you gather in.... That is the tops, dear Manuel,' Anouk confides. 'And Varnak's far from that.'

*

They stop – every face is white with dust. They laugh – white faces – that's as far as it can go.

Anouk bunks by Manuel, 'No one's alone,' he thinks. 'It's not where I'd have chosen....'

'Nor would I,' says Anouk, cosying up.

There's fights, but no one's bothered, 'Go where you want,' says Manuel.

It's hot, it's very hot. 'It's worse for me,' says Anouk, unbuttoning a blouse and thrusting Manuel's hand inside.

'My!' he says, 'it's fur – so thick and silky – and the colours...! How...? It can't be wolf, or leopard, but....'

'I think it's retro-cat,' she says. 'If you follow stars, especially those in uniform, they off-load on to you – ambition, other inconveniences....'

'Houses will come, for sure,' says Manuel – he's at a loss. Doesn't believe that things will change – and that's a busted hope!...

'You thought you had a strategy,' says Anouk. 'A plan. Instead, you broke the moral codes, when they were in your way. Now, it's too late, you're just a wastrel, like the rest of us.'

Manuel thinks back in life – for sure, there's theft and pride, and anger too. Sloth and lust are absent, greed as well. Indifference and doubt – those are not sins. You'd say he's well ahead regarding sins, but all the same....

It's very hot, barracks are hotter than tents would be.

After a while, the Chinese workers come. 'See,' Anouk says. 'They'll bring our house, for sure.'

They don't. They raise the barracks on to piles of bricks.

They're mostly silent, they don't sing. 'It's for the snakes, we can't be left to rest upon the ground,' says Anouk.

No one's seen a snake. Not ever, not round here.

'Will China save us?' Manuel wonders. 'If there's war?' and Anouk says:

'Oh, at the end – they'll live here too. They'll fight to save their cities, pull them down if they are threatened.... Their land has no resource, it's barren – if there's soldiers come, they will resist ... even if they've only past and future, empty time to save, they'll do it. The worst thing is to be occupied, then liberated. Worst for anyone, so worst for us. It leaves a problem with all sides.'

'And even worse,' says Manuel, gloomily, 'is first conscripted, do the massacres, then beaten, occupied, and liberated by another lot, and educated: it will take years.'

'That's plausible,' says Anouk, admiring. 'You are wise. And Varnak is no help, of course – he's not up to making war and peace – he sails along wherever there's a wind....'

\*

There's not much food, nor much to do. There's little stalls, you barter if you've stuff. There's not much cash. 'This is the best,' says Anouk. 'It's crap. But all the same.... And I shan't dig so we can grow our food. It would be the start of something worse.'

'It isn't easy answering that,' says Manuel.

'That's good,' says Anouk, sharp, 'because it's not a question.'

She whirls and preens. 'See! Someone taught me how to dance. It may be useful. The guy said so.'

'A Chinese guy?' asks Manuel. 'Are they here for charity, or as punishment?'

'We've free time here,' says Anouk, continuing to whisk around. 'So we could start our civilisation – except, that needs a structure. We're not Mayans, so our time has only present. They could build pyramids because they had past and future too.'

'You could get snakes, Anouk, you've got contacts,' says Manuel. 'If that brings us civilisation. They are full of time, snakes – people like to get shot of them, they wouldn't cost, they don't get paid, they intrude. Nothing to use them for, even if they tell you secrets ... watch they don't sting you, but they're best ignored ... besides, we're safe up high, prepared.'

'I could look up guys with snakes,' says Anouk. 'Tell me, is it civilisation the Chinese will bring? We don't have it, nor do guys like Varnak. What's so special about it, civilisation, anyway? There's workers, and there's people like me, afflicted with fur, like fucking animals. What more do people want, what does "more" involve? Religion, conscription, human sacrifice? Magazines that no one reads?'

'You're exceptional, Anouk,' says Manuel, not liking getting close to her. 'Your pelt. It's not a gift, it's a regression. Being cast out. The fur might go away with treatment.... It's the way you live, have lived. No one is keen on hybrids anywhere.... True, the signs can make us all reflect – what you portend, where you came from, were treated, all that stuff. But, in the end – you're inconvenient. You can't explain yourself....'

'You've lost your argument,' says Anouk, shedding tears. 'If I had wealth and learning you bet life would be different ... as it is, we hybrids, as you call me, we don't strip off, and no one paints our picture....'

'I hope it lasts,' says Manuel. 'Our peace. Our hardship. Our being overlooked. Alas, money's been spent on us. That's poison. We're international – there's competition between peoples to ship us in and ship us out....'

'To help?' says Anouk, not convinced. 'Transform us?'

'To help themselves, and make us useful,' Manuel says. 'I never wanted to be useful – *art brut* now seems to me the best: art for its own sake, without future hopes, or acknowledgments to history.... Spontaneous combustion, Anouk. I never wanted usefulness – just to be central; at the centre of the world.... But – best be very careful now. Hide your fur: it's beautiful, between us shared; show no one else, don't draw attention, don't try to make a buck by flaunting it, don't let them shave it off and take a sliver of your soul, then see their slicer go in deeper, deep into your bones and then some spoonfuls of your mind and sessions in an office all your life and then beyond, your essence slabbed like humble pie, petrified into an aspic – amber, jade or chert ... like Lenin's brain, bottled in a retort, stoppered in, made sure it can't escape and do it all again, better this time, and drive those fourteen armies out that's after him, old fox....'

'Yes, yes,' says Anouk, 'but you must admit – it's future! And attractive. They'll come, the uniforms, and change it all. You will be a little boss and me a curiosity....'

'It's not our thing, Anouk,' says Manuel. 'Respect's a fine objective when they spit on you, but a chimera when it means you are a boss or artefact: terrible reckonings await....'

'You're right,' Anouk says. 'No one created me, I did it all myself, for no profit, no display. An emanation. My inspiration: every breath a serenade, and every nap a nocturne.... No tweak, no gallery, no glass coffin, display case – nothing, no show and no parade. Mine, mine alone: then on with more and more. Or nothing more at all.'

\*

It makes no difference, of course.

Guys, saying they don't know: not where they came from, what they do, nor who's responsible for anything: guys come. They count and measure. Guys without a memory take it all back to somewhere where there's bigger deafs and dumbs, and something is prepared that's wide enough to cover Manuel, Anouk, with ash and leaves, all in one night.

Meanwhile, Robbie in his tapsalteerie kilt runs up and down the sewer pipe, the scaredy rat! – and curses Manuel, and looks for tiny coins, wind-blown as ash-leaves, he could put upon his lids, under his tongue, and so at last glide out, afloat on the dark river ... into the light.

*

'Meaning, Manuel, meaning!' Anouk pleads. 'You're the smart one, drifting, rebounding, taking out your secrets when you're alone, turning them over, like a beach-bird examining stones for crawling things – you're pregnant with those meanings – cough them up!'

Manuel laughs, 'Oh Anouk – it's probably a private thing ... Destiny....!' He thinks of Masha; the vanman's black-stubbly face, 'What's your uncertainty? Anxiety's your horse. What could reassure, coming from me? I'm a spectator, seeing all sides, siding with none ... sweeping away....'

'Let's take extinction first,' says Anouk. 'Is that our destiny? For me – it's good. Down we all go, together, the tinies and the roarers – us, who're somewhere in between in sound and size.... All in together, a huge carrion pie. It gives me an importance – yes! The last. Valediction. The first – if there is something else – I'd be the first! The first they'll find....'

'It need not be, Anouk,' says Manuel, remembering solutions, palliatives.... Anouk jumps in, 'Yes, yes, I know! Be prudent and repair ... but we are not like that! Live lean and parsimonious? That's not our style. Tomorrow's dinner, do we consider that? No – we eat the cubs today, the tenderness appeals. If nature won't provide tomorrow – we'll be the carrion. Some animals, they roam afar to kill their prey, some polish off their neighbours. Some are born – to follow up my thought – born Americans, some are Chinese. Some leap and pounce, others swallow, swell, digest.'

'That's your answer, then, Anouk,' says Manuel, much irritated. 'You're a spectator too – too stupid to run away, too much the fatalist, the moralist, to join the predators.'

'We hybrids,' Anouk says, 'don't live as long, as short, as others might. I'd want someone, something, to stay with me, to see my body is not eaten. Stuffed, is worse... Sent to coroners around the world, a piece for each, a trophy....

'I need an end, a proper one. As for meaning: – "lives and dies". What more meaning can you have? – a beetle or the universe – all rolling balls of crotte, horizon to horizon, deathless crotte, the beetle who becomes his ball....'

'Don't be deceived, Anouk,' says Manuel. 'I won't watch over you. I'm untrustworthy and faithless.'

'And I am meat,' says Anouk.

\*

Doctors come. You can't tell who, or where ... they wear those little masks. A dreadful sign:

'We weren't sick before,' Anouk says. 'Now, everybody takes a test. We feel the same – but they can tell where we came from, or what they can remove from us. Some of us they take away, entire. Maybe those are Toltecs, portending danger, sent off to where the eagle and the jaguar have gone....

'Do I look Toltec, Manuel?'

'Some perhaps they take to disassemble them,' says Manuel, seeking to avoid her glance. 'A good arm, a useful leg, a twist of sturdy ganglia – cheaper to take them from the living than have the sick go into therapy.... Then there's the resisters – easy to see the awkward ones....'

\*

One day, Anouk's not there, not any more, not as she was, at least. It's commonplace, not even fantasy. She's never seen again, not as she was.

She was a hunter, Manuel thinks: nothing died because of her.

\* \* \*

The little houses come – the barracks are nearly emptied out – it's best to stay together, someone says.

My! Here's Gaston, the soldier. He was listed as a corpse. No medals, no religion, service minimal, rank? none bestowed.

'It's just provocation,' Gaston says. 'Just getting in supplies. Preparing. It's just the countries. They take against you, they're vindictive, they're not personal but they seem to take things personally, their people tag along....'

'I was wrong,' says Manuel. 'In olden days, the city and the street were one. Now, they're seperated. I thought I could reach the city from the street – it's never so, the traffic is one way – and me, I'm from the street down to the sewer, then to the holding pen, the purifying ponds. I'm now disposable, Gaston – I slide! I must be smooth....'

'It could be, Manuel,' says Gaston laughing. 'You're viscid. They thought snakes were slimy, but it isn't so – maybe you're not the snake, you eat the apple, get the lesson wrong. It's the species, Manuel, we're mostly so. You can say yes or no – it's all the same. It doesn't change, our stance is meaningless – it's just our legs: they feel more comfortable at ease than at the "present arms". That's all.'

'There's always a last chance,' says Manuel. 'Let's leave the camp before they tidy up the last of us, and purify....'

'You've been lucky, Manuel,' says Gaston. 'You've maybe slid a little, but you're still running, still looking for the Start. The others – have done much worse – the women – my dear!' and he cackles, rises to falsetto. 'The soldiers! Those that do well, like Varnak, climb up a pile of broken bricks and wait to tumble down: – those sharp broken edges, each one gets your liver....

'The system finds it hard to pick out ones or even twos of us. There's floods and famines – outside its reach, propensity: then there's the births, the trains, the roads, the oil, the regions, and the epidemics – for each of us, it is a lottery.... Sometimes – there's an aim, it seems, but mostly not, nature or the bureaucrats, they don't know you, how scared and spiteful. If they did, it wouldn't signify. So, if they call – it's pretty much pure luck. A lottery, they say, where there's no winners and no prize – just to avoid the moving finger is enough. Being missed out – that's the best ... and you're the master, Manuel, at dodging, skittering down, keeping your nose clean, and sticking out the silt to breathe. It isn't happiness. No life of Bloom, no blooming life – accessories is everything, you live on hoping all your stuff does not go obsolete too quick, or that you're not a plagiarism, written up and sold in someone's anecdote.'

They ponder this.

'I don't write things down, Gaston,' Manuel says: 'A clock's enough, no diary. The encampment – well, nothing happened, except the ebb and flow. While I was writing nothing down, I might have thought how great the people are, the country too, and songs in bars and lore in general. People do! They spend their lives writing down their lives, and make careers that way. Meanwhile, a huge war might have slipped right by, beneath their gaze and underneath their noticing. It could have happened so to me, but it did not.

'Our dictator – still at college, failing a course and bribing profs – despising them, their arrogance, venality ... all's yet to happen, it is evident. The End – that fits post mortem sales, director's cut, the proofs, the topping out: if it's not written, striped on, it won't happen, not at all.'

'Oh,' Gaston says. 'It's been written, you can bet. Into the hopper, everyone! A fricassé, meat loaf for giants – or in the bin, for worms.... I saw it on the wall – a wide red river, meticulous, it flows down from a throne and seeks out every runner, burns like a nettle shirt.... Doesn't discriminate, nor rationalise....'

'That's a picture, Gaston,' Manuel says. 'We all draw those on walls. And on our bodies too. What we have now – is slide. You'd think if mud slides, you just step away – it isn't so: it comes down like a wall, a wind, a continent. We're in the mud, become the mud. No one has fingered us, or stamped our document, but here it comes ... the mud.'

'We'll head out towards that line of trees,' says Gaston. 'Machines can't get in there, the dark wood. We'll be safe.'

And the two of them, that's what they do.

\*

No one follows them. They lie side by side, in peace, two princelings beneath the curtseying trees.

'We could join up,' says Gaston.

'Join?' asks Manuel. 'What to what?'

'Us. An army. A band, a gang,' says Gaston. 'It's the coming thing. See – proper armies cost, and they are visible, their badges: all kinds of heavy things. There's even rules. A militia, though, is lithe: a presence, an idea. It represents; it's simple. Someone's behind you – but how far behind? What does that someone want from you? Moreover, you are paid. It's no more dangerous than sleeping rough out here. And mostly, that is what you do – you sleep. Be rough. Be tender. There's no extradition, if you choose your place....'

'But,' Manuel says, much afraid, 'I've the fear of being taken hostage. It is a metaphor, I know – but there's degrees ... discomfort and uncertainty. I know, that's what we have right here – but there is much much worse. Enrolled. Someone's chosen for you, chosen your side. You don't know if it's right....'

'Well,' Gaston says, 'that is the point. Besides, that way, we are redeemed. Whatever we have merited – the barracks, being helped and relocated, locked up, experimented with – all is wiped out. No more regrets, or guilt – that's all to come, if come it does....'

'But we're the victims, Gaston,' Manuel says. 'Someone else should pay, if anybody does – not us.'

'Remember – the *Oba* and Benin,' says Gaston. 'The victim always pays, and pays two times. You must be cleansed of what the others do to you.'

'Suppose – I did it all myself,' says Manuel.

'Then you can punish and redeem yourself,' says Gaston, irritated. 'Over and over. You're a case extreme – and rare.'

*

'Listen', says Gaston, losing his small patience. 'Everyone is frightened, everywhere and all the time. It can happen any time, one time – it will. Enrol – and you can be exactly what you want – guilty or innocent, deserter, warrior. You can liberate, found nations: build a fort, be burnt alive, die in the sand, run charities. It's the only trade you'll ever have that gives you power – see if comes from the barrel of a gun. You will have one of those – use it to prop the tent, or as a splint, a crutch, a table leg. Shoot your brother, if you want.'

'I'm terrified,' says Manuel. 'It must be real, because I never felt this way before – being on a parapet, just out the egg; so, cast yourself – the air will bear you up, and you have wings. Wings you've never seen – and so....'

'Jump!' says Gaston, walking off. 'It's nature. Fifty per cent is guaranteed at least one jump. Remember too – it doesn't mean a thing is real because first time it strikes you so. It's the contrary. What's real needs hammering in, over and over, till you're sure. Now, come. They're taking names – that red tent with the prayer flags. Invent a name, and give it them.'

And that he does.

\*

'Now there'll be lectures,' Gaston says. 'Then how to crawl with guns. Who's on our side, and we on theirs, up to a point, they say....'

'It doesn't sound like it's for me,' says Manuel. 'I'm only good for listening. Click! – an ivory ball kissing another similar, rolling off, trying to avoid a pocket, the abyss. That's me. I'm not proper, not a round shape you'd like to play with. Trust, righteousness – that's all gone by, too late now. I just have life, and other people shave me off a slice of theirs....'

Gaston's not convinced, or, better, he's not interested.

There's lectures – where and how to bank your pay. The law of nationalities: who can try you, when, what to do if you get caught, what to do if you catch someone. That's the interesting part. There's nothing about hostages, or being prisoners. 'You see,' the lecturer says. 'You are a hinge. A hinge stops a door from falling down. The door is closed, the hinges keep it so. And if the door is opened, it's because the hinges turn with it. That's all.'

'Of course it isn't all,' says Gaston. 'They tell you that to show if you're in trouble, they won't help.'

\*

There's a movie: 'This is the finest movie there has ever been,' says the guy.

Gaston calls him 'Sarge' – he doesn't mind, he doesn't understand, he doesn't care. 'Put these in your ears,' he says. There is no sound, not from anywhere.

The colour, sometimes a little over-cooked, sometimes it's shades of anthracite ... there's nothing special, it's where we all came from, got our eyes and hair and genes, skills in running, fast, away, indifference to suffering, ourselves and others, doing puzzles, playing games, prayers and superstitions, accepting defeat, overeating at a victory, the same spot of yellow grass and stuff like beetroot tops, the glacier ending in a splash and crumble, you don't hear the grinding as its years sing out, and there's the black brown huts leaning together on the slope, a hairy pony tied, the brown and black people looking straight down the lens as if they're stills, the tilted stone-girt fields, eaten bare, a track sketched out half-hearted and there's beasts at every bend, desperate, unmannered, they'll eat you or a lizard any day, the lizard's best because you eat it all at once, don't have to fight to keep a carcase, remember where you left what isn't finished, have to eat the tripes, the shit, of anything full-grown, you hear the bears and jackals and the vultures over there, beyond the crest, and down the scree go aged people dragging loads, to be defrauded in the market, pay some tax, start trudging back....

'They don't look happy,' Manuel says to Gaston.

'Are you happy?' Gaston asks.

... there's big faces, rutted and pimpled, you get those down the mine ... there's little groups of guys with scythes, old guns ... a flag. Silently, they wave the weapons, open and shut their mouths, a revolutionary song perhaps....

It's over. Endless sadness. Little trees, tiny with being far away.

'That's who we join?' asks Manuel.

'Oh no,' says the Sarge. 'That's all gone, all over, the people and their fields. The houses don't have beams you carry off, they drop down where they stand. Everything goes, has gone; that was fifty years ago, you don't have anything to do with all of that ... even if you wanted to....'

'It's so moving....' Gaston says, weeping. 'The prayers ... the warriors....'

'I didn't see....' Manuel starts.

'You must see it many times,' says Sarge. 'First off, you miss the detail, and the sounds.'

'They're like us,' says Gaston. 'Exactly. They've moved, been paid some to move some more, then not paid, so's they'll have to move again....'

*

'Your unit,' says the Sarge, taking most things as set, for granted, 'isn't you. It's not the you yourself you live in, know about. It's proxies – just remember that. You – are a presence that gets snapped, snapped from above, so far up you'll never see it, guess what it records, why, what can it be – vulture, wasp – or just a lark, windhover.... You're proxies – you are someone else, and they are you. Probably – elsewhere. You are the fight that carries on, but you don't fight – that's not the point. The point is settling; a settlement we make when all the folks have gone, moved off, changed into something else, another nationality, another homeland, all that stuff.'

'I told you, Manuel,' says Gaston, 'we're not real people, we're not the people in the film. We're standing in, we can do quite what we want, it isn't us, we are the first resort, it's what's behind us that's the last resort, resort where we can all relax and lie upon the sand, forget, and be forgiven, live to fight or liberate another day....'

'I understand all that,' says Manuel. 'It's action. It's what the lives I've seen – the people in the street, walking up and down to reach elusive cities – what they lacked. Action: decisive; permanent in its effect. Exactly what I waited for, and plotted, stole and lied to reach.... And now you tell me what is evident: we'd not be real, not really us, although we seem to promise exactly what real people would have done; brought justice, fairness, sharing of knowledge.... Some cleansing deaths.

'And yet it isn't so – we bring vendettas: oppression sitting in the hut, the factor taking half of everything that grows, and if there's nothing grows – a half of that as well.... We are the judgement first, then the apocalypse, dear Gaston.... If we want, maybe you or maybe me ... we'd be real people, but we're not.... What stops us, Gaston...?'

'Oh Manuel!' Gaston laughs. 'That's quite another movie, pretentious, false. You and I, we're nothing more than those same idlers, who listened to poor Anouk's chattering, and understood why she was she. A curse fell on us, Manuel. Pity without a remedy: a falsity, a dead-end alleyway....'

*

'Now,' says the Sarge. 'Decide. Who's in, who's out, or if you'll sit here in the wood and do philosophy.'

'Redress....' Manuel begins.

'There is none, Manuel,' Gaston says. 'Even if you've power, cleaned the barrel, and reloaded.... You'll never shift the mountain – things piled on top of circumstantial things. Too heavy to be

weighed. You, Manuel, should realise, you're small – think back –
even, you were born small,' and Gaston laughs and laughs.

'It worries me,' says Manuel, and thinks 'here they come again'
– the vanman, Masha, what you can do, don't want to do, your limit
and the mountain you can't budge. 'It's like we're lions,' he says,
'Deciding who to hunt, or maybe give it up, that life – a day or so,
and rest, stop killing ancestors – although you can't, most are
already long long dead, or moved away, changing their names and
languages, in shanty-towns or camps or attics in Manhattan. Ours –
a life of wandering, of living, letting live, killing, dying ...
nomads....'

'Exactly so,' says Gaston. 'Militarised nomads. Our flocks
forsaken. On our horses, terrible and swift.'

*

'Are we at the point....' asks Manuel, quite desperate. 'Three guys
stop the atom plant from blowing up ... just. That was one life gone,
and theirs of course, but we may well have fewer lives than cats. I
grant you, will we roast or freeze or rot – we probably shan't know,
we'll be going, or be gone. The next lot – they'll have a little more
of truth. That was the theory – we're top dogs, top pigs, top wolves
– because we want the truth. Some even said "we make the truth" –
but those aren't many now, who think that way. It is clear, we make
the mess, and something else is truth, spun out by something, a
truth not found in temples or in mosques, but nonetheless.... There
is: there is the truth, like it, want it, or not, however it might look,
what it can do.... Found, extruded, manufactured....

'Then there's my search – the people I have found. The women,
mostly – they kiss, they slide away. I'm snookered, over, over – the
colours – fade. The touch, alignment – sighting on the cue ... and
then they're gone! The sorrow, Gaston, the regret – it's not like the
irritation that you feel when a proposition or a lemma turns its back
– but.... What does it matter? Sometimes, not much to me; and
usually, not that much to them....'

'You'll never end the story of yourself, my friend,' says Gaston,
checking out night-vision stuff, and pulling on tall buckled boots.
'Your mind, my dear – it's like a taiga – birch trees and snow –
every horizon seems identical and infinitely far. Join me, join up –
the impact's certain – a provocation, pretext, quite exposed, we're
messengers of good and bad, and – depending who you are, of bad

and good. This is the best you'll have, the least ambiguity there is. Decide! Listen to our Sarge: – the time is limited!'

\*

'It's not for me,' says Manuel. 'I'm sure. You're in a cloud, pulled up by some god's machine – but you're still mortal, treading on the fluff – and then? You drop like Icarus, or cast some lightning bolts. What if they bounce back?
    'It's dark. There's enemies, you've no defence....'
He elaborates some more, the images bear fruit, more dreadful crawlers show ... he's terrified ... and the truck moves off – his partner waves farewell....

\*

And Manuel runs. Be left behind another time? Alone ... Too much! The truck has slowed, he clambers up. 'I can desert,' he thinks, 'There's always that.'
    He doesn't mention it to Gaston.

\*

'What's your trade?' another Sarge asks Manuel.
    'Oh, geopolitics and strategy, interrogation, spotting spies....' says Manuel.
    'Then here's your broom,' the Sergeant says. 'Sweep this piece of desert clean of sand. Your mate is in intelligence, he'll tell me when you're done.'

\*

'It's the hunting season,' says the Sarge – 'Gaston leads – he's got his pips....'
    Gaston laughs. 'A fat apple from the snake,' he says. 'Now, remember, if you shoot, try it when they're in the act of coupling. That's when they are distracted – you would say there's pleasure, but prudence tells – you can't ascribe emotions across cultures. Be very careful how you generalise. Ah! – to generalise. The general's our goal, career grade. Now, it's true, we're few, but we are

someone else – and so, if we are hit, they'll say we're all a general....'

There's merriment, and general ribaldry – they sing the song, and Manuel moves his mouth – he can remember only the obscene words, and those run round his head.... It's action, but there's ambiguity. They make hard progress up the scree – for sure, there's guys that's watching them from Mars, or nearly there: alighting, they plod on, a little band in thick disguise....

'There is a line,' shouts Gaston down the file, 'in the ecological, between the massacre and the cull. Be very careful, not to overstep ... We get to lay them out, the cadavers, their hands arranged as if for prayer, a sweet surrender, and there's solemn guys around who sound their horns. It's quite totemic, and of course we mustn't cook them –' and everybody laughs.

'What if we hunt them all?' asks Manuel.... 'The forest will be bare: or, rather, this stony sealess beach will barren be ... like – before life crawled ashore, before the troubles, clash of plates, and this reared up, became a mountain range. Those prints of animals extinct, the ones that nearly flew and almost walked, undisturbed, waiting for another future.... Left abandoned, betwixt sea and air.... Patience! – we humans, if only we could wait as long as them, to come erect, crawl up the hill and start again, or build Jerusalem, Raqqa – whatever town we choose to call, Harbin, Novosibirsk.... Instead – we hunt ... where does that end?'

'It's just the same,' says Gaston, 'if we kill them all; every one. The guys will blow their little horns, the flag will rise, I'll maybe get another pip ... a bit of nature that could serve – we ate it! That is all. We must deny there ever were those bodies anyway – it's wisps we hunt, ghosts, people who would rather not be there.... A cull; it's natural....'

There's talk without a thread, but everyone is sure, behind them there are armies poised, friends, foes, in-between, ambassadors at work, opponents cruel and bigoted ahead, a provocation is required, for sure....

'The net!' shouts Gaston. 'Manuel! You're in the net.'

There's just a wire, caught in his feathered hat, but then a tower of dislocated things, a stupa of irrelevancies, castle of winds, a crash of lids and spoons, of tinsel clowns and jars of whortleberries, wavers – like a heavy-loaded pelican, an albatross – and whirlygigs, binds him like a fly in web, there's rattling of churns, a crunch of bakelite – cat's-whisker radios – it's all around and over him, and Manuel sheds a tear, powerless; he struggles, but there's tape and buttons ... he despairs.

'Leave him,' shouts Gaston. 'Manuel, if we remember, we'll return for you.'

The others laugh, trudge on. Manuel hears the song again, this time the words obscene and clear ring out, and he joins softly in ... Maybe they'll find some hostages, slaves to be freed, and prisoners to take, guys seized between their fighting and desertion....

*

The warriors? Gaston? They're never seen again. Not one of them. No record, and no claim, no fate to mourn, investigate, no cairn, no medals coined, no prayer, no grandchild bodgering memorials, no wall, no obelisk, no poem and no book.

'No Gaston,' Manuel says: 'My inspiration?'

The encampment – it's been trashed, the stuff has gone. A guy is waiting – 'Out! Out of here!' he shouts. 'You're criminals. Not summoned, and not wanted. Your backers, like your mates – all scum....'

'It was to rescue hostages, they said,' says Manuel, much stressed. 'In my case – I followed a philosophy. There was no scientific path to take – it seems that science eradicates the foxes, but attracts black birds....'

'Out!' shouts the man, gesturing. 'Give me your clothes!'

It may be safer so. Manuel strips off, the guy takes everything – the boots, the crumpled feather in the hat, the shoulder flashes and the little flag....

In the ruin – a sheet's been left, a dishdasha, as it were, and Manuel winds it round. Even the broom has gone – maybe the most desirable kit of all. The sand is back.

*

'We're all called Ali here,' says Ali, 'except you, Manuel. You may rise to general indifference – but you are not one of us, nor either one of them. Listen. The job is this. We cook the eggs. We cook the chickens. We cook the male chicks, feed them to the snakes. We keep the snakes.'

'General indifference,' says Manuel. 'It isn't bad. I'd a friend well on the path to be a general. It's better than the street ... the clean-sweeping, where you see everything, and mustn't tell....'

'Possibly,' Ali says. 'On the street, you have to fight, and maybe die. The street's demanding. Here, we eat street food, we're in the flow. I don't say it does you good.' He rhapsodises: 'Once there were big powers, deciding everything. Now – there's scores of middling powers as well, with middling ideas – ruled, kept quiet – by despots, crackpots; potheads and mopheads.... A melting-pot of hopes deluded, talents frosted in the bud, illusions of a purpose, a significance, a special recognition.... Even the big guys stop sometimes, they think "what for?", before they raise another army, find more people to enslave.... Billions of middling people, all with middling ideas, hanging in everywhere, overwhelming everyone and every plan, big boss and middling....

'And the thing is, Manuel – no one's going to make it. We're all poisoned, we eat it, more and more, the venom – our doctors spit it in our eyes, we breathe it in, rub it on our wounds – we love a fry-up, a boiling-bee, and it's us! jumped on the charcoal, seethed in the bain-marie ... the generals, they worry about bombs, how much they cost, how they cripple all who load them up – but we've been done bad to at conception, in the cradle, doomed, yes, all doomed, mutilated and deformed, started bad and going twisted.... Soon, much much too many of us – then too few. So very few: in hunting parties, seeking each other out.... Hoping to start again, but no! The kitchen's closed, the garden's bare, we all have buboes, ulcers too....'

'I know,' says Manuel, 'I've been in one of those patrols....'

'Your friend – I'll bet he's disappeared!' says Ali. 'You, they, need to find the exit, especially the nobs. Mostly, generals get let off – you win, and you retire; and if you lose, you're in the pail, out with the garbage, dinner for the dog! Look at Vienna – in the museum, those big pictures of defeats! That's indifference, for sure. No generals were hurt in making those pictures – that's what they claim. Hunters in the snow – draws the admirers, but – at least we're spared the massacre.... It is my favourite....'

'I know,' says Manuel. 'It's everyone's. It's harder than it looks, in sand ... to hunt....'

'Every morning,' Ali insists, 'Do you hear noise? Birds rejoicing. Owls retiring? And do you feel good? in yourself?'

'There's chirping,' Manuel says. 'But from the kitchen. Until the water hots up.'

He thinks – feel good? Feel bad? The mind ramps up at dawn – the body – no! The body wants to cry forfait....

'Exactly,' Ali says. 'Think – when we shall be the only living things – we humans, onward. Upward. True humanism – that way you'll see who believes, truly thinks – "Us, we alone, we are the tops, we rule the globe" – and perhaps the snakes; crawling and drooling, like they wanted jobs – like you, Manuel ... perhaps they think like us. I devote myself to them. Preserved for their wisdom and humility....

'As a species – we hate life. We're true-born natural Nazis – we'd like to finish off misshapen ones, make room so we can take a run at those resembling us. Collective combat, or individual, captivates for centuries: the epic where no one counts the cost – poor Polyphemus, poor monsters in the Ramayama – destruction beyond reckoning. Just one is saved, my dear Ganesh: decapitated lord of accident, of the mistake.

'Imagine – no fields, seas clogged, no trees, no pollen – no buzz, no bite, no busy bees....

'Fancy a slice of thigh? A breast? You'll have to take it off yourself. Or maybe your partner would oblige.... And yet – be very very careful. We take in bad stuff, from the off. It's like those Nazi docs devised: we're sterilised by hamburger.... Remember what they say – "like rats that ravin down their proper bane..." What use is cannibalism – we're equal, every one identical! Poison, Manuel: that's what we serve, it's what they, we, love; gigantic, flambé, an elixir, whopper, borne under napkins at Maxim's. Venom. Extinction, Manuel.'

'When we're all alone, and all on top,' says Manuel, 'perhaps....'

'No, no,' says Ali, 'Look! There's camps set up to send the peaceful somewhere else, and camps that want aggressive guys reformed. There's camps to re-educate the peaceful guys, and camps bombarded where's there's warlike ones.... There's whole countries that's a camp – and every country has a part at least that's camp, or people living over somewhere else who work for you, go back to sleep in airless cubicles and dormitories.... You – everybody – knows it's so. I tell you this so you'll feel bad, don't think that you're my friend, I'm pleased you came, I'm glad to see you go. We can't be trusted, Manuel. The smaller goes the world, the more there isn't space. When there is just one left, a Crusoe on his rock – he wouldn't know one prophecy, one clue to leave to – who?

'Friday's been long gone, the goats consumed.... You're poor, Manuel – you should trek on, and keep your ideas quiet....'

'I've no ideas,' says Manuel. 'Though they may come, I don't expect they'll bring me peace – but I'm not where I was, nor where I'm going to be.... It moves, Ali, the whole swarm moves, like hornets looking for a bole....'

'Try working in a camp,' says Ali. The other Alis laugh. 'They need a cleaner, always, who can speak their tongues.'

'I only know one song,' says Manuel, 'with the obscene words. But – I guess Gaston might be in a cubicle, locked up, for sure....'

\*

The sign says. 'Ali's: Fly with our wings', and Manuel does, or tries to. After a week – he flies.

Every tense tale requires short-order cooks. There's always someone who shows up anew – and no one stays for long.

The snakes? What for? Oh, Ali likes them. He collects.

\*

The camp is tall, lit up, white, by night. The guys play games all day outside, and when it's dark, the tarmac's full of dogs, looking for food. Beyond the fences there's fields – abandoned Indian corn, brown husks.

'New Life'. That is the message – does for bigots, warriors, and deluded guys who started off without a ticket to their goal, or with a ticket but no goal. Manuel looks everywhere – there's young guys, look alike, no beards, no military uniforms, but shirts with mottoes from a guru, or an insult – there's teams for basketball, beach volley, soccer too – and – they run! O how they run, the murderers! Manuel gets dizzy with the speed. The women in the camp next door – they're mostly covered up against the dust and flies ... no shout, no song. No Gaston; none of his patrol shows up. Not as prisoners, not in transit, nor as garrison....

\*

'Fantastic!' says Vivette. Her badge says 'Vivette'. 'We were at school.... You're Manuel.'

'I was at many schools,' says Manuel. 'In the beginning, I was first person, without shame, I was the "I". Then – I objectified myself, no longer an extraordinary – I repeated everything. I repeat myself. Whole strands of happenstance recur – names, banalities, greats and littles. I perform the rites like everybody else, less convinced than most.'

'You wouldn't kiss me,' says Vivette. 'Behind the green chalkboard.'

'Even now, that kiss is not the greatest trip,' says Manuel.

'The people here,' Vivette says. 'I'm worried, how they'll all end up.'

'They've ended, Vivette,' says Manuel. 'That is not the point.'

'Ali's wings!' she says. 'That's what we need. Let me try on those wise snakes in the pails beneath the sink: garters, belts, a parure, a turban or foulard. Like the superb couple, in the poem, who proclaim, declaim all afternoon ... under the palms.... Beauty, Manuel, you and I.'

'No, Vivette,' says Manuel. 'It's too late for that, for Ali, his fast food. His wings are singed. I've met everyone alive, and survived each fall. I've loved men and women: a continent. Nothing has left a mark. Maybe you do remember me, or someone like. The memory lives from the past, a foetus, growing tattoos, a breastplate, greaves, a throwing stick – ready to be born, a hero....

'It's not so. What's born is something, someone, else; it didn't start with me or you – what emerges from your head is pale, and wilts. The armour rusts. It's a sick shoot I swear, Vivette.'

'Ali is wrong,' Vivette says. 'He's been taken in, like you, and all the rest – there is no doom. There's crisis, like there always is and has to be. Capitalism. It's blocked. It will unblock. The world won't end. You think it's capitalism, causing our disaster. All will be sorted out, you'll see. A new phase, expedients – and we'll sail on. This planet, this universe – is made for capital. Maybe every universe is planned like that. Life, in capitalism: the default system of creation.... It'll be resolved, for sure: a war, collapse, dictators of all kinds – then things run smooth, the planet's saved, some animals reprieved, though we are not.... And on we go again, to more illusions – salvations, redemptions, apocalypse and judgement – but meanwhile ... we work: you clean the street, and on and on it goes. You'll die quite soon, and being right or wrong won't count....

'Old Karl was wrong as well, but understood at last: a little band of rebels won't take over, change the rules. Crisis after crisis – that's how it goes on, that's how it grows! Perhaps the chance was missed to try a different plot, but – centuries ago! ... Two humans left? – they'll start it off again – the snakes, the patch of grass, fruit trees ... and – away it goes! You read it all at school, the many you frequented, or dropped in....'

'Wise snakes?' asks Manuel. 'That's what it takes?'

They laugh. Of course – the remedy for present discontents and fears will come, and generate still more of them, and so and so.... Maybe there's nothing else, that will not come. Maybe what is forever twists around and bites its tail, and yours, and mine....

'I call it "capital", Manuel,' Vivette says sternly. 'The 'ism. What Marcel calls the Time – "my life, in fact it's me"'.... Mademoiselle de Saint-Loup, the whole basketful: the vanman, Masha, Gaston – do you see?'

'I see what you see, Vivette,' Manuel says. 'But – I've gone beyond all that, giant steps. More than an epic, more than an epic text – I'm striding far beyond, ahead....'

'Oh, you're so stupid, Manuel, you always were, you never took your chance,' says Vivette, laughing, starting to cry. 'You think we're dinos, could survive six hundred million years if only we could cut the poison out. You haven't understood. We're super-smart. We do all life, all history, in decades: – invent and finish quick! We don't fossilise, Manuel, we're bon mots, unjustified and stark.'

'Decide, Vivette,' says Manuel, annoyed. 'Does it end? Start over? End quick or drag?'

'I'm not so clear on that, Manuel,' she says. 'I'd look to you to help me out.... You think – I do. I move – you linger. That is how it's been for you. You had regrets before the tragedy, the guilt before your peccadillo, your real betrayal before the trivial arrived: the vanman before poor Masha....

'You were the one who lived in metaphor; you've had your fun. Now, you must change. I'll take you to the mountain, you'll be my Faust – gazing at the little fiefdoms down below. And I'm a Marie-Antoinette. I have a hobby flock of sheep. Now – for sure you'll say, "there are no lambs, no males. The sheep are young, all females making cheese, we throw their wool away, there is no call for it." There is no secret, Manuel: we eat the rest. But – see me with my hair piled up, my crook – I play the martyr; my sheep – my spirits. I'll show you, Manuel – how it was when we were very young, and you chose solitude....'

Manuel's amazed – 'Oh no, Vivette,' he says. 'I'm not afflicted. Not love, affection, liaisons dangerous or bland: no threat, no trickery. I've hit the wall. That's all. I can't proceed. I don't want you, a past, a spectre wandering....'

'It's nature, where you're going: where you, all of us, ends up. It's history, that you're part of, like in a crowd of extras, just a face. No body, but still there,' she says.

'Be sure, Vivette,' says Manuel. 'I'll shake the little bell, it has no clapper, but we hear it go ting-ting, and so we'll find where you have gone: if you are dead, the sound will wake you, show where they buried you, and who's nearby, and if you're walking round, the lot of you. Bone fields, Vivette. That's what we have, to plant our seed.'

'I understand,' Vivette says. 'It's too late. What you say's the same as everyone – the joy has gone. If it must end soon – let it end sooner. There *is* a ladder – but all the way up, if there's a top high in the clouds – it's all rickety – the weevils in the wood, the terns that peck at your pant legs.... We didn't always think like that – we had delusions....'

'I told you, Vivette,' says Manuel, impatiently. 'You must fill every moment – with intensity. What does it signify? Vigour, that's important. Lots of notes – made Mozart's reputation. See everything, meet everyone, carry, be carried – let them slide off your back, you too – you're burdensome, I'm sure they've told you.... We have that in common.... All futures – they have been imagined. Scoop us out at birth, give us a mechanism, stainless and eternal click and clock. Replace us all, make us go tender? ... everything has been foretold, so if we have no future, none is needed anyway....'

'And when you've heard everything,' says Vivette. 'You're ready for the start.'

'Exactly so,' says Manuel, walking away.

\*

Marisu wears an enormous afro, like in the sixties – so big she hardly gets it through the door. Her face is ivory, the afro black, shimmering like a cloud of bees. From the little bus, after her, come women smoking little pipes, a guy carrying a coypu in a plastic bag. They jump down carefully; inside, there's a fug.

'Let's see your hut,' says Marisu, impressed and irritated. Here, there's not much.

'It's where they did the auctions,' Manuel says. 'One beast at a time, so it's small. A pen. The boards – it's really turned to slats. I have the counting-house.'

It's a cupboard size, up at the back: a tiny amphitheatre of benches – and that's it.

'You found your destiny then,' says Marisu.

What is it, destiny? Is this it?

There's a bread shop – and a photo shop, looks like it's closed: 'My magazine enjoyed your pic,' says Marisu. 'I'm here to see the rest.'

'They're in this pile,' says Manuel. 'The insects get them if you don't protect....'

'It's that it seems you still use film,' says Marisu. 'Mostly, pics come by nothing to our desk.'

'Oh,' Manuel says, shuffling his prints – 'Amateurs. Computers. I can't handle the technology. I'd like to do the silver stuff. Prints, negatives, and plates....'

'There's always room for paper, books. Though I guess the insects....' Marisu says, and laughs. She looks through the folder: 'Everything you see – it's through a film. There's what you see, and something else. Everybody – all the others – just looks through the glass.... But – these are all alike, the face, the photos! The same one, or very similar....'

'You'd say it was a study,' Manuel says. 'There are vendettas here, you never know – they get aggressive, guys without work. Don't look them in the eye, not anyone. They don't like to linger while I snap.'

'It must be frightening,' says Marisu, disappointed, unconvinced.

'Oh it is,' says Manuel. 'It is, we are. Very frightened all the time.'

*

There's shouting. The bridge is down, the bus won't leave again that day, the detour – is too long, and dark.

'My films?' asks Manuel. 'Have you remembered? Brought them...?'

'Films?' asks Marisu. 'No films. Next time. Next time, if there is....'

She sits, combs out the afro: she has a little bag, with wigs, red, white: she puts the white one on. Her face is pale pale amber.

'These little towns,' she says. 'No villages...?'

'No,' says Manuel. 'Little houses in what was the forest. Just isolated? Just towns now, what is left.'

'It's very orderly,' says Marisu. 'Though limited. Order – is the key. The city longs for it....'

'Oh yes,' says Manuel, 'your despot – the whole club of them. "Bring order to the street...."'

'Well,' says Marisu. 'If you don't understand us, you don't understand a thing. A moderate tyranny – try it, maybe it will fit.... We wanted pics of simple folk, in simple places – that was you. Things, people, needs – they go on and on, predictable. But – you've not done as much as we had hoped....'

'No, nothing: nothing has been done at all,' says Manuel. 'I started here because guys had thrown their cameras away, but still they wanted weddings, deaths, the rites, recorded. The locals snap what's ephemeral – they let others engrave their birth and death. Then, the guy who had the shop ... he left...

'I improvise....'

'Maybe I should go look for that guy – I bet he'd help....' says Marisu. 'He didn't improvise.'

'Maybe you should,' says Manuel, 'I've been looking for people all my life. If I had a sack to put them in .... ! But there's no one, and yet I feel their weight on me. Your hair, Marisu – it probably doesn't weigh a thing, and yet you are ponderous – you're a shape-shifter, but the heft remains the same. I'm scared. I'm a Siegfried who doesn't know there's been a hatch of dragons in the wood....'

'The dragons may not know the script,' says Marisu. 'He should watch out, your Siegfried, the wood is rotten, no hiding-place, just firewood. There's a platoon of Siegfrieds tramping round – their swords – tangled in the ivy – talk about self'-inflicted wounds! That's their speciality! For any one of them, hero or dragon, the end may come too soon, no time to start the conflagration, burning all the gods....'

'I'm just starting,' Manuel says. 'I started, then I had – I'm having – to start again.'

'Yours is a poor move,' says Marisu. 'More slump than move.'

'I'm what I look like,' Manuel says. 'It's my job. The camera's. But there's more than truth, appearances.... Your bosses – they are crooks, aspiring to be criminals, and, when criminals, wanting to be a plague.'

Marisu's amused – 'Wanting or not,' she says. 'The toys accumulated give anyone the chance ... to be exactly that: plague, famine, poverty – it's all available. Remember Jean-Paul S: "the Apocalypse supposes the existence of serial gatherings and institutionalised groups." No visions, Manuel: the Apocalypse is permanent, until it ends....'

*

They're blocked. They scrutinise each other. Their faces? No, no hint of how to leave. It's bus, or nothing. Nothing, under this roasting sun...! Wait.'

The guy who left? – not Sean. Sean – the wise guy, though less wise than snakes ... he must be hoping for parole by now. Liffey and Paulie – pegged out, roasted, unleavened, their time a fossil in the rocks....

*

'If you want,' says Marisum, 'we could promote you. We could make you anything ...'

'The kingdoms of the earth again?' asks Manuel: 'Fame, riches, power. All I need give – is everything. The pampered victim for a year – and then the sacrifice.... For what?'

'Oh, we don't know that,' says Marisu. 'We push you up the hill. If you fall, too bad. Nothing – that's what you get from failure. Or success. But guys hate failure, love success. It's the species, Manuel – I'm sure you've often heard it said.'

'I'd not want fame....' says Manuel, doubtful.

'You'd be forgot,' says Marisu. 'We'd want that. You too, forgotten and forgetting, and everyone as well; involuntary.'

'But a following – to get it ... all those guys, in jail, beaten in the street, censored, silenced ... starved and tortured,' Manuel says. 'It's a scourge, a punishment of innocence....'

'It must be so,' says Marisu. 'That's how a side is picked. It takes a while. And then ....'

'... banal ...' says Manuel, mumbling. 'It would be something. Nothing, too. Beating and death. And *facho*....'

'Well, all's up to you,' says Marisu. She pulls a slat, to show it's not nailed in: 'I make the offer – if it were me, maybe I'd not accept. Stay here. More people come.... You could snap each one.... Here – is ruined. People leave, complain, ask your advice. You've convictions, I should guess – be sure to choose the one heatproofed against the times.'

She pauses, laughs: 'No, I'm not cruel! You're a Pushkin, without money. A progressive who trades in serfs. Talent? – how'd we know? Try! It costs you nothing, you've no cash. We'd make you hero, on the stage. Write on air. Grimace on it, do pratfalls on it. Everybody does: only, you do it in your way, your special way.'

'If this is my dream,' says Manuel, 'it's so modest it will break my heart.'

'It could be one of your women's dreams,' says Marisu. 'Though women don't have dreams.'

'I'd settle for a horse – and a leather hat,' says Manuel. 'Though I can't ride.'

'A horse that takes two,' Marisu agrees. 'Like in epics. Or I'd be left here.'

'I don't want to stay here,' says Manuel. 'But I don't want to leave. Is it like changing hair? You're now here, now there, you, another you, yet nothing moves? Like that?'

'You know it is,' says Marisu. 'I'm your bad fairy. I don't give discounts for your innocence. Buy me, ride me round the block. I'm your new Pontiac – the minute you get inside, you lose twenty per cent, in taxes paid. Surely you'd heard of that?'

'There's no way of refusing intimacy,' Manuel says. 'Not politely. Let's do what must be done, before we take the bus.'

And that they do.

*

'What did it mean?' asks Manuel, 'to copulate? I realise I always ask.... Sex, love, desire, relationship.... What do you have when you've had any one of those? The answer's never interesting.'

'In the auction pen,' Marisu says, 'first they stroke the horse, the beast, the bull, the teeth, the hooves – then the screwing happens in the counting house.'

'There's usually a scam:' says Manuel: 'I can guess what's yours. And as for mine ... I'm working on it.... You must have realised – there's is no dark room here – this office lets light in, like a brake; branches and fronds. I'm a fine photographer, but I've lacked the means. I can't develop, I can't print. Everything's done elsewhere, so nothing keeps me here.'

'Truth to tell,' says Marisu, speaking out bold. 'It was not for you I came. I'd hoped the photoshop – the guy – could balance out my hair. And fix my nose, give me some height, less weight....'

'He could,' says Manuel. 'Though once you leave this magic place – it all reverts. It isn't real, what they touch up on you....'

'No, no,' says Marisu, 'don't lecture me on real and not. Besides – you've had me, as they say, I gave myself to you. Of course – you've gained nothing; and I am much the same.' She laughs –

'Decide! – take my offer, or moulder here. Have us make you over, lift you up, turn you into something good, and tempting too. As for the photoshop – any result is fixed in time, and if you have the knack to reel it back – you're there, the better you: the figurine, the portrait in a frame! Time is circular, Manuel: – go far enough, it starts to bend, it boomerangs – and there you are, back where you started, but you're different! More experience, more wary. More beautiful, more perfect still....'

*

'I don't want what's going to happen to me, Marisu,' says Manuel. They're on the bus: 'What may happen. What you want.'

'You always want what happens to have happened in the past – it will,' she says, and laughs. 'I only took your hand, back there, no big idea....'

'I thought it was much more,' says Manuel.

'That's an interesting thought,' says Marisu: 'More ... I'm sure you have imagination, that gives you everything you'll ever want.

'Anyway, what you were, what difference does it make? A communist? A terrorist? They'll make out it's the same. Religion, secession? Once it's gone, it really doesn't matter. Smell! you can smell the terrorists from here, they rot beneath those ruins....' There's big grey heaps: it could be Mosul, could be Mindanau, Madrid, or – maybe Warsaw.... Earth-movers, pecking at the mounds.

You wonder how they'll ever move it, rubble. In Berlin they made a mountain out of it.

'Of course it matters, what you were,' says Manuel. 'It matters more than what you are right now. It's obvious. They're not supposed to bury you, just drop you in a hole.'

'You know how it would end,' she says. 'If you choose the losing side – you're landfill. I don't say that you're wrong, or could avoid. You can make poems out of losing.'

'I don't like this talk, before I've started,' Manuel says.

'I'm your horse,' she says. 'You bought me back there. I'm in your blood, you can't deny me, not anything. You bought, but didn't pay.'

\*

'There's a demo, a manif, over there,' says Manuel. 'I don't suppose I could join in....'

'Of course you can,' says Marisu, 'I'll wait right here.'

'You see,' says Manuel, tying a cloth around his face, finding a miner's helmet to protect his head. 'You'd only recognise what it's worth, if you could go back, put it in a context.... Or, if I've missed it out, something, it'll be an oversight.'

An anomaly, perhaps. The people demonstrating – they're indigenous. They're painted red and green. No significance politically, it's just the colour cycle of the maize.

'Where's the kids?' asks Manuel. 'They should be out here begging....'

'Oh,' says Marisu. 'They're in the Pied Piper camp – see – it says, 'Detention, Cleansing, Sales': they fit them up and send them off.'

It's suburbs now – a tall house here and there has fallen, but mostly you can see in side streets little markets, on the strip there's bars and cop cars, roasteries and joints of every kind ... It looks like home, except, perhaps, the streets have not been cleaned, there's piles of pink and yellow bags that smell and spill....

The sign says 'Rally'. It's a spectacle, no motors, not a command – there's rows of guys already on the stage.

'They're like my friends,' says Manuel, and –

'No!' says Marisu, 'they're not your friends. They're candidates, like you.'

'So, I'll say anything,' says Manuel, and Marisu says –

'No! I'll interview you; be very very prudent, don't do your rant against the monotheisms, don't say you're a communist, nor that you're a fascist, or a liberal, still less that you could be anyone – if necessary, say you have an open mind and could end up as anything, fixing everything.... Those isms, those museums you once visited – chase them away, hunt them like foxes. One fox – set snapping at another fox's heels.'

'But – do I want this, Marisu?' asks Manuel, quite overwhelmed.

'Oh, no one asks,' says Marisu. 'I guess I don't want, but someone has to wave the flag and clean the streets, besides, this is Apocalypse! That's what we promise, that's what comes! Think of balloons – some coming out your mouth, others not high up, but restful, consoling. Don't you think of them that way...?'

'Oh,' Manuel says. 'I think French Revolution – those gas balloons with leaflets dropping over Grimsby and the Vatican....'

'There! Words you must use with care – French, Revolution. Remember, Manuel,' says Marisu. 'The movement's called Apocalypse. It's up to you to make it fly.... Remember, too, that winning isn't everything, it's worse. Being second, even third – it's good. You get an office and some cash – and anonymity....'

'You're a wise horse, Marisu,' says Manuel, feeling quite attached.

'I'm pleased you spotted that,' says Marisu. She opens her hand – the thumb is tiny, the forefinger like a crab's, with blunt serrations, thick and woody, greenish like a shipwrecked bone left on the shore – and there in the thumb's crotch there is a tiny horse, blue, its legs bunched up, not a seahorse, but hunched, its legs a spider's, little watch springs, go go go, those say. 'We all have something, Manuel,' she says. 'That holds the little cameos, the totems if you like – to have a place to perch.'

'Oh no,' says Manuel. 'I don't agree. A tattoo's not an affront to whoever made us, the design, not like carving on school desks, as if you wrote "Boulle" on chests, on woods and scales and nacre evidently his ... the smart ass quip, a name in copperplate, a flower that never fades and so's never had a scent, a flagrance, or its modesty.... No! It is the skin, the suit you have to wear, are wrapped in it at birth, your shroud and swaddling, and buried so, its browns and wrinkles, lots of blots, carrying your years in poison blue – skin! Marisu, the rustling cope that shreds and tears, blisters and blusters, scuffs, roughs, flakes, swells, boils up and crepes, like omelettes and like cauliflowers, and is stamped ... stamped in red and purple, a parcel, bill of way and weigh, delivery to mister death who stamps it paid.... Skin – holds us together: in – do not tamper, respect the tribe but not the fashion, what's prescribed, not sold....'

'No, no,' says Marisu, who laughs and adds, 'How you exaggerate! All candidates must state their wish, indelible, unseen – a manifesto – old Karl had his in Roman on his back, he didn't even write the half, the rest was pencilled in by women, comrades: Engels too ... until he felt the rhythm, when all was nearly lost, he heard the beat, the rock, the bang and scrape of nature, of rabbits two by two who made a multitude, of nature in sere haps, indifferent cruelty: a providence! He sensed – a Providence, a tickety-tock. Invented what the Marxist century had buried – the hidden watchmaker! A clockwork god in threestep, two paces and a jump. Dialectics, Manuel! He heard it in the earth – and was mistaken. Dialectics – that's us; and has to be and we alone excogitate it: that's our invention, that is how we move, and stand upright. But Friedrich thought instead it was all natural, like limbo dancing, blowing smoke rings ... no marvel, then, that Marx took to his bed and screwed the servant girl: Engels descending, falling! Nature! Not us, but wolves and foxes, dancing in the moonlight with pointy hats stuck on their pointy heads....'

'Yes, Marisu,' says Manuel. 'I always gagged at that myself. Poor Marx – those boils raged like a strip mill every night. That cursed book, apocrypha.... The Engels spell, the bad angel ... even molecules can do it, dance until dawn ... the rocks the laws are written on, those too!'

*

'Look, Manuel,' says Marisu. She shows an arm – it's like Lascaux, the horses, bay and tawny, pintos, mustangs – all naked, heaving in a ferment, gold and red, carnelian and ruddy.... 'You see?' she says. 'I believe in lots and lots of everything, abundance.'

A shoulder – it's a troop of blacks and greys, those knobbly sticks of legs quite inappropriate – 'And on they go – here's Indians, and Mongols,' and there's hordes, those Scythians have grown into their mounts, they face both ways, the mount, the rider – the horse runs forward, the archer like a turret gunner picks them off behind – at day's-end, they sleep, hunkered together like blundered nursery toys fused into one.... Down her flanks stream the military steeds, at the trot, close order, abandoned as the empires fold, they seek a water hole, in arid wastes where Hereros used to be ... her nipples serve as salt licks, the navel's maybe ... slightly brackish – and down and round they roam – 'All over? Everywhere?' says Manuel marvelling. With burnished accoutrements, in charge and flight, the guard imperial, caparisoned in gold ... dobbins for drawing carts and coal and ploughs, dogcarts and growlers, hansoms, landaus ... no riders who direct, no vehicles which humiliate – a mass in movement, from the world's sweet centre: Chach, Merv, Balkh, Khorasan and Badakhshan, – markets, horses for China, Syria and Bactria, India and Arakan, tamed and – 'For forgetting, yes, of course,' says Marisu. 'A celebration, a frozen frieze, now that they've gone.'

'I never saw these,' Manuel says. 'When we were holding hands. Your claw – a grip I'd not forget: for clinging on, remembrance. And, Marisu, when you are dead – where will they go?'

'Ah, that's the snag,' she says. 'I could be flayed. The pope might like my skin, a vestment to bless his pets, his animals in ... But then again – I misbelieve, I'm miscreant ... it nags. I'd maybe write my will upon my skin, and leave them to roam free ... they'd sometimes cluster round about my tomb maybe....'

'No, no,' says Manuel. 'You're like Ali. You collect, Marisu – it's superstition. But I wouldn't face the needle. If I could tell you "no", I would – but then again ... you do it, or you don't, like everything we do or don't.... Engrave: that's how you know we were. Once, we existed.'

He goes on, says reluctantly: 'It is a splendid show; Marisu, you're a parade, the world in movement as it was.... The horse – tamed, sacrificed, bowed; for ever *asvamedha*. But – it's poison, Marisu, an atonement that will kill. It's poison ink, worse than on books. Your life is sacrificed.... For sure I'll not put a slogan on my butt, to show, if I should lose my voice ... or destination.'

'At all events,' says Marisu, 'nature will suffice for me in life, then kill me, as it does....

'I often hear that tale about old Karl. It never wavers: guys like you, the moderate commies, never persecuted, and never hurt, how you repeat it!.... The point is – not that the dialectic's natural, but that it can be mastered, by almost anyone.... Even you....'

'Oh come,' says Manuel. 'There's horses everywhere.'

'No,' says Marisu. 'You keep on seeing them – it doesn't mean there's lots. They're athletes, in movies, niches, in Kosovo and in Peru – but they've gone, the major part, to where we'll end....'

'I'm sure it isn't so,' says Manuel. 'Nostalgia, death wish. We are so numerous, we humans – though it's true, they said we should change the world. We have. We didn't understand it, obviously – maybe I'll go back to the philosophy....'

'Like you had when leaning on your broom?' asks Marisu, not kindly. 'You're here to change it for the better. Which way? Which way to turn the world....'

'I feel the weight,' says Manuel. 'Like the donkey strapped to its beam, round and round the threshing floor....'

'You're an antique, Manuel,' says Marisu. 'And me? I'm a memorial.'

'A tombstone,' Manuel says. 'What is my message for tonight?'

'Don't say "let it be like it once was,"' says Marisu. 'Like a stupid. Be banal. Say – "like it should be now".'

'I'll say it,' Manuel says, 'but nothing makes me a believer.'

There's pomp and strut. The guys, they primp and rant and reassure. There's much applause, maybe the most's for Manuel. He doesn't win. Nor come in fourth. Or tenth.

What a relief. How inconclusive too.

\*

'You didn't show,' says Marisu. 'You didn't place. A poor performance – and you ran for us, our colours.... Didn't you get coked up? The others did – barrels of the stuff behind the scenes....'

'You're not the only time I've had connection with a horse,' says Manuel, hoping to stop her anger. 'Though I don't quite remember who, or how. I'm clean: brain, flat as a blancmange. No fantasies, and no regrets.'

'That will happen more and more,' says Marisu, irritated. 'Memory. It's a Loki, a malignant wisp. Remembrance, a past – it flows away, until you're wholly emptied out. It doesn't mean you're clean. You don't say a bottle's clean, when you have drunk it. Empty, that is all. It's like the street – that isn't clean – just there's no one hanging round.'

'This doesn't get us somewhere, Marisu,' says Manuel.

'If you don't understand your life,' says Marisu, 'what else could you understand? Who could do it in your place? It's trivial, but you fall down on trivial things, so how....'

'Those guys, coked up – they ran for glory, for legitimacy, for the greatest power,' he says. 'They did the act. They'll have to stick with that. What did they understand? That they could jump the obstacle in front of them?'

'Why come, if you didn't have commitment?' asks Marisu. 'You and me ... in all that grass – savannah? Pampas? What did it do for you? A sneeze?'

'It's my weakness,' Manuel says. 'Attaches me to you. Something you find almost in everyone – a fascination. Curiosity. There's a time, "Fascination", though "curiosity" is not, though that is always close to us.... It's why we came up from the south in bands. Not families.... And found the horse. And sat on him, bound him, raced him, charged pikemen on him, kicked him, made him into glue, made her bear foals, until she too became a blanket. Where we left, Africa, they didn't ride. Just chariots. Pulled along. Though later on, in the Maghreb....'

'Enough!' says Marisu. 'That's not what I want from you. "The full body of the intense earth" – it thrills me, and I find instead I'm threatened with – the body of the despot. "Terror replaces cruelty", and we must change with the times, Manuel. You don't – and it's unavailing. You ought to realise – "from clean to empty", that's your tiny shift, that's where you've moved.'

'An empty despot?' Manuel asks. 'That's what you had in mind for me? Win the tournament, start drinking blood from skull-cups, fortify the emptiness?'

'You're wrong,' she says. 'You can cut off the head, you can't cut off a body made of lead. From tin to lead, tin soldier to a solider one ... come in the box, thousands, in caftan, kilt or suit. Don't minimise....'

'But you are fine with them, or some,' says Manuel. 'You're not an opposition, and extinction doesn't faze you.... It's what you expect. Soldiers to the last.'

'You said it, Manuel,' she says. 'It's fascination. I hold fast,' and she hoists her claw, waves it, 'snap snap' it goes. 'Voting – is folklore,' she goes on. 'You had despotism in your grasp – the despot has to sweep, sweep civilisations into heaps, a pile of skulls a hundred metres high: must be a tempest, or a cold north wind, liar, knave or fool, or all of these, meaning well or willing bad – it's despotism, Manuel, that is the joust! I wanted so – to see you struggle, see you fight. Just my fascination – for maladies without a cure....'

*

'This? This is our runner?' asks Charmaine, Marisu's boss, hair shined and piled up high, lucent, bejewelled, like bread rolls with poppy seeds; a single slink suit, off the shoulder, nearly off a breast.... 'He's the one, who wouldn't ink his slogan on his bum?'

'Oh Charmaine,' Marisu laughs, joshes Charmaine, she's on fair terms, but scared she'll get the sack.... 'They don't all do it. This guy, Manuel – he's fairly much a patsy. Lost his faith in Lenin long ago, and gyres in emptiness.... A solipsist....'

'So we've no candidate.' Charmaine declares. 'Some *facho* will walk it.... Send all of us to dig or drown. You said our guy would be a lion, from way out there ... composing visuals, every peasant registered and in a drawer....' She torments herself. 'This gentleman,' she says. 'Seems docile.'

'He's not the one we aimed for,' says Marisu. 'That one had left: he composed, made things up – this one just drops the shutter.' She rocks and keens. 'O Charmaine – the misery, misery of everything. The countryside – the people. They hold their money very dear. You need payback....'

'You're right!' says Charmaine, illuminated from within – the Word! – 'Payback'.

'Apocalypse will come – not at all our responsibility, though we may find ourselves pulling ancients in a broken cart; on the hoof, escaping retribution.'

'Too bad my friend Sean didn't win,' says Manuel. 'We all loved Sean.'

'Sean was a thief, I hear,' says Charmaine, brusque. 'What does that make you, Manuel?'

'No one could hate my friend, my Manuel,' says Marisu. 'Nor me.'

'Of course they can,' Charmaine says. 'Especially you, dear Marisu. The point is having people hate you, and you to hate them, even more – hate them back, in spades; see where it goes. The guys who win these contests laugh with you, laugh at you, whip it up. Everybody running, all each way – stampede!'

'Why did I follow you, dear Marisu?' asks Manuel. 'I didn't want this, and I had the counting-office, the auction house ... windy and dry....'

'We all do what we do not like,' says Charmaine. 'If we didn't, we'd be slaves. Slaves of somebody; who knows who?'

'I hadn't realised it was so bad,' says Manuel. 'Here, and on the way. Back there, there was no cash, of course....'

'Ah yes,' says Charmaine. 'Cash. The countryside – they hold their money very dear, they say.'

'The winners will insult us, say we undermine, we are a plague, bacteria – even if we weren't,' says Marisu.

'Now, now,' says Charmaine. 'Let's not be babies, eh? We're agents, Marisu, agents don't have a boss. And they don't boss anybody; who knows what they do? This guy,' and she holds Manuel to the light, 'is street fluff. If you wore pants, Marisu, you'd find him in your cuff.'

How to take that?

Manuel says, 'Coming here – there was a lot of ruins. Clearing them away – an industry, producing nothing....'

'Oh, those ruins are the economy,' says Charmaine. 'No one's responsible. If it was daub and wattle, you wouldn't even notice what fell down.'

'I give Marisu all rights to handle me, to sell or rent....' says Manuel. 'Seeing as I've no qualifications, no qualities, no cash....'

'We could grind you up, I guess,' says Charmaine, laughing. 'And spread you on the fields. But there's economies that haven't worked, and revolutions too – they leave a lot of dust and stones, bodies underneath that you'd not like to find.... It sometimes goes that way, that things end so, in multitudes cast down, but – nothing finishes: it takes another turn.'

She doesn't say she's disappointed in him, probably in Marisu as well.

*

Ten percent of nothing is – what everybody knows.

*

'Listen, Manuel,' says Marisu. 'If you stick with me, forget about the big change, the putsch, new world, and future written on the coins. That's all been tried, and here we are....

'The *écolos* will clip the wings. We've reached an end. No one will try to fly again, tie feathers on their slaves and drop them in the sea.... And after, if we should survive, we shall live modestly and well, revive some animals, and walk to where we hoe the fields that cover almost everything to feed us all.... We shall be brothers, sisters, all of us, from everywhere....'

'I've heard all that,' says Manuel. 'First, though, will come Apocalypse.... If we survive, then – palliatives and more machines: big errors: resentful children of the genocides ... vendetta, massacres; and of course, it will be good and true, it won't be beautiful....'

'We're finished here,' says Marisu. 'Life won't be good for candidates who lost, insulting guys who won.... Forget the past, everything you thought, it's all quite different now, the objective's just the same, of course, as always unattainable.... Forget everything, Manuel, except how you began, sweeping so's to con a job from someone up above, steal enough to start your life, don't look for Sean, or Paulie, Liffie – just hurry on and up – and off! It is time to go,' and she pushes Manuel out, and Charmaine says, 'Don't forget, an agent has no boss, remember, remember Marisu.... The people, sovereign – elect their despot, bare their necks, shoulder their long guns....'

'Yes, yes, Charmaine,' says Marisu. 'I promise, if taken, I shan't ever mention you....'

'To horse, to horse,' says Manuel, but Marisu, she doesn't laugh at all.

\*

'Oh, how you exaggerate,' says Marisu. 'Stop it! Ruins are the marks that good and evil leave. They show the battle-lines of justice. Be happy with them. Now, let's find a place where we can hide, and I can do my business.'

'It's not just I don't see myself attached to you, dear Marisu,' says Manuel. 'I've never reconciled myself – to the mortality.... All around. Everything: it disappears. How can anyone live so, a reasonable life? You're stood upon a sea, at once you start to sink – those dime-and-quarter fishy eyes, they stare unfriendly as you drop – the monsters must resent their throat's too small to take you in. And down you go, swift, down to where it's dark.'

'Let's go this way,' says Marisu, and pulls him by the sleeve. 'Behind us  the Apocalypse. Down here, it's empty, and been partly cleaned. When we're safe, you can decide – with me, or without me. I know – I'm really not a guide. But,' and she laughs. 'Nor are you.'

'For me, it started as a miniature,' says Manuel. 'The art show, and outside, the crowd, some looking for a lark, a bit of trouble.

Then you realise – it's all come from far away, this is just a little scene, toy theatre ... and maybe you're not up to it, living small, the being calm, surviving well and strutting round, that it's a sequence, millions of such shows, a press behind each turmoil, lynching, every tantrum.... And then it all goes small again, like in a peepshow: when you pay for time, you watch the longer if you have more cash, and then the shutter falls, a guillotine; and your time for now is up, the lovely lady disappears, the shutter on the camera drops, blinks, leaves the memory, and outside in the street you see the distance isn't empty, isn't just a view, indifference: ... that something, big as a reactor, or a tower of Babylon, is waiting there in fuzz and flies, and we – we have to take that road, I know, it looks the cleanest, but I promise, Marisu, it's not the emptiest.'

'Your perspective, Manuel,' says Marisu. 'It's wrong – you're up so high, that it all blurs below. You're living *now*, you must discriminate and judge, that's what it's all about, and then you act, you stumble, they shackle you – but that is how it is, and so you learn why it all happens as it does.'

'I might agree,' says Manuel. 'Except – we're running, Marisu! Escape!'

\*

'A place built up like this,' says Marisu. 'They have to clear the animals away. In the film, they tranquillise them, put them in a palanquin and take them to a forest, tall and feathery, and every shade of green.

'It isn't so, Manuel. They shoot them: they can't stay here among the people, and if you take them from their habitat, they're sad, they pine, they starve. They die....'

\*

The sign says 'Teleportering', and, smaller – 'at your own risk, and ours'.

'Remember, Manuel,' says Marisu. 'You're ordinary. It's not a good, to be a symbol, or be typical. It simply means you're dross. Undifferentiated. You mention thefts – so's to wriggle out from under them. The murders in the hunt, or casual neglect – you hide beneath a rug of words.'

It's a cellar.

Even if you're Marisu, unknown in any detail, you're just a curiosity, sweating, terrified, in off the street.

The guy with the machines before him says, 'I'm Angel – I lift you up, and drop you down – down a wormhole, if it helps, though you may end up a worm,' and he laughs. 'I lived in cellars during both our wars, when we were bad, then when we started being good. Every house was bombed right down to stumps, but every cellar held, and now I wouldn't be without.'

'Teleportering's a myth,' says Manuel.

'For things, maybe, but not for words,' says Angel, putting back his 'phones, 'They're mightier than swords, they say. I can deliver them. Everyone alive or dead – has an address. You're mediocre, Manuel, like the lady says, but if you have messages – obscene, transfers of cash, a call to war, surrender or atrocity – I'll send them anywhere, anonymous, and you'll sit here quite safe....'

'We'd prefer to have you send *us* to a place....' says Marisu, confused.

'Of course,' says Angel, 'to a glade. With corner-store to hand. A bee-loud glade, the stings removed?'

'Fireflies too,' says Manuel. 'Stone house, reserved for one. My white dog in the yard.'

'Seriously,' Angel says, hearing nothing of their talk, 'being a worm is best. You propagate by being cut in half, so you can be half good, half bad – and so it will go one, throughout the generations, join one good army, one bad, like the despots – beheaded – there's good brain, wicked body, or cut in half again... I told you. Worms. You're not a despot, I suppose?' he asks.

'He'd like to be,' says Marisu. 'They all do, the nonentities,' and she ogles a lad down in the gloom, who's eating something pickled from a newspaper.

She whispers to Manuel, 'Chechens. Remember them? There isn't much they have not seen – but then, that goes for us, back to seeing, fearing, and recoiling. They're maybe more used to action....'

She tells Angel, 'Find me a place, Angel – I mediate. Work for both sides, an intermediary – except ... I'm *banco* too, the dealer ... holding the advantage.'

'You're small,' says Angel, not listening. 'You'd fit down a wormhole, frequenter of the up- and under-worlds, a wanderer in both. They're not dissimilar – down below, you talk with animals – those that are left, and have the time for chat.... Pray at the shrine

for goddesses, find the horn of plenty you can blow, play a game
that has no rules.... At first, you'll be an Alice, hoity-toity, but it's
your home, you'll prosper.'

'There's not much room to mediate,' she says. 'Just up or down.
And Manuel? He talks of purity, but from the start, he's grubby:
where does he belong? Not up or down...? And – we both might
disappear. Who'd look for me? Nature's so profligate....'

'I lied,' says Angel, addressing them direct. 'There's no room
here, and no geography. No choice of worlds, just here, and not
here, this is not a station, there's no rails, no train. I can know
anything – what can I do with it, this knowledge, everybody has a
store ... quite useless.... Live with nothing, you're still you, nothing
is nothing, and when you send it round the world – it's nothing still,
that is, it's immaterial, we live by it, it makes us hear the sounds
and see the pictures, and since it's nothing, there is nothing you can
lose, if it's here or there. There's traffic, and it takes a while to
shunt it round, but the sounds are not the sounds of couplings,
squeaking and clanging, they're the sounds of waiting in the dark,
until your message leaves – and you're still here, and you don't
know who reads it, if you know them, if they understand, what
alphabet it's in, or just a string of numbers. It's not an easy time,
although there's nothing happening, not that you can see. You have
the choice, of course.... Leave as you are, or I could advertise you.'

'That would be fine for me,' says Marisu. 'An ad. Even if it
means becoming very very small. Painless adventures, hatches of
monsters – take me in, however crowded you are here, however
little food....'

'Wait over there,' says Angel. 'It may take a while....' and she
sees rows and rows – in the gloaming – of babushkas, sitting on
their sacks, rheumy eyes expectant....

'I have no destination,' Manuel says. 'And I don't need
miniaturising. If I can leave....'

'Go with God,' says Angel, pushing him up the stairs, out into
the light and heat. He is alone and lonely.

*

How does he live? Involving in the everyday – it brings you
friends, and not to mention enemies ... remember what the poet
said, release yourself into the flow, a bubble in prosecco,
sometimes in champagne ... into the nation – ah, romanticism, what

a dance you had them prance and strut, but didn't have them heed
how it all ended up – in flames and ruins ... archaeology in the
river-bed, a fumbling in the mud.

\*

A gathering at the crossroads – it's dangerous, you'd maybe be a
target there – or else you're planning something, to go and get
someone. These people know each other – some are wearing caps,
but it's not forethought, not political, just fashion, they are not
organised, maybe discussing news, a danger, or an edict ... waiting
for someone, they'll know who it is and what they stand for, safety
or danger. At all events, they know much more than Manuel, more
than he'll know or feel, ever. Half-hidden at the back is Marisu, the
best place to be, with a crowd, shows you're one of them and not
especially afraid.

'I couldn't wait,' she says to Manuel. 'Angel is right –
behaviour's changed, the weather too – the cellar is the ideal
lurking place. My body though – I couldn't dispense with it, it
didn't fit in the machines, even if he makes your brain a barley
sugar, there is still the chance someone will find you, suck you out,
could even be a dog.... So – you can wait down there, hunkered for
generations.

'I knew you'd have to take this road, it isn't safe. These people –
think there is a spy....'

'I'm sure they're right,' says Manuel. 'There always is.'

'You might be flattered, Manuel,' says Marisu. 'The cellar was
so dark.... I clung to you....'

'You should have stayed,' says Manuel, angry and anxious.
'You left me, I was glad, you leech on everyone, and now you're
back, there's all to be unravelled, and in the end, there's just a
Ariadne thread remains ... no use for anything except to turn
another kink, a bend in the labyrinth – the labyrinth, your home,
you are an agent, it's your universe of deals that will not hold, of
lives shut in a drawer expiring when you dust the folders off and
there is nothing in them, empty files with someone's name
outside....'

'I've no one else,' says Marisu, starting to cry. 'I've family to
nurture – they don't even know my face. I ask you to do nothing
except be beside me, companion until this tricky place is left,
pretend, pretend, Manuel, it's the most concrete thing you're asked

to do, together we're more plausible, and we can leave here, then separate....'

'What family?' asks Manuel. 'Get them to walk you out, I want no liability....'

'Oh, they're all small or ancient, Manuel ... if I could help them, naturally ... Don't mistake me – I love humanity,' she says, she pleads. 'To be precise – I love the Russian people ... German musicians, French cinema ... I used to love those huge steaks in America,' she says. 'But of course, you can't – so, I love cows instead.'

'I fear people,' Manuel says. 'And you mistrust them, yet you negotiate....'

'Oh, not just trust or not,' says Marisu. 'It's this clump of guys stood round – a bomb attracted, drops in the middle, a mortar's best – or they're in someone's service, looking for me ... or even you .... we should depart and quick....'

'It sounds quite solipsistic, Marisu,' says Manuel. 'You can't live life in such simplicity.'

\*

'Oh Manuel,' says Marisu. 'We'll starve, without the everyday. Forget the sex – it's food we need....'

Ladies and Escorts, says the sign – a throwback, nostalgia paradise. The wooden floors, the pickled stuff, the smell of entrails – escorts in plenty, lady – only Marisu. Manuel sees – a table, with four Indians. They're talking Choctaw – 'I'm not fluent, but I have some words,' says Manuel. 'Let's have a game of shuffleboard – I'll show you.'

They are keen, they've just been paid, and want to spend it all as fast as fast – fasts's how the board goes first – Manuel's a genius – his guards, his hangers, taking-out – the Indians are fired, amazed. They slow the board right down – the rocks slide slow as though they're glued ... but still he wins – 'A gift,' he says, 'Rare, limited....' They sand the board – so fast the rocks are meteorites, they touch, explode....

'Manuel – you could have been an Indian,' says Marisu.

'Oh no,' says Manuel. 'That's a rare gift, quite limited – but there's the everyday, my dear, accounted for –'

But as they leave, some guys, from greed, rev up their wheels – a StratoChief – and drive at them.... Marisu is hit – she spirals up,

the sky is full of flying horses – for sure she's dead – but no, she's
fit enough to run with Manuel, who says – 'Those Indians – they'd
give us all the cash they had. It was my show, attracted greed ...
that motor aimed to take our cash. First my vanity at the board, then
the malign ....

'Now, back to business, Marisu, back to themes I once discussed
with Tatiana, the future, and the universe, and how to picture it and
put us in, our twisted figures, our rare skills, however limited ...Our
quiddity, turned into cash ...'

'There's nothing to buy, nowhere to buy it either,' says Marisu,
and weeps. She hurts.

'Here's seeds,' says Manuel, shaking a dried head and gathering
some, 'Though I don't know what to do with them. They have a
timer, and they know their spot, and exactly what they'll look like
when they're ripe, and how they'll finish up.... Except ... when they
grow, where shall we be?'

'Yes, Manuel, for them you are a pantheon – what you don't
know about them trumps what they know about themselves,' says
Marisu. 'That's their life, as well as ours. It seems to me – it's
better not have seeds, and the uncertainty.'

'It doesn't follow, Marisu,' says Manuel. 'The future's a black
hole. It shows we're not created for philosophy.

'But – see, there's a host of people, falling, fallen, trudging,
along this risky road. It's best to make some friends....'

'I'm not so sure,' says Marisu. 'Friends – are patched and
brittle.... But I can't think of anything to do, to walk, to stay.... I
hurt. You, Manuel, you're a fly, eyes all round your head, a jerky
gait. Omnivorous, incontinent. And me – I'm broken up. There's no
safe choice – when you live by greed – some greedy guy tries to
kill you in the parking lot.... There used to be a void ahead of me,
and now it's passed behind. I used to think I could be anyone, but
now – there's someone, anyone, who wants to take my place....
When I am not, dark figures step forward, do everything and more
that I have ever done. *Si j'étais vous* ... you fantasise about an
interchange of selves, but now – you, the unknown – are me....
Who are you? What will you do, as me?'

'It's nothing consequential, Marisu,' says Manuel. 'It's only –
all inside, you broke. But the skin, the picture's perfect still.'

'What happens, Manuel?' asks Marisu – a gasp. 'For you, it's all
symposium, there's no one dead, just not invited.... My horses, they
can't move, escape.... The only other dead was Masha, something

unexplored in there, you carried on, indifferent, and so – the nugatory child you never knew must die as well....'

'That's mawkish, Marisu,' says Manuel. 'The child I never knew, I didn't want. We all go on and on, but you can't say we're not explored because we're not together till the end....'

'Well, Manuel,' says Marisu, a croak. 'What was in me? And unexplored?'

'Nothing,' says Manuel. 'It's all outside, inked in. Your life is on your skin. I have to leave you in the ditch – the horses don't come off, but it is wrong to bury you with all the horde still galloping.... Identity – it's just a trick. I thought that I was "I", but now, I'm Manuel, and no one questions what it means to live inside oneself.... The inside you is dying, Marisu – what do we do with what is left outside?'

'Forget all that,' says Marisu, rallying. 'The problem isn't mine. That bar – a piece of re-creation; and those Indians – they exist no more. Even that StratoChief's a museum piece....'

'It's good it's been a mystery,' says Manuel. 'It makes your life unique....'

'My skin is that,' says Marissu. 'Unique – each steed now more than just unique – extinct. Each one's a memorial, but who remembers? What exists to be remembered, Manuel?'

'I could flay you, Marisu,' says Manuel.

The two consider that awhile.

'It wouldn't be for love of me,' says Marisu. 'Nor of the animals. I wouldn't even make a pair of shoes.'

'In any case it wouldn't be appropriate,' says Manuel. 'Nor practical. Charmaine – now, she's a type who follows fashion.... I could ask her....'

'You'd be insulting us all round,' says Marisu. 'You are a builder, Manuel – you lay a stone and hope it brings another stone. You have a plan, and then a brick attracts a brick.... You have a starting-place that tells you all the further moves.... You have a destination. You talk in order to refine. Your fly's eyes – they see all that's circling round – those threats, the swat, the other flying beasts – you save your life ten times a day....'

'That's right,' says Manuel. 'It's not exalted, but it works....'

'And I have none of that,' says Marisu. 'I am the rotting rind, you'll feed on me....'

\*

'It's the times, Charmaine,' I say. 'We were punished, we turned on people here, then there, we were ruined, ruins we sent everywhere for punishment.... Find unhappy people, make them more unhappy still, and then you find the ruins have come to your door, there's only punishment but you've forgotten what it's for....'

'Yes, yes,' says Chamaine. 'The body – where did that end up?'

He wonders if she and Marisu were lovers – for sure, they didn't like each other much, so lovers it would have to be....

'The skin?' asks Manuel. 'There could have been a wish, a will. In this case – the skin – it was the will and that was what was willed. I don't think she'd something else, we didn't know what's best ... to do with the picture and the rest. A gift? Or – nothing. Let it dry up like a fig, wrinkle, change colour, tear.... In itself – the image is nothing, what it represents – it isn't there. Or maybe – not anywhere. A celebration of a thought. Should it endure? And should we scrape it off – the picture or the thought? Nothing has prepared me.... In life, what did it mean, in death ... her thoughts, what she thought she might have seen, imagined...? It's a question we all ask, Charmaine, and there are answers willowy and whimsical....'

'And so,' she says, 'you left it in a ditch. At least you covered it?'

'A sheet of tin,' says Manuel. 'There's no reply, no question and no voice. Leave it, Charmaine, forget it, forget Marisu – nothing she wanted did she have, so – no need to look, there's nothing to dispose.... They took her cash – our cash....'

'Of the dead,' says Charmaine, 'they say their life was hard. Marisu's life, instead, was bad. She told you....'

'No, nothing, we didn't talk,' says Manuel. 'We didn't get along, it doesn't matter, if there was sex it was because we didn't like each other, so it stopped, in any case – it doesn't matter, none of it. People rake over it as if it does, they do theology, leave flowers, sacrifice to inexistent gods, take bullets for some principle that isn't, or for cash they cannot spend, or isn't paid. So, does it matter? You're another simple little soldier, Charmaine, well-equipped and fitted out – reason and the truth don't trouble you, they are not visible, you aren't a scientist who tramps in leaky boots on sinking causeways – error, my friend – doesn't even trouble you....'

'Be very careful, Manuel,' says Charmaine. 'You have to love us, love the people, respect their striving and their will, or else....'

'I know,' says Manuel. 'What I say – it's irrelevant, it's contradicted by my life, I know....'

'The pity is,' says Charmaine, 'that Marisu lived a bad life, knew it so – and there's no picture of her skin ... you could have found a camera....'

'Let's say it all rubbed off, faded long ago,' says Manuel. 'An adolescent's jape, that you pretend it signifies.'

\*

'You dress the part, Charmaine,' says Manuel. 'What is your part?'

'I'm an agent,' Chamraine says, 'I fix everything. Marisu – she worked for me, she fixed the rest.'

'Fix me!' Manuel says, suddenly adrift. 'Stop the waves! Stop these tragedies – they're hunks of stale black bread, it's habit makes me gather them, stash them, inedible, in my sack.'

'I'd have to fix a lot of other people too,' says Charmaine, grinning – her long incisors sidling out, 'to make a pedestal for you.'

'Then do it, if you can,' says Manuel. 'If it's true that you know....'

'Of course I know,' Charmaine says, tipping him a wink, closing her office door.

\*

'I'm a therapist,' Finley tells Manuel, 'but I don't believe in cures. It's beating time: you do something to cheat the nothing that awaits.'

'I'm a great spiritualist,' Manuel joshes him, like they're two genius blues singers meeting up, with not much left for them to do.... 'But if the Spirit is a *We,* and "the external expresses the internal" – my life, every life, is a disaster. Look around.'

'Exactly so,' says Finley. 'Mind. It's all in us, us thinking: if we don't do that, the spirit has to lurk somewhere – probably in our shoe.'

'Listen, Finley,' Manuel says. 'I have an agent, but no contract. If you have a plan, I could keep schtum, she'll never know ... and you won't owe a cent to anyone.'

'Reclaiming,' Finley says. 'We can show – that history is reversible. The desert: – flowers. It snows again. Wolves sing. We all cool down.'

'"Show"?' Manuel objects. 'To people? Have it copied? Repeated, sequestered, licensed?'

'We'd avoid all that,' says Finley. 'Especially people. Saying something's right, and that it's a start of something else, maybe anyone can discuss, put their two cents' worth in: that, we eschew. Rather, we seek a wrong end. Break the sequence – contest a conclusion, replace premises. How does that appeal?'

'It's what I've been creeping to,' says Manuel. 'I've not been pure, nor good nor true. I've thought. I conclude, that thinking and concluding – they don't fit. Conclusions happen, usually you've not thought of them....'

'Yes!' says Finley. 'That's slick! No one thinks in order to be admired for it. People seek admiration, so they do not think. We shall conclude; our end will come, but what we've done is quite indifferent to us....'

'Oh Finley,' Manuel says. 'You're diving into thickets. Start from the simple thing you have in mind: that's where the spirit is, it can't be elsewhere....'

They contemplate each other. What luck, a meeting, casual.... The meeting – maybe that was luck, but is the consequence so lucky? You read the question in their eyes....

'Here's my plan,' says Finley. 'Just as I have it jigging in my mind.'

'Who's to share it?' Manuel asks. 'Only me? We'll succeed – everyone will want to share ... and then, it's something else: a state, parade, a chorus line.... A plan that changes contexts, habitats – we're in a contradiction there....'

'Manuel,' says Finley, squeezing both his arms and puffing propositions in his face, 'You're right. I propose a contradiction. I think, and that is a sufficiency. Then – I do, I act. I dig and sculpt. Agriculture. Where's the sense? Thinking's internal, yet here am I, proposing an interlude in which I save the globe from what is happening, what will happen – by my actions, physical and dusty. Why should I care? Aren't I departing from my thoughts?

'I'm not nice; not good and warm, about me there's a smell of sticky drugs, the inside of spittoons.... My deity is Moloch, but it's clear I don't have faith in anything beyond myself, my mind, my spirit .... my philosophy, it has no consequence, no consolation, prescribes nothing except more and more of it, refinement, undo what's done, accept the flaws in argument....

'The real! Ah, dear me! The real – is knotted up with contradictions that's not at all in logic, but no less, they are destructive: plenty runs to glut and stupor, famine ends with cannibals....

'You are cold, incompetent, Manuel. Maybe you're as brilliant as me – yet I am steam, I blow up reactors, volcanoes, I expand, I dissipate. And my end is drip and drizzle.' And he slumps.

'I've been in the cleaning biz,' says Manuel, to fill the void. 'Anywhere can be reclaimed, and edenised, animals made plush and happy....'

'Yes,' say Finley. 'My science guarantees it too. That is why we'll find a place that can recover, be reclaimed, made pristine – but! all around there's predators, waiting for their off. And sand, white sand, dead corals, waiting for their wind, to invade, obliterate. What *is* – it isn't there by chance: you can paint it over, but it's there ... make a movie of it, doesn't alter anything: you've changed the tense, from is to was, that's it, that's all. The century won't change because you rig your clock.'

'The poor? The refugees? What shall we do?' Manuel asks, 'When they show up?'

'We're not a destination,' Finley says. 'Besides, how could we respond? We're refugees too. I'm poor – I'm much much poorer, Manuel, than you, and you have nothing, and no skills, no country that you want, none that will take you – what's your lesson? Ours is an experiment that proves exactly what you know – the past produces where we are – an impasse. An impossibility.'

'It's convincing,' Manuel says. 'For sure, I've not saved anyone....'

'And no one asked you to,' says Finley, triumphantly. 'Now's your chance! I need you, Manuel – maybe there are others too ... need me, need you. Too bad! Don't help – just dig. Earth. Bring earth, plant trees, the birds will come and sing, and prime our hearts. "Sex. Land. Bugs" – their slogans, melodies. They don't feel pity. Duty, that is all. Family happiness.

'Cuckoos – you could make them heroes of a book, a message. Some birds – monogamy; others – free as air. Responsibility – and freedom, its reverse.'

'They'll eat the bugs,' says Manuel, 'before the bugs eat us.'

'It's almost true,' says Finley, slapping at his throat, a necklet of pustules round, insistent, a ruby-red volcanic archipelago: 'In our domain, we'll have a temperate year again – one quarter each for frost, then babies, raging heat, then booze and fog. It used to come quite naturally – no one designed it so. It will come again: and then no more.

'No pity, Manuel, it doesn't work, it won't help you, nor me.'

They stare at the imagined patch of sand and scrub. It will flower and rhyme again.... 'There!' says Finley, pointing. 'A fox! Steady, my red friend! We're all animals together – moderation and respect...! And, Manuel – there's Concita,' and he waves, gesticulates, 'She's straight like you, strayed in, maybe you can try each other out.... You'd prefer something mechanical, I'm sure – ungendered, Cartesian. You want her body, but you say she'll share you thoughts! Impossible – as if she, or anyone, were able to get inside.... You've not shared anything in all your life, so, frankly, a machine to screw would suit.... A machine that thinks? How would you tell? How share, communicate? We can't all be thinkers, Manuel. We're recruiting hands, farm servants. Half the year they'll trade their lore before the fire with you, you'll watch the turkeys and the hams spin smoking in the chimney.... Dull, my friend: dull, dull, dull....'

'You're right,' says Manuel wearily. 'The end: the consequence of the present – it's inevitable. We can show it need not be so, but it *is* so.'

'You haven't got the argument quite right,' says Finley. 'But you're not a pro, so it's beyond you. But you're right enough not to have me bother to set up the scene. Ahimé! The people, the animals, Manuel – we could have made them live, even if ... it doesn't last.'

'With your conviction, Finley, it's a project you could realise, over and over, driving to the limit – remaining yourself cool, tough as a stone. Philosopher's stone, of course,' says Manuel.

'Yes, Manuel,' Finley says. 'It will not work. It works, of course, but time's against us – we go where we must go....' He turns away, softly says, 'And you will not be an "I" again, all those people ending in your care, discarded, dropped, mislaid – you, making up scenarios, then living them, deserting, soldiering on.... Manuel takes no responsibility – an "I" would suffer terribly ... regret, guilt, memory....'

Both weep. Different scenes, pleasant, horrible, appear to each.

'I didn't say that you would like me,' Finley says.

'I'll go on,' says Manuel. 'There is no end to me, the living me – though anywhere can be an end. Once you have been – that's it. Oblivion's normality....'

*

'I've signed on,' says Finley, wiping his eyes. 'A military rocket – I could pilot it. I know where the moon's located; further still – they're all lit up.... The smartest of us, and the clods: in a pod. Driven.... There's a selection course; besides, those rockets may be needed round about, to exterminate a country – or just to possess a forest of them....

'I've always hope; I ride, I gallop, on ideas – I don't commit to putting brick on brick. Remember too ... ruins are normality, my friend.'

*

Returning to somewhere you've been in before – it isn't good, though it's inevitable –

'*Vernissage* – images and installations – The Universe by Tatiana – everywhere....'

*

'A genius,' says Tina, a pupil, follower – a hanger-on.... 'A life of great utility....'

'I know her work,' says Manuel. 'And her. I've seen every type the species has; I've travelled everywhere. Every crime, and every mystery – I've witnessed them, recorded them.... I'm a certain kind of person – a spokesman, the narrator. I don't partake – but that is good. I'm a telescope – I study Time, Variety. And prospects too.'

'It doesn't matter,' Tina says. 'No doubt you've suffered, as you contemplate the suffering around you, what is to come ... there's no merit in that study, none at all. Tatiana's work will last long after the Universe has disappeared. I'm sure you've heard how images are made to last longer than what they represent – their double, ghost, their other....'

'It wasn't good with Tatiana,' Manuel tells Tina. 'When I realised that the cleaning was in vain. It won't be good, Tina, the time I'd spend with you. That vision.... Tatiana's Universe!... She's vindictive and controlling....'

'Oh, I agree, I think you have to be those things,' says Tina, much impressed with Manuel, and quite hostile.

Manuel says to her:

'I've not begun to tell the story, not as it should be told. It won't comfort you.'

About the author

John Fraser has lived in Rome since 1980. Previously, he worked in England and Canada.